In 198. Chan married a Hong Kong national in a traditional Chinese wedding ceremony in Eastern China. In 1993 she and her husband moved to Hong Kong and lived there for ten years. She has seen a great deal of Chinese culture and come to appreciate the customs and way of life.

In 2003 she closed down her successful IT consultancy company in Hong Kong and moved back to Australia. She decided to use her knowledge of Chinese mythology, culture, and martial arts to weave a story that would appeal to a wide audience.

Since returning to Australia, Kylie has studied Kung Fu (Wing Chun and Southern Chow Clan styles) as well as tai chi and is now a senior belt in both forms. She has also made an intensive study of Buddhist and Taoist philosophy and has brought all of these together into her storytelling.

Kylie is a mother of two who lives in Brisbane.

Kylie's website is at www.kyliechan.com.

Books by Kylie Chan

Dark Heavens

White Tiger (1)
Red Phoenix (2)
Blue Dragon (3)

Journey to Wudang

Earth to Hell (1)
Hell to Heaven (2)

地獄到天堂

JOURNEY TO WUDANG
BOOK TWO

HELL TO HEAVEN

KYLIE CHAN

HARPER
Voyager

Harper*Voyager*
An imprint of HarperCollins*Publishers*
77–85 Fulham Palace Road,
Hammersmith, London W6 8JB

www.harpercollins.co.uk

This paperback edition 2012
1

First published in Australia by
Voyager 2010

A catalogue record for this book is
available from the British Library

ISBN: 978 0 00 736577 7

This novel is entirely a work of fiction.
The names, characters and incidents portrayed in it are
the work of the author's imagination. Any resemblance to
actual persons, living or dead, events or localities is
entirely coincidental.

Printed and bound in Great Britain by
Clays Ltd, St Ives plc

MIX
Paper from
responsible sources
FSC www.fsc.org FSC˚ C007454

FSC™ is a non-profit international organisation established to promote
the responsible management of the world's forests. Products carrying the
FSC label are independently certified to assure consumers that they come
from forests that are managed to meet the social, economic and
ecological needs of present and future generations,
and other controlled sources.

Find out more about HarperCollins and the environment at
www.harpercollins.co.uk/green

The Turtle raises its head above the water
and watches the glittering coloured lights
beneath the blazing stars of the Northern
Heavens, wondering why it is there.

The Serpent chokes on the polluted water,
drifting to the bottom amid the mud and
oil, listening to the many engines moving
overhead.

They cry. There is no answer.

CHAPTER 1

I was in my office, trying to ensure a fair allocation of funds from the increased Northern Heavens tax revenue, when the intercom on my desk buzzed.

'There is someone here for you, ma'am,' Yi Hao said. 'She's very upset and says she needs to see you right now.'

'Who?'

'Zara. She says she knows you.'

'Send her in.'

Yi Hao opened the door and escorted a young Chinese woman in, then left, closing the door behind her. The woman was about twenty-five, with long, snow-white hair and matching brows and lashes, incongruous against her golden skin.

'Sit, Zara,' I said, gesturing towards one of the visitors' chairs. 'What's the problem?'

Zara opened her mouth to talk, but didn't make it very far, instead collapsing into great racking sobs. I went around the desk and put my hands on her shoulders to comfort her, and she leaned into me, still weeping. I pulled a tissue from the box on my desk and handed it to her, and she blew her nose loudly.

The rest of the stones are accusing her of being complicit in Lady Rhonda's destruction, the stone in my ring said. *After what happened to Gold, and the activities of Demon Prince Six, we even suspect our own of treachery. It is a sad situation. The Tiger's Retainers have been interrogating her, that is why she is distraught.*

I sat in the other visitors' chair and put my arms around her, and she clutched me.

'Let it out,' I said. 'I can wait.'

She continued to yank tissues out of the box, and eventually ran out of steam.

'My stone told me what you're going through,' I said. 'It must be very tough. You can stay here as long as you like, Zara, we can look after you.'

'I am a possession of the Emperor of the West, I must return,' Zara said in a soft Putonghua accent.

'If you want to stay here, I can ask him to release you. All I have to do is say the word.'

She looked up at me, her eyes red and her face full of hope. 'If you could shelter me until this blows over, please, I would appreciate it.'

'Done,' I said, then to the stone: 'Tell the Tiger.'

'Ma'am,' the stone said.

Good, take her for a while, see if you can get anything out of the stupid bitch, the Tiger said. *We need to find the real Rhonda! My wife is out there somewhere and that stone doesn't know anything, she's fucking useless.*

You made sure yourself that she was the real Rhonda, I reminded the Tiger via the stone.

No! the Tiger said. *Not possible!*

Tell the Tiger what Kwan Yin said to me, I said to the stone.

... The Lady said that Rhonda was a victim of her heritage, same as Lady Emma is, Lord Bai, the stone said. *That wasn't a demon copy of your lovely lady. It was really her. Please, sir, talk to Kwan Yin.*

Fuck, the Tiger said, and went quiet.

I turned back to Zara. 'I have the word of Kwan Yin that it was the real Lady Rhonda that was destroyed by the Elixir of Immortality,' I said. 'I didn't realise anyone was giving you trouble about this, Zara; if I had known I would have told them.'

Zara let out a huge, shivering sigh. 'I thank you, my Lady. You have saved my honour.'

'Will you stay here with us?'

She glanced up at me. 'May I switch off for a while in a corner somewhere?'

I nodded. 'If that is what you wish.'

Zara addressed the stone in my ring. 'Jade Building Block, will you tell the others what Kwan Yin said?'

'I already have; it should be filtering back to you through the network already,' the stone said.

She dropped her head. 'I have been disconnected from the network for the last three days.'

The stone was silent for a moment, then: 'Reconnect, dear one, hear what they have to say.'

Zara concentrated for a moment and her face cleared, then she collapsed weeping again.

The stone in my ring took human form and stood behind her, his hand on her shoulder. 'Come to the armoury with me, Zara. The section for the Celestial Weapons is completely soundproofed and just what you need.'

She nodded and rose, then bowed her head to me. 'Thank you, Lady Emma, my honour is yours.' She went out with the stone, who nodded to me as he closed the door behind them.

I turned back to my computer just as a body landed on the floor with an almighty thump. I jumped up and peered over the desk, then relaxed; it was Leo, prone on the floor. He floated into the air, came upright, then sat in the chair across from me and collapsed over my desk.

'Keep trying, you'll have it soon,' I said.

'That's what Meredith keeps saying,' he said, his voice muffled by the desk. He pulled himself upright. 'I thought I'd have it first time! I've spent enough goddamn time in here gossiping with you — I should have the image straight in my head.'

I waved one hand at him and turned back to the computer. 'Just make less of a noise when you hit the floor, okay? I'm trying to get some work done here.'

'Humph,' he said, and disappeared with a rush of air that rustled my papers.

'And less of a tornado when you leave,' I said.

I'm working on it, he said.

Without the stone, I couldn't respond. I pressed the intercom button for Yi Hao.

'Yes, ma'am?'

'Pass on my congratulations to Lord Leo, please, he just learned telepathy.'

'Oh, ma'am, that is good news. I will do it right away.'

Really? You heard me?

I pressed the button again.

'Ma'am?'

'Please tell Leo: Yes. And tell him that I don't have my stone on me right now, so I can't talk back to him.'

Can't talk back to me, eh? Let me have a think

4

about all the things I could say to you while I have you like this.

'Bastard,' I said under my breath as I returned to my work.

I heard that.

Later that day, Leo dropped me off for my lunch meeting at the Mandarin Hotel with the planet Venus, the Jade Emperor's emissary. He pulled up across the road from the Landmark in Central, blatantly illegally using the Pedder Street informal lay-by outside the Pedder Building. I hopped out and walked up to the corner to cross the road, pulling my scruffy silk jacket closer around me; the late winter wind off the harbour was cold. Every shopfront in this area housed a famous designer label and the window displays struggled to outdo each other in artistic extravagance. Some of them didn't even show the products on sale; instead they focused on the 'lifestyle' they represented. Leo had been hounding me to go shopping with him along this strip to replace what he called my 'gruesome' wardrobe, but I'd managed to avoid it.

I entered the Landmark and took the escalators up to the pedestrian overpass across Queen's Road into Alexandra House, an unremarkable office building with a plain, tiled lobby full of people like me who were just passing through. I walked across another enclosed pedestrian bridge over Ice House Street to the Prince's Building, which was all shiny white tiles, glittering glass and jewellery shops displaying gemstones the size of pigeon eggs. Stern-looking Sikh security guards armed with sawn-off shotguns stood at the doors.

I passed a couple of tailor's shops and took another pedestrian overpass to the Mandarin Hotel. A huge

5

crystal chandelier adorned the staircase that swept from the ground-floor lobby up to the second floor. The Mandarin's coffee shop had been on the ground floor, with large windows looking out onto the street and providing a fascinating view of life in Central — the immaculately dressed tai-tais on their way to their daily salon visit, the couriers riding their heavy Chinese-made bicycles with full-sized gas bottles in the front basket, usually wearing nothing but a pair of filthy shorts and a grimy towel around their necks. Recently, however, the coffee shop had been moved up to the mezzanine floor and renamed something that sounded more upmarket — and was therefore unpronounceable. The cheesecake was the same though, which was why I'd arranged to meet Venus there.

Theoretically I had precedence over him as First Heavenly General (Acting), but it was politically sensible to arrive there first and do him the honour of waiting for him. The waiter guided me to a table next to the window overlooking the street, and went through the tedious rigmarole of spreading my napkin, offering me the over-priced bottled water of the day, filling my huge balloon wine glass with chilled water from a silver-plated jug, and handing me a menu that was mostly blank paper in an expensive leather folder. Finally he established that I was there to meet someone and left me to wait for Venus.

Venus arrived five minutes later, accompanied by a pair of Retainers who had taken the form of burly Chinese bodyguards. He was in the form of a mid-thirties Chinese, slim and elegant, wearing a tailored grey silk suit, his long hair held in a traditional topknot and flowing to his waist. The waiter escorted him to my table, did the napkin and water thing, then hurried back to the entrance to take the bodyguards to another table nearby. A couple of diners noticed the bodyguards and took surreptitious photos of us with their mobile phones, probably hoping to catch a minor celebrity meeting with his foreign mistress to sell to a gossip magazine. Unfortunately for them, all they would get would be movement-blurred images no matter how still they held the phone.

Venus toasted me with his glass of water: 'Lady Emma.' It was a polite alternative to the traditional salute in a modern setting. I nodded and toasted him back, then we checked the menus. The options hadn't changed much since we were last there so I just folded it and waited for him.

'Lord Leo wasn't able to join us?'

'I asked him to come along, but he said he had some errands to attend to at the bank,' I said. 'He's still establishing his identity, and the bank is giving him trouble about the new accounts.'

'He doesn't need to worry about these Earthly issues any more,' Venus said. 'Why hasn't he taken up residence on the Celestial where he belongs?'

'He says he belongs here with us, his family,' I said.

Venus nodded his understanding. 'He is unusual in his swift return to what he was doing before he was Raised. Do you think it has something to do with his Western heritage? Most Chinese are well aware of what lies in store for them should they attain Immortality. Westerners, however, seem to have little idea.'

'That may have something to do with it,' I said. 'What did Meredith do?'

'I have only recently made Master Liu's acquaintance, I'm afraid. You should probably ask her. I'd venture a guess that she was assisted by her husband.'

I nodded; that made sense.

'Leo must start to take his place among us, Lady Emma. He should be at your side when you are undertaking your official duties in the Northern Heavens. He is the Retainer of the First Heavenly General now, not a simple human bodyguard.'

'Try telling him that,' I said. 'And good luck.'

The waiter approached us, ready to take our order, and I opened the menu and pointed. 'Vegetarian pasta.'

'Hainan chicken,' Venus said, and I choked with laughter. He looked at me. 'What?'

'Very good,' the waiter said, and took our menus. 'Wine?'

'No, thank you,' we said together, and the waiter nodded and left.

'What's so funny about Hainan chicken?' Venus said.

'Do you know what *steak frites* is?'

'It's a restaurant in New York.'

'No, the dish itself.'

Venus nodded. 'Steak and chips. Horrible Western meal.'

'Well, Western restaurants all over the world do steak and chips, from the most down-market greasy-spoon diner to the top five-star hotel restaurant. It's everywhere, they just make it with less or more expensive ingredients and trimmings.'

'And this has to do with Hainan chicken how?' Venus said, then his face cleared. 'It's the same, isn't it. You can go get Hainan chicken from one of those chain cafeterias, or from a noodle shop in Tsim Sha Tsui, or from a top-class hotel like this. It's the same dish, just with different trimmings.'

'And everybody orders it!'

'Well, it's good,' Venus said.

'Not when the chicken's so underdone that the bones are red,' I grumbled quietly.

'Chicken is best underdone, it is tough when overcooked,' Venus protested. 'You are with a Celestial, you have no health risk!' He realised he had been speaking too loudly and dropped his voice, his face alight with mirth. 'The best chicken is done so that the meat is just cooked and the bones are still raw. It is a shame that in the last ten years or so they have become concerned about things like bird flu and have started cooking the chicken all the way through. Terrible waste.'

Our dishes arrived; mine was a monstrous plate of ribbon pasta with a thick creamy cheese sauce and large pieces of broccoli, carrot and mushroom. Venus's Hainan chicken was presented on an elegant platter, with one dish holding the gently boiled and cut-up chicken; three small sauce bowls; a bowl of rice that had been steamed in chicken stock; and a bowl of the stock as a soup.

He gestured dismissively towards the meat. 'See? Overdone. Cooked all the way through. At least they have chilled the skin so that it has become jelly — white chicken.'

'You do realise that if they roasted the chicken, the skin would become crisp and juicy?' I said.

'I have had Western chicken before,' Venus said. 'It is good, but different. This,' he waved his chopsticks over his food, 'is the way chicken *should* be done.'

We ate in silence for a while, the waiters occasionally topping up our water glasses. Venus raised his head, his face blank, then returned to his chicken.

'They're checking on me,' he said. 'I am never left to my own devices for even two seconds.'

'I know the feeling!'

'At least you're not telepathic,' he said with humour.

'No, so when they contact me with an emergency, I have to call them back on my mobile, or wake up this goddamn cranky stone.'

'I resemble that remark,' the stone said.

'Isn't the correct term "resent that remark"?' Venus said.

'It's a lame Western joke,' the stone said. 'Emma uses it all the time.'

'So my Western lameness is rubbing off on you,' I said. 'Compounding your Eastern lameness, making you even more lame.'

'I have never heard anybody speak to a Building Block like that before,' Venus said with wonder. 'Or a Heavenly General, for that matter.'

'Get used to it,' the stone grumbled. 'She's so blunt sometimes I wince.'

'That's *you* rubbing off on *me*,' I said.

'Conceded,' the stone said.

Venus shook his head over his rice.

We didn't get down to business until the coffee and cheesecake, but Venus was such a charming companion that I didn't mind the wait.

'Generally the news is good,' he said. 'The residents of the Northern Heavens have made their feelings known about your solution to the energy problem; you have gained a great deal of political mileage with this one.'

'It had nothing to do with me,' I said. 'It's the Xuan Wu's children who have made it happen.'

'Regardless, you are the one who brought them together,' Venus said.

'I've established a small team of Celestials to search all the nearby oceans for any other children of the Xuan Wu who may have been enslaved by Six,' I said. 'We found one turtle and three snakes. I hope we find them all; but they themselves say that when their father is back, he'll be able to find them quickly.'

'That is good news. Any reports on the locations of the other two demons in that group?'

'I have people in Thailand working together with the Phoenix's people to search for the Death Mother,' I said. 'It appears that both she and the Geek have gone to ground.'

'The Geek is somewhere in Shenzhen, correct?'

'Yes.'

'I don't know which is worse: the urban jungle of Shenzhen, or the tropical jungle of Thailand.'

'Exactly.'

'Anything else major happening that I need to know about?'

'Not really. Simone is settling nicely into her new school. Leo is learning very quickly; only yesterday he started using telepathy.'

'Really?' Venus's face went slack for a moment, then he snapped back and grinned. 'He told me he'd come have lunch with us next time, but only if I'm buying and I wear something ... to quote him ... "really cute".'

'Stone, tell Leo that he is *such* a man-whore,' I said.

Venus's eyes went wide.

Oh snap, Leo said. *Can you do me a favour and come up to the bank when you're done there and scare the living daylights out of these assholes for me? I need backup!*

Venus obviously heard it too. 'He did *not* just ask you to go rescue him?' he said.

I shrugged. 'Apparently I do "angry gweipoh" extremely well.'

'What is that? Angry "foreign grandmother"?'

'You don't see them as much any more, but back before the Handover they were everywhere.'

'The Handover?'

'Hong Kong to China, in '97. Anyway, imagine this. You have a wealthy English lady, probably from an old, titled family, who's always had everything her own way. Back in England, tradesmen came to her house at the snap of her fingers, she paid them very well for the finest-quality work, and was treated like a princess by everybody. She comes here and the quality of the work is slapdash, tradesmen turn up at eleven at night, customer service is sloppy everywhere, and *nobody* treats her like a princess. After a couple of years of this, she gets angry with the whole thing. The minute anything isn't exactly as she wants it she throws a huge tantrum to get things moving. Well, that's what Leo wants me to do for him over at the bank.'

'Sounds like some of the local women as well,' Venus said wryly.

'Yeah, I saw that YouTube of the woman throwing a tantrum at the airport too,' I said.

We were interrupted by a woman loudly arguing with the waiter about the items on her bill, and shared a smile.

I finished my coffee, caught a waiter's eye and drew a circle in the air to indicate that I wanted the bill. He nodded and turned away to retrieve it.

'Nothing else exciting happening?' I said. 'Sounds like things are reasonably under control for a change.'

'The Demon King still tries us, but for some reason

his attempts lately have been half-hearted,' Venus said. 'Oh! Er Lang.'

I sagged over the table, picked up my fork and drew circles in the remains of my cheesecake with it. 'Tell me the worst.'

'He has once again petitioned the Celestial to have you removed from your post, citing lack of competence.'

I shrugged. 'Situation normal then.'

'Don't be concerned, Emma, the Celestial supports your efforts. The recent rejuvenation of the Northern Heavens is a demonstration of your suitability for the role. Remember, if the Kingdom flourishes, it indicates that the sovereign is worthy.'

'Martin and Yue Gui should be running the place in name as well as reality,' I said. 'They do all the work and I'm the one getting the credit; it's wrong.'

'That is the way it should be. You are the supreme ruler, and they manage the day-to-day affairs for you. The generals have been freed from the more tedious administrative tasks and can concentrate on defending the Heavens, which is probably why the Demon King has slowed his efforts. It is an excellent result all around.'

'I'd just like to know which demon it was that gave Yue Gui to me in the first place,' I said. 'It could have been Six, hoping to plant a spy, or another demon trying to undermine Six's efforts by telling us about the nest under Golden Arcade.'

'I'd say most likely it was either the Death Mother or the Geek, using one of Six's stone-implanted Shen as a spy and at the same time undermining Six's own empire. You can ask them yourself when you catch them.'

The waiter brought the bill and I pulled out my wallet to pay.

Venus knew better than to give me grief about the bill. 'My turn to pay next time.'

I nodded. 'Remind me before we order so I can get something extremely expensive.'

'I will,' he said. After the waiter had left he turned around to his bodyguards and nodded. 'We're done.'

One of the bodyguards rose and came to us. He stood fidgeting for a moment, then said, 'Lady Emma, ma'am, I have heard very much about you from Lord Venus. May I ask you a question?'

'Sure, go ahead,' I said.

The waiter came with the folder containing the receipt and my credit card, and I nodded and removed them.

'Do you give private tuition, ma'am?' the bodyguard said. 'My skills are weak with sword, polearm and spear. My broadsword is terrible, and I completely fail at chain staff —'

'You exaggerate; your martial arts skills are the match of anyone,' Venus said amiably.

The waiter stared at us.

'Would you teach me, ma'am?' the bodyguard said. 'Could I come down to the Academy and learn from you?'

'There are plenty of instructors at the Academy who are better than me,' I said. 'Venus has my secretary's number; just give her a call and she'll arrange something for you.'

The bodyguard fell to one knee and then rose again, to the bemused stares of nearby diners. 'I would appreciate it if you could spare some of your own time, ma'am.'

'Let me see what I can work out,' I said. 'I really am too busy to take on private students.'

The bodyguard nodded, grinning broadly. 'Thank you, ma'am!'

'Did you just ask this gweipoh for private tuition in martial arts?' the waiter asked the bodyguard in Cantonese.

'Yes,' the bodyguard said. 'She is the *best*!'

'I'm not the best, and you know it,' I said. 'There are many, many better than me.'

'Have you been in any famous movies, ma'am?' the waiter said.

'Not a single one,' I said. 'I'm just a teacher. Nothing special.'

'A foreign woman who teaches martial arts is something special,' the waiter said with humour. He bowed to me. 'My name is Jimmy, ask for me next time you come.'

'I'll be sure to,' I lied.

I rose and Venus did as well, and we shook hands. 'Lovely to catch up with you, Venus. I'll have my people arrange something next month; sooner if something major turns up.'

Venus bowed slightly to me. 'My pleasure, ma'am. You'd better hurry and go rescue poor Leo.'

I picked up my bag. 'Poor little Leo. Scared of the big bad bank.'

CHAPTER 2

I took the escalators from the enormous open area under the bank building up two storeys to the general banking hall. Leo was parked in his wheelchair next to one of the flat, square leather waiting seats, holding a stack of papers in his lap.

I sat on the chair facing him. 'What's it all about?'

'They say I can't open an account without proof of residence.' He waved his documents. 'These are all in *your* name. I have nothing that shows that I live here.'

'Stone, can you do something about this?' I said.

'Let me talk to Lok about it,' the stone said.

'I forgot how annoying the racism here can be,' Leo said irritably. 'The teller took one look at me and frowned. Then, when I started talking to her, she actually turned away.'

'It might be the speech impediment too, mate, it makes you a bit hard to understand the first time.'

'Bah. Do you have any idea how much concentration it takes to get rid of that?'

'Enough that it's not worth it and people will have to learn to deal.'

'Pain in the ass.'

'I have some documents for you; I've put them into Emma's bag,' the stone said.

I opened my tote and pulled out some freshly printed and folded papers: electricity, gas and phone bills for one of the apartments at the Old Folly, all in Leo's name and backdated six months. I scrunched the documents a few times to make them appear older, then handed them to Leo. 'Here you go.'

He flipped through them and nodded. 'Okay, let's try this.'

He turned in the wheelchair and rejoined the queue to speak to the tellers. I stood beside him. A few people openly stared at him as we waited, but we ignored them. Finally we reached the end of the queue and a light indicated a free teller. Leo wheeled himself to the window, which was too high for him to comfortably see over. He raised himself on his arms to speak to the teller.

'Can we talk to someone about opening an account?'

She stared at him, uncomprehending, then glanced at me.

'You do speak English?' he said.

She continued to look blank.

'I want to open an account,' Leo said more slowly and clearly, trying to work around his speech impediment.

The teller spoke to me, ignoring Leo. 'What account type you want to open?'

'My friend wants to open a savings account,' I said.

The teller pushed some forms across the counter to me. 'Ask friend to fill in forms.' She leaned back and waited for us to leave.

Leo raised the documents he was holding and put them on the counter. 'I've already filled them in. The account is for *me*.'

The teller took the forms and skimmed through them, then looked at me. 'He needs proof of Hong Kong residence.'

'I'm right here,' Leo growled, frustrated.

I gestured towards Leo. 'Talk to him then. Like he said, he's right here.'

The teller stared at me.

'This is for *me*,' Leo repeated. 'I have all the documents and I want to open an account.'

The teller jumped up from her chair and quickly walked away.

'What the *hell*!' Leo said.

'No, it's fine. She's rushed off to get help.'

'Why didn't she say something?'

'It's considered politer to rush off and do it for you, rather than dither around telling you that they're going to do it,' I said. 'They're used to being chastised for wasting time.'

Leo rested his hands on the arms of the chair. 'Well, *that's* stupid.'

The teller came back with a young man in a suit. He leaned over the counter to speak to me. 'You want to open a new account?'

'No, *I* do,' Leo said.

The young man appeared to see Leo for the first time. 'Wait here, please,' he said and walked away.

Leo thumped the arm of his wheelchair.

The teller retook her seat and pressed the button to indicate that she was free. A local man came over and leaned around us to talk to her in Cantonese, so we were forced to move to one side.

'Let's just go to the other bank next door,' Leo said, and wheeled himself around to leave.

The young man opened a door near us and nodded. 'Please, come this way.'

Leo hesitated, then shrugged and wheeled himself through the door, with me following. The young man led us to a small, glass-walled meeting room with a tiny round table. He sat and pulled out a pen, then gestured for us to sit.

'So sorry. Yes, we have all the documents here. Do you have your ID and proof of residence? Rent notice, electricity, phone bill ...'

'Here,' Leo said, and passed his passport, Hong Kong ID card and the new documents across the table.

The young man flipped through the documents, checking them against the forms that Leo had filled in, and nodded. 'Thank you, sir, this is all in order. How much were you looking to deposit to start the account?'

Leo opened his mouth to answer but I tapped his hand. *Tell him to say a million dollars,* I said to the stone.

'Uh ... one point three million dollars,' Leo said. *Geez, let's make it something more believable than just a round mill,* he added silently to me. *Besides, if you're gonna foot the bill, I'd better make it worthwhile, eh?*

'One point three million Hong Kong dollars?' the young man said, his eyebrows raised.

Leo grinned evilly. 'No, American dollars. Will I have to convert it?'

The young man looked down at the papers, then up at Leo. 'We can provide you with a Premier account for that, sir. With a platinum credit card, priority service and special offers. If you have two million, we can provide you with private banking, which has a range of extended services.'

'No, Premier is fine,' Leo said.

'Normally I would move you to the Premier Banking office floor,' the young man said, 'but in this case it would probably suit you better to do it here, and I can show you through when we're done. Is that suitable?'

Leo relaxed. 'Quite suitable.'

The young man nodded. 'We will give you a multiple currency account, but you will need to deposit one million Hong Kong. The rest you can keep as US.'

Leo waved one hand airily. 'No, convert it all to Hong Kong dollars, I live here now. Let's go ahead.'

The young man nodded, took a business card holder out of his breast pocket, rose and held out a card to Leo with both hands. 'Leave it with me for a moment, sir, and I will return shortly with the account information for you, and show you where your Premier Banking service centre is.'

'Fine,' Leo said, and the young man went out.

'Money talks,' I said.

'He's googling you,' the stone said with humour. 'He couldn't find "Leo Alexander" so he's now looking for ... oh, this is funny.'

'What?' Leo said.

'He thinks you're Mike Tyson,' the stone said. 'He's looking up photos of Mike Tyson.'

'Humph,' Leo said. 'I am ten times uglier than that mother.'

'Hear, hear,' I said.

'Emma didn't do Ugly Gweipoh, she did Rich Bitch instead,' the stone said, disappointed. 'I like Ugly Gweipoh better.'

'Ugly Gweipoh tends to involve burning bridges,' I said, 'and Leo did the Rich Bitch, not me! If we did

Ugly Gweipoh we would be branded as trouble, and Leo would have problems getting his money out to buy his expensive loafers.'

'You fill my shoes with sand again and I'll never forgive you!' Leo said. 'Those were Armani!'

'You filled my shoes with sand first,' I said.

'Shoes from K-Mart in Australia *do not count*,' Leo said.

I raised one foot. 'Yes, they do.'

He buried his face in his hand. 'I give up.'

'I thought you liked to avoid stereotyping,' I said.

'Stereotyping is one thing. Dressing like a street sleeper when you have a fund of several hundred million dollars —' He stopped as the young man returned.

The bank employee looked from Leo to me, then sat at the table with a glossy folder containing all of Leo's account information. He passed me a business card. 'Maybe I could interest you in some private banking as well, ma'am? If you have several hundred million dollars, we can help you to manage those funds and ensure that they grow for you.'

I took his card with a nod. 'Thank you, but I already have a private banking advisor here.'

The young man shook his head and flipped open the folder to explain the account details to Leo.

Michael stood on my right in Training Room Four, watching as I raised my left hand and summoned demon essence to fill it. 'That's it. Demon essence.'

Michael raised his left hand and chi glowed around it. He grimaced and the chi disappeared. He dropped his head in concentration and the chi reappeared around his hand, this time a deep purple, almost black.

'That's interesting. Can you do black?' I said.

Michael concentrated again and the chi became a light blue. He shook his head. 'Nope.'

'Okay,' I said. I released the Murasame from my right hand and it floated above the floor; the sword was fussy about being dropped. 'Take my hand.'

Michael took my right hand in his left and used the connection to observe my demon essence. He gasped. 'Damn, Emma.'

'I know,' I said. 'I need to spend some time on the Celestial Plane.'

'Soon!' Michael said. 'How do you control that?'

'I have no idea. Seen enough?'

Michael nodded and released my hand, then raised his own again and dropped his head, concentrating. The dark blue chi reappeared and he shook his head. 'I don't think I can do it.'

'Of course you can't. You're my son, and I'm too yang to produce anything like that,' the Tiger said from where he'd appeared on the other side of the room.

'Tell Lok to freaking *inform me* before letting this bastard into the Academy,' I said to the stone in my ring.

'That is no way to greet an old friend,' the Tiger said. He approached us, hands out. 'Peace. Michael, I need to talk to you.'

Michael turned away. 'I have nothing to say to you.' He bowed slightly to me. 'It's kind of a relief that I can't do it, Emma. I'll see you later — I'm having dinner at your place tonight.'

I nodded to him. 'I just wish I wasn't able to do it either.'

'Look, it's about your mother,' the Tiger said. 'Can we put this aside? We both loved her, and I need your help to find out why she died.'

Michael rounded on the Tiger. 'It's obvious why she died. You killed her!' He swept one hand through the air. 'Or one of the other wives killed her in a fit of jealousy. Either way, she's gone and you're responsible.' He spun to leave.

'I know I'm responsible,' the Tiger said. 'And Emma is a clue as to what happened. I need you to help me find out what made your mother different.'

Michael ignored him, opening the door to exit.

'Emma, I need you too,' the Tiger said. 'Come to the lab and donate some DNA. We need to find out what killed Rhonda so it doesn't happen to anyone again.'

'I'm a demon,' I said. 'That's what would kill me.'

'You're not listening to me, either of you!' the Tiger shouted, and Michael stopped halfway through the door. 'Michael, what killed her could kill you!' He pointed at me. 'And you! I want to save your fucking lives here, humans. For fuck's sake, let me!' He dropped his voice. 'I want to ensure that no Celestial Worthy is ever destroyed again by taking the Elixir. They should gain Immortality, not die! Hell, boy, you'll probably achieve Immortality by yourself. But if you ever want that fucking Elixir, you'd better be damn sure that it won't blow you up.'

Michael dropped his head. 'Like it did my mother.'

'I loved her,' the Tiger said, his voice full of anguish. 'She was my world. And now she's gone, nothing means anything to me. The only thing keeping me going is the thought that I can stop this from happening to you.'

'Let me think about it,' Michael said without looking up. He walked out, softly closing the door behind him.

'Emma?' the Tiger said.

'I'll think about it too,' I said. 'I can only travel to the Celestial Plane as a serpent. I'm contaminated by the demon essence ...'

'We might be able to remove the demon from you if we study your DNA,' the Tiger said.

'Maybe. Either way, let me think about it. I'm scheduled to spend some time on the Plane next week, visiting the Northern Heavens for an update on how things are going and some hearings. I might stop in at the West to help you out.'

'I can always send some scientists down here to take some samples if you don't want to come to the West,' he said. 'Your choice. I just want to make sure that when Ah Wu comes back, he can fulfil his promise to you.' He waved a hand after Michael. 'This kid will be my Number One one day, and the finest I've ever had. But to get there, he's gonna need Immortality, and we need to be sure that the Elixir won't kill him.' He disappeared.

I retrieved the Murasame from where it was floating in the air and put it back into its black scabbard. What the Tiger didn't know was my memories of being imprisoned in a hospital-type lab being infused with demon essence had affected me; I'd suffered nightmares ever since. The idea of being the willing subject of lab experiments was something I found hard even to consider.

When I got back to my office there was an email waiting for me that made me sigh.

To: Emma Donahoe
<emmad@newwudang.com.hk>
   From: Evarocks <eva95@zqphoenix.com.id>
   Hi Emma,
   I haven't heard from Simone in ages, is she okay? Me and Sylvie kinda miss going around with her. I emailed her a couple of days ago and she didn't reply.
   If she doesn't want to be friends any more, could you tell her it's okay, I understand, but just to tell me and I'll stop contacting her to do stuff?
   Thanx
   Eva

I stared at the screen for a moment, then replied.

To: Evarocks <eva95@zqphoenix.com.id>
   From: Emma Donahoe
<emmad@newwudang.com.hk>
   Bcc: Simone Chen
<darkchaos4682@gmail.com>
   Hi Eva,
   I think it's mainly that she's so busy with school at the moment — because of the change of schools mid-year she's flat out catching up with the rest of her class. I'm sure that when things settle down she'll be back in contact with you.
   Emma

I quickly composed another email:

To: Simone Chen <darkchaos4682@gmail.com>
   From: Emma Donahoe
<emmad@newwudang.com.hk>

I bcc'd the message to you so you could see,
but she doesn't know I sent it on to you.
I remember when you were five years old and
didn't have a single friend in the world. How
things have changed.
E

I would get the Silent Treatment when she got home from the shops later, but it would be worth it.

CHAPTER 3

About four that afternoon, Simone contacted me telepathically. *Emma, I'm going to call you on your mobile. Can you play along, please?*

My mobile rang and I answered it. 'Yes?'

Simone sounded incredibly giggly and silly. 'Emma, can you come pick me up at Festie? I'm here with my friends and we're done.'

'What? Why?'

I wanna be normal for a change, Emma, can you just do this for me? I want them to see me getting picked up like a normal kid.

'Just come and get me, please, Emma,' she whined.

'I suppose. I'll meet you at the lay-by.'

'You'll have to come to the car park, the lay-by's closed for some stupid roadworks or something.' I heard her friends giggling in the background, and one of them said something. 'Can you meet us under the P and S?' Simone added. 'Right down the bottom, close to the doors, please, we have a lot of stuff. Oh, and can you give Sarah a lift home too?'

I sighed with feeling. 'I suppose.'

'Thanks, Emma!' she said, and hung up. *Thanks, really, Emma*, she added silently. *I wouldn't ask if you had a class, and I won't ask again, okay?*

'Tell her she can ask as much as she likes if it makes her feel good about being normal,' I said to the stone.

Simone's voice was giddy in my head. *You're the GREATEST, Emma!*

'You won't be the greatest when she gets your email,' the stone said.

I rose and collected my bag.

'Not sending Leo?' the stone said.

'Nah, he's with Meredith. It'll do me good to get out of the office, even if it is to go through the tunnel.'

It took half an hour to wend my way through the Cross-Harbour Tunnel traffic and reach the top of Kowloon City and the massive shopping mall of Festival Walk. The mall didn't look much from the outside, a regular two-storey rectangular monolith, but inside it plunged to six storeys below ground level. I entered the spiralling ramp down to the car park, travelling a long time before I reached the boom gate. I pushed my credit card into the slot and wound my way to the bottom floor, another three levels down. The car park was deserted this far down during the day, and I pulled up next to the lobby at the bottom of the escalators below the supermarket.

Simone wasn't there so I pulled out my phone to call her. There was no signal so I left the car and went towards the escalator lobby. As I opened the door to enter, my hand was grabbed from behind and I was swung away from the door. I didn't really register who had attacked me; I just knew they were human not demon: three Chinese men, all of them menacingly close. The one holding my wrist was grinning at me.

28

I didn't mess around; I moved as quickly as I could and took them down. I pushed just above the heart of the man holding my wrist and his knees buckled, his eyes went blank and he collapsed. I used a simple throat block to make the second feel unable to breathe for a few seconds, and used that time to hit the third under the ear on a pressure point that put him straight to sleep. I returned to the second and shoved him in the solar plexus, knocking him unconscious as well.

I was bending to check their unmoving bodies for ID when I heard panting and running. I looked up, preparing to defend myself again, and saw the Nemesis, Peter Tong. He was wearing a designer polo shirt and a pair of slacks hitched under his bulging stomach. His face was swollen with exertion and one flailing arm held a small pistol. I moved into a long defensive stance, ready to take him down before he could shoot me.

He stopped, bent over his knees to pant for a while, then stood again. 'What happened?'

'Put the gun down,' I said.

He waved the gun again and I ducked as he pointed it at my head. 'No! I'm here to defend you!'

I moved close to him, put my foot between his feet, bent my knee into him and pushed him onto his back, taking the gun at the same time. He smelt of cooking oil and expensive aftershave.

'You idiot, you could have killed me,' I said. I checked the magazine; it was empty. 'You run around with an empty gun? What *are* you doing?'

Simone and her friend Sarah came down the escalators and hurried to us.

'Oh, Emma, were you attacked?' Sarah said, waving her arms theatrically. 'What a stroke of luck that Peter was here to save you!'

'Wait a minute,' I said, and looked from the Nemesis, still gasping on the ground, to Sarah. 'How much did he pay you to do this, Sarah?'

'Oh, you know about it? Three thousand dollars,' Sarah said. She went to Peter and held out her hand. 'Come on, pay up.'

'What happened?' Simone said. She studied the goons on the ground. 'These aren't ... These are ordinary ...' She was silent for a moment, thinking. 'You were mugged by three men, Emma?'

'Yeah, and Peter came rushing with his dinky cowboy gun to rescue me,' I said.

'Wait, he paid Sarah?' Simone took her friend by the shoulder. 'He *paid* you to set Emma up?'

'Nobody was going to get hurt. It was just a little demonstration to show Emma how much she needs a man in her life to defend her,' Peter said. He clumsily pulled himself to his feet. 'What if these men had attacked you and I hadn't been here to scare them off?'

'*You* scared them off?' Simone said with scorn.

'Look! They all fainted with fear when they saw me!' Peter said.

I passed the gun to Simone and she held it as if it were something contaminated. I moved into a serpent-style stance: legs spread, and palms flat and facing down like the head of a snake. I jabbed a few times at the Nemesis's eyes, making him reel back with shock, then lightly hit him with the tips of my fingers, not enough to hurt him but enough to make him feel it. I struck his chin, throat, shoulders, chest, and then made a flurry of strikes at his stomach, not hard enough to do damage. I changed to monkey style and swept low, taking his feet out from under him, and catching him just as he was about to hit the ground. I lowered him to the floor so that he didn't hurt himself, and stepped back.

'I took them down myself,' I said. 'I'm a master of seventeen different styles of Kung Fu.'

Sarah stared at me, then turned to Simone. 'Do you do martial arts too?'

Simone hesitated, then raised her chin. 'Yes.'

'*Why?*'

'It's fun,' Simone said.

Sarah turned back to Peter. 'I did what you asked me to. Where's my money?'

Peter pulled himself back to his feet, then hunched over, grimacing with pain. 'I'm horribly injured! You beat me! I need an ambulance — and a lawyer!'

'You're a good thirty centimetres taller than me,' I said. 'Nobody's going to believe that I hurt you, particularly when there isn't a mark on you.'

He raised his shirt, revealing his white, glutinous abdomen. 'I'm covered in bruises!'

'No, you're not. Get over yourself.' I turned away from him. 'I think you need to find a lift home, Sarah. Or was this loser going to drive you as well as pay you blood money?'

'My driver's on the way to pick me up anyway,' Sarah said with a toss of her head. 'I don't need to call *my* stepmother for a lift. My *real* mother can't drive, she doesn't *need* to. We have a driver; we don't drive ourselves around like domestic helpers.' She turned to Simone. 'Next time I think I'll go shopping with someone *interesting*, not some freak who does martial arts.'

She swung her bags as she turned to go up the escalators, then turned back to Peter. 'I know who you are, loser, and you owe me. If you don't pay up soon,

I'll get my boyfriend and some of his friends to spray-paint your store in Central. The *inside*.' She swept away.

'Well, thank you very much,' Simone said, grabbing her bags and storming towards the car. She turned back to yell at me. 'Just go and ruin my life one friend at a time, Emma, why don't you!'

I pointed at the unconscious goons on the ground. 'How much did you pay them?' I asked Peter.

He pulled down his polo shirt to cover his stomach, his face red. 'I never paid anybody! I protected you from these ... these ... *thugs*!'

I moved into a serpent stance again. 'How about protecting yourself from *me*?'

He opened and closed his mouth a few times, then ran away into the escalator lobby, his arms flailing.

I returned to the car. Simone was sitting in the back, leaning against the door and weeping. I reached into my bag, pulled out a packet of tissues and handed it to her. She took it without looking at me.

I switched on the ignition and drove up towards the surface.

Do you want me to recall that email? the stone said.

No.

Your call, I suppose.

Yes.

We drove home in silence.

Later, at home, Simone came into the office and sat across the desk from me. 'You are such a cow,' she said.

I didn't look away from the screen. 'Thank you.'

She sighed and put her head in her hands. 'Sarah is the *least* snotty of the snotty bitches in my grade.'

'No, she isn't, Simone, you are.'

She was silent for a moment, then swept back her honey-coloured hair and sat back in her chair. 'I just want to be a normal kid. Is that so hard?'

'I desperately want to be a normal human. Not a demon. Not a snake. Just a woman. Sometimes we have to deal with what we're given.'

'Thanks for pointing out all the horrible things that have happened to you because of me.'

'I think it's more because of your father,' I said mildly. 'Particularly the snake thing.'

'When he comes back, our lives are gonna be twenty times weirder again, aren't they?'

'Probably.'

'I really don't want a weird life, Emma. Sometimes, I don't want him back; I just want to have a normal life here without him.'

I turned to face her. 'When he was living with your mother, she wouldn't let him do *anything* Celestial in front of her. That's one of the reasons we're in this predicament in the first place —'

'You can't blame Mummy for this!' she protested.

'I'm not blaming her. I've heard a lot about your mother, Simone, and she was a wonderful, strong, smart woman who put up with an awful lot of bullshit from your dad and his assorted cronies before she put her foot down and told him she'd had enough. She wanted a normal life too. He did his best to give her that, and he did incredibly well. Jade's told me stories about how your mother sacrificed so much — her career, her travel, everything — and he made the sacrifice too of not taking True Form, of not travelling to the Plane nearly as much, and of staying here with you.'

'They should have known it would end in disaster,' Simone said, her voice small. 'Daddy should have known. Celestials can see the future. He should never have promised Mummy not to take True Form, that was so *stupid*.'

'He can't see the future when those he loves are involved. He's said that.'

She glanced at me. 'Really? He didn't know whether we'd live or die?'

'He said he could see the possibilities, and they were all nasty. The other Celestials wouldn't tell him. The minute your mother was murdered, he knew things were heading downhill fast and did the best he could to salvage the situation.'

'I wonder how things would be if Mummy was still alive,' she said. 'She could have taken me to the Plane ... Daddy would be at full strength ... we would be a family.'

'I've said that myself more than once.'

She dropped her head. 'Oh, sorry, Emma.'

'Nothing to be sorry about. But when your father comes back — and he *will* come back, Simone — you'll have your family again.'

'And the weirdness will get twenty times worse.'

'You missed my point. He's quite capable of being normal and having a mundane family life if that's what's required of him. He did it for your mother, he can do it for you. Well, as normal as is possible in this crazy town.'

She brightened but didn't reply.

'There won't be the low-energy issue, and you won't be a tiny child who can't travel to the Plane,' I went on. 'It'll all work out.'

'Maybe,' she said. 'But in the meantime, I have to go

back to school tomorrow and be labelled a martial arts freak because I told Sarah the truth.'

'You know what, Simone? I think every other girl — and boy — there will think you're the coolest kid ever 'cause you can do the arts, and they'll ask you for demonstrations. Then, by the end of the week, they'll have forgotten all about it.'

'I will *not* give demonstrations.'

'I don't either.'

She smiled. 'That was a pretty convincing demonstration you gave the Nemesis.'

'Did you see his *tummy*?'

She laughed, and it was wonderful to hear. 'It was like vanilla pudding, oh my God, so *flabby*!'

I dropped my voice to a low purr. 'Sexy.'

She laughed even harder.

'Don't cut off your friendship with Eva and Sylvie just because they're Shen, Simone. If you do that, you're no better than Sarah. They can be ordinary kids, just like you, and you can go shopping with them just like ordinary girls. They like you.'

She paused, thoughtful. 'I guess you're right.'

The entrance to the Palace of the Dark Heavens was a huge gate at the end of a long, tree-lined avenue. The road widened there to form a circle so people could be dropped off; and in the circle's centre was a round pavilion, about four metres across, for those who arrived directly.

When Simone and I landed there was a sedan chair waiting for us next to the pavilion, a couple of tame demons standing unmoving and patient between the carry bars. Two officials in black robes were there too, and two black, heavy-set Chinese horses stood behind the sedan chair, saddled and bridled but not tethered to anything.

The officials bowed low, saluting at the same time. One stepped forward and spoke. 'Regent of the Dark Northern Heavens, Lady Emma, Dark Lady, First Heavenly General, Serpent Who Wears the Stone of the World. Princess Simone, Only Human Child of the Xuan Wu, Wielder of the Seven Stars. We welcome you to your palace and trust you will be comfortable during your stay. It is our desire to fulfil your every wish. The hearths are warm and the servants ready to do your bidding. Please allow us to guide you to your home in the Northern Heavens.'

I bowed my serpent head to them both individually. 'True Lord Xu, Religious Master of Ten Thousand Magical Arts and Giver of Supernatural Aid; True Lord Yu, Religious Master of Meritorious Magnificence, Original Lord of the Transmission of the Salvific Miracle, I am honoured by your welcome and greet you most cordially.'

'I honour your welcome, my Lords,' Simone said, and saluted. 'All appears to be in good order, in alignment with the forces of the Celestial and pleasing to the spirit.'

Lord Xu gestured towards the sedan chair. 'My Ladies, if it pleases you, I have arranged this transportation to your abode in the Heavens, guarded and guided by ourselves to ensure that you reach your destination in safety and comfort.'

We nodded again and I replied, 'This transportation is most suitable for our needs and we are pleased to take it to our palace.'

The officials bowed to us again, and we walked — or in my case slithered with as much dignity as I could muster — to the sedan chair. I coiled up in my 'senior' place on the seat facing forward and Simone sat facing the back. The curtains over the windows closed by themselves and there was a lurch upwards as the demons lifted the chair. There was barely room for Simone's knees to clear the seat on my side. She leaned back and closed her eyes. The jingling bits and creaking of leather indicated that the officials had mounted their horses. The sedan chair lurched again and began its horrible swaying progression towards the palace entrance.

'You had it exactly right,' the stone said. 'Well done.'

'It's a freaking script,' I said softly. 'It's all acting.'

'It is an important ceremony that emphasises and enhances your rule over the Northern Heavens and attunes the energy flowing in the palace to your own,' the stone said. 'The whole thing is vital to the health of your rule and the Heavens themselves.'

'That is the biggest load of bull I have ever heard,' Simone said without opening her eyes.

'How does the Tiger put up with all this?' I said.

'The Tiger revels in it,' the stone said. 'Michael's told you about the Harvest Festival, hasn't he?'

'Yeah, he says it's like the German Oktoberfest,' Simone said. 'Just a huge excuse to get drunk.'

'The Tiger performs many rituals during the three days of the festival to ensure the safety and wellbeing of his family,' the stone said. 'Michael would be aware of that if he were further up the hierarchy of sons. For those lower down, it's just a big party.'

'It's kind of disturbing the way they wear cloth patches to indicate their relationship to the Tiger so no incest takes place,' Simone said. She opened her eyes and grabbed the side of the sedan chair as it lurched particularly violently; one of the carriers had stumbled slightly. 'I mean, what if they met each other outside the palace and got it on? It's so *wrong*.'

The stone hesitated slightly, then said, 'Is this something that concerns you, Simone?'

She leaned back again, her expression stiff. 'Maybe.'

'The tradition of "calling" is a way of avoiding this. Mortals do it to mimic Celestials.'

Simone looked interested. 'Really? I thought it was just about using the title to show respect.'

'It's more than just establishing the pecking order in the family,' the stone said. 'It's a way of confirming exactly how closely you're related. Junior members of the family greet senior members by "calling" them — Poh Poh, Yeh Yeh, Wai Poh for the grandmother on the mother's side. They establish themselves immediately so everybody present, from other branches of the family too, can straightaway see where they sit in the family network.'

'Jade told me a story about that,' Simone said. 'When my mother's parents first came to visit us in Hong Kong, I went up to my grandmother and "called" her — Poh Poh probably; I don't remember it myself. I was used to "calling" everybody in my family, but it confused them. She just stood there and said "What?"'

'And you were standing there waiting for the "good girl" response that kids always get when they "call" their grandparents,' I said with amusement. 'Culture shock both ways just in the first few words.'

'So it's actually a way of establishing links?' Simone said. 'I never thought of it that way. I thought of it — like you said — as the "pecking order" in the family.' She grinned. 'Human families have it easy. What about your sister's son who's a couple of hundred years older than you and also a tree? What do you call him?'

'Jerk-off,' I said quietly.

Simone nodded with mock solemnity. 'Very well, Lady Emma, when I next "call" my nephew, I will greet him as "Jerk-off".'

I stretched out on the cushioned seat. 'You won't have to; I'll probably already have done it.'

The chair lurched again and I nearly slid off the silk cushions onto the floor. I coiled up again, tightening my grip on the silk. 'Dammit, I hate these things!'

'I'm not surprised Daddy bought the car,' Simone said.

The sedan chair stopped suddenly and I landed on my back on the floor in an undignified heap. I raised my tail to give me the leverage to crawl back onto the cushion but it was too late. The curtains flipped open and there we were: Simone sitting like the princess she was, and me in a three-metre-long tangle at her feet.

The officials had dismounted and stood on either side of the door to escort us out. I flipped so that I was the right way up, shook my head, and slithered out of the chair and onto the pavers in front of the palace.

Yue Gui, Simone's big sister, and Martin, her big brother, waited for us in the forecourt of the palace. They were dressed in Tang-style silk robes: Martin in black and silver; Yue Gui in pink and gold. They bowed and saluted us. Simone and I stood opposite them and bowed back.

'Welcome, She Zheng Zhi, Gong Zhu, Regent and Princess,' Yue Gui said.

'We thank you, Gong Zhu and Wang Chu, Prince and Princess,' I said.

'Jie Jie, Ge Ge,' Simone said, 'calling' her relatives.

'Mei Mei,' Yue Gui and Martin both responded with pleasure.

Simone's shoulders slumped slightly. 'Can we *stop* with the formal protocol BS now?'

Martin gave her a quick, friendly hug, then smiled down at her with his hands on her shoulders. 'Yes, we're done. Come inside and have some lunch.'

I held back. 'Is Sang Shen here?'

'No,' Yue Gui said, amused by my dislike of her son. 'He's still under house arrest at home, serving his sentence.'

The four of us sat at the round, six-seater table with a couple of demon servants to attend us. We were in Martin's apartments in the palace: a courtyard house attached to the rest of the complex by a breezeway. It was on the western side of the complex, towards the centre, next to the main apartment occupied by Xuan Wu when he was present. The informal dining room had a pleasant aspect over a small garden next to the high internal defensive wall for Xuan Wu's residence.

'I could provide you with a variety of different foods, Emma,' Martin said. 'It doesn't have to be *alive*. Snakes eat dead food too. I've seen you eat waffles. Why don't you just try it?'

'Just give up, Ge Ge,' Simone said, sounding bored.

'My serpent form doesn't need to eat,' I said for the millionth time. 'You should know this yourself, Martin, we reptiles ...' My voice trailed off.

'Yes. We *reptiles*,' Martin said, jumping on the point. He gestured towards Yue Gui. 'We are all reptiles together. Even Simone has a reptilian form. Do not be ashamed of it! And by the Heavens, Emma, do me the honour of accepting my hospitality while you are in this form!'

'Well, I don't need to eat for days on end as serpent,'

I said. 'The food I eat as a human keeps it satisfied. If I'm going to start eating as a snake, then I'll try things at home and let you know.'

'This should be your home,' Yue Gui said. 'When the Dark Lord returns, I'm sure it will be.'

'Is it *his* home?' I said.

They were silent at that.

I continued. 'No, Wudangshan is his home. This is one of his offices. And for me it will be too. For *you*, this is home. Both of you. And you should be named as rulers together.'

'That would interfere with the alignment of the Heavens and would not be accepted,' Martin said stiffly. He relaxed. 'Father will return, and he will retake his place on the throne of the Northern Heavens.'

'Do you have any idea how long it's going to take him to come back?' Simone said.

Martin and Yue Gui shared a look.

'You do!' Simone said.

'You know they aren't allowed to tell us mortals the future, Simone,' I said, miserable.

'Actually, nobody knows,' Martin said. 'Father is too elemental, too powerful and too aligned with the forces of nature to be predicted. He is so much a part of the fabric of the universe that he cannot be seen in divination. It is like trying to predict the course of the Earth around the Sun — the Cosmos just says "It will happen, leave it alone."'

'Both of us have caught glimpses of him though,' Yue Gui said, and Martin nodded agreement.

'You have?' Simone said, visibly brightening. 'You've seen Daddy?' She jiggled slightly with excitement. 'Did he say anything?'

'We have caught *glimpses*,' Yue Gui said with sympathy. 'His Turtle and his Serpent are at opposite ends of the world. They cry. They seem to be searching for one another — and for you.'

'And for you,' I said.

'We are reptiles,' Yue Gui said. 'We lay our eggs and leave them. That is the Way.'

The demons cleared the dishes, and Martin poured more tea all around. I flicked my tongue above it to test the temperature, then carefully lowered my snout into the bowl to drink without tipping it over.

'See? Told you you'd get there in the end,' Simone said, waving her own teacup. 'It just took practice.'

'And if you used a larger bowl you wouldn't have any issue with it at all,' Martin said.

I pulled my dripping snout out of the tea bowl, then wiped it on a napkin laid on the table for me. 'I'm not drinking out of a dog's bowl, thank you very much.'

'Dragon bowl!' Martin said.

'You are argumentative today, Ming Gui,' I said sternly. 'You need to take some time and meditate on your faults; you are lacking in filial piety towards your senior. You should be more modest and obedient.'

Simone nearly spat out her tea, and Martin's mouth flopped open with delight.

Yue Gui toasted me with her teacup. 'I could not have said it better myself, ma'am; you are quite correct in your clarification of Ming Gui's faults. He should write a ten-page, seven-legged essay outlining his shortcomings and his plan for reparation.'

'Be careful,' Martin said with good humour. 'I may just do that, and make all of you read it.'

Simone shook her hands over the table. 'No, that's

really not necessary!' She brightened. 'But you can write an essay for me on the reproductive variety in different species of annelids.'

'Worms?'

'Worms.'

'Wait, the whole phylum? That's a hell of a lot of worms! Their reproductive variety is astounding — did you choose this topic yourself?'

Simone nodded. 'I like worms.' She sagged slightly. 'But you're right, it's a huge topic.'

'When's it due?' Martin said.

'Two weeks from tomorrow.'

He put his hand out over the table. 'Sounds like fun. I'll help you. Deal?'

She shook his hand. 'Deal. You like biology too?'

He shrugged. 'Most interesting field of science there is. Some Celestial biology makes Earthly biology look very tame in comparison.' He turned to me. 'Now that we're finished, I think it's time to move to general matters at hand. There aren't many cases for you to hear; I'll provide you with a list in the morning.'

'Is Sang Shen still going on about me living in the wrong part of the palace?' I said.

'No,' Yue Gui said. 'I talked to him and offered him a compromise.'

'Which is?'

Martin cut in. 'Emma, if we move the fittings from the Serpent Concubine Pavilion into the Pavilion of Dark Celestial Bliss, will you move there?'

'That's what I've been asking for! It would solve the whole problem, but they said the fittings couldn't be moved without disrupting the fung shui of Dark Bliss. The pavilion was designed to be occupied by a human not a snake.'

'We have a fung shui master who says it can be done with some alterations to the layout to counteract the excessive yang of a snake presence. It will mean making the northern part of the pavilion larger, adding a water feature of some sort and choosing more turtle motifs in the decoration.'

'Sounds very nice,' I said. 'How much will it cost?'

He hesitated. 'Ten jin of Celestial jade.'

'*Ten jin*?' I said, horrified.

'That's, like, ten ounces, isn't it?' Simone said. 'About a million dollars? That's a bit over the top.'

'No,' I said. 'It's ten kilos. A hundred and sixty ounces. Ten *cattys*!'

'That's ... what ... sixteen mill?' Simone said. 'To add one room and a water feature? That's ridiculous.'

'We could have the whole goddamn pavilion knocked down and rebuilt for that,' I said.

'It's made of aged Celestial teak and ebony from the plantations on the southern shores of the Northern Heavens — the trees from there take five hundred years to grow,' Martin said. 'The fittings are Earthly black and white jade trimmed with pure silver. The multicoloured floor tiles are semi-precious stones — topaz, garnet and tourmaline — and it will be hard to find stones that large again.'

I rested my head on the table. 'I'll just stay in the concubine quarters. It's only Sang Shen who's making a fuss about me moving.' I raised my head. 'Look, tell him that I'll be happy to move into the Empress's quarters, but he has to pay the ten jin to have it altered.'

Yue Gui nodded. 'Good idea. I will tell him.' She smiled slightly.

'You really love tormenting him, don't you, Jie Jie,' Simone said.

Yue Gui shrugged. 'He is in my custody to serve a sentence. And serve a sentence he will.'

'Speaking of living quarters, there is one other matter, and then we have nothing else until tomorrow,' Martin said. He pulled himself upright and spoke more formally. 'Lady Emma, now that the Northern Heavens have been restored and are no longer a frigid wasteland, it would be most fitting to harmonious Celestial alignment if your family — your parents — were to be living in these Heavens rather than those in the West. This is where they belong as your family, and it is your filial duty to serve them closely. This is best achieved by them moving here.'

I stared at him, shocked. My parents had been living in the West for ten years and now he wanted them to move to a completely new — and strange — place?

'I can't see Nanna and Pop wanting to do that,' Simone said mildly. 'They've made a lot of friends in the West over the last ten years, Martin. I really think they're more comfortable in the West.'

Martin opened his mouth to argue but I cut him off. 'I will take the matter under advisement and discuss it with my parents.'

He nodded. 'Very good, ma'am.'

CHAPTER 4

That evening Simone and I spread out on some beanbags in the Serpent Concubine Pavilion and watched a DVD together, she in her pyjamas and me stretched out next to her in serpent form. When the movie finished, she switched off the DVD and spread her arms. 'Hug, Emma.'

I slithered next her and she held me close, my head resting on her shoulder.

'I worry I'm gonna squeeze you and hurt you,' she said. 'You're kinda soft and squishy under the scales.'

'I think my ribs are pretty springy, and you've never hurt me yet,' I said. I wished I could smile, but opening my mouth made my fangs slide down, which wasn't a good look.

She kissed the end of my nose. 'I'm going to bed. See you at breakfast.'

'Night, Simone.'

She disappeared; she would travel invisible to the apartment she'd commandeered so that nobody would see her in her pyjamas. There were no human-suitable beds in my quarters.

I slithered into my own bedroom, which had a

recessed floor area filled with beanbags, and a couple of infra-red heat lamps above to provide heat without light. My quarters were generally kept at a warmer temperature than was comfortable for humans but very pleasant by reptile standards. I put my head next to the edge of the sleeping recess and the stone from my ring, now in the filigree crown on my head, reached out a long green tendril and lifted itself and the crown onto the recess ledge. It grabbed a paper seal from the stack there, reached towards me and stuck the seal onto the top of my head between my eyes.

I stretched out under the ray lamps and performed a mild meditation cycle, moving my serpent chi through the length of my body. The serpent's chi was different from both human and demon essence; darker and brighter at the same time, and colder because of my cold-bloodedness.

The stone moved around the edge of the recess so it was closer to my head.

'You'll be asleep yourself; you won't know if the seal slips,' I said drowsily.

'You're too casual about the consequences of losing that seal,' the stone said.

I began to drift off, my vision blurring. 'I'm more comfortable as a snake anyway; I doubt I'll lose the form.'

'I'll make sure you don't,' the stone said, but I barely heard it.

The next morning I joined Simone in her apartment while she ate breakfast. She was already in her school uniform, and she checked the art deco mantle clock on the rosewood side table as she scooped up her cereal.

'You still have time,' I said.

She nodded, but finished quickly and bounced up. 'I have swimming training after school so I'll be late back.'

'Stay down there. Monica and Leo can look after you,' I said.

She hesitated, then shrugged. 'Okay. I'll come back on the weekend.'

'How's the swimming going?'

'I'm second best on the team,' she said proudly. 'We have a meet in two weeks.'

'Book me in,' I said.

'Already did.' She came around the table, put her hand on the back of my neck and kissed the top of my head. 'See you on the weekend, Emma.'

'I'll call you later,' I said.

After she'd gone, I took myself over to the palace's administrative centre. The Serpent Concubine Pavilion was on the western side of the palace complex, with only the servants' quarters and the support areas — the laundry and kitchens — further north of it. There had only ever been one Serpent Concubine in the entire history of the palace, and nobody would say much about her. John had never bothered to have the Serpent Pavilion returned to a human-style dwelling, and nobody had spoken much about his reasons for that either. The servants wouldn't even tell me whether the Serpent Concubine had died or had left him; they all suggested that I contact the Archivist for the full story.

The palace was divided into two rectangular areas: the residential section took up the northern half; the administrative section, the southern half. A four-metre internal wall with a single gate separated them, entirely blocking off one side from the other. Tradition called for the Emperor and his most senior advisors — and consorts — to be carried around the complex in sedan chairs, but John had never bothered with that, preferring to walk through the complex so he could check the status of the different areas as he passed. He was a very early — by a few hundred years — practitioner of 'management by walking around'. In more recent times, apparently, he'd taken to riding a motorbike around the complex, occasionally doing outrageous jumps over some of the decorative semicircular bridges in the gardens. The resulting skid marks on the pristine white marble had caused the domestic demons much grief.

John's welcome in the various sections of the palace would have been very different from mine. As my three-metre-long snake form slithered through the gardens, the demons either froze with terror or skittered away. I'd gone through all the support sections the first time I'd visited the palace, greeting the demons and trying to allay their fears, but to no avail. Maybe their reaction had something to do with the Serpent Concubine; they might have had bad experiences with snakes in the past. Or maybe it was just that I brought back nasty memories of the Snake Mothers in Hell. Then again, maybe it was just because I was a snake.

I reached the wall that divided the residential and administrative areas. The gate building was set on top of three terraces, each bordered with black marble balustrades. The building itself was around ten metres to a side, built of gunmetal-coloured stone with a traditional upward-curving, black-tiled roof. It had thick hardwood doors on both sides reinforced with metre-wide black metal studs. I slithered up the three flights of stairs and found the reception area empty, except for four humanoid demon guards at the gate's two doors. They stood to attention as I passed and thumped their chests with their fists, but their expressions weren't happy.

The administrative section of the palace was much more open and formal. The main buildings sat on three-tiered terraces in the centre of the rectangular area, while smaller buildings — for the support staff — flanked the sides. At the far end of the dividing wall was another gatehouse: the main entry into the palace. The long avenue up to the palace was visible through the gate's open doors.

A group of officials were waiting for me with a sedan chair, all of them on one knee. I nodded to them and swiftly slithered around them to avoid the chair. They jumped up and followed me, then stopped and saluted again when Martin appeared on the top balcony of the central administrative building. He waved to me and came down the steps.

'Rise,' he said to the officials as he came closer, and they all rose and bowed again. He waved them away. 'I will guide Lady Emma to the hearings.'

I accompanied him up the stairs.

'The petitions should only take a couple of days,' he said. 'Since the energy has returned to the North, the residents have had much less to complain about and the petitions have dried up.'

'That's wonderful news,' I said.

We entered the Pavilion of Dark Justice together, and all those present fell to one knee. The pavilion was rectangular and made of gunmetal-coloured polished stone with a black roof, same as the other buildings. The doors to the hearing room opened in front of us; inside, officials sat behind desks and gathered the information required for the day's proceedings. The petitioners would wait their turn in luxuriously appointed waiting rooms along the sides of the pavilion, with demon servants shuttling backwards and forwards to tend to their needs.

Lily, one of the court administrators, rose from her desk and walked to the doorway. 'All salute Regent General Da Na Huo and Tai Zi Ming Gui, the Bright One.'

The staff fell to one knee and saluted us.

'Rise,' I said. 'Return to your duties.'

They returned to what they'd been doing without any fuss.

'They finally got it,' I said with relief.

'Well, some of them have worked for more traditional Shen,' Martin said as we entered the hearing room and climbed the dais to the throne. 'An order like that could be a trick to see if they were truly showing respect.'

'Sounds stupid to me,' I grumbled under my breath as I pulled myself up onto the black silk cushions. 'Okay, what have we got?'

Lily approached with a document printed from one of the computers in the office. 'Not many changes to the list I emailed you last week. Three disputes on the ownership of demon servants, as in the email. One new case, not previously mentioned: about the parentage of a particularly fine colt that was born over at the House of Ling only yesterday —'

'The mare dropped?' I cut in. 'I must go have a look.'

'It's palomino, Emma,' Martin said.

I hissed with amusement. 'Somebody's stallion's been sneaking around! No way could that mating produce a palomino.'

Lily winced. 'There is some suggestion that the colt was fathered by a horse demon.'

'Do we have horse demons here?' I said.

Both of them nodded.

'You have a list, right?' I said.

Lily nodded again. 'On my desk, ma'am. There are three or four possible fathers.'

'The owner of the mare is petitioning ... for what?' I said. 'We just do a DNA test, establish the father, slap a fine on the owner of the demon stallion for failing to control the animal, end of story.'

'The owner of the mare is petitioning that the owner of the stallion be reprimanded for not controlling his demons. She says the mare has been ruined by carrying a demon foal and she wants a very large sum in compensation.'

'I see. When's the hearing on that?'

'It's one of the last — I knew you'd want to see the files first,' Lily said. 'You must order the DNA test and then decide on how much to fine the owner of the stallion.'

'It's possible the owner of the sire may claim the colt as well,' Martin said.

'As soon as you provide me with all the details, and we establish the colt's parentage, we'll take it from there,' I said. 'What else?'

'One other petition delivered just yesterday — Sang Shen —'

I hissed with frustration. 'Sometimes I almost wish he *had* been executed!'

'Sang Shen has raised the price of the leaves from his mulberry tree exponentially,' Lily said. 'The Blue Dragon has requested a mediation to discuss renegotiating the contract for provision of the leaves.'

'He's a tree, they're his leaves, he can set the price. Tell the Dragon to get lost,' I said.

'He's charging ten times the weight of the leaves in Celestial Jade.'

That stopped me. 'That's *insane*!'

'The worst part is that the Dragon is prepared to pay something close to this, but he wants to squeal about it first.'

'This is a bad precedent. Other leaf suppliers will raise their prices to match Sang Shen's, and the rise in costs will drive up the price of silk,' I said, lowering my head to think. I looked up at them. 'Ensure that this is a completely closed court; this is an extremely private matter between Sang Shen and the Blue Dragon. Nobody must know that the Dragon's silkworms eat the leaves from Sang Shen's tree.'

'I think part of this lawsuit is Sang Shen trying to make it known that he *is* the provider of the leaves,' Martin said.

'That sounds like him,' I said. 'He vowed to the Dragon that he wouldn't reveal himself as the source of the leaves, but he's been dropping heavy hints in the public domain ever since. He's followed the letter of the agreement but definitely not the spirit.'

'You could reprimand him for that and order him to fix the price of his leaves,' Lily said.

'That would not be fair to either of them. I must hear this in secret, and emerge with a judgement that's fair to both of them.'

'What if neither of them agrees with your decision?' Martin said.

'If both of them are upset about the decision, then I think I've succeeded in mediating it fairly,' I said.

* * *

Three days later, on the evening before the final day of hearings, I was settling down to sleep when a demon servant crept into my quarters and hesitated beside the door.

'Don't be afraid,' I said gently. 'Tell me.'

'The Lord of the East, the Blue Dragon Qing Long, is here and requests audience, madam,' the demon said, its voice barely above a whisper.

'Show him into the formal salon,' I said. After the demon had gone I tapped the stone with my nose. 'Hop back on — the Dragon wants to talk to me.'

The stone grumbled quietly as it floated its setting onto the top of my head. I twisted my head a couple of times to make sure the crown fitted comfortably, then I slithered to the salon. The audience chamber was the place where the Emperor and his concubine would formally meet and discuss any issues arising from the management of the household. I couldn't imagine John ever using it — he wasn't a fan of formality — and so wasn't surprised that the furniture, which was probably at least a thousand years old, appeared as new. I slid up onto the black and silver silk cushions of the throne, which was two metres long and intricately carved with serpents.

The Dragon was escorted in by the demon; he fell to one knee in front of me, saluting. 'This humble servant greets his master,' he said, then rose again.

I bowed my head. 'You are welcome, my Lord. Please, sit and drink tea with me.'

A stool that looked very much like a piano stool was brought for the Dragon, and a small table with tea was placed in front of him. The demons were so quiet and smooth in their movements it was as if the furniture arrived by itself.

I stretched out on the soft cushions, enjoying the sensation on my serpent belly. 'What can I do for you?'

The Dragon raised his teacup. 'Finest Celestial tea I've had in a long while, ma'am.' He sat slightly straighter. 'I know you don't like wasting time on formal protocol, so I'll get straight to the point. I hear that you are living in this pavilion designed for a concubine rather than in the Empress's Pavilion as is fitting.'

'The architect estimates a cost of ten jin of jade to make the necessary alterations to the Dark Bliss Pavilion. I'm just as comfortable staying here, so we won't be making the changes,' I said.

He nodded, unsurprised. 'That is a great deal of money, ma'am. But if you extended the Pavilion of Dark Bliss, the fung shui aspects would be perfectly aligned. As well as that, you would have more room for your clothes, your make-up, all your feminine necessities —'

I cut him off. 'Snakes don't need clothes or make-up. Where is this going?'

'One day you will be able to take human form here, ma'am, I'm sure of it. If you were to extend Dark Bliss as they have suggested, it would not only improve the harmonious resonance of the building, it would provide you with more space for all your needs.'

'I fail to see where this is heading, Dragon.'

'I would hate to see a beautiful lady such as yourself unable to make herself as attractive as she possibly can for the return of her lover. I would like to help.'

'You want to help? How?'

'How about I pay for the additions to the pavilion? It would be my pleasure, ma'am. I know that the

Northern coffers have been drained by the recent difficulties, while the East remains strong. Let me do this thing for you.'

I hesitated a moment, studying him, then said, 'And what do you want in return?'

'Well, I will have more of a budget for the renovation if I do not have to pay such ridiculously exorbitant prices for the leaves for my silk factories.'

I stared at him, stunned.

He shrugged and smiled slightly. 'You are a beautiful woman, Lady Emma. It is such a shame that you do not have the space to allow you to enhance your appearance to the utmost — for your Lord, of course. With the space for proper baths and personal care staff here, you would always look your best. I can provide you with clothing assistants, make-up artists and hair designers. You will want for nothing.'

I opened my mouth then closed it again.

'So, would you like me to pay for the alterations?' the Dragon said, his face full of hope.

'I tell you what,' I said, 'I will take your offer into consideration when I am hearing the case tomorrow.'

He bowed his head again. 'That is all I can ask for: some small amount of consideration for the care I am taking of you.'

'Yes, I'll be *absolutely damn sure* to remember that you tried to *bribe* me to give you a sympathetic outcome,' I said with force. 'I've half a mind to find in the tree's favour without even having a hearing. In fact, I should double whatever price he's asking for his leaves.' I moved my head and the first metre or so of my body closer to the Dragon's face. 'You insult me by attempting to corrupt me. Is this the way you do business in the East?'

The Dragon replaced his teacup. 'This is the way I do business everywhere, because it's the way business is done.' He disappeared.

'Asshole!' I said, and slithered down off the throne and headed back to my sleeping quarters.

'You should do what you said you'd do: find in the tree's favour tomorrow,' the stone said.

'No, I'm going to hear this case fairly and impartially,' I said. 'The fact he's tried to bribe me doesn't change the facts of the case, and I will hear it based on the facts rather than on how much I *intensely dislike* the two parties involved in it.'

'Which one do you hate more?' the stone said.

I slid into my sleeping pit. 'If I had a choice of which one I'd hang upside down over a scorpion pit, I'd choose both of them.'

'Would you like me to order you a scorpion pit? I can get one about three metres across, filled with the most enormous, highly venomous scorpions you ever saw. Hours of fun for the whole family.'

'You're worse than they are,' I said, and stretched out to sleep on the cushions.

CHAPTER 5

The next morning I entered the court for the final day of hearings. The guards fell to one knee and saluted me, then rose and held their swords in front of them. I nodded to Lily and Martin, slithered up the dais and onto the chair behind the desk. A demon servant took up position next to me, ready to turn the pages of the documents, saving me the embarrassment of having to turn them with my mouth.

'First case today,' I said, 'the horse one; about time we had something interesting. Bring the case of Ling versus Toi.'

Ling and Toi entered the room and kneeled before me; they were both dragons in human form.

'Up you get,' I said, and they rose, their expressions suspicious at my informal tone. 'I'd like to hear from your own mouth, Mr Toi, exactly what the *hell* you were thinking when you did this.'

Toi, a slender, elderly gentleman in a black silk robe, was the owner of the demon stallion. He bowed his head slightly to speak. 'This was an accident, Lady Regent. The stallion concerned broke from its restraints in the middle of the night and went to

Honoured Miss Ling's residence under its own volition, probably drawn by the scent of her fine mare in heat.'

'You had the stallion restrained?' I said.

'It was in a high-walled stall, but it managed to escape,' Toi said. 'I do not understand how such a thing could have happened, ma'am. I provide the best accommodation for my beasts. This will never happen again.'

I turned to the woman, who also wore a black silk robe, probably dressed down to show her distress. 'Miss Ling, you claim that the mare is ruined and request compensation of ten jin of Celestial Jade. Has the mare been injured by bearing the foal and cannot bear any more for you?'

'She has been contaminated by the demon essence of the stallion,' Ling said, her jaw clenched with anger. 'This foal is half-demon and an abomination. I will never be able to sell another foal from the mare, as any future foal will be tainted by the fact that the mare has been covered by a demon. The mare is worthless.'

'I have investigated this claim — something along the lines of a Celestial urban myth — that once a female animal has been impregnated by a demon, the demonic essence remains.' I nodded to the demon secretary and she pulled out the folder containing the DNA samples. 'I have scientific evidence that this is not true: the mare's future offspring will not be contaminated in any way.'

Toi gave Miss Ling a triumphant look.

'That's as it may be, ma'am,' Ling said, 'but everybody still believes it, and my mare's foals will no longer be as prized — or as valuable — as they once were.'

'Madam,' Toi said, 'please, go to the stables and view the colt. It is exceptional. I do not dispute that it is the progeny of my stallion, but I *do* dispute that the foal is an abomination. The mother is quite capable of bearing many more fine foals, both pure animal and half-demon.'

I checked the notes in front of me. 'You request ownership of the colt and have offered Miss Ling two jin of jade for it. She is asking for ten, which is the value of the mare and any future progeny she would have borne.'

Miss Ling spread her arms. 'This mare is only seven years old, she had many more years of fruitfulness in her. This is a tragedy.'

'If he paid the ten jin, would you give him the mare and the foal?' I asked Miss Ling.

She nodded, sober. 'That I would, ma'am.'

'I would like to see this mare again and view the colt.' I called towards the back of the courtroom: 'Hey, Lily, do we have time this afternoon? What else do I have on?'

'Only one more, scheduled for 2 pm, ma'am,' Lily called back, to the shock and amusement of those present. 'The closed hearing.'

'Only one more? That's a relief.' I slithered down off my chair. 'Get the demon driver to bring the car around, I want to have a look at these horses.' I nodded to Lily. 'Arrange the usual witness and note-taking rigmarole, will you?'

'Sure thing, ma'am,' Lily said, and went out to organise the details.

I saw Toi and Ling share a lightning-fast look and realised this whole thing was a setup. I stopped, nearly changing my mind about seeing the horses — but what the hell. Foals were cute. I raised my snout to them. 'Want to come in my car?'

They bowed, formal again, and agreed. I sat in the front next to the driver, and Toi and Ling sat side by side in the back.

These two ever been an item? I asked the stone.

If the stone could sigh, it would have. *Emma, with people who live this long, I think everybody's been an item with everybody else at some stage. These are both dragons, and not related to each other; he's spawn of Qing Long and she's one of the daughters of the Dragon King. Of course they've 'done it'.*

I turned my head to see them. 'I think I should just cut to the chase here. Do you want to give the foal to me or to Simone?'

Ling opened and closed her mouth a few times, then glanced at Toi, speechless.

'I have no idea what you are talking about, ma'am,' Toi said.

I rested my chin on the top of the car seat. 'You two want to dispel this myth about demon essence ruining animals. You arranged for the stallion to "escape" and impregnate the mare. I've heard how fine this mare is, Miss Ling; the White Tiger has been trying to arrange for his own stallions to cover her — he's jealous as all hell about her. You're taking me to look at her so I fall in love with the foal and want to take him as my own — or as Simone's private riding horse. If I take the foal, your mare will become even more prestigious and people will be forced to overcome their prejudice about demon essence contaminating livestock if they want to buy any further foals from her. Am I correct so far?'

Toi sat back, his face full of shock. 'I'd heard how intelligent you are, ma'am, but this is exceptional.'

'I just put two and two together,' I said. 'It's a great idea. You should have contacted me before. I would be happy to take the foal and prove to the Celestial that this myth is untrue. Stone, is Simone out of school yet?'

'No, she's still in class,' the stone said. 'Lunch isn't for another hour or so.'

'Too bad, she misses out on cute baby horses,' I said.

Noooo, Simone wailed in my head. *Cute babies! I love cute babies!*

Ling and Toi shared a grin.

'How about I take this one, the demon spawn,' I said. 'Simone can take the next one, the progeny of one of the Tiger's stallions or something, a pure animal horse that she can ride here in the Heavens. I'll have to take mine down to the Earthly and ride it there; I can't really do much as a snake.'

'That's what we were hoping for, ma'am,' Miss Ling said. 'We would gladly give each of you such a steed in return for your endorsement that the myth is untrue.'

I hissed with amusement. 'I won't let you give them to me, I'll pay you fair recompense for them. It is not right for the ruler to take gifts from the subjects.'

They bowed their heads, obviously delighted at the turn events were taking.

'I think the prestige you'll gain from me and Simone both riding this mare's progeny will override any prejudice people have about the demon thing,' I said. 'I'll arrange for the Tiger to make his most prized stallions available to you —'

'He already did, ma'am,' Ling said, cutting me off, then bobbed her head. 'I apologise for interrupting.'

'Is he in on this too?' I said.

'He may have had something to do with this, yes,' Toi said.

'I am going to tear his whiskers off,' I said. 'Trying to put one over on me. Who does he think he is?'

I love you too, baby, the White Tiger said into my ear. *I told these two morons that you'd see through their little plot, but they thought you'd be as stupid as his dad — Qing Long — and they'd have to go through all this roundabout bullshit to get where they wanted to be. Stupid assholes, both of them, typical dragons. But it's a good cause: this mare of hers is a freak of nature, exceptional animal, and his stallion is one of the finest demon horses anywhere. Anything to make people get over this 'contaminated by demon' bullshit! Oh, and if you like, I'd be delighted to train the little bastard for you when he's old enough to be backed.*

Miss Ling's estate sat on the hills to the south of the capital of the Northern Heavens, with large post-and-rail paddocks and a central equestrian complex. She provided riding, racing and war horses for the Celestial community, and had recently diversified into competition horses as well. Her longstanding rivalry with the White Tiger was well-known throughout the Celestial and there were sometimes bets placed on which of the two would win a particular equestrian event.

The foaling yards were close to the main house for easy monitoring. We entered the stable block and Miss Ling guided us to the mare in question; she was located in one of the stalls, its floor lined with sawdust bedding. The foal was with her, gambolling around the stall. Its legs looked impossibly long and it seemed unable to control all four at once; each splayed out in a different direction and the foal glared at them, as if ordering them to behave. The mare watched with bemused tolerance and obvious affection.

The mare was an eventing horse, a thoroughbred that excelled at both dressage and show jumping. Miss Ling had won a couple of Earthly competitions riding her, and there had been much speculation in the Celestial about the price the foal would command when Miss Ling had the mare serviced with frozen semen from one of the world's top eventing stallions.

'The stallion that provided the semen was black, with no dilution gene, and everybody knows it,' Miss Ling said. 'This mare is bay, and also has no dilution gene, so a palomino or buckskin from the cross is impossible.'

'My demon stallion is palomino, however,' Mr Toi said. 'There was a reasonable chance that he would throw a dilute foal, which would be a loud signal to everybody that my horse was the father. We succeeded: the foal is palomino, red dilute, and a fine little horse. Everybody in the Celestial is aware of the parentage, and they'll have to get over their prejudice about demon foals if they want to take advantage of this mare's progeny in future.'

'It was worth the risk,' Miss Ling said. 'We planned to gift this half-demon foal to you; then give a natural-horse foal from one of the Tiger's stallions to Princess Simone. After that, future progeny will be ...' She searched for the word.

'A free-for-all,' I said. 'Everybody will want one.'

'We're hoping that some may even want full brothers to this one as well, since you or the Princess will be riding it,' Mr Toi said.

'How dark's the dad?' I said. The foal had a cream body with a lighter cream mane and tail; it would take a while for his adult colour to show.

'The stallion is a very brilliant gold with a

completely white mane and tail,' Mr Toi said. 'This little fellow will probably be just as rich a colour.' He leaned on the stable door to watch the foal. 'My demon stallion is one of the finest mounts on the Celestial — smart, reliable and loyal. If this foal shows any of his traits he will be exceptional.'

'Sometimes such a mating can produce a fully natural animal,' Miss Ling said. 'But we've had the foal tested and he has demon essence flowing through his blood.'

'What are the general implications?' I said. 'Will I need to take any special care if I have him as a saddle horse?'

Ling and Toi both shook their heads.

'My stallion is highly intelligent, to the point of being self-aware,' Toi said. 'And this foal seems to have the intelligence of an extremely smart animal. I don't think you'll need to give him special attention, and he won't ever talk —'

'You stay away from my mummy!' the foal yelled, sounding like a small boy. He was standing in front of his mother, gangly legs spread wide for support, his tiny carpet-like tail twitching with aggression and his teeth bared.

'Well, how about that,' Toi said with amusement.

'I'm not going to hurt your mummy,' I said to the foal. 'I like horses.'

The foal lowered his bulbous forehead, still glaring at me. 'You look like something that would eat horses.'

I lowered my head as well. 'Well, I don't. Usually I take the same form as these two people here, and I look after horses.'

The foal looked back at his mother, who was apparently accustomed to all sorts of Celestial creatures viewing her and was unperturbed by my presence. He glanced from Ling to Toi, unsure.

'Your mummy isn't worried about me,' I said.

'Mummy's not real smart,' the foal said. He backed up slightly so he was closer to her. 'She don't talk.'

'This foal just became worth ten jin of jade all by himself,' Toi said, still amused. 'He's smart and courageous and isn't afraid to speak his mind.'

'I can't take him as a saddle horse now,' I said. 'He's much too valuable as breeding stock.'

Ling and Toi both shook their heads.

'No, no,' Toi said. 'Half-demon horses aren't useful as breeding stock, they're always sterile. We can geld him for you and you can use him as a riding horse, no problem at all.'

'I don't feel good about doing that to a sentient creature,' I said, watching the foal.

He overcame his fear and approached me cautiously and with curiosity, although his tiny tail still flapped with agitation. 'Are you talking about me?' he said.

'Yes,' I said. 'We think you are very beautiful and all of us want to own you when you grow up into a fine, strong horse.'

He stared at me with round, liquid eyes. 'You think I'm beautiful?'

I lowered my head even further so my nose was level with his. 'I think you're the most beautiful little horse I've ever seen.'

'Aww, gee.' He dropped his head and turned away. He skittered back to his mother, butted her belly a few times with his nose, and began to suck noisily, his tail going round like a propeller.

'He may not need gelding if he gets the right training and the hormones don't fill him full of attitude,' Toi said. 'We'll just have to see how he goes. If by six months he's attacking people on sight and mounting everything he can, you can make the decision then.'

'He's a total sweetheart,' I said.

'So, would you like to take him as your own and give Simone the next one?' Mr Toi said. 'We'll have the mare covered by a natural horse that's the right mix of quality and temperament to give Princess Simone a saddle horse that's smart, reliable and has enough talent to do anything she likes with it.'

'She may want this little guy,' I said. 'I'm not too fussed either way. Let's see what happens after she's taken a look at him.'

Ling and Toi both stood formally with their hands in front of them and bowed their heads to me.

'Ma'am, you have done a great thing here. With both you and Simone riding horses that are half-brothers from this mare we will finally be able to destroy this prejudice that exists about half-demon animals,' Toi said.

'I can't believe anybody would be prejudiced against something as exceptional as this foal,' I said as we made our way to the main house.

'He is exceptional, ma'am,' Ling agreed. 'It is very unusual for a half demon horse to talk.' She nodded to the demon servant that opened the door for her. 'Most half-demon horses are small, weak and dull. But Mr Toi's stallion is different, and I hope all his progeny turn out to be as exceptional as this little one.'

'Where did the demon stallion come from?' I said.

'He just turned up,' Toi said.

We sat on the rosewood couches in the living room and a demon servant brought tea. Miss Ling poured.

'I was demon-hunting in the mountains of Fukien when I came across this stallion,' Toi continued. 'He was injured, and appeared to have been pierced by some sort of lance several times. I tamed him and brought him here. He's been a fine, intelligent and brave steed for me and is now my preferred mount when demon-hunting. He is completely fearless.'

'He talks too?' I said.

'That he does, ma'am,' Toi said.

Miss Ling shrugged. 'We took a gamble that Mr Toi's stallion would sire something special. This is his first covering and the results are beyond expectation.'

'Our plan worked out far better than we could have hoped,' Toi said, and he and Ling shared a smile.

'If the Dark Lord were still ruler here, would you have discussed your plans with him from the start?' I said.

They both paused for a moment, thinking, then Miss Ling nodded. 'Probably. He is always straightforward in his dealings and works hard to overcome prejudice in all its forms.'

'But because I'm a woman, you felt you needed to play this charade?' I said.

They both appeared concerned and I rushed to reassure them. 'Don't worry, I'm not upset about this. I just want you guys to feel that you can approach me the same way you could approach John ... Xuan Wu. I want to build a good relationship with the citizens of the North.'

'It was more that you are from the Earthly, ma'am, and Earthly politics usually involve manipulation instead of honest dealing,' Toi said. 'You are not resident on the Celestial and not an Immortal. People on the Earthly are usually out for themselves first, working to promote their own interests.'

'Well, I'm not like that,' I said. 'I work for the good of the citizens of the Heavens first. I don't feel I'm doing a terribly good job, but hopefully by the time Xuan Wu returns I won't have made a complete mess of it.'

I lowered my snout and delicately sipped my tea; it was sow mei, my favourite. I felt a quiet rush of satisfaction at managing to drink it without spilling any.

'What the Dark Lady is trying to say,' the stone added, 'is that none of you need to play games to get things done. All you have to do is contact her, say what you need and she'll work hard to get it for you. You should pass the word along.'

'Uh ... yeah,' I said.

One of the demon servants, appearing as an elderly man in traditional black and white, came to us and bowed. 'The Princess of the Northern Heavens is here.'

'Show her in, don't make her wait!' Miss Ling said, gesturing quickly with one hand.

Simone came in and leaned over the back of the sofa to kiss the top of my serpent head. She smiled at Ling and Toi. 'Can I see the baby?'

They both rose and formally bowed to Simone but she waved them down. 'Please, you know I don't like this formal rigmarole. I'd just like to see the foal, if I could.'

'You're supposed to be in school,' I said.

'They won't notice I'm gone if I run back quick enough. It's nearly lunchtime anyway.'

I slithered off the couch and onto the floor. 'Do you mind if she takes a look too?'

'Not at all,' Miss Ling said, and guided us back out to the stables.

The foal was curled up at his mother's feet, dozing. He pricked up his ears when we entered but didn't open his eyes.

'He's *so* pretty,' Simone whispered.

'Would there be any issue with him travelling between Heaven and the Earthly if Simone decided to take him?' I said.

'He was born here so can travel to both Planes when he is old enough,' Toi said. 'He can be tamed with the Fire Essence Pill if he shows demonic tendencies.'

'Then he would probably be a better match for you, Simone,' I said. 'I can only ride on the Earthly, so I might as well get a natural horse.'

'Can I go in and pet him?' Simone said.

Miss Ling nodded, smiling slightly. 'Of course. Take care of his hooves when he tries to stand up.'

She opened the stall gate and Simone carefully approached the foal. He opened one eye and looked at her with curiosity. 'You smell nice.'

'He *talks*?' Simone said in disbelief.

He dropped his head, shy. 'Is that wrong?'

'No, no,' she said. 'It just means that you're special.' She kneeled and raised one hand cautiously towards him. 'Can I touch you?'

He raised his nose to sniff her hand, then licked it. 'You taste good too.'

She carefully ran her hand over the soft hair of his mane between his ears and down the front of his face. He nuzzled into her hand. 'You feel nice. I like you.'

Simone's face softened.

'I can't take him now,' I said with amusement. 'She's smitten.'

'When you grow up to be a big, strong, beautiful horse,' Simone said gently to him, 'will you let me ride you and take you all over the place and show everybody what a special horse you are?'

He studied her appraisingly. 'You won't be too heavy?'

'Not when you're all grown up,' she said.

He pulled himself clumsily to his feet and she quickly moved back to avoid his tiny, sharp hooves. He stood and watched her, his tail flicking, then he glanced towards me, Ling and Toi. 'Do I get to choose who rides me?'

Simone put her hand out towards him. 'I think you can choose between me and the snake lady, who loves you just as much as I do.'

He shoved his forehead into her hand. 'Then I choose you, 'cause I really like you.'

She bowed her head as she stroked his ears. 'My name's Simone.'

He licked her hand again. 'I don't have a name.' He dropped his head and eyed her shyly. 'Can *you* give me a name? I'd really like that.'

'I'll have to think of something that's as impressive and handsome as you are,' she said. 'I can't just call you Freddo Frog or anything.'

'Freddo Frog! I *love* that!' He gambolled around the stall, flicking his tail. 'I'm Freddo Frog, the wonder horse. I belong to Simonny, the wonder girl!' He turned to her and reared, then dropped and kicked out his tiny back feet. 'Freddo Frog and Simonny!'

Simone fell to sit on the straw, hysterical with laughter. Freddo lay down next to her and rested his head in her lap, gazing up at her. 'Thank you, Simonny.'

She cupped his head with both hands. 'You're welcome, Freddo. Can I come and visit you every day?'

'I'd like that,' he said.

Sorry, Simone mouthed to Miss Ling over the top of his head. She switched to silent speech. *You should choose a stud name for him; you can't call him Freddo Frog!*

'Ling's Golden Freddo (DX) it is,' Miss Ling said.

'DX?' Simone said.

'It's an indicator we put at the end of the stud name to show demonic offspring,' Miss Ling said. She turned to me. 'What does Freddo Frog mean anyway?'

'It's a small chocolate bar that you can buy in Australia,' I said. 'Simone loves them.'

Ling gestured with her head towards Simone and Freddo. 'I think this is love as well.'

'You have to go back to school, you know that, Simone,' I said.

Freddo popped up onto his feet again, excited. 'Can I come with you?' He stamped his hooves and looked from me to Simone. 'Can I?'

'Your mummy won't be able to come with us,' Simone said. 'You should stay with her here — she has good milk for you to grow big and strong.'

'Oh yeah,' Freddo said, eyes wide. 'I'm *hungry*!'

'Oh, he's definitely your horse,' I said to Simone as Freddo started nursing again.

Simone rose and brushed off the sawdust. 'You don't mind, Emma?'

I moved back as Miss Ling let Simone out of the stall. 'Not at all. He's perfect for you; a steed fit for a princess.'

Freddo stopped feeding and turned to look at us. 'You're going, Simonny?'

'You eat and then have a big sleep so you have lots of energy when we play tomorrow,' Simone said.

72

'Okay!' Freddo returned to his mother, his tail frantically waving as he sucked.

'We need to get back to the palace, I have one more hearing,' I said. I bowed my head to Ling and Toi. 'Please, if there is anything you need that I can help with, do not hesitate to contact myself, Ming Gui or Yue Gui.'

Ling and Toi bowed, their hands held formally at their waists. 'We appreciate your time and presence, my Lady,' Ling said, 'and look forward to serving you in future.'

Simone put her arm around my neck as we made our way back to the car. 'Let's have lunch with Martin and Yue Gui before I go back to school,' she said. 'Five dollars says Martin tells the story about the archery contest again.'

'You're on,' I said. 'He only told that one yesterday, no way would he think to bore us with it again.'

Simone grinned. 'Five bucks, all mine. I'm rich!'

CHAPTER 6

Sang Shen entered the courtroom accompanied by his mother, Yue Gui — Simone's older sister — and a single demon servant. The Blue Dragon was attended by five lithe young women in multi-layered Ming robes. Both Sang Shen and the Dragon stepped forward, kneeled and saluted me, then rose again.

'Sang Shen,' I said.

Sang Shen saluted. 'This humble Shen is present and honoured.'

'Qing Long.'

The Dragon glared at me with his turquoise eyes, flicked his long hair over his shoulder and gracefully saluted. 'This ...' I watched with amusement as the words stuck in his throat. 'This humble Shen is present and honoured.'

'The applicant will present his case,' I said.

Sang Shen gestured towards his demon servant and the servant passed him a scroll. He opened it and read aloud: 'This humble tree Shen provides mulberry leaves whose quality and purity are unmatched on any Plane. Since this Shen's death sentence was suspended, and the Heavens have been rejuvenated by your own most wise and generous self, his leaves have become even richer and more beneficial, and the silk produced by worms fed on these leaves is unparalleled in quality, the finest silk that has ever come out of the East.'

'That's *because* it's the East,' the Dragon said under his breath.

'The respondent will remain silent until given leave to speak,' I said with relish.

The Dragon flicked his long hair again and subsided.

'This tree Shen therefore has raised the price of his leaves accordingly.' Sang Shen closed the scroll with a snap. 'If the buyer does not wish to pay the premium, then the buyer may look elsewhere.'

'Bluff,' the Dragon said.

'You were warned,' I said.

The Dragon bowed gracefully to me, making a point of bowing low.

'You may state your case,' I said to him.

'This is extortion,' the Dragon said. 'The leaves are not worth this amount. This criminal is still being held at your pleasure, ma'am, and he does not deserve to accrue wealth while paying for his crimes.'

'What does that mean — "held at her pleasure"?' Sang Shen said. 'I resent the implications of this slander!'

'It means that I have had you incarcerated to pay for your crimes,' I said. 'It's an archaic English term. He's been doing his homework, probably to try to ingratiate himself with me.'

'No more than this tree Shen has infiltrated your family and tried to ingratiate himself with your stepdaughter,' the Dragon said.

'That was unnecessary; he *is* family,' I said. 'And so are you, East Wind. Let me summarise the case. Sang

Shen wishes to charge a premium for his excellent leaves; and Qing Long says he doesn't have the right because he's a prisoner of the Court of the North.'

'This is true,' the Dragon said.

'My leaves are truly excellent,' Sang Shen said.

'Geez, that sounds so wrong,' I said. 'Okay. Record my judgement.'

Sang Shen and Qing Long exchanged venomous looks.

'You two go and set a value for the leaves together. Sang Shen gets ten per cent of it, held in trust until his sentence is served. The rest is to be converted into Earthly currency and donated to Earthly charities as proceeds of a convicted criminal. No details of this case are to be discussed outside this courtroom.'

'He'll just inflate the price by ten!' the Dragon protested.

'Then refuse to pay,' I said.

'Ten per cent makes the sale of the leaves scarcely worth it,' Sang Shen said.

'Then refuse to sell,' I said.

Both of them glared at me, furious. The Dragon waved one arm in disgust and turned away. 'This is not a fair result. You have made the product even more expensive.' He stormed out without saluting and his attendants stared after him, dumbfounded.

'How am I supposed to make a living with you taking the majority of my income?' Sang Shen shouted, his brown face livid with rage.

'You're a convicted criminal by your own admission and you should not be earning a fortune while incarcerated,' I said. 'Remember, Sang Shen, this agreement you made with the Dragon is confidential. I am warning you now: if anyone discovers that the

Dragon is buying the leaves from you, I will hold you responsible and you will receive none of the income from your leaves.'

He made some incoherent, spluttering noises, then stormed out as well.

Yue Gui's face glowed with suppressed amusement as she came up to the bench. 'That was the most fun I've had in a while. Well done, Emma, you thoroughly pissed off both of them. What a triumph.'

'He's your son, Yue.'

'And it's about time he grew up.' She saluted me and turned to address the Dragon's servants. 'Why are you still here? Follow your master.'

One of the women stepped forward and bowed with her hands clasped in front of her. 'By your leave, ma'am, we have a favour to ask of the Dark Lady.'

'Come forward,' I said.

The five of them walked towards me with tiny steps, delicate ladies-in-waiting. The lead attendant stopped next to Yue Gui and the others stood behind her.

'My Lady,' the lead woman said. 'My name is Purple Jade.' She bowed again, obviously nervous, and looked back at the other women. 'We have a request for you. We wish to ask you this thing in confidence.'

'Don't be afraid,' I said gently. 'Just ask.'

'We would prefer to speak to you alone,' she said.

'Yue Gui is Councillor of the Northern Heavens and one of my most trusted aides. She will keep this matter confidential. You may speak freely in front of her,' I said.

Yue Gui bowed slightly. 'I thank you, ma'am, but if this matter is to remain confidential ...'

'No, stay. You can advise me if this turns into a Celestial matter,' I said.

'The Dragon is a harsh master!' Purple Jade said, almost an explosion of emotion. She stopped, seemingly surprised at her own outburst. She pulled herself together. 'We would request that we be allowed to work for you, ma'am. Please, we wish to be freed from his service and to serve you instead.'

The other women nodded, their eyes downcast in deference.

'Are you demon servants?' I said. 'I see you as humans, not demons, but if you are tamed demons then you're his possessions and I can't take you.'

The woman glanced at Yue Gui. 'This matter really should be confidential, ma'am. It is between us, you and the Blue Dragon. We are human, not demon. We are third-generation servants of the Qing Long. Our mothers and grandmothers were servants.'

'Wait,' I said sharply. 'Are you paid for your services? You're not forced to work for him?'

Purple Jade nodded, still nervous. 'We are paid, we are free to choose to work for him, ma'am. He pays extremely well. We would be happy to tell you the details of our arrangement with him, but not in front of the honoured councillor.'

'Phew,' I said. 'For a moment I thought that asshole had human slaves. Would you like to return to the Earthly and live normal lives?'

'No!' she said, eyes wide at the concept. 'We live long and illness-free lives here on the Celestial Plane. We do not wish to descend.' She bowed lower, trembling. 'We just request that we be allowed to join your service instead of his. As his sovereign, you are within your rights to requisition us.' She leaned in to whisper: 'You and you alone. Please, ma'am. We know a place we can go to discuss this in private.'

'Right, this is getting way too obvious. Summon the Blue Dragon,' I said.

The women squeaked with dismay and stepped back. The Blue Dragon stormed into the room, strode up to my bench and quickly saluted. 'You summoned me, ma'am?'

'Check these servants of yours to see if they're demon copies, please.'

The Dragon turned his turquoise eyes on the women and they stopped pretending to be servants and straightened. The lead one raised her arms. 'Now!'

The other four changed from women to fake water elementals, two metres tall and roughly human-shaped. One of them flew up and engulfed me in a sphere of water. I held my breath but knew I wouldn't last long. Then everything went black and suddenly I could breathe again. I tried to move but I was encased in something.

I have you, the stone said. *I'm strong to water. I think they forgot that I'm here.*

'Can you lift me out of the water elemental?'

I'm doing as much as I can. These people had better find a way to destroy these elementals quickly, because I can't bring any more air from outside for you.

'So that's a no and I'm suffocating,' I said.

Just relax. They're fighting them. Sang Shen came in as well, and he's helping. Yue Gui has called guards. Oh, good, she's lifting us ...

I felt the vibration as the stone hit the ground, and it split open in front of me. The Dragon had taken True Form and stood beside Sang Shen facing the four water elementals. The woman leading them had gone; probably already destroyed. Yue Gui changed to turtle form and stood on the other side of Sang Shen, who had summoned his spear and held it towards the elementals.

'Can you talk? Turn and we will spare you,' I said to the fake elementals.

They didn't reply, they just changed form to spheres, obviously planning to engulf us and drown us. One enclosed Sang Shen, who stood rigid inside it, his nut-brown face blank with concentration. The Dragon tried to take a bite out of one, but it oozed around his jaws and reformed over his head. Yue Gui was enclosed by the third, and the last one came for me.

I slithered back out of the way. I couldn't fight these in serpent form, there was nothing to hit.

Sang Shen loaded his spear with shen energy, making the tip glow blazing white, and the elemental exploded into a cloud of steam. The Dragon thrashed his head around, trying to free himself from the globe of water but unable to shake it off. Yue Gui's turtle face was serene as she glowed white with shen energy and made her elemental explode. She concentrated and the elemental coming for me exploded as well.

Sang Shen thrust his shen-loaded spear into the sphere engulfing the Dragon's head and water splashed everywhere as it disintegrated.

The guards ran into the room, but it was too late: the Shen had taken care of it. We all stood there panting and staring at each other.

The stone folded up and floated back into my crown. *I need a nap. Hold my calls, please.*

Sang Shen pulled the shen energy out of his spear, held it upright in front of him and pointed an accusing finger at the Dragon. 'They were *yours*!'

'They were demon copies,' I said. 'More and more of them are showing up. They're almost undetectable.

My stone was probably too worn out from changing form to record them. Your servants are probably dead, Qing Long.'

'I'd like to know when that happened,' Qing Long said with menace. 'Those girls were some of my best.'

'You walked out and left them here,' Sang Shen said.

'They can look after themselves,' Qing Long said. He changed back to human form. 'There's no way of detecting these copies?'

'My staff have been sharing the information on this for a while,' I said. 'You have to run regular sweeps through your human staff to detect them; they're not immediately recognisable as demon copies. Didn't you get the information?'

The Dragon swiped one hand through the air. 'I'm far too busy to read every memo that crosses my desk. I have staff for that.'

'Then I suggest you go back, find that memo, read it and check the staff who are supposed to pass that information on to you,' I said.

The Dragon's expression changed from angry to concerned and he disappeared.

'They were trying to get you alone,' Yue Gui said. 'They can only be destroyed with shen energy.'

'And I can't manipulate energy at all in this form,' I said.

'Are they everywhere?'

'No, they show up in groups whenever their master's planning something. First time I've seen copies that can change to elementals though. Usually they're copy humans that turn out to be demons.'

'Something new,' Yue Gui said. 'Always a bad thing.'

CHAPTER 7

After the Sang Shen and Blue Dragon hearing I headed out from the main administrative building to one of the smaller buildings skirting the large courtyard. The building was a row of rooms all opening onto the terrace overlooking the courtyard; it reminded me of an Australian motel — all it needed was the cars parked out the front. The room at the far north end of the structure, closest to the residential part of the complex, was my office; and instead of bumping up the stairs, I gripped the balustrade and slithered up it.

Firebrand, the other administrator, and Lily were there already, going through the massive piles of documents related to the cases I'd heard over the past three days, deciding which needed to go down to the Earthly for future reference and which didn't. There was a pile on the desk at least twenty centimetres tall.

'That's not the papers going down with me, is it?' I said.

Lily and Firebrand shared a look, then both pointedly ignored me and continued shuffling through the transcripts.

Simone and Leo appeared at the door, Simone holding the handles of Leo's wheelchair.

'Ready to go yet?' she said.

'It's only three o'clock, you haven't finished school yet,' I said. 'What are you doing back here?'

Leo glared up at her. 'You're ditching school to take us? You should go right back down there, missy.'

'Okay,' Simone said, and disappeared. She reappeared a moment later. 'But it looks like you're ready to go and I'm the only one who can take you.'

I sighed with resignation. 'Okay, but just this once.'

'Sure thing, ma'am,' she said. 'Just this once, until next time.'

We landed outside my parents' house in the Western Heavens. Simone guided Leo's wheelchair to the front door, then pressed the doorbell. We heard footsteps and Simone grinned and yelled, 'Nanna! Pop! We're here!'

My mother opened the door and hugged and kissed Simone, then crouched to kiss Leo on the cheek. 'Here's our beautiful girls and our handsome man. We've been waiting for you.'

My father came up behind her and Simone hugged and kissed him too. He held his hand out to shake Leo's. 'Leo, mate, good to see you.' He squeezed Simone around the waist. 'How's my little girl?'

Simone jiggled with excitement. 'I just got a new horse! He's only a baby and he *talks*!'

'A talking horse, eh,' my father said, bemused. 'Come inside and tell us all about it.'

My mother reached one hand towards me. 'Come on, Emma, don't hang back. You're part of this family too, so come on in.'

I took the smallest serpent form I could and followed Leo's chair inside.

'So you're Immortal now, eh?' my father said to Leo as he handed him a large mug of instant coffee. 'But you're still paraplegic. How does that work? I thought Immortals were like gods or something, all perfect.'

'Emma can tell you how it works,' Leo said. 'She knows more about it than I do.'

'They remain in the form they were in at the moment they were Raised,' I said. 'That's why John's hair's always coming out — he was Raised straight after a big battle and his hair was a mess.'

'Why Chinese men — particularly warriors — choose to have long hair is completely beyond me,' my father said, shaking his head. 'It's always coming out — must be a damn nuisance.'

'You can ask John about that when he returns,' I said with humour. 'He'd occasionally lose his temper about it and have something of a rant.'

'I can't imagine John losing his temper, he was the coolest man I've ever met,' my mother said.

'*Is*, Nanna,' Simone corrected her. 'He's not a *was*, he's an *is*. He's out there somewhere, and he's going to come back for us.'

'Sorry, sweetheart,' my mother said, and patted her arm. 'You know what I mean.'

Simone gave her a friendly squeeze. 'Yeah, Nanna, I know.'

Everyone sat at the dining table, and I took a larger serpent form and rested my coils on the floor. My mother put a bowl of tea in front of me and I sipped it, enjoying the fine flavour of the Tiger's best tea.

'Can you do Immortal stuff, Leo?' my father said.

Leo grinned, then his wheelchair rose about five centimetres above the floor, hovered and dropped with a rattle. 'I'm getting there. I can walk if I need to, but it takes a lot of effort. It's easier to do the black lion thing. I occasionally change into a lion at the Academy so I can get around easier. It's fun — it freaks everybody out.'

'A black lion,' my father said with wonder. 'I saw you at Rhonda's wedding, you were huge. Congratulations, mate, it was a sight to see when you were Raised.'

'And then poor Rhonda exploded everywhere,' Leo said, his face falling. 'Michael's still getting over that. He's refusing to believe it was his mother; he won't give up searching for her. Kwan Yin even told him it was really her, but he wouldn't listen.'

'I hope it works out all right for him,' my father said.

'Your brother was here,' my mother said to Simone. 'He said we have to move to the Northern Heavens. Something about Celestial Harmony.'

'You don't have to move there unless you want to,' I said. 'Martin's just being old-fashioned.'

'Well, that's a relief,' my father said. 'Because we're happy and settled here; we have a lot of friends in the Tiger's family and we really would prefer not to move.'

My mother flipped open her mobile phone and texted someone. 'Just telling Jen you're here, Emma, she wants to see you.'

I shrank my serpent form slightly smaller so I could only just see over the table.

My mother glared at me. 'Don't be like that, Jen's as proud of you as we all are. Look at you, some sort of general, and Regent, whatever that is. Everybody talks about you in the same sort of voice they used to talk about John.'

'What, you mean scared?' Leo said with amusement.

My father pointed at Leo with triumph. 'Damn straight.'

My mother tapped him on the shoulder. 'Brendan! It's rude to point.'

'And bad luck,' he added, still amused. He leaned on the arm of his chair to speak conspiratorially to Leo. 'Did you know that this is villa number four? It has 3A on the letterbox, but everybody knows it's number four. Nobody would live here until we arrived.'

'We Aussies don't care about silly things like bad luck numbers,' my mother said, busying herself making more tea and pulling out a packet of Australian biscuits. 'The Tiger's pleased he finally has someone living here.' She waved the biscuits at Simone. 'Tim Tam?'

Simone jiggled with delight. 'I haven't had one of those in *ages*.'

'Oh, *those* evil things,' Leo said. He raised one hand. 'A couple over here too, ma'am, if you please.'

'Emma?' my mother said.

'Oh, Emma doesn't eat in snake form,' Simone said dismissively.

'Good. More for us,' my father said with a wink.

'Why not? That means you never eat while you're up here in Shangri-La,' my mother said. 'That's just silly, Emma.'

'Yeah, she goes for days at a time without eating,' Simone said through a mouthful of chocolate biscuit. 'She's probably starving right now; she's been up on the Celestial for three days and hasn't eaten a thing.'

'So go find me a live rat or a bird,' I said softly.

They were all silent at that.

The doorbell rang and my mother's face lit up. 'There's Jen now.'

My sister Jennifer and my friend Louise came in. Jennifer grimaced when she saw me, but Louise came right up and tapped me on the head.

'That you?' she said.

'No, I'm a wild, venomous python and I'm going to eat you,' I said.

'Cool, it is you,' Louise said, and sat at the table. 'Oh my God, are those Tim Tams?'

'Help yourself, love,' my mother said, and Louise didn't need to be asked twice.

Jennifer stayed on the opposite side of the room from me, her face rigid with restraint. 'Uh, hi, Emma. Good to see you.'

'I didn't know you had a snake phobia,' I said.

Jen grimaced again. 'Sort of.'

'Chicken,' Louise said with a grin. 'Emma's not gonna hurt you, Jen. Oh,' she turned to face me, 'the reason we're here is to invite you to a party in the main part of the palace tonight. Can you come? A lot of the girls would love to meet you.'

I hesitated. Simone was right: I was starving and couldn't wait to get home to eat. But it would be fun to spend some time with the girls. 'Sure.'

'Cool. Oh, and by the way,' Louise leaned closer to me and grinned, 'pythons aren't venomous.'

'Just mention the Nemesis and this one becomes extremely venomous,' Simone said, still munching on the biscuit. 'It's just like a Harlequin romance: she hates him but he pursues her, sure that one day she'll see exactly how great he really is.'

'He'd be great turning green and foaming at the mouth,' I said quietly.

'See?' Simone said with triumph. 'Venomous!'

The party was held in the Tiger's Grand Audience Hall, which was filled with wives of about the same age as Louise — most of them wearing skin-tight miniskirts — together with many of the Elite Seraglio Guards, some in uniform and some in designer outfits, obviously off-duty. A dance floor had been set up at one end of the hall, complete with disco ball and laser lights. One of the Tiger's sons had set up double turntables and was acting as DJ. I felt the music vibrating through the floor beneath my coils.

Louise and Jen guided me out through the French doors along the side of the hall into the garden decked with coloured fairy lights. A buffet had been set up here, and many of the wives stood around eating or sat at the tables on the lawn.

'Isn't this awesome?' Louise said. 'We have one of these every couple of weeks; we alternate with the twenty-somethings. Sometimes the Tiger wanders in and then it gets *really* wild.'

A trio of giggling women approached us cautiously.

'Excuse me, but are you, like, Emma?' one of them said.

I bowed my head slightly. 'Yes, I'm Emma.'

'The Dark Lady? The real one?'

'That'd be me.'

'We were wondering,' she glanced at her two friends, 'if there was, like, anything you need? Anything we could do for you? How about some PR work or secretarial stuff?'

'I can type,' one of her friends said.

'I worked in a fashion magazine before I met the Tiger,' the other one added. 'I can help out if you need it.'

'Why would you want to work for me?' I said, suspicious. Then I realised what they were after. 'No, I'm sorry, I won't tell the Tiger to give you more time if you do things for me. I don't work like that.'

'How about I share my skills as a personal shopper and you have a quick word with Tigger on my behalf?' the first girl said.

'I think I just said no,' I said.

'Louise,' one of them said in a drawn-out whine, 'tell her to get us more time with him. We'll let you in on the deal.'

'Honey,' Louise said, 'she won't even talk to him on *my* behalf and I'm supposed to be her best friend.'

Another group of wives approached, five of them this time. 'Is this Emma?' one said.

'Yeah,' replied one of the women from the first group. 'The real one.'

'Hey,' said one of the newcomers, 'I just wanted to say thank you. You helped us all out and we appreciate it.'

There was a chorus of assent from the other wives.

'What did I do?' I said.

One of them turned to address the rest of the women in the garden. 'Hey, guys, this is Emma! The Dark Lady! The snake one!'

More wives gathered, smiling with encouragement. Some of them burst into spontaneous applause, a few of them cheering.

'What did I do?' I repeated. 'Is this because I defeated Demon Prince Six?'

'No, silly,' one of the wives said. 'We want to show our appreciation because you got that uppity bitch Rhonda out of our faces and now we're all equal again.'

'Yeah!' some of the others shouted. 'Way to go, Emma!'

I slithered away and back into the hall as fast as my coils could take me. Louise and Jennifer had to run to keep up.

'Emma, wait!' Louise shouted after me.

Suddenly the music stopped and all the lights in the hall came on. I stopped, dazzled by the brightness.

'Emperor present. All show respect!' a Horseman shouted from the main entrance. In a single smooth movement all of the women and guards present fell to their knees, their heads bowed.

The Tiger walked in, came to me, fell to one knee, saluted, then rose again. 'Hope my girls are showing you a good time, ma'am.'

I pulled out the oldest excuse in the book. 'I need some air.' I turned to Louise and Jennifer. 'I need to talk to the Tiger alone, if you don't mind.'

'Whoa, listen to the boss lady,' Louise said. 'Top-secret, superhero god stuff, eh?'

I slithered out of the hall, the Tiger following me. When we were some distance from the crowd I stopped. 'They just gave me three cheers for killing Rhonda,' I said, my voice hissing with frustration. 'Bitches.'

'That they are,' the Tiger said, glancing back at the hall. 'Not many women aren't. Particularly when things get tough.'

I glared at him. 'That goes for me too, I suppose.'

He put his hands on his hips and smiled slightly. 'You more than any of them.'

I turned away. 'Make it quite clear to them that I had nothing to do with Rhonda.'

'I have. They need someone to hero-worship, and you're it. Some of them have started learning the arts from the Masters here. You've even inspired some of them to talk back to *me*.'

'I think Rhonda would have had something to do with that as well,' I said, turning back to look at him. 'Now I see why she said you had to be dragged tail-first into the twenty-first century.'

'I love the twenty-first century; health care is at an amazing level. Used to be if my wives went down to the Earthly for a trip, they'd come back with all sorts of nasty shit and die in no time. Now, just about everything's curable.'

'Doesn't it bother you — you living so long, and them ageing and dying?'

He concentrated on me. 'You worried about Ah Wu ditching you because you're getting old?'

'Actually, no. But it must be hard to lose so many that you love.'

'Meh. They live a good, long, healthy and luxurious life here, and they die and I move on.'

'Damn, you're a callous bastard. Don't you mourn them?'

'I prefer practical. I lose a few a year — I'm not spending all my time mourning them, that'd be a waste. They live a good life. That's worth celebrating.'

The sweet scent of fresh, young blood wafted over the lawn and I raised my head. 'What's *that*?'

The Tiger sniffed the air. 'Just some birds.'

A woman walked past with a couple of small children, both about five years old. She wore a traditional long silk tunic with matching leggings, and the children wore pantsuits in black cotton with toggles and loops, their hair shaved except for a topknot each. When the woman saw the Tiger she dropped to one knee, bowed gracefully, then rose and continued.

The scent was coming from them; the children in particular exuded the wonderfully sweet, rich scent of fresh blood. It drew me closer. The woman saw me approaching, grabbed the children's hands and ran. I didn't think; I just pursued them. One of those children would keep me satisfied for weeks, and the feeling of swallowing it whole would be precious indeed. If I grabbed it and squeezed hard enough, it might even take bird form and be even more delicious to eat.

One of the children tripped and sprawled on the grass. The mother saw how close I was and changed to phoenix form. She spread her wings protectively over her children and burst into flames.

Something grabbed me by the throat from behind and hurled me to the ground, holding me there. 'Go,' a voice said, a throaty rumble, and the phoenix changed back to human form and hurried her chicks away.

The pressure holding me down didn't give way. 'Now listen to me,' the voice said, and I recognised it as the Tiger. My senses began to return and I shrank with horror at what I'd nearly done.

'You can let me up,' I said.

'Not quite yet, she's still too close,' the Tiger said. 'Listen up. You'd better fucking start eating when you're on the Celestial Plane or I'll make a complaint to the Jade Emperor. That was a mighty close call there; she's one of my oldest and most respected wives.'

I didn't reply, still stiff with shock.

'Did you fucking hear me!' the Tiger rasped.

'I hear you, I'm just ...' My voice trailed off. 'I can't believe I just did that.'

'Start eating on the Celestial Plane,' the Tiger repeated with force.

'Can you help me?' I said, my voice small.

'The people in the Northern Heavens are the ones to ask,' the Tiger said. 'Go talk to them. They've had experience with Ah Wu's Serpent. My staff just bring me big, bleeding chunks of African wildlife.'

He released my head and I raised it, then turned to him. 'I am so sorry, Lord Bai Hu, please accept this small serpent's apology.'

'Apology accepted,' he said gruffly. 'Go home to the Earthly and have something to eat. Then, when you have time, come back and talk to your Retainers here about food in the Heavens. If this happens again I'll make your life complete hell.'

Simone transported Leo and me back to our Hong Kong apartment later that evening. She was flushed and excited from spending time with the family.

'I'd better head to bed,' she said. 'I have a test first thing tomorrow.' She hesitated. 'Are you okay to take human form, Emma?'

I changed and shook myself out. 'No problem at all.'

'You could at least conjure some clothes with no holes in them,' she said, and slipped out of the living room before I could think of a suitable retort.

I went into the kitchen. Monica opened the door between the kitchen and her room; she was already in her pyjamas. 'Can I get you anything, ma'am?'

'It's okay, go back to bed,' I said. 'I'll make some noodles for myself.'

She came into the kitchen and closed the door behind her. 'I'll do that for you, ma'am.'

I went to her, opened the door and pushed her back into her room. 'No, you won't. It's late, and I can look after myself. I know where everything is. Go back to bed.'

She grimaced. 'At least leave the dishes for me to clean up, ma'am.'

'Whatever you say,' I said, not meaning it.

She went back into her room and closed the door, and I proceeded to raid the fridge for some ho fan, baby bok choy and vegetable stock to make myself some soup noodles. I checked the use-by date on the cans of cat food in the bottom of the cupboard; they were still good. Maybe this time they would get eaten before they needed to be replaced.

Leo wheeled himself into the kitchen and I waved the cooking chopsticks at him. 'Want some?'

'Nah, I ate in the West while you were at the party,' he said.

He went over to the drip coffee machine set up on a low benchtop on the other side of the kitchen and poured himself some strong black coffee. He inhaled deeply as he brought the mug to his mouth. 'Need to get one of these sent up to the Northern Heavens — they don't have a single decent coffee machine there. The only coffee I could get was some sort of awful coffee-coconut mix that they make on Hainan Island.'

'Oh, I tried that, it was foul,' I said. 'When do you think you'll be able to carry yourself up there?'

He took another sip of coffee and made the wheelchair spin around by itself so he was facing me. He grinned with pride. 'Getting there, won't be long.'

'You moved the chair too fast — you've spilt coffee in your lap,' I said, and turned back to the noodles.

'Dammit!' Leo said, and whizzed out the door towards his bedroom.

CHAPTER 8

The next morning Yi Hao followed me into the office and placed my large desk diary on my desk. She was wearing a smart navy business suit with a white shirt and matching navy pumps. 'Not many appointments today, ma'am. Things have settled down here very well recently.'

I dropped my tote bag into my desk drawer, sat down and grimaced when I saw my overflowing in-tray. Then I grinned up at her. 'Looking professional, Yi Hao. You'd pass for a local businesswoman.'

She fidgeted with pride. 'Some of the younger students have been helping me.'

I leaned on the desk. 'Do you want to go further than just being my secretary? You can go study if you like.'

She appeared horrified. 'Ma'am, please do not wish such a thing on me! It is a dream come true for me to be acting in this capacity for you. Now...' She looked down at the diary, professional again. 'You should tell me when you give humans my phone number, ma'am. A man called Chang called me and I had no idea what he was talking about. He is being held on the first floor until you decide what to do with him.'

'Chang?' I said, confused. 'I have no idea. What does he look like?'

'Big!' Yi Hao exclaimed. She spread her arms. 'He looks like a ... a ... *big man*!'

I searched my memory. 'No idea. Okay, I'll go down after we've been through the diary. When's my first appointment?'

'In half an hour you have a meeting with General Ma.'

'Good. Did you give us at least an hour?'

'Yes, ma'am. After that, no more appointments.' She gestured with her head towards the in-tray. 'You'll need some time to deal with this.'

I sagged over the desk. 'You all hate me.'

She touched my arm. 'You know we don't, ma'am. Now go check on this human that you seem to have collected.'

I went down to the first floor, the armoury, the most secure area inside the Academy building. Master Liu, dressed in jeans and a scruffy Batman T-shirt, was waiting there for me with a massive Chinese man, nearly as tall as Leo and heavily muscled. He was sitting morosely in the holding room but jumped to his feet when he saw me. 'Lady, help me!'

'This was Demon Prince Six's driver and general assassin-about-town,' I said to Liu.

Chang grimaced. 'Tell your janitor here that I am not a criminal. I was under an oath, but now I am free.'

Liu's mouth flopped open with delight. '*Janitor?*'

Chang glared at him with derision. 'I want to speak to you alone, ma'am, without this lackey around.'

'What word did that come out as in English?' Liu said.

'Lackey,' I said.

'It was far more obscene and derogatory in Chinese,' Liu said.

I turned to Chang. 'Remember when I told you that Liu Cheng Rong hadn't died six hundred years ago; he'd attained Immortality?'

Chang made the most lightning-fast double-take I had ever seen. He glanced from myself to Liu, then swiftly fell to his knees in front of Liu and touched his head to the floor. 'This humble, worthless piece of dung profoundly apologises for this insult and prays that you will allow him to assist you with his skills as a Shaolin master.'

Liu's face went thoughtful as he looked down at Chang. 'Hmm.'

'I was a disciple of Shaolin before I lost my way, Master. Please, help me to retake the oaths and return to the Path,' Chang said, still with his forehead on the floor.

Liu rubbed his bearded chin. 'Interesting. How long have you been outside the temple?'

'Six years,' Chang said with misery. 'I made some terrible mistakes and I want to atone for them.' He glanced up at Liu. 'Master, please help me.'

Liu gestured to him. 'Get up. Tell me what you have done.'

Chang rose, a swift and elegant movement. 'I have killed,' he said, almost a moan of despair. 'I have broken my vows. I wish to retake them and follow the Path once again.'

Liu rubbed his chin again, studying Chang. 'What was your reason for straying?'

'Wealth,' Chang said. 'I saw the wealth of the West and wanted it for my own. I have since learned that wealth is an illusion and cannot bring true joy. For the last three years I have lived in misery, serving one who was truly monstrous and evil.'

'If you believe in the concept of evil then you still have a long way to go,' Liu said.

Chang's face crumpled and he dropped his head. 'The temple gave me only empty words and hollow rules. I have yet to see the full truth inside them.' He looked back up to Liu, full of hope. 'Help me to see the True Way.'

'Very well,' Liu said. 'But it will not be easy.'

'Tell me what I need to do, Master.'

Liu concentrated for a moment, and Lok appeared out of the armoury. 'What?' he said. 'I don't have all day. I have three junior weapons classes this afternoon and half those dipshits don't return their weapons when they're done with them.'

Liu gestured towards Chang. 'I got you a new assistant-cum-janitor. Give him all the worst jobs.'

'About time,' Lok said, and raised his snout towards Chang. 'You look like a nice strong one, you can do the heavy lifting for me. Not having opposable thumbs is a pain in my doggy ass.'

'I am fully trained in the arts of Shaolin!' Chang protested. 'I was in the temple for twenty-three years! I'm better than any human I've fought, I was teaching juniors at Shaolin, and you want me to work as a *cleaner*? Assisting a dirty demon *dog*?'

'Forget it,' Liu said, and turned away. 'Never mind, Lok.'

'What an asswipe,' Lok said, heading back to the armoury. 'Dirty demon dog indeed. I had a bath last week. Nearly killed me.'

'I'd be wasted as a janitor,' Chang said. 'I can help

out with the martial arts training here. Use me! Help me to find the Way!'

'You are so far from the Way that you do not even see the Path when it is placed before you,' Liu said.

Chang turned to me. 'Lady, don't waste my talents.'

'Come with me, I'll see you out,' I said.

I went to the lifts and pressed the button to go down to the lobby. What a waste — so intelligent and talented, and so damn proud he couldn't see the redemption being offered him.

'I need an assistant,' Lok said, pausing. 'You should make him stay.' Then he gave a full-on dog bark of surprise.

I saw the glow reflected off the lift doors and turned to see what was causing it. It was Kwan Yin in Celestial Form, seated on a lotus blossom, a radiant field of shen energy pulsing around her. Chang fell to his knees and prostrated himself, while Liu and I quickly dropped to one knee. Lok bowed his shaggy head.

'You do not need to bow to me, Emma, we are family,' Kwan Yin said, her voice sounding the same as it always did. She changed from Celestial Form to her normal human form of a middle-aged Chinese lady, slim and elegant in a white silk pantsuit. She held her hand out to me and raised me, then pulled me into a gentle hug. 'You are like the promised to my own child.'

'And you are like another mother to me,' I whispered into her ear. The fragrance of lotus and jasmine floated around her. I pulled back. 'Has something happened?'

Ms Kwan gestured towards Chang. 'This has happened.'

Chang didn't look up from the floor; he lay there as if frozen.

'One of the most intelligent prospects we've seen here in a long while,' I said. 'Gifted with language, very perceptive, and one of Shaolin's finest practitioners. Shame he never managed to perceive the gist of the Teachings.'

'He is full of pride,' Ms Kwan said.

'That he is,' Liu said.

'But he has potential,' Ms Kwan said.

'Not while he's so damn up himself,' Liu said with amusement. 'Are you going to fix him, Lady? I don't think he deserves it.'

'All deserve what they receive, Liu; you of all people should know that,' Ms Kwan said. She gestured towards Chang, who still hadn't moved. 'Rise, Chang, let me see you.'

Chang pulled himself together and rose.

'You have been given an opportunity here, little one,' Kwan Yin said to Chang. 'You need to learn humility. If you will be guided by these Immortals, you have a chance to become much more than you are. You say that you wish to retake your vows and return your feet to the Path. Are you sincere?'

Chang bowed his head. 'I am sincere, Lady. I am weak.'

'You are not weak,' she said, 'you are too strong. You are rigid and unyielding. You will break before you bend. You need to learn to become weak. If you let them teach you, you will learn.' She raised one hand towards him, palm up. 'Will you retake your vows and serve with humility?'

He opened his mouth to reply but she turned her hand around so the palm faced him. 'Before you answer, Chang, be aware that if you say yes, you will not be living with dignity or esteem. You will be performing menial, dirty tasks in the service of a dog, living without luxury for many years. Are you willing to debase yourself to learn?'

Chang hesitated, his expression full of conflict.

'You like your comfort,' she said with amusement.

'That I do, my Lady,' he said, looking miserable. 'I have experienced poverty and hardship and I do not wish to relive them.'

'Very well. Yes or no?'

'What will happen to me if I say no?' he said.

'Nothing,' Liu said. 'We will take you downstairs and let you go.'

'What will become of me then?'

'You will live a life of case and comfort. You will be employed as a bodyguard by wealthy humans, and return to the life you knew while you were serving Six. You will have wealth and women and luxury, as you did then,' Kwan Yin said.

Chang's expression cleared. 'That life was meaningless! Yes, my Lady, I will retake the vows and serve the dog.'

'Serve well,' Kwan Yin said, and disappeared.

'General Ma is here, Emma,' the stone said.

'I have to get going,' I said.

'We can handle the rest,' Liu said. 'I know you just agreed to work for the dog, Chang, but *are you sure*?'

Chang didn't hesitate. He strode to Lok and fell to one knee before him. 'Master.'

Lok made a small barking sound deep in his throat. 'Good.' He turned to head back to the armoury. 'Come with me; you can help me find out who didn't return their weapons.'

'Send him up to me later. We'll have a small ceremony for him to retake the vows,' Liu said. 'Remember the precepts as well, Lok: he won't be eating after noon, no alcohol, no girls ...'

'You don't need to remind me, I know the whole deal,' Lok said.

I pushed the up button on the lift. 'I'll see you guys later.'

'Oh, and if you happen to be in the markets anytime soon,' Lok began, but the lift doors closed on me. *Cow's heart!* he finished inside my head.

General Ma and I went down to the coffee shop on the ground floor of the Academy building for our meeting; he'd developed a taste for hazelnut lattes and couldn't get enough of them.

'Now, you have to understand that there is minimal discourse between the Platforms,' Ma said, waving his latte. 'Just as the Earthly Plane is the World of Ruin to the Celestial, so the Celestial is considered Ruin to the higher Platforms.'

'But you move between worlds without difficulty,' I said. 'So the residents of the higher Platforms must come down to the Celestial now and then.'

'That they do. But we never announce ourselves as Immortals when visiting this Plane,' he said. 'And most of the Bodhisattvas do the same when they come down to the Celestial.'

'But it's different — you aren't allowed to tell people on the Earthly that you exist,' I said. 'Everybody on the Celestial knows that Bodhisattvas exist, and people like Kwan Yin visit you all the time.'

'There is nothing to stop us from revealing our Immortal nature to those on the Earthly,' he said. 'But you tell someone you're a Taoist Immortal and watch them make your life a complete misery for the next hundred years or so, wanting you to share the secret. Totally not worth it.'

'I thought you weren't allowed to tell people anything?'

'There are topics we're not permitted to discuss. Our existence is well-known, however, so that's not off limits.'

'I see,' I said. 'You're not allowed to talk about death, the afterlife, stuff like that.'

'Maybe,' he said, smiling knowingly.

'So Nu Wa is on a higher Platform, for Bodhisattvas? Can I even go that far?'

'No, Nu Wa exists on the Celestial, in the Kunlun Mountains in the West, same Plane as the rest of us Immortals,' Ma said. 'You won't have to travel to a higher Platform to see her.'

'So I *can* go see her without too much difficulty. I can just ride a cloud with Simone.'

'She's up too high. No cloud can carry you that far. You have to walk the last two hundred li or so.'

I shrugged. 'Okay, I'll walk.'

'In the snow.'

I shrugged again.

'As a *snake*, Emma.'

'Oh.'

'No other serpent has been that far. I suggest you start working now on a way to keep you warm while you make the trek.'

'Something all-over and padded maybe,' I said. 'And Simone can carry me.'

'I doubt if even someone as powerful as the Princess can carry you all the way,' he said. 'Ever seen a documentary about climbing Everest?'

'No *way*. It's that high?'

'It's twice as high,' he said.

'But that would mean it's in the lower part of the stratosphere! There wouldn't be enough oxygen to breathe!'

'Exactly.'

I dropped my head. 'Geez, this is crazy.' I remembered what John had said. 'What about the Three Pure Ones? He said to see them first.'

'They are on the First; you do not visit the higher Platform first. You should see Nu Wa on the Third — the Celestial Plane — before even thinking about visiting the First.'

'The Second is the Heaven of Perfection and Enlightenment?'

'Where the Buddhas exist, yes. The Three Pure Ones are on a higher Plane again. They are not living beings; they are more like concepts that occasionally choose to take human form and annoy the hell out of the rest of us.'

'What's the highest Platform like, Ma?'

'The First Platform is so far removed from reality — from space–time as we know it — that it is difficult to describe it as even existing.'

'Have you been there?'

'Once or twice, when Ah Wu was in serious trouble and we needed some really high-end help. It's not a place I'd recommend to anyone; the experience of being there twists your mind and can affect your sanity.' He finished his latte. 'Before you run off to do this stupid thing, I have made an appointment for you to see the Archivist. He may be able to help you.'

'Thank you,' I said with feeling. 'I've been trying to see him since just after John died, and he's ignored me completely. I even pulled rank and he *still* ignored me.'

He opened and closed his mouth, then smiled. '"John died". That's a strange way of putting it for those of us in the know. Ah Wu is not dead, he still shows up now and then.'

'On the Earthly, you cut someone's head off, they're dead. I've made a habit of saying that John *died* so people on the Earthly don't try to have me committed; and people on the Celestial see it as a joke in extremely poor taste.'

'So you win either way,' he said, understanding.

'I'm getting old and forgetful,' I said with a grin. 'It's easier to tell everybody that he died, but sometimes I talk to the office staff of Chencorp about him coming back and they think I'm crazy.'

'You're not getting old. You look younger every day. You need to find a mountain with a nice spring and some —'

'I don't have time for pine nuts and springwater. Go *away*,' I said. We rose and shook hands. 'Thanks, Ah Guang, I appreciate your time. And props for getting the Archivist to talk to me.'

'No problem at all,' he said.

When I reached the door, I found it was stuck closed. The clatter of cups and the murmur of conversation ceased and the room became eerily silent; everybody in the coffee shop except Ma and myself had disappeared.

I didn't mess around: I summoned the Murasame and it appeared in my hand. Ma took Celestial Form: a red-garbed warrior with flames on his robes and bright red hair down to his waist. A pyramid-shaped gold brick appeared in his left hand and a sword in his right.

'Do you know what's caused this?' I said.

'Wong Mo,' he said, and gestured towards the door. 'Incoming.'

Life continued as usual outside the shop windows; nobody noticed that I was holding a long black sword and standing next to a ten-foot-tall, red-robed god.

The doorbell rang. Ma was right: it was the King of the Demons, in normal human form, wearing a maroon silk shirt and black jeans, his blood-coloured hair held back in a ponytail. He spread his arms. 'Emma, sweetheart, you don't need that thing with me. I'm here to help.' He saluted Ma. 'Magistrate Ma of the Only True Power.'

Ma nodded back. 'Wong Mo.'

I dismissed the sword. 'Now I know why Simone hates being called "sweetheart".'

The Demon King gestured towards the table where Ma and I had been sitting. 'May I speak to you alone, Lady Emma?'

'Anything you have to say, you can say in front of my most trusted lieutenant,' I said.

'Bah, she should be *your* lieutenant,' the Demon King said to Ma. 'You're a heavenly general, one of the leaders of the Heavenly Host, right hand to the Dark Lord himself, and here you are babysitting a young female mortal.'

'Just goes to show how far apart we are,' Ma said. He moved to stand behind me as a Retainer.

I sat at the table. 'Now, what did you want to talk to me about?'

'You're searching for ways to clear the demon essence from you. Just let me do it, dear Emma, and you can be ready for him when he returns.'

I rose again. 'If that's all you're here for, you're wasting your time.'

He spread his hands without rising. 'Maybe we can negotiate something.'

'As long as it involves me prostituting myself to you, we have nothing to talk about.'

He didn't move, hands still spread. 'As I said, maybe we can negotiate something.'

'What do I have that you want, except for demon spawn?' I said.

'Oh, many things,' he said, jolly. 'Safe passage Above, certain Celestials who have been a complete pain in the ass to me, some homely women ... There are any number of things I could name.'

'I do not negotiate with demons,' I said stiffly.

He leaned over the table and grinned at me. 'You're doing it again.'

'Good,' I said. 'That means I know exactly how to deal with you.'

'Whatever,' he said, and rose.

Noise clashed around us and the people in the coffee shop reappeared. Ma quickly changed back to his usual human form.

'Let me send you some suggestions of what would be a suitable trade for your humanity,' the King said. 'Have a look through, and if you see something you like, let me know. You still have my phone, don't you?'

'Yeah,' I said. 'Neat trick how it always changes to the latest model.'

'Only the best for my Emma,' he said, and disappeared.

'Doing what again?' Ma said.

'Sounding like John,' I said.

He nodded. 'That you do sometimes.'

'Do you think I'm his Serpent, Ma?'

'You've been in the same room as his Serpent, ma'am, and not even he can be in *three* places at the same time.' His face changed to thoughtful. 'No, I take that back. I don't think there's much that he can't do.'

'Thanks for that, that was just what I needed to hear,' I said. I nodded to him, more serious. 'And thanks for hanging around.'

'I would have been more comfortable leaving and letting you face him alone as a display of my faith in you,' he said. 'But protocol demanded that I remain in my capacity as Retainer.'

'I know, and I appreciate it. Either way.'

'I've given your secretary the details of your appointment with the Archivist,' Ma said. 'Talk to him before you go traipsing off to see Nu Wa; you may be able to avoid seeing her altogether. The Heavens know, last time someone visited her it caused a war.'

'Nobody's been to see her since the Shang/Zhou?' I said.

He shook his head. 'Nobody's been brave enough.'

'Would a visit annoy her? I really don't want to walk into the home of one of the most powerful Shen in creation if she's pissed.'

'Impossible to tell. Nobody's spoken to her in thousands of years. Even before that, she was a recluse. You know the stories: she is as ancient as time and as powerful as nature. Approach her cautiously.'

'If the Archivist can help me, I won't have to approach her at all.'

'That would be the ideal situation.'

He saluted me quickly and we went out together. I took the lift back up to the Academy; he disappeared.

CHAPTER 9

When I returned to my office the White Tiger was stretched across the doorway in True Form. Even lying down he was nearly a metre tall.

I glared at him. 'What are you doing here? I just left your palace last night. And how am I supposed to get any work done when I can't get into my office?'

'You and Ah Wu are as bad as each other, working your asses off,' the Tiger said without moving. 'A *real* leader delegates everything and spends their time eating and screwing. I only need to work at most about ten minutes a day, and even then it's just "yes" or "no". When are you going to learn?'

'I prefer a more hands-on approach and less eating and screwing,' I said. I gestured towards him. 'Get out of the damn way.'

'Yeah, well in your case, with the vegetarianism and celibacy, you might as well be hands-on and keep yourself distracted. I don't know how you do it.' He rose, stretched out his front legs like a house cat and scraped his claws on the carpet. 'I need to talk to you.'

'Don't tear up my carpet!' I said.

He moved to one side and I opened the office door to let us both in.

'Shall I order a cat-scratching post, ma'am?' Yi Hao called from her desk.

'Yes, please,' I called back, and closed the door on her giggles.

'Oh, very funny. I eat demons like that for breakfast,' the Tiger said.

I opened the office door again. 'And a giant-sized cat collar and bell,' I added.

Yi Hao screeched with laughter.

I closed the door and sat behind my desk. 'Just the person I wanted to see. I need help.'

He took human form, leaned against the wall, crossed his arms over his chest and scowled. 'I told you to talk to the people in the Northern Heavens about feeding your serpent.'

'Not feeding the snake. John told me to go see Nu Wa, and I think I'll need a hand with that.'

His expression changed from suspicious to resigned and he flopped to sit in the chair across from me. 'That's a big ask. Anyone with any sense stays well away from her.'

'It shouldn't be that bad, Bai Hu. It's only on the Third Platform —'

'How do you know about the Three Platforms?' he said.

'Oh, come on, Bai Hu, its full name is Seven Stars Sword of the Three Platforms. Do you think I'm stupid?'

He rubbed one hand over his face. 'I keep forgetting exactly how much you aren't.'

'So I need to see Nu Wa on the Celestial, but I'll need a hand getting there because of the cold. You're the perfect person to help, being the Lesser Yang.'

'I pull out full yang anywhere near you and you'll be incinerated. Like being in the centre of a nuclear blast. Maybe you *are* stupid.'

'She's up about twice as high as Everest. It'll be bitterly cold, there won't be enough oxygen for a mortal like me to breathe —'

'So wear a spacesuit,' he snapped. 'I'll even provide one for you.'

'And I have to go in serpent form since it's on the Celestial. Do you have a long, narrow spacesuit you can lend me?'

He sighed loudly, leaned back and put his hands behind his head. 'The things you ask for. A snake spacesuit. Now I've heard everything.'

'But you have ordinary human spacesuits?'

'Of course I do. Some of the wives are thrillseekers and love being taken up into orbit. After a nasty accident where I became ...' he hesitated '... distracted, I decided to make them wear spacesuits when I take them up there.'

'I do not believe you sometimes! Someone died because you can't keep your mind off your gonads?'

He shrugged. 'Can't stop me being what I am.'

'Where do you have the suits made? Maybe I can get a special suit designed.'

'I'll see what I can do. A human suit might be okay; if you can make yourself small enough, we can just pop you in. Leave it with me. But I want something in return.'

It was my turn to be suspicious. 'What?'

He grinned. 'The blood sample you promised you'd give me when you visited the West. You never coughed up. So you're coming down to the shoebox that passes for an infirmary in this place and giving me some *right now.*'

'I never promised any such thing.'

'Beside the point now, 'cause if you want something to keep you warm and alive when you visit Nu Wa, you'll provide it anyway.'

'Oh, okay.' I went around the desk and opened the door. 'Yi Hao, is Edwin in the infirmary?'

Yi Hao's face went blank for a moment, then she nodded. 'He's there, ma'am, and asks if there is a problem.'

'Tell him we're coming down to give the Tiger a blood sample from me. It isn't enough that the damn cat gets our best students when they're fully trained, now he wants my blood as well.'

'That's a lie and you know it,' the Tiger growled behind me. 'The Jade Emperor gets your best graduates and you leave me with the rejects.'

'If you don't want my rejects, let me know, because there are more people asking for our graduates than we can spare. I'm sure some Celestial residents would be delighted to take them.'

'Just give me the damn blood so I can get the fuck out of here,' he said.

'Mind your language in front of my rejects.'

'Humph.'

After we had given the blood sample to the Tiger, I asked him: 'Do you think you can carry me to Wudang? I have a couple of things I need to do. Won't take more than thirty minutes.'

'Which one?' he said.

'Celestial.'

He studied me appraisingly. 'No. You're too fat.'

I changed into serpent form. 'I love you too.'

* * *

112

We landed in the main forecourt of the Celestial Wudang Mountain, an area about a hundred and fifty metres to a side and tiled with dark grey slate. It was used for the grandest displays of martial arts and the regular Taoist ceremonies held at the Mountain. The Hall of Purple Mist, majestic with its black roof and polished slate walls, stood to our north, facing Imperial south. To the east and west stood Dragon Tiger and True Way Halls. The Golden Temple rose on the highest peak behind Purple Mist, at least another hundred metres above us. Its gold walls and roof shone in the brilliant Celestial sun.

The Tiger put his hands on his hips and looked around. 'I haven't been here in a while. Good job on fixing it up.'

I slithered towards True Way, heading to the part of the complex where the forge was located. 'I don't like coming up here. It's too quiet.'

The Tiger stopped and I waited for him. The only sound was the breeze whispering through the buildings and the rustle of the pine trees that covered the hillside around us.

'I see what you mean,' he said. 'Wudang was never this quiet. There was always the noise and shouting of the Disciples, and the drums and chanting in the temples.' He shook his head and caught up with me. 'Spooky.'

We walked together along a narrow path that cut into the hillside. About three hundred metres on we came to a soaring arched bridge that straddled the deep gorge between the peaks. The breeze carried clouds below us, making the deep green pines in the gorge disappear and reappear. I led the Tiger around the edge of the peak and through a narrow passage to the next peak. A complex of smaller buildings, without open areas for practice, stood at the end of the passage. There was more noise here — no voices, but the gentle background sounds of people busy about their lives. As we neared the forge, the smell of burning and clanging of metal being struck became apparent.

'Good to see the Wudang forge back up,' the Tiger said. 'Must send some orders in.'

'Go right ahead,' I said. The revenue from the sale of some Wudang weapons would be welcome. 'Tell your friends. We have plenty of demons trained and working; we can handle any size order.'

He grinned at me. 'You give me good price, okay?'

'Yeah, dream on, Devil Tiger.'

We walked down four flights of stairs, flanked by small cypress trees, to the forge itself, with its well-worn rough stone bricks and clumsily put-together walls. The demons working there dropped to their knees when we entered, touching their heads to the floor; a couple of them fled in terror.

'You may rise,' I said to the head demon. 'I've come to check the status of the sword being forged for the Black Lion.'

The head demon pulled himself to his feet and grinned broadly. 'We will be fitting the handle tomorrow, ma'am, it has nearly cooled sufficiently. Please, come and see.'

He guided me past the cowering demons to the racks in the oven where weapons were gently cooled from the forging process. Cooling them too fast would make them brittle. He gestured towards a single black sword resting on the highest rack by itself. The simple metal spike that would be the base for the handle looked incongruous protruding from the slender black blade.

The Tiger eyed it appreciatively. 'Is it too long?'

'The Masters say it's the best length for him,' I said.

The sword was almost two metres long and Japanese katana style. There'd been some discussion about the most suitable blade for Leo to wield, and the consensus among the Masters and the forge staff was that for someone of his size, the light and slender but balanced and deadly katana style was the way to go. I hoped Leo would appreciate it.

The handle sat on another rack nearby. It hadn't had the final leather wrap put around it yet and its studded black metal gleamed in the lights of the forge. It was decorated with the head of a black lion, mouth open to reveal its fangs. The lion's eyes were covered with a strip of red paper, so that a demon could not possess it before it was blessed and its spirit entered it.

'What are you going to wrap it in?' the Tiger asked the head demon.

'Ray skin,' the demon said. 'Maybe even some thick sharkskin if we can get our hands on it.'

The Tiger glanced up from the handle. 'Don't wrap it yet. I have some skin taken from one of the biggest sharks that ever lived. I caught it a couple of hundred years ago, with my own claws, off a tiny fishing boat in the South China Sea. I had the skin tanned; it's not black, but you can dye it. It would be perfect.'

The demon grinned with delight. 'My thanks, sir, that would be more than suitable.'

'Thanks, Tiger,' I said. I turned to the demon. 'When are you planning to put it together?'

'We were planning to wrap and fit the handle tomorrow, sharpen the blade the next day, and then have it blessed three days from now,' the demon said. He bobbed his head at the Tiger. 'Now we will wait until the sharkskin arrives.'

'I'll have it here for you tomorrow,' the Tiger said.

The demon shrugged. 'Then it will be right on schedule.' He nodded to me. 'You can present it to Lord Leo anytime after that, ma'am.'

'I'll need to send out invitations, so at least five days after that,' I said.

My next stop was the mess hall, where the head caterer, a human Immortal, was preparing food for the demon workers.

'The sword will be ready in three to four days,' I said. 'Can we hold the presentation ceremony in about nine or ten days?'

He quickly checked the calendar. 'Neither of those days are auspicious, but the day after, eleven days from now, is a good time to give gifts.'

'Done,' I said. 'I'll have Yi Hao give you a list of who to invite.'

He nodded. 'Looking forward to it, ma'am, it's way too quiet around here. I'm sure the demons that turned from the service of One Two Two will be delighted to see the Disciples back here where they belong, celebrating.' His smile faded. 'Is there any word on the possibility of changing you back so that the Academy can be moved back here? That is what we all want to see, ma'am, the buildings and courts full of students again.'

'I have some leads that Xuan Wu himself gave me,' I said. 'They sound difficult but I'm determined.'

'That's good to hear, ma'am.'

I led the Tiger back along the narrow path cut into the side of the cliff and to the main forecourt in front of the Hall of Purple Mist.

'Before you take me back down, could you give me a few minutes alone in the temple?' I said.

The Tiger changed to True Form and stretched out on the stones in the sunshine. 'Go right ahead. I'm not going anywhere.'

I slithered up the narrow stairs to the temple. The Celestial version of the Golden Temple was double the size of the one on Earthly Wudangshan. Statues of the Xuan Wu — the snake/turtle combination of John's True Form — guarded each side of the entrance, the snake wrapped around the turtle's shell and disappearing into it where they touched. Inside the temple was a statue of John in Celestial Form — a black-skinned human with wild hair and a small goatee, sitting on a throne and holding a sword across his knees. The sword was Seven Stars. A snake and turtle were beneath each of his bare feet. An altar was laid out in front of him, holding two vases of flowers, cups of wine and burning incense. A screen stood behind him.

I curled up my coils and sat in front of his effigy. His black fierce face gazed at me and he seemed ready to leap up and cut off my serpent head with the sword.

I meditated on the lives of those who had died because of the battle between Heaven and Hell. Charlie, Rhonda, Regina: women who had died caring for others rather than fighting, the way so many women in the world's conflicts died. The Disciples who had died defending the Mountain — the stronghold against the forces of Hell. April, whose naivety had killed both her and her child. The fox spirit who had died trying to hide herself and protect her child, who had died anyway. All the stone Shen destroyed by Six. It was a long list and I wished I could shed a tear for them all, but it wasn't possible in serpent form. Many of them had chosen their path and died with honour, but for some their deaths were what those in the military blithely called 'collateral damage' and dismissed as part of the necessity of war.

Even though John was God of the Arts of War, he had never revelled in war and had always sought negotiation first. He was a study in contradictions, being the greatest fighter in existence and at the same time holding a deep abhorrence for killing. It didn't stop people from dying, however. Always so many people giving their lives, even more so recently because John was no longer present to protect them.

I raised my serpent head. I wasn't a fighter of his calibre but I would do my best to protect those who needed protection. I nodded to John, and his statue stared fiercely back at me.

I turned. I was on top of the highest peak in Celestial Wudangshan and the view was breathtaking. The mountains below me spread as far as I could see, their bases covered in mist and their peaks jagged and sharp. Something to do with the altitude and the geography made it seem that all the lower peaks were facing this highest peak and bowing to it. I turned back to glance at John's statue and bowed to him. My warm, caring, generous, reptilian god.

I went down the stairs to the waiting Tiger.

'Okay, I'm ready to head back to work,' I said.

'Did he appear to you?'

'No.'

'I'd expected his statue to take on a life of its own and come charging down to carry you away.'

'He's in two pieces at opposite ends of the world. Not very likely to happen.'

'Has he appeared to anybody recently?'

'Not since Chinese New Year.'

'Okay.' The Tiger touched my snout with his nose

and carried me back to the Academy. He bowed on one foreleg and disappeared.

Gold was waiting for me outside my office. He jumped up as soon as I appeared and followed me inside. I sat at the desk and he shut the door and sat across from me, his face alight with excitement.

'I can see you have something to tell me, so go ahead,' I said.

'I have a lead on Shenzhen. It seems that peasants are travelling there to work in the factories, and not leaving. At all. Ever.'

'Couldn't they just be falling through the bureaucratic cracks?' I said. 'This is all done on paper, I've seen it. When you go through immigration at Lo Wu, you fill in a mountain of bureaucratic forms that they don't even look at. They just stamp them and then put them in a box for filing. There must be some pieces of paper that don't make it through to data entry, even if they *do* have a computer system.'

'They do, and I'll have to investigate more; all I have at the moment is a hunch. A stone I know was working on the update of the China Bureau of Statistics' databases and, in a fit of nostalgia, looked for a human ex-lover. He found her — but once she moved to Shenzhen her records disappeared; in fact, she's disappeared completely. Normally people have to continue to pay taxes in their home province even if they move to the city to work, and she stopped doing it. He checked her residential, health, work permit and family planning records too — and found nothing. She's gone. No death record either.'

'More than one person has disappeared like this?'

'Several hundred.'

I grimaced.

'I know what you're thinking, ma'am: there are millions of people travelling into Shenzhen, and many of them want to disappear to avoid being sent back to their villages or to avoid paying taxes back home. But there seems to be some sort of pattern to the disappearances, and we want to do some analysis on the data.'

'How big's the database, Gold?'

It was his turn to grimace. 'Huge. Even the current year's data is in the terabytes. Older data is kept separately. It's a nightmare.'

'You'll have to go down to crunch that.'

'Even with three stones linked up, it would take about a day completely offline. Possibly longer.'

'Do you have a couple of friends who'd be willing to do this? I know how you stones hate being used as computers.'

'Calcite — my friend who worked in the Bureau of Statistics — will help. We just need to find one more.'

'Don't look at me,' the stone in my ring said. 'I'm not leaving Emma alone after what happened last year.'

'Oh, good point,' Gold said. He went quiet for a moment, thoughtful, then stopped moving completely, not breathing or blinking.

'Gold, stay alive,' the stone said.

Gold came back with a start. 'Oh, sorry.'

'This has you more upset than usual,' I said. 'It's not often you forget to live.'

'This sounds like a threesome,' the stone in my ring said.

Gold wiped one hand over his face. 'Not a threesome. She's my great-great-granddaughter.'

'Five generations?' my stone said.

Gold nodded.

'And you worry about her? You've been human way too long,' the stone said.

'Her great-grandmother was one of my wives at the tea plantation,' Gold said. 'When the Celestial found out that I'd helped steal the tea, they only gave me five minutes to put my affairs in order before I was taken to the Celestial Plane. I never really had a chance to say goodbye to them and to make sure they were cared for. The demon servants took off, then the local warlord found out I'd gone. He kept my wives as his own, but when he found that one of them was pregnant he threw her out, leaving her with nothing.'

'She did well to survive.'

'She was forced to do things that I'm not proud to be responsible for. Now our descendant, Ah Fua, has disappeared.'

'This is ridiculous. I bet she doesn't even keep a tablet for you,' the stone said. 'Five generations is way past any accountability.'

'Her mother does. She has an ancestral tablet for me at home, and one for my whole generation in the temple. Ah Fua doesn't need to do it because her mother does everything, even sweeps the graves. They're good, diligent children.'

'Do they know?'

'Of course not, Dad. Now, if we've finished with the interrogation, I'd like to find another stone who can help locate Ah Fua.'

'I wonder if Zara would mind helping,' I said. 'She's still in hiding in the armoury, it would keep her busy.'

Gold's face lit up. 'She says yes.' He grinned broadly. 'I'll go arrange it.'

CHAPTER 10

Simone, Leo and I had dinner together that evening, just the three of us.

'The appointment with the Archivist is tomorrow after school,' I said to Simone. 'Don't forget. I'll need you to take me.'

She gasped, her eyes wide. 'Oh, no! I've arranged to take some of my friends out on the boat after school tomorrow!'

'You never asked me,' I said.

She stuck her chin out at me. 'I don't need to. It's my boat.'

'Point taken; but I'm your guardian and you're not an adult. Therefore I am legally required to be aware of where you are at all times.'

'I'm going on the boat after school tomorrow,' she said, stubborn.

'I think an adult should go along with you, just in case,' I said.

'You have to go see the Archivist, and Leo's ...' Simone hesitated, obviously not wanting to hurt Leo's feelings. She changed what she was going to say. 'Leo's no good on the water.'

Leo grimaced but didn't say anything.

'How about Michael then? All the girls will think he's the coolest thing ever.'

'I told them girls only; they wanted to bring some boys but I said no, just all girls is more fun,' Simone said. 'They'll get really annoyed if I bring Michael. I don't need anyone along, Emma, really. The demons will look after us.'

'I'd like to go,' Leo said.

Simone's expression softened. 'You sure?'

He nodded with a false smile. 'Sounds like fun. I want to meet your friends.'

Simone shrugged. 'Okay. We can have fun pretending we're related.'

'Sounds like a plan,' Leo said, his smile becoming more genuine.

'I still need to get to the Archivist. Can you drop me there and be back in time for your cruise?' I said.

'How far is it?' Simone said.

'I have no idea,' I said. 'I thought General Ma was going to tell you where it is.'

Simone unfocused, concentrating, then snapped back, obviously happier. 'It's fine, it's just next to the Celestial Palace. He said you can take the stairs in Wan Chai and then someone can summon you a cloud to take you the rest of the way. I don't need to take you.'

'Can Ma do it?'

She concentrated again. 'No, he's busy. I'm asking around ... what time is it tomorrow?'

'Three.'

She nodded, still concentrating, then snapped back. 'Your stone is supposed to have all of this info, Emma. It's gone to sleep again, hasn't it?'

The stone didn't reply.

She shrugged. 'Michael will wait for you at the Celestial Palace at about two forty-five and take you across on a cloud. Problem solved.'

It was quicker to walk the kilometre or so from the Academy to the Celestial Gateway than to drive. I walked along Hennessy Road, the air thick with the fumes of the passing traffic and burning my throat and eyes. At Southorn Playground — a concrete soccer pitch painted green, used by locals to sit and talk, and by young people to play basketball and soccer — I took an escalator up to the pedestrian overpass. The overpass straddled the busy streets of Wan Chai — Lockhart Road, Jaffe Road and then finally Gloucester Road, five lanes each way and packed with cars and red taxis. The overpass led into the mezzanine floor of Immigration Tower, which was full of Filipina domestic helpers suffering the tedious all-day wait for their work visas. Before I'd met John I'd often spent the whole day here myself, waiting for hours in the cockroach-infested halls rich with the ripe aroma of the over-used toilet facilities, being shuffled from counter to counter and interviewed by bored or aggressively irritated immigration officers. The waiting areas had recently been upgraded, but the bored bureaucrats behind the desks remained the same.

The walkway continued out of Immigration Tower and into Central Plaza One, an office tower that had once been Hong Kong's tallest building. It was triangular in cross-section, and each wall had a bank of lifts to go to a different section of floors. All of the fittings were triangular to fit with the theme, including triangular gardens on the ground around the tower. I walked through Central Plaza, across another small walkway and into the office tower connected to the Convention Centre. I passed a number of international convention attendees, their large identity cards strung around their necks. They were loudly discussing some sort of plastics manufacturing in American and French accents.

I turned right out of the Convention Centre complex and walked across another road to Great Eagle Centre, which sat right on the edge of the water. It and its twin tower, Harbour Centre, had massive advertising signs spanning their first to third floors — they were visible from all over the harbour and featured in any night-time Hong Kong postcard scene. I could see the Star Ferry pulling into the Wan Chai ferry terminal below me, and a few double-decker buses waited in the bus station. I took another overpass to the Hong Kong Exhibition Centre, then an escalator down to the ground. I'd walked more than a kilometre without touching the ground.

The Hong Kong Exhibition Centre had a large open area on its ground floor and a rectangular fountain with dragon-head spouts. Behind the fountain stood a replica of Beijing's Nine Dragon Wall, the gate to the Celestial Palace.

I didn't immediately approach the wall; instead, I went to the roadside, where two large bronze statues of qilin stood facing the traffic. Known as kirin in Japan, they were Celestial creatures with the body of a horse, the head of a lion, the horns of a deer and the feet of a goat; most interestingly to me, they were also covered in scales like a reptile. Westerners often referred to them as Chinese unicorns, and although their appearance was not very unicorn-like, their nature was similar. They were divine creatures of pure light, fleeting and rare, not even composed of yang or yin but somehow transcendent of universal essence. It was regarded as a blessing to see a qilin. I never had, and knew that only very few of my Celestial acquaintances had ever seen one.

I turned away from the qilin and walked up to the Nine Dragon Wall. As I approached, the wall grew from two to four metres high and spread to twice as wide. The marble balustrade guarding the front of the wall descended into the ground and the sounds of human life around me ceased. The dragons came to life and writhed to the centre of the wall to greet me.

I reached into the large Sogo shopping bag that I'd brought with me and pulled out a range of local snacks. I waved one of the boxes. 'Strawberry pocky is who?'

'Me!' said a gold dragon; it whipped its head out of the wall and took the box of pocky in its mouth. The lid opened and all of the iced biscuit sticks flew into its mouth at the same time. The box disappeared.

'Damn, you're greedy,' I said.

'Any more in there?' the dragon said, eyeing the Sogo bag.

I raised a box of tiny hollow koala-shaped biscuits filled with icing. 'Koalas?'

'Chocolate?' one of the purple dragons said.

'Mine!' another dragon said, and snatched the box out of my hand, then slithered to the end of the wall to enjoy the biscuits in peace.

I raised another couple of boxes. 'I have strawberry and vanilla koalas here ...' They floated out of my hand to two more dragons. I checked inside the bag. 'Chiu Chow iced mini biscuits ...'

'No *way*,' a blue dragon said, staring wide-eyed at me. 'Really?'

'Give them to him, he's from Swatow,' said a purple dragon through a mouthful of koala.

I passed the Chiu Chow biscuits to the blue dragon and checked the bag again. 'I feel like Santa at Christmas. I have ... barbecue beef, spicy pork, Portuguese egg tarts ...'

Two of the dragons started to squabble over the barbecued meat slices before I'd even taken them out of the bag. The winner approached me triumphantly. 'I'll take the pork. He can have the beef.'

I passed him both bags of thinly sliced barbecue meat, then waved the cake box containing the egg tarts. 'Anybody?'

The box floated out of my hand and down to a corner of the wall where two dragons were sitting together, their eyes wide with pleasure.

I looked inside the bag again. 'More pocky — man pocky, the dark chocolate stuff; ordinary chocolate, strawberry, hazelnut, pineapple ...' I glanced up. 'I don't know how you can eat pineapple pocky, it's *horrible*. I have pork floss, dried squid, preserved lemon ginger ...'

'Ginger!' a gold dragon said, and I threw the paper-wrapped pieces to him. The pork floss — cooked and shredded pork — and the dried squid were claimed by a couple of dragons who were already enjoying their biscuits. The remaining boxes of pocky floated to the ground beneath the wall, opened and all the dragons shared the sticks.

'I have a bag of White Rabbit candy for all of you to share as well,' I said.

'Did you check the date?' a green dragon said suspiciously.

'It's definitely from after the powdered-milk scare, there won't be any melamine in it,' I said.

The dragon nodded. 'Good.' Its head dropped slightly. 'Is that all?'

I pulled a large glossy cardboard box, elegantly decorated with printed flowers and wound with ribbon, from the bottom of the bag. 'Cakes!'

Three of the dragons rushed to me and held the box floating in front of them. The ribbon unwound and the handles pulled apart, revealing a variety of small individual slices of cake. I'd chosen the most expensive ones: multi-layered chocolate; elegant sponge with mock cream and topped with glazed fruit; and the inevitable whipped hazelnut creation. The dragons shared a look then all opened their mouths into wide dragon grins.

The wall split apart in the middle, revealing a set of stairs that appeared to be made of cloud but were solid underfoot. The dragons relaxed, enjoying the food I'd brought them.

I reached into the very bottom of the bag. 'Oh, and I have some salty plums.'

Two dragons rushed me. I ducked to avoid their blows as they had a brief scrap over the plums. Another dragon sneaked up, took the plums out of my hand, winked, and slithered to the end of the wall. I went back to the fountain, put the Sogo bag into a bin, and proceeded to the bottom of the stairs. I changed to serpent form and had slithered up the stairs before the two fighting dragons noticed that the plums had already been taken.

The sounds of the dragons ceased and silence engulfed me. Cherry trees lined the wall of the Celestial Palace, nearly as high as the wall itself and adorned with pale pink blossoms. The air was filled with their pink fluffy petals, blowing in the Celestial breeze and covering the ground with a thick, soft blanket. The air was cold; it was early spring, the time when the cherry trees blossomed to give their promise of a warmer future.

I slithered through the piles of petals to the gate of the Celestial Palace, where Michael was waiting for me.

'I thought you'd been held up,' he said. 'I was ready to call you and find out what had happened. You're gonna be late, Emma.'

'I was busy bribing the Nine Dragon Wall,' I said.

He was suddenly more curious. 'What do you bribe a wall with?'

'Pocky.'

'Ah, the great tool of corrupters everywhere. My mom used to bribe me with pocky when we first moved to Hong Kong.' His face fell and he looked down. 'I'll get you that cloud.'

'I miss her too, Michael,' I said as a small cloud materialised above us and floated down to land on the cherry blossoms.

'Thanks,' he said.

'I miss you as well,' I said. 'Take your time, but when you're ready, I'd love you back with us, where you belong.'

He didn't look at me as he stepped onto the cloud and gestured for me to join him. 'I'm just not ready yet. After all that's happened, I need to spend some time being a normal guy on the Earthly. I have a good job in a finance company in Wan Chai, did you know that? And I have an ordinary human girlfriend. Sometimes being ordinary can be the best thing in the world.'

'I know exactly where you're coming from, but let me know if you're ever ready to return to us.'

'I will. Is Simone meeting us there?'

'She's not coming, she's having a boat party with her schoolfriends.'

Michael grimaced. 'You should go along. I know what sort of stuff happens at those parties. I went to one of those schools before I dropped out and you employed me.'

'Leo's there.'

He visibly relaxed. 'It'll be all right then.'

The mist of the cloud surrounded a sturdy platform, and I curled up on it. 'Simone's one of the most powerful creatures in creation, Michael; a group of ordinary humans can't hurt her.'

'They can break her heart.'

I nodded my serpent head. 'You have a point. But Leo is there to make sure they don't.'

'I just wish she had the brains to realise that Celestial High is where she should be!' Michael said, frustrated. 'She would learn so much there, and not just about her talents. She knows *nothing* about demons.'

'Go on and tell her.'

He grimaced again. 'Yeah, I know how far that'll get me. I never went there myself, I have no first-hand experience, I'm living as a normal human on the Earthly ... My opinion isn't worth squat.'

I chose my words carefully. 'I think she'd probably value your advice. You're like a big brother to her. Feel free to talk to her about this. I'm not happy about this school either but she's determined to go to a "normal" school and we don't have any other choice on the Earthly. If I try and force her to go to CH she'll just ditch school altogether, same way you did.'

He was silent at that.

The cloud lifted from the ground, giving me a view of the entire Celestial Palace complex. In many ways it mirrored the Forbidden City in Beijing: rectangular buildings with gold-tiled roofs, small courtyard gardens, and a system of high red walls throughout that separated the large formal ceremonial buildings from the smaller residential and administrative areas. Hundreds of cherry trees bloomed between the buildings and walls. The Grand Audience Chamber sat on top of the hill, its white walls and gold roof shimmering against the brilliantly blue Celestial sky.

'I'm surprised there's no analogue for Tian Tan, the Temple of Heaven,' I said. 'That's as big a tourist attraction in Beijing as the Forbidden City.'

'Haven't you been there?' Michael said, amused. 'It's half an hour away in the other direction.'

'It's only the last couple of months that I've discovered I can come to the Celestial in serpent form,' I said. 'I'm still finding my way around. I'm always getting lost in the Palace of the Dark Heavens, and the demons are too terrified to put me on the right path. I spent half an hour wandering around last week, no idea where I was.'

The sky darkened from midday blue to the rich violet of evening, and a few stars shone around us.

'What's happening?' I said.

'The Archives are always in the dark. Dunno why, but it goes from evening to night as you approach.'

'Are we time-travelling? Moving faster through the day?'

Michael chuckled. 'You *do* need to spend more time on the Celestial. Nobody can time-travel, Emma, especially not me. You can't go breaking the fundamental laws of the universe like that, it just doesn't work. We're only moving into an area where it's always night.'

'John's time-travelled. I saw a shadow of him as he was when Simone was a little girl, just last year in a record shop. He recognised us.'

'Wow,' Michael said quietly. 'That's just ... wow.'

The sky darkened to the deep blue-purple of night and the stars came out fully, blazing with the brilliance of high altitude and clear air. A cluster of lights coalesced into view some distance away, and slowly grew as we travelled closer. The temperature didn't drop as I would have expected at night; it remained warm and pleasant, the breeze full of rich night-time fragrances.

'I've never met the Archivist, but Dad says to take it slowly with him,' Michael said.

'Yeah, he's completely ignored my precedence so far. I was only able to arrange this meeting with Ma's help,' I said.

'You have some powerful friends, ma'am.'

'And some powerful enemies as well.'

'I wouldn't call Er Lang your *enemy* as such ...'

'I wasn't talking about him. There are plenty of guys on the Celestial who have issues with my gender, my serpent nature and my mortality. They might not like me, but they're out in the open about it. Your real enemies are the ones who pretend to be your friends.'

'Oh no!' He clutched his heart theatrically. 'You've found me out! I am your sworn enemy, your nemesis! Now I cannot let you live!'

'You are so lame sometimes,' I said. 'But not nearly as lame as the real Nemesis. Did you hear what he did?'

'The ambush at Festie? That was real classy,' he said. 'And the girl who set that up was supposed to be Simone's *friend*.'

I dropped my serpent head. 'Talk to her about Celestial High, please.'

'Will do.'

As the cloud took us closer to the Archives I could see that it was a floating series of walkways between large flattened rocks holding bookshelves and racks of scrolls. A particularly large rock in the centre, suspended in the night sky, held a traditional administrative building, its metre-wide veranda reaching right to the edge of the rock. Walkways spread from the central building to the other floating rocks. People became visible on the walkways and I suddenly realised that what I'd thought were small walkways of about a metre across were actually at least ten metres wide. The central building had originally appeared about three hundred metres to a side, but it could easily have been three times that.

'I've seen something vaguely like this before,' I said, confused. 'Walkways in the night sky.'

'The Archivist is a huge fan of Diablo II,' Michael said. 'He suddenly remodelled the Archives one day based on a level of the game.'

'No *way*.'

'There are even replica monsters roaming around,' Michael said. 'I heard that when Diablo III came out, the Archives were unavailable for three weeks.'

He guided our cloud over the walkways to the central building, and floated it up to the edge of the veranda so I could slide onto it.

'I'll stay with you as Retainer,' he said, summoning his sword and clipping it onto his back. 'I took the afternoon off work, told them I was having physical therapy for the limp.'

'What's the prognosis on that?'

'I'll get there.'

The doors opened by themselves, revealing the foyer: a rectangular room about ten metres wide and five deep, with a polished dark wood floor and red wood pillars holding up the roof with the complicated bracket structure used in traditional buildings. A few rosewood sofas, decorative chairs and coffee tables were placed around the room. Large rosewood shelving units on either side held a collection of vases from all dynasties. Doors led out to the left and right, but nobody was present.

'And they complain about *you* breaching protocol,' Michael said.

'Any idea which way to go?' I said.

Michael shook his head. 'Never been here.'

I turned left. 'I'll go the yin direction then, just to be contrary.'

Michael opened the door on the left for me. The lower half was dark rosewood, but the top half was a random lattice of wood with paper between the slats. I slithered through the door and into a corridor running down the side of the building. To the left was a dead end, so I headed right. The air tasted of old, dry paper.

Michael unfocused, using his Inner Eye. 'The Archivist's office is at the end of this corridor, on the right. There's a similar corridor on the other side so it didn't matter which direction we went. The office takes up the back wall of this building, and the middle — where these doors are — holds what looks like the oldest and most valuable records.'

Keep your Inner Eye to yourself and both of you get your asses down here, the Archivist said into my head. From Michael's expression he'd heard it too. *Let's get this over with so I can move on to something important.*

'Charming,' I said, and slithered to the end of the corridor, Michael following me.

Michael opened the last door on the right for me and I went in. At first I thought we'd gone in the wrong door: several rows of bookshelves stood in front of us, with an aisle between them. About half the documents on the shelves were scrolls bound with red ribbon; the other half were old-fashioned books. A very few ancient books made of bamboo slats, bound vertically and held together with string, were rolled up for storage on the end shelves.

'Get a move on, I don't have all day!' the Archivist shouted from the centre of the room.

I glanced at Michael. The Archivist sounded like a young woman, but Michael had definitely said 'he'. Michael missed my look and waited for me to proceed. I slithered down the aisle between the shelves and arrived in a large open area in the centre of the room. The Archivist sat behind a huge rosewood desk that was covered in books and scrolls, a brush and ink stone to one side. There were trolleys all around the desk holding more books and scrolls. The Archivist was in the form of a twelve-year-old Chinese boy wearing a traditional black silk robe. He had round glasses and wore his hair in a long pigtail. He finished the document he was annotating with brush and ink, hung the brush on the brush stand and glared at me.

He waved me impatiently towards him. 'Hurry *up*, will you; you really are very slow.'

I nodded my head. 'Archivist. Thank you for seeing me. I need your help.'

'Yes, yes, you want to know what you are,' the Archivist said, shuffling documents on his desk. He stopped and glared at me again. 'I don't know. Nobody knows. Now piss off.'

'I'm a snake. I don't piss, I pass solid urine; you should know that,' I said.

He glared at me again, then leaned back in his chair and laughed. He took his glasses off, wiped them on the sleeve of his robe, then put them back on. His laughter eventually faded to an evil chuckle.

'Tell me where the stuff is and I'll have a look myself,' I said. 'Anything about serpent Shen, anything about Rainbow Serpents, and anything you have about Australia's first settlers. I also need to know if it's possible to remove the demon essence from me.'

He gestured towards one of the trolleys. 'It's all there. I had the staff collate it for you before you arrived.' He waved at a set of large double doors. 'There are some reading rooms through there; they have computers with internet access, and there should be a stack of blank disks if you need them.'

'My stone will take notes for me,' I said. I nodded to him again. 'I thank you, sir.'

He gazed at me appraisingly. 'You treat me with the respect due to an adult despite my appearance.'

'You treat me like shit even though I'm First Heavenly General,' I said.

He banged his hand on the desk and laughed again. 'That I do,' he said. 'Who'd have thought a little human girl would be teaching me about respect.'

I moved closer to the desk and looked him in the eye. 'Come down to the Earthly with a sword in your hand and I'll give you a fine lesson in respect.'

He gasped with laughter again. 'The Celestial didn't *tell* me! If I'd known how much fun you are, Emma, I would have let you in here a long time ago. All I'd heard was that you were an uppity bitch who doesn't know her place.'

'That I am.' I glanced at the trolley. 'Is this everything? You didn't hold anything back because you're pissed at me?'

'I'm not pissed at *you* so much as annoyed at having to do this pointless task,' he said. 'Nobody knows what you are: accept that. Just *be* what you are; that is the essence of the Tao.'

He waved one hand and a demon appeared next to the desk. 'We do not have anything on removing demon essence from humans because that has never happened.' He turned to the demon. 'Do a full cross-indexed search on Lady Emma's topics: serpent Shen, Rainbow Serpents, and settlers in Australia — we may not have anything on that last topic. When you have it, take it to reading room two.'

He rose gracefully from the chair and came around the desk. In his twelve-year-old form he reached only to chest height on Michael. 'Let me show you to the room and you can do the rest yourselves. You might be a hell of a lot of fun, Emma, but I'm not going out of my way to help you on this pointless quest.'

CHAPTER 11

The reading room contained a mix of modern chairs and tables with computers, and rosewood couches and armchairs. A coffee table to one side held a teapot with cups, as well as a thermos jug with coffee, powdered whitener and sugar.

Michael and I sat and flipped open the documents. He looked at the books, having hands; I used my head to unroll the scrolls. They were readable regardless of their language, a benefit from being inside the Archives building. Many of the documents were very old, but some were recent articles published in academic journals; all of them were mind-numbingly tedious. After about half an hour, a demon tapped on the door and came in pushing another trolley of documents for us to study.

Emma, Leo said into my head. *Emma, I need you back down here right now. It's horrible ... they brought boys along and one of them tried to drug Simone ...*

'What is it, Emma?' Michael said.

'Tell Leo to share with you,' I said.

Michael concentrated for a moment.

One of the boys tried to drug Simone — one of the girls helped him — oh God, Emma, it's awful ...

'Take it easy, old man, start from the beginning — someone drugged Simone?' Michael said, his voice fierce with urgency.

He tried to rape her. The girl slipped a roofie into Simone's drink, Simone felt tired, she went down into the cabin at the front of the boat to sleep it off ... the boy followed her ... It sounded like Leo took a deep breath. *She wasn't unconscious, and when he tried to ... when he tried to ... she yinned him! She took half the boat with him. Fortunately it was the front end, and everybody else was at the back in the lounge or on the roof on the sundeck — but she's killed him for sure, and the boat sank!*

'Where are you now? Where's Simone?' Michael said.

Water police, Leo said with misery. *I herded them all onto the life raft, and the water police picked us up — the boat's on the bottom of the harbour, with the front end blown completely off, and Simone's taken off and won't reply when I call her, and this boy is ... he's ... she killed him, Emma. What do we do?*

'I need to get back down there right now,' I said to Michael. 'But nobody except Simone is big enough to carry me. You need to take me back to the Celestial Palace, and then meet me at the Nine Dragon Wall in the car.'

'One of the Academy drivers will meet both of us there,' Michael said. He concentrated for a moment.

Water Police Headquarters in Central, Leo said. *Across the road from The Centre.*

'That's not too far from Wan Chai, only about a fifteen-minute drive,' Michael said. 'Let's go.'

'Contact Gold, ask him about the legal implications on the Earthly of the boat exploding in Hong Kong and the children being put in danger, and of this boy disappearing while in our care,' I said to Michael as we rode his cloud back to the Celestial Palace. 'Ask him to also check the Celestial implications of the fact that Simone's killed this kid — the Celestial will know she's done it and they'll want to pursue her for breaking Celestial law.'

'Done. Gold says he'll meet you at the water police station. All the kids are there, and their parents are on the way. There's a lot of hysteria from the parents already there, Emma, and Leo's bearing most of it. They're blaming him.'

Michael stopped at the top of the stairs leading back down to the Earthly. 'It would be a shame to lose all that information the Archivist put together for you, Emma. Let me go back and put it on some disks for you.'

'Thanks.'

'I'll pass them along to you later,' he said.

The dragons were silent as I slithered down the stairs. I changed back to human form and walked to the kerb to meet the car.

'Good luck, Emma!' a voice called behind me — one of the dragons. I turned to thank it but the wall had returned to its normal form, the dragons unmoving. I nodded to them and got into the back of the car. Marcus was driving; Monica, who'd obviously been crying, was sitting in the front.

'I heard what happened, ma'am, and I'm sorry we didn't go along to watch over the Princess,' Marcus said as he pulled away from the kerb.

'No need to apologise, Marcus, Leo was there,' I

said. 'We could never have predicted that this would happen.'

'Have we heard from little Simone?' Monica said.

'Nobody's heard from her, Monica, but she's just run away. She's fine.'

Monica dropped her head and blew her nose with a soggy tissue. 'She's not fine, ma'am, a *horrible* boy tried to have his way with her and she *killed* him. No little girl should have to face things like that.'

Marcus thumped the steering wheel. 'Trying to hurt *our* little *Simone*! She is so innocent, and he tried to take that innocence! He deserved it, the little ...' He dissolved into Tagalog, roundly cursing the boy involved.

It was mayhem at the water police headquarters. Parents hugged hysterical teens, shouting over their heads at the policeman behind the counter. When they saw me enter, the parents mobbed me. I pushed my way to the counter, the parents shouting abuse and threats at me. Gold was already there and he looked relieved when he saw us.

I yelled to the police officer, 'Where is Leo Alexander?'

'Why you ask about that dark-lei?' one woman shouted. 'Why you not ask about my daughter? You nearly killed my daughter!'

'You are killer, just like that neeg-la in the wheelchair!' a man shouted. 'He kill that boy and that girl with rubbish boat and now he *hides*!'

'Who are you?' the policeman said, straining to be heard over the noise.

'This is Emma Donahoe, the majority owner of the boat,' Gold shouted over the counter. 'I'm her lawyer, Gold Gam.'

'That's right, gweipoh, bring a lawyer, because we are going to sue you for everything you own. Go back to your own country!' a woman yelled behind us.

The policeman nodded, and went through a door behind the counter. He opened a door in the wall and gestured for us to enter. He stopped Monica and Marcus. 'Family only.'

'Lock her up!' a Filipina shouted. I turned to see her. She was clutching a sobbing blonde girl; she was obviously the domestic helper come to collect the teen.

I went through the door and the policeman led us down a corridor to an interview room where Leo was waiting. He sat at the table, his face grim. The room looked more like a corporate meeting room than the rooms you see on crime dramas on television. It held a large, eight-seater table with conference chairs around it, and had windows giving a grand view of the harbour. The water police had recently moved to this new building in the reclaimed land of Central.

'Sit here,' the policeman said, and went out, leaving us alone.

I put my hand on Leo's. 'She's alive, Leo, we know that for sure.'

He grabbed me and pulled me into a clumsy hug; the handles of his wheelchair got in the way and dug into my ribs. 'She's killed someone, Emma, how is she ever going to live with herself? God, poor Simone, she's so young to face so much.'

I held him tight and buried my face into his shoulder. 'She'll survive, Leo, she's the strongest of all of us.'

'We need to find her and set it up so that she *can* survive this,' Gold said. 'We can't have the police thinking her dead; her identity will be lost and we'll have to make another one for her.'

'Always thinking of the practicalities, two steps ahead,' Leo said. He took a deep breath. 'Any word?'

I shook my head.

The policeman came back with a stack of forms and accompanied by another officer from the regular police force, who was carrying a thick file.

I tapped the stone and covered it with my hand.

Gold is coaching Leo in what to say, the stone said. *We're getting the story straight and making sure it will keep the police happy. All you have to do is insist that the boat was safety-checked, and that you don't know what happened because you weren't there. We will fix this.*

The two officers sat at the table and the marine policeman nodded to the regular police officer to begin.

'I'm Lieutenant Cheung,' the regular policeman said. 'We need to complete a full report on what happened. The coroner will be involved, as both the young boy and girl were killed in the explosion.' He glanced down at the file. 'Simone Chen is the girl who was killed, is that right?'

'We can't be sure she's dead, Lieutenant,' I said.

'I think we can, ma'am, because you've lost all of your family now.'

I hesitated. 'No, my parents are fine, and my sisters ... Nothing's happened to them, has it?'

He flipped open the file. 'Michelle LeBlanc, died 1999. After she died, you moved in on John Chen Wu, but he died in 2004, leaving you in charge of the family assets in trust for Simone Chen, who's now —'

I jumped to my feet. 'Just a goddamn minute! Don't try to suggest this is murder! Simone's out there somewhere and we're going to find her.'

'We'll raise the boat and find out exactly what happened, ma'am. Now.' He turned to Leo. 'How long have you and Miss Donahoe known each other?'

'Okay, look,' Leo said, and rapped his hand on the table. 'I haven't told you the whole story, but I will now. This is how it happened. I'm in a wheelchair, I can't go up or down stairs, so I was stuck in the main saloon of the boat. I saw Simone and ... Brian?'

'Bevan,' the policeman said.

Leo nodded. 'That's right, Bevan. They'd gone into the cabin. I never saw them go in — one of the other kids must have distracted me while they sneaked in. They'd closed the door but a wave jarred it open and I saw them. They were naked, and they were getting ready to light up some marijuana cigarettes —'

Quick. Shocked. Now, the stone said.

'She was having *sex* and smoking *pot* on the *boat*?' I yelled at Leo.

Yes, blame him. Good.

'Look, I'm sure Simone gets up to a lot of stuff that you don't know about, Emma. This is the first time I've actually caught her in the act,' Leo said. 'I've smelled smoke in her room before, and you know those times when she says she's having a sleepover with a girlfriend ...'

'She's with a *boy*?' I shouted.

'Ma'am, everybody outside can hear you,' Gold said, trying to calm me. 'I think the press have turned up.'

I made a hugely obvious effort to control myself. 'I hope you stopped them, Leo.'

'For the sex part, it was too late, but I told them to throw the pot over the side and get dressed,' Leo said. 'Then I wheeled myself to the back of the boat to check

144

on the kids on the roof ...' He hesitated, and took a deep breath. 'That was when the whole front of the boat exploded.'

'Was anybody cooking on the boat?' the marine policeman said.

'We warmed up some pizza in the boat's oven,' Leo said.

'Gas?'

'Yes.'

'Did you smell any gas?' the policeman said.

Leo grimaced. 'Yeah, I did, and this is my fault. I should have made sure they didn't light up; instead I just told them to throw the drugs overboard and walked away. I was embarrassed because they had no clothes on, and I was really upset to see Simone like that. I smelled the gas, but I thought it was just from starting up the oven — it hadn't been used in a while. It would have been okay if they hadn't lit up ... but they did.' He put his head in his hand. 'This is all my fault.'

'You *walked* away?' Lieutenant Cheung said. 'You can't walk!'

'Wheeled. Walked. Same thing for me.'

'When was the boat's last safety inspection?' the marine policeman said.

'Two months ago; you should have the records of that,' Gold said with confidence. 'I can retrieve the documents from my files.'

'And when was the last gas-bottle swap?' Lieutenant Cheung said.

Gold hesitated. 'I don't know. The crew arrange that.'

'Was it due for a new hose?'

Gold appeared embarrassed. 'I don't know, sir. That was the responsibility of the crew. It is possible they may have forgotten to have the hose replaced.' He grimaced. 'And we see those advertisements on the television all the time saying that hoses need to be checked.'

The marine policeman glanced at the regular policeman; he appeared satisfied but Lieutenant Cheung obviously didn't want to let it go.

Oh crap, this is the policeman that interviewed you when that copy of you was found in a dumpster about nine years ago, the stone in my ring said. *He was after you then, and he has the seniority to really go after you now!*

Leo and Gold shared a look; they'd heard.

The door opened and another policeman stuck his head through. 'Girl turned up alive,' he said in Cantonese. 'Boy is dead. They washed up on the shore in Pok Fu Lam. We have an ambulance down there picking them up.'

'Simone's alive, ma'am,' Gold said. 'They found her.'

If you can burst into tears of relief right now that would be helpful, the stone said.

'Oh, thank God. Thank God,' I moaned, and put my head in my hands.

Gold leaned over and patted me on the shoulder. 'She is being taken to the hospital?' he asked the policemen in Cantonese.

'Yes. Queen Mary,' the marine policeman said.

Cheung was staring at me, obviously not believing my relieved act.

'She's in Queen Mary Hospital, ma'am,' Gold said.

I jumped to my feet. 'Let's go!'

'We need to take statements first,' Cheung said.

'Can't this wait?' I said. 'I want to see my stepdaughter —'

'Did you marry this girl's father?' Cheung said.

'No, we were engaged, but she's like a daughter to me.'

'Humph,' Cheung said and looked down at the folder he had on us. 'Then don't call her your stepdaughter. That is wrong.'

'Then she's a little girl who means the whole world to me!' I snapped.

Cheung glared at me. 'Sixteen is not little girl.'

'She is to me!'

'Can we see her and come back to do the paperwork?' Gold said in Cantonese. 'We just want to be sure she's okay.'

Cheung turned his glare on Gold. 'No. You fill in the paperwork first. I want to hear all the stories.'

The marine officer snorted with disgust, roughly put his papers together and rose, shoving his chair back. 'Can I talk to you outside?'

Cheung rose as well and they went out of the room together.

'Let me relay,' Gold said softly. His voice changed to that of the marine policeman: 'This is chee seen. Crazy. This is the third gas-bottle explosion in the last year on a boat from this bad batch of gas-bottle hoses. You see conspiracies everywhere.'

'This girl's mother, grandparents and uncle were murdered in Ho Sheung Heung. Then her father had his head cut off after this gweipoh moved in. Now the little girl nearly dies on their boat. Can't you see what's going on here?'

'I think you see too much, my friend. With all due respect, this really looks like a standard gas-bottle incident. We'll raise the boat and find a blown-up gas oven.'

'We'll see,' Cheung said. 'Let's take their statements. Miss Donahoe with me; Mr Alexander with you. I bet you a hundred that their stories fall apart after ten minutes.'

'You're on,' the marine policeman said, and they came back into the room.

'Miss Donahoe, you will give your statement to me,' Lieutenant Cheung said. 'Mr Alexander, go with Senior Marine Constable Tin. Mr Gam, stay here, please. An officer will keep you company while you wait.'

Don't worry, it's all under control, Gold said silently. *Go with him, and I'll help out.* He continued speaking to me as Cheung led me down the corridor to another room similar to the first. *What they'll do is take extremely detailed statements, asking the same questions over and over, asking for a detailed time line, that sort of thing. They'll be trying to find a hole in your story, or any discrepancy between your statement and Leo's.*

But I wasn't there!

Even so, they'll want you to tell them exactly what you were doing and when, and tell them over and over without changing a single detail. If you're lying, you'll eventually make a mistake or contradict yourself. If you're telling the truth, your story, no matter how detailed, will be consistent. Hang tough, Emma, we can do this.

I just want to get to Simone.

Gold's voice changed slightly in my head. *The Celestial has summoned all of us. We have a hearing in the Celestial Palace in four hours.*

Oh no, not right on top of this, I said. 'Poor Simone,' I added out loud.

'She is a lucky girl,' Cheung said.

'I don't know whether I should hug her or punish her when I do see her,' I said ruefully. 'I thought she was better behaved than this.' I sat at the table in the interview room and put my head in my hands. 'I've failed as a parent. Sleeping with boys and smoking pot — how could she do these things?' I sat up and wiped my eyes. 'This is all my fault.'

Bravo! the stone said, the hint of sarcasm in its voice made all the more cutting by its British accent.

'How is the boy?' I said. 'You said they found them both?'

'The boy is dead,' Cheung said. 'Head injury from the blast.'

The boy was Jade, Gold said. *The real Bevan was yinned, gone completely. Jade won't be back for a while; she's in the tenth level of Hell now.*

I rested my head in my hands again. 'Oh no, that's awful. What am I going to say to his parents?'

'Worry about that when you get there. Right now,' Cheung opened a folder and pulled out some forms, 'I need you to give me a statement. So why weren't you on the boat?'

Repeat after me, the stone said: *I was at the Immigration Department …*

'I was at the Immigration Department,' I began, and followed its coaching for the next forty minutes.

Finally, after he'd grilled me on my movements four times, Cheung closed the folder. 'I'm sorry to have to put you through this, Miss Donahoe,' he said, and smiled. Smiling made him seem much more human and approachable, and I relaxed slightly. 'I think I've been mistaken. You obviously do care for Miss Chen and you're doing your best to look after her. I will have to pursue this further when the boat is raised, but in the meantime please go visit her in the hospital. If there's anything else I need, I'll be in touch.' He rose and held out his hand; I rose too and shook it. 'I wish you good luck in talking to Miss Chen,' he went on. 'She will probably need counselling after this.'

'I'll arrange it. I just want her to recover and be happy again,' I said with feeling. I nodded to him. 'Thanks so much for being understanding, Lieutenant. I hope you see that I really do care for Simone very much.'

'Oh, I do,' he said, and opened the door for me. 'This way.'

Is he lying as much as I think he's lying? I asked the stone.

Twenty-four-carat lies. He's after you; he's convinced you and Leo have been picking them off for their money, Leo being the brains and you the muscle. Watch your face!

I carefully controlled my expression. Leo the brains and me the muscle. Yeah, right.

Oh, well done, Emma! the stone said, even more sarcastic now. *Way to go, he didn't miss that triumphant smirk!*

Geez. And I was doing so well.

Emma, do me a favour, dear, get that demon essence cleared out of your system so you can go live on the Celestial Plane ...

I know. Where I won't have to deal with over-zealous police officers.

Exactly.

And what about Simone, who wants to live on the Earthly?

The stone was silent at that.

150

Fortunately, the parents had left by the time we returned to the reception area. Monica and Marcus were sitting on the plastic chairs waiting for us.

Gold didn't speak until we were some distance from the station, walking through the pedestrian overpass that would take us across Gloucester Road to the car park under The Centre. 'Marcus, take Monica and Emma home. I'll take Emma's form and drive Leo up to the hospital —'

'No!' Monica and I said at the same time.

'Emma, you can't touch Simone. If you don't rush up there and give her a huge hug, it will look very bad,' Gold said. 'Let me do it, and then I'll bring her home.'

'I want to go too!' Monica said.

'My Boxster is only a two-seater,' Gold said ruefully, 'and neither you nor Leo can drive it.'

'I'll drive Marcus home in the Boxster, and you three can go ...' I stopped. 'Okay, that won't work. I would definitely wreck the love of your life, Gold. We'll do it your way.'

Gold let his breath out, obviously relieved.

'How about we all go?' I said. 'You take my form, Gold, and give me your form.'

'Yes!' Monica said. 'We can all go and see her!'

Gold shrugged. 'That would work.'

We arrived at the car park, and paid at the shroff office before taking the lifts down. I hesitated before walking out of the lift.

'What, Emma?' Leo said.

'This is where I was attacked by that Mother and put into the hospital,' I said.

Gold hesitated for a moment, checking. 'No Mothers here.' He grinned. 'Except for Leo.'

'Damn straight,' Leo said, and wheeled himself to the car.

'You still here, stone?' I said.

'I'm here.'

'Contact Lok. Tell him about Jade.'

'Why?' the stone said.

'Because she has *three children*.'

'I will take them, ma'am,' Monica said. 'We can look after them.'

'They're dragons, Monica.'

'They're children first, ma'am.'

'Can't do anything underground, Emma,' the stone said. 'It will have to wait until we're out of the car park.'

'I'll do it,' Leo said. 'Lok says it's under control. Jade arranged for them to go stay with their father. He came and collected them from the Folly an hour ago.'

'Their father?' I said.

'Qing Long.'

CHAPTER 12

The hospital complex in Pok Fu Lam was enormous. We parked in the multi-storey car park near the entrance to the main building. Gold got out of his Boxster, then changed into me. He concentrated on me and the world around me grew a glimmering pearly halo as I took on his form. Gold walked ahead of me to the lifts to the hospital's main entrance.

'I need to work out more,' I said as I followed him.

He turned. 'Ma'am, you're nearly forty. You're allowed some spread. Besides, you know more than anyone that appearance means nothing. Nobody can match you with a sword.'

'Oh, come on, Gold,' I said as we waited for the lift. 'Just about anyone can take me down — I'm a human. I might be a match for another human, but against a Shen I'm usually overmatched.'

Gold gave a resigned shrug.

'And tidy up your hair,' I said. 'I never have it all coming out like that — you're exaggerating!'

'He's an exact copy,' Leo said. 'Stained shirt and all.'

Gold proudly displayed the T-shirt I was wearing, which had an oil splatter along the bottom.

'I spilled some oil on myself last time I oiled my weapons,' I said, the excuse sounding feeble even to my ears.

'That's why we have aprons for that sort of thing,' Gold said, turning back to the lift and giving me a discomforting view of my growing behind.

The hospital's main lobby was tired and worn from the passage of so many people through it. There were about twenty bored-looking people sitting in chairs on one side, and a few patients wandered around in plain white cotton pyjamas.

We went to the reception desk, which was heavily barred with a small vent at the bottom to talk through. Gold leaned in to speak to the receptionist in Cantonese. 'Chen See Mun, please. Simone Chen. We're her family, to pick her up.'

The receptionist stared at Gold in shock, and Gold started, then grinned. 'I've lived here all my life.'

The receptionist turned away, frowning, and entered the details on the computer. She leaned into the vent to speak to us, still frowning. 'Third floor, wing F.'

Gold nodded. 'Thank you.'

We looked around for a sign that would show us the way. Nothing. Gold turned back to the receptionist, whose frown deepened. 'Follow red arrows!' she barked, and turned away.

The floor was marked with arrows set into the worn linoleum, and we followed the red ones to the lift. A few people were waiting in the lift lobby, next to a collection of abandoned gurneys and wheelchairs set to one side. The lift arrived and those waiting rushed inside before those inside could get out. There was some grunting and tussling, and those inside managed to fight their way out of the lift as Gold and I held the doors open for them. We went in and Gold pressed the third-floor button.

On the first floor, the doors opened and someone at the back of the lift, who'd rushed to get in first, elbowed his way to the doors to get out.

On the third floor, the corridors spread from the lift lobby in all directions and we stopped, confused. There was a nurses' station nearby and Gold walked to it, the rest of us following. A couple of harassed-looking nurses sat there fiddling with paperwork. Both of them ignored us for a moment then one of them came up to us.

'Visiting hours seven thirty. Family only; maximum two people. Wait until then,' she said.

'We're here to take Simone Chen home,' Gold said.

She sat at the computer terminal, flipping through the records. 'Simone Chen.' She pointed down the corridor without looking away from the screen. 'Third room along. F3.'

'Thank you,' Gold said, and we all headed in that direction.

'Two people only!' the nurse snapped. She gestured in the other direction. 'Waiting room there.'

'Me and Gold,' I said, Gold's voice sounding strange in my ears.

Monica handed me a shopping bag with a change of clothes in it for Simone.

The ward room was grey and grimy, with stained painted walls and four chipped metal beds, two on each side of the room. The bathroom reeked of urine and damp as we passed it. The furthest bed on the left had the curtains pulled around it; the closer bed on the left held a middle-aged woman, asleep. Simone was sitting on the closer bed on the right, dressed in her hospital pyjamas, talking to a policeman who was making notes in a folder. It was Lieutenant Cheung, getting her story before we could coach her. In the far bed on the right was an elderly woman, also in the regulation pyjamas; she was sitting up and listening to every word Simone said with an expression of deep concentration.

'Oh, guys, thank goodness you're here,' Simone said. She hopped off the bed and ran to Gold who was still in my form. They held each other for a while, Gold patting Simone on the back and Simone clutching him.

'This little girl, very bad behaviour!' the old woman said loudly in English, waking up the sleeping woman. 'You teach her wrong! Need to punish her, she is very bad girl!' She nodded and settled into the bed, then waved her finger at us. 'You should spend more time correcting her, make sure she does right thing! Study more, be good girl, find *nice* boy!'

Simone turned in Gold's arms to speak to the old woman. 'Oh, go die in a fire.'

'Humph!' The woman crossed her arms and looked away, then released a torrent of abuse in Cantonese. 'Bad girl! Treats elders with no respect!' She glared at Gold. 'You teach her right way. *Chinese* way. Treat elders with respect, do as she is told. She very bad girl!'

Simone released Gold and turned to speak to Lieutenant Cheung. 'Are you done with me?'

Cheung held out the clipboard with the paperwork. 'I need you to sign this please, Miss.'

Simone stomped to him, grabbed the clipboard and scribbled a signature on the bottom of the form. 'I can go now?'

Cheung nodded and Simone came back to us. I handed her the bag of clothes and she went into the bathroom to change. She wrinkled her nose as she came out. 'It's clean; they say the smell is from a faulty drainage system.'

A nurse with a kind face came in. 'You are going now?'

Simone's expression softened. 'Thanks for looking after me, Lydia. I'm going home.'

The nurse touched Simone's arm. 'Take care, Simone. Talk to a counsellor, okay? That was a terrible thing that happened.'

Simone nodded, took Gold's hand and led him out of the room with me trailing behind.

'Why, of all the stories that you could have made up, did you have to decide on *that* one?' Simone growled under her breath as we returned to the nurses' station. 'You really do hate me, don't you? Having sex, smoking pot — dammit, Emma, do you *want* me to get up to that sort of stuff for some reason?'

'The stone and I made up that story,' Gold said. 'Emma had nothing to do with it.'

Simone stopped and put her hands on her hips. 'It will take me a long time to forgive you two for this. You've destroyed my reputation at school — I don't know how I'm ever going to go back there! They'll all think I'm a *slut*!'

'"They" being the same people who tried to drug you and date-rape you,' Gold said.

Simone raised her hands with exasperation and continued towards the nurses' station. 'It was just a couple of them.' When we reached the station, she leaned on its ledge and covered her face with her hands. 'And I *killed* someone. I *killed* him!' Her shoulders shook as she lost control, weeping into her hands.

Gold put his arm around her and concentrated. Monica, Marcus and Leo came rushing from the waiting room. Monica bundled Simone into her arms and held her as she cried, and Marcus patted her back.

Gold went around the counter to see the nurses and I followed. One of them held out a clipboard with a stack of paperwork on it without speaking. Gold picked up the pen that was chained to the station and signed my name at the bottom.

The nurse checked the papers. 'No medication, you can go.' Her expression softened. 'I hope you'll be all right, Chen See Mun. That was bad.' She sat and started to key the details into the computer.

We went down in the lift, Simone still clutching Monica. She continued to hold her tight as we walked back to the car park.

Monica stopped when we exited the car park lift. 'I smell gas!' She looked around, concerned. 'The smell is very strong, ma'am!' She spun back to the lift and pressed the button. 'We need to get out of here right now!'

'I don't smell anything,' I said.

The rest of the group smelled the air and then shook their heads.

'Why only Monica then?' Gold said.

'We need to get out of here, it's very bad!' Monica said.

Simone stiffened, then grimaced. 'This is *all. I. Need!*' she shouted, and stomped towards the car. 'Monica, stay there. There's no gas; it's just a demon clearing the area before it shows up.'

Simone stood in the middle of the car park lane, put her hand out and summoned Dark Heavens.

The demon appeared. It was about ten metres long and so tall it nearly touched the roof of the car park. It looked like an insect, with barbed front legs and a bulbous head, but it was made of silvery metal, reflective in the brown haze of the afternoon.

'What the hell is *that*?' I said. 'I've never seen one of those before.'

'It's some sort of elemental/demon hybrid,' Gold said, then jumped back in shock as the demon raised its spike-ended feet and tried to impale him. It swept him aside, knocking him into the wall, and came straight for me.

I moved back. I didn't want to fight this thing; its essence would definitely turn me into a Snake Mother.

'Change, Emma, there's nobody around,' Simone said. 'You can fight as a snake.'

The demon heard her and tried to impale her on one of its feet, then turned back to me.

There was a metallic clatter as Leo discarded his wheelchair. He came to stand next to me. 'I think the snake thing is a good idea,' he said.

The demon approached me with obvious menace and I concentrated, taking snake form. As soon as I changed to snake, the demon stopped, appeared to stare at me with its eyeless head, then cast around, swinging its head from side to side. It swung, its feet clicking on the concrete, to face Simone; then quickly spun and rushed Gold, who'd changed back to his normal form.

Simone raced after it and slashed it from behind with Dark Heavens. A wound opened in the demon's hindquarters, then closed up again, the metal element moving like mercury. It raised one foreleg and dropped it on Gold, who turned to his stone battle form, raised one arm, changed its shape to a rough shield and blocked the demon's blow. He changed his other arm to a lance and skewered it.

It backed quickly off the skewer and the puncture wound healed like the slash that Simone had made in it. It hesitated, rotating slightly as it worked out whether to attack Gold or Simone. Then it rushed Gold again, this time raising both front legs and attempting to pin him against the wall. Gold changed to a pebble and flew so that he was next to me, then reformed in his battle shape.

Simone joined us to face the demon as it turned to attack again. It lowered its head to bite at us, and she ducked under its chin, raised the sword, filled it with shen and swiped its head off, leaving a blank silvery neck. The head liquefied as it hit the ground, turning into something that resembled mercury before it dissipated. The legs collapsed and the body hit the ground.

'That thing was like the goddamn Terminator,' Leo said.

'In more ways than one,' Gold said as the demon rose again and a bulge appeared in the smooth neck. It grew a new head and lifted itself back onto its legs.

It raised its legs again, and this time grabbed Simone, holding her with one leg each side of her. She took both legs off with her sword and it dropped her. She fell hard on the concrete.

Rage filled me.

'She's had enough to deal with today — leave her alone!' I shouted at the demon, and rushed it. Suddenly I was three times bigger, three times meaner, and *mad as hell*.

'Emma, what ...' Gold began, but I barely heard him. All I knew was this thing was going to *die*.

'... if she doesn't come around soon, I'll take her in the back of the Mercedes, and Monica and Marcus can take a taxi,' Gold was saying.

'I'm here,' I said. I felt something soft and warm behind me; my head was in Leo's lap, and he was sitting on the floor of the car park next to the Mercedes. I pulled myself slightly more upright, leaning on him for support. 'I blacked out again? I thought I'd stopped doing that!'

'Can you stand, Emma? We have to be on the Celestial in two hours,' Gold said.

'They'll cut us some slack ...' I began, then stopped. 'Okay, they won't.'

Leo, still sitting behind me, put his hand on my shoulder. 'You okay? Not dizzy?'

I rose. 'I'm not dizzy at all. I feel just fine. That was really strange; why did I black out?'

Leo tried to get up as well, failed, and then gave up. 'Lost it. Someone get my chair for me?'

'You turned into something ... else,' Simone said as Gold brought Leo's chair and helped him into it. 'It was ... big.'

'I wasn't a snake?'

'Yeah, you were a snake,' Leo said. 'Who's going with you, Gold?'

'I'll take Monica,' Gold said. 'You can take the rest.'

Leo nodded, and opened the driver's door of the Mercedes to get in. Gold helped him, then folded the wheelchair and put it into the boot.

'You were a snake, but you were *huge*,' Simone said. 'Like a freaking big Shen or something. It was you, but like ... not you. Really strange.'

'Did I talk?' I said.

'Yeah, mostly just saying how much you wanted the demon to die,' Simone said. 'You sounded like you were having fun.'

She got into the front of the car, and I went around to get in the back next to Marcus. 'So who killed it?' I said. 'It is dead, isn't it?'

'You took it apart and ate it, and had a lot of fun doing it,' Leo said. 'Never seen anything quite so disturbing in my entire life.'

'What I'd like to know,' Simone said, 'is why that demon went for Gold.'

'It went for me at first,' I said, then stopped. 'I was still disguised as Gold.'

'Exactly, and when you changed to a snake it went straight for the real Gold,' Simone said. She turned in her seat to look into the back of the car. 'Is your stone awake, Emma? Jade Building Block, are you awake?'

'No, go away,' the stone said, sounding like a cranky old Englishman.

'Geez, everybody hates me today,' Simone said, and turned back around. 'Got any tissues, Emma?'

I reached into my bag and passed her a pack of tissues. She took them with a nod.

'I'm sorry, little one, you've had a terrible day,' the stone said, more understanding. 'What did you want to know?'

'Whether you took a recording of that demon,' Simone said, her voice thick with tears.

'No, I didn't,' the stone said. 'I should have. Gold didn't either, he was busy defending himself.'

'It's just that ...' Simone said, and her voice trailed off. She took a few gasping breaths. 'It's just ... it's just ...'

'What, Simone?' I said.

'You looked like *Daddy*,' Simone said, and collapsed into sobs.

'What?'

'She has a point, Emma, your serpent form there did look a lot like the Dark Lord's Serpent,' the stone said.

'No.'

Oh no, damn girl, don't be his Serpent now when Simone needs you, Leo said.

It was well past dinnertime when we arrived at the Wan Chai gateway to the Celestial. Monica had tried to coax Simone to eat something, but, like the rest of us, she hadn't been interested. Marcus parked the car and came with us to the podium level, where he sat next to the fountain to wait for us. We approached the wall and it changed, but the dragons didn't gather at the middle in the way they usually did. They remained in their places without speaking.

Michael appeared next to us as the wall separated. He went to Simone and took her hand. 'You all right, squirt?'

'I swear I'm going to yin you if ...' Simone started, then shrugged. 'Just don't freaking call me squirt, okay?'

He released her hand and nodded, then turned to face the wall. 'I got your back, Princess.'

'Thanks, Michael,' she said, her voice small. 'What do you think they'll do to me? You spend more time around them than I do.'

'Not any more.' He walked around her to the wall.

'Michael, stop and tell me,' Simone said.

Gold went to stand next to Simone. 'We'll plead manslaughter, that you had no intention of killing him.

163

Normally the sentence for killing a human is execution, but since you're not Immortal and it was in self-defence, they won't do that.'

Simone studied Gold's face carefully. 'Are you sure about that? And if it's not execution — then what? Prison? This is way worse than what you did.'

'I honestly don't know, Simone,' he said. 'Just remember — it was in self-defence. They will have to be lenient because of that.'

'It wasn't really self-defence — my life wasn't at risk at all, he had no chance of hurting me,' Simone said. She began to tremble. 'I had no reason to yin him — it was total overkill.' She laughed, and there was a brittle edge to it. 'Complete overkill, because I killed him, and nearly killed everybody else. One day I'm going to lose control of it and destroy the whole freaking world.'

I changed to snake and went to her, butting her with my head. She grabbed me and held me so tight she nearly strangled me.

'It'll be all right, Simone, believe me,' I said.

'Thanks, Emma.' She took a deep breath and walked up to the wall, and Michael fell into step behind her. 'Here we go.'

I slithered up the stairs after them, and Leo concentrated and floated his wheelchair over them and up.

The cherry blossoms still flowered at the Celestial Palace, but it was dark and the cool breeze was brisk. The stars blazed brilliantly in the clear sky. As we approached the ten-metre high palace gates, they swung open outwards.

We entered. An official that I'd never seen before was waiting for us just inside the gates, and saluted us. 'Princess Xuan. Your matter has been scheduled to be heard in Courtroom Four. Please follow me.' He turned, said, 'Courtroom Four,' loudly, then disappeared.

We all repeated the words and followed him.

Courtroom Four was a building located at the back of the Celestial Palace complex, with a small garden around it and a bridge over a tiny pond. The building was about four metres to a side, dwarfed by the four-metre-high external wall of the palace, which stood a couple of metres from it. The official bowed slightly and gestured for us to enter.

This is highly unusual, Gold said. *I've never seen this building before, and it's very informal for a serious hearing like this. The number four is ominous.*

I nodded my understanding and went in.

Inside, it looked more like a Chinese living room than a courtroom. Rosewood sofas with thick silk cushions were set in a circle around a large, heavy, Ming-style coffee table. The walls were decorated with calligraphy scrolls — there must have been more than ten of them — all in the Jade Emperor's own hand. There were a couple of delicately brushed ink paintings of Taoist mountains, which also had the Jade Emperor's seal on the bottom. Tall plant stands under the scrolls held large vases of spectacular chrysanthemums; each blossom had to be nearly thirty centimetres across.

The Jade Emperor himself, in a simple yellow robe, was filling a kettle with water from a large jug. He sat the kettle on a small gas burner and waved for us to enter.

'Come in, come in, sit down,' he said. 'No formality, this is just to talk.'

Kowtow anyway, Gold said, and the humans quickly fell to one knee and saluted. I bobbed my serpent head and Leo saluted from his chair.

The Jade Emperor waved one hand at us. 'Up, up, let's talk about this.' He turned and flicked his robe, then sat on the sofa closest to the tea set. 'Please, sit.'

We all took seats on the sofas around the coffee table. I curled up on the silk cushions and Simone sat next to me, one hand resting on my coils.

A stone Shen in human form appeared sitting at a table to one side, and the Jade Emperor waved one hand at him without looking at him. 'Good, he's here. Now, Simone, tell me in your own words what happened.'

'Um,' Simone said, then took a deep breath. 'I had a boat party. The girls brought boys along, even though I told them not to. The boys were already there so I let it go. They brought beer, and I was really annoyed at them. One of them tried to get me drunk, he kept putting beer in my Coke, and when I wouldn't drink it he got one of the girls to put something, like a drug or something, in my Coke. I was really sleepy so I went to the front cabin, and he followed me in, and tried ...' She took another deep breath. 'He tried to rape me. I got really mad at him and yinned him, and took half the boat with him, and it sank.'

'You killed him?' the Jade Emperor said.

Simone nodded, then jumped as Gold corrected her. 'Yes, Majesty.'

'Very well. Your words are validated by the records; we already knew what happened, but it's good to hear a succinct and truthful account. Now.' He leaned back. 'What to do with you?'

Simone cringed.

'What I think we should do ...' the Jade Emperor began, and the kettle whistled loudly. He leaned forward and took it off the heat.

The tea set in front of him was set for Chiu Chow tea; the teapot was black with tannin and only five centimetres across. Each cup was a shallow bowl of two centimetres across. The pot and cups were held on a large tray that had slots to allow the water through into another tray underneath. The Jade Emperor pulled the lid off a cylindrical pewter tea canister and filled the tiny teapot to the brim with the tikuanyin tea, packing it in tightly. He filled the teapot with hot water, put the lid back on, and poured the tea into the cups.

'What we'll do is this,' he said, rinsing the teacups with tea and tipping the liquid out into the tray. He filled the teapot again and quickly poured the extremely strong tea into the tiny cups. He gestured for us to help ourselves, taking one of the teacups himself and sipping its contents with obvious enjoyment.

'Majesty,' Gold said, lifting a teacup and toasting the Jade Emperor with it. 'Please understand that this was not premeditated, and Simone was acting in self-defence. She could honestly have thought her life was at stake and was defending herself. Therefore the Celestial has every reason to be merciful in its judging of this matter.'

'Oh, come on, we both know she was in no danger. But you did the right thing, Simone,' the Jade Emperor said. 'Normally in this sort of situation you should bring him up here for us to deal with, though. We'd try him and execute him for this attempt on you.'

'But he couldn't hurt me! He was no danger to me! There was no reason to execute him,' Simone protested.

'He was a danger to your *honour*, madam,' the Jade Emperor said. 'That is worth as much as your life. You were right to summarily try and execute him for the crime of attempting to dishonour you.'

Simone stared at him, speechless.

'According to the Laws, he should have been brought up here for trial, but as Celestial Princess you are perfectly qualified to judge such a case yourself and hand down a summary sentence,' the Jade Emperor said. 'I'll have it entered into the records as such. An attempt was made on your honour, you defended yourself, convicted and executed the felon. As it should have been. Your first case heard as Princess of the Northern Heavens, and handled with aplomb. A Celestial commendation will be entered on your record, and your dominion will receive commensurate compensation.'

'That's not right. I *killed* him, that was *wrong*,' Simone said. 'My honour? That's just plain medieval!'

'Wait a moment,' the Jade Emperor said. He waved one hand at the stone Shen and he disappeared.

The Jade Emperor took the kettle off the gas and filled the tiny teapot again, then filled the cups. 'All right, now we're off the record.'

'I wasn't expecting to be *commended* for killing this guy,' Simone said.

'Of course not. But rules are rules, and you're a ruler, and have the power of life and death, as we all do. Technically, that case should have been heard by the Blue Dragon, as Hong Kong sits on the edge of his dominion, but he's staying extremely low and quiet during this whole thing.'

'So that's all?' Simone said. 'I get a commendation and sent home with a pat on the back, saying that I did the right thing in killing this guy? No punishment or anything?'

'No. The one person who should be severely punished here is the Blue Dragon.'

'Qing Long didn't have anything to do with it!'

'Qing Long is supposed to be teaching you how to control your yin, Simone. As the Lesser Yin, he can give you quite a few handy tips on ensuring that this never happens again. I don't like the idea of you destroying the world in a fit of pique, young lady, and I'm going to order him to give you some tuition, and I'm ordering you to take it.'

'But he's such an —' She bit off the rest of it.

'Asshole,' the Jade Emperor said.

Simone giggled, then bent over her knees and let go. The Jade Emperor joined her and they laughed together.

She stopped laughing and heaved a huge sigh. 'Why do I feel so much better now?'

'Because I want you to,' the Jade Emperor said. He gestured towards the tea. 'Drink, drink, it's good Iron Buddha.'

'Normally I don't like this really strong Kung Fu tea, but this is different,' Simone said. 'It's kind of fresh.'

'Really good tikuanyin has a very slight edge of orange blossom in the strong fermented flavour,' the Jade Emperor said. 'And, of course, this is the finest you can find.'

I leaned my head towards the table, studying the teacup, calculating whether I could try the tea without knocking the whole thing over. Simone reached over, picked up the teacup and held it in front of my nose. My snout was too large to sip from the cup, so I just lapped at it with my tongue. The Jade Emperor was right.

'Qing Long will be in touch with you in a week or so to arrange some yin tuition,' the Jade Emperor said.

169

'While you're here, anything else that needs discussing?'

We all shared a look and shook our heads.

'Well then, that's sorted.' The Jade Emperor rose, and we did too. I slid off the cushions onto the floor. 'I must come and see what you're up to at Wudang Mountain, Emma. I heard some very interesting things are happening over there.'

'You are more than welcome, Majesty,' I said, bobbing my serpent head. 'But please, give us some notice before you come so we can organise a suitable reception.'

'No need for that,' he said, waving me down. 'Oh! I have heard complaints that you are corrupting the Hong Kong Nine Dragon Wall. With Japanese candy, I believe? Now they are demanding this from all Celestials who pass.'

'They were completely corrupt already,' I said.

'You have a point.' He led us to the door. 'It's good to see all of you, particularly you, Lion.' He patted Leo on the shoulder. 'You must spend more time up here and learn the way of the Celestial. There is so much more that you could do if you put your mind to it. Oh!' He turned to Simone. 'I nearly forgot! Simone, you are hereby ordered to attend the Celestial Upper School for Shen of the Third Platform. That's an *order*, dear. Stop messing around and go learn something useful. Face the fact that you are what you are.'

I braced myself for the explosion, but Simone just sagged slightly. 'Yeah, okay. I suppose this has been coming for a while and I've just been putting it off.'

'Good.' The Jade Emperor looked around at us, jolly. 'Er Lang keeps complaining about all of you, but I think you're doing a splendid job.' He disappeared.

CHAPTER 13

Simone's friend Eva was waiting for Simone as we exited the meeting room, along with Sylvie the snake Shen and her dragon girlfriend, Precious. All three of them rushed to hold Simone's hands and shoulders.

'What's the damage?' Sylvie said, trying to sound unconcerned and failing.

'I'm to be commended for protecting my honour,' Simone said miserably.

The girls shared a look, then Precious said, 'I keep forgetting that the Jade Emperor is so goddamn old.'

Simone's mobile rang and she pulled it out of the pocket of her jeans.

'How does that still work — it's been in the water for hours,' Eva said.

'It's a Celestial phone, works on both Planes. A variation on the network I built that rides Celestial Harmony,' Gold said.

'Sounds fascinating,' Sylvie said. 'You must show me one day, Lord Gold.'

'My pleasure,' Gold said.

Simone listened to the call for a while, then dropped the phone and bent double, sobbing. Her friends crowded round her again and held her as she cried.

'That ...' Simone took a deep, gasping breath, struggling to get the words out. 'That was Pinky ... Bevan's girlfriend. She just told me that she hates me forever ... and she's going to get someone to chop me. She cursed me and said she hopes I die because I'm a murderer.'

'Just ignore her, Simone. She tried to drug you so he could rape you,' I said.

'She's *right*,' Simone wailed.

'Simone ...' Eva bent to look into Simone's eyes. 'Simone, you need to get away. That's why I'm here. Mom wants to lend you one of our nicest places — a villa in Phuket. All yours for a week. Go out to the Phi Phis, relax, sit by the pool, all on us.' She patted Simone's shoulder. 'You can have it as long as you want it. Okay?'

Simone gasped without speaking and nodded.

'Sound good?'

Simone nodded again.

'Good. You can fly straight there, I can give you the details.'

'I'll fly commercial with Emma. We can go together,' Simone said.

'What about the private jet?' Leo said.

'We sold it,' I said. 'We don't need it. It was just to keep John safe while he was weak, and it cost a fortune to keep running. Simone can carry herself and me short distances, and we fly commercial for long distances like London.'

'Makes sense,' Leo said.

'No handbag, no tissues,' I said to Simone.

172

She nodded, straightened and wiped her eyes. 'Tell your mother thanks, Eva. Do you guys want to come along too? It's a whole villa.'

Sylvie and Precious shared a meaningful look.

'No way are you two using this as an excuse for a tryst,' I said. 'Different bedrooms and no funny business, just a straight-up girls' fun holiday.'

'So I'm not invited?' Leo said, pretending to be hurt.

'Of course, you're one of the girls,' I said.

He grinned. 'Good.'

'Nah, you guys go have some quiet time,' Precious said. 'We have school and shit. We'll meet up with you when you start at CH, Simone.'

Simone nodded, her voice still thick from crying. 'Okay.'

We could fly directly to Phuket from Hong Kong as it was such a major Hong Kong tourist destination. The airport was large, clean and modern, and even catered for Leo's wheelchair with ramps throughout. A demon met us at the exit from Customs, and the Phoenix herself was waiting outside the terminal, next to a large bright red Mercedes van driven by a smiling demon appearing as a local man. The Phoenix was wearing a traditional Thai outfit of red silk shot through with orange and yellow highlights that appeared and disappeared as she moved. Her skirt was pencil-slim and reached to her feet, with a decorative gold border at the bottom. Her blouse had short sleeves and a round neck, with a similar decorative border along its bottom and a sash of matching red and gold silk over one shoulder.

She pressed her palms together and greeted us with a slight bow. 'Sawatdee. Welcome to the gracious south, where the holy light of Buddhism was born, and the people are more gentle and civilised.'

'Have you ever said that in front of the other three Winds?' Simone said, amused.

'All the time,' the Phoenix said. She gestured towards the van. 'The villas are at Bangtao Beach.'

It was a twenty-minute drive to the resort. We passed plantations of trees, all of them with large sloping scars on their trunks and cups at the base.

'Oh, rubber trees,' Simone said with interest. 'Never seen them before.'

'It is a minor source of income for the island, after tourism,' the Phoenix said. 'Here we are.'

The lobby was a series of pavilions with pyramid-shaped roofs spread around a large resort-style pool. The staff bowed their heads low, raising their hands to touch their faces. The Phoenix went to the desk and picked up our keys, then took us out to where the demons had loaded our luggage onto a golf buggy.

The villas were all constructed around a central lagoon. 'So much water!' Simone said as we were driven to our accommodation. 'The main area has that big pool, and you have this lagoon ...' She stopped and realised. 'Oh.'

'Wait until you see your villa,' the Phoenix said.

It had the traditional high-pitched Thai roof with flame-shaped decorations at the bottom of the arches, and a small sign outside: 'Madam Emma Donohoe, Lord Leo Alexander and Princess Simone Chen'.

The entry hall opened into a large, high-ceilinged room lined with polished timber; the interior walls were smooth and white with dark wood surrounding frames. All of the soft furnishings were a rich dark red silk, and an ornamental table held an arrangement of bird-of-paradise flowers that was nearly two metres tall. The floor-to-ceiling windows were open and looked out onto the villa's private pool, which had a glass-walled spa set into it. Its infinity-style edge meant that the far end appeared to merge with the lagoon. There were a couple of timber sun lounges set next to the pool.

Simone took a running leap and dived straight over the spa into the pool. She travelled underwater to the far end, kicked off without surfacing and swam underwater back to us. She surfaced, floated out of the pool, dried her clothes and landed lightly on the polished timber floor. She took a deep breath. 'Okay, where are our bedrooms?'

The Phoenix gestured down a corridor. 'Your bedroom is this way, miss.'

Simone gasped when she saw the room. It had its own pavilion, with a king-sized bed covered in plush cushions, floor-to-ceiling glass on three sides, and high courtyard walls two metres from the glass to give the room privacy. The entire area was surrounded by a blue wading pool, the water only half a metre deep; a pair of plastic chairs sat in the pool on either side of a table holding a decorative flower arrangement. Simone appeared to be contemplating diving into this water as well, then changed her mind. She turned back to the Phoenix. 'Is this because your family stays here?'

The Phoenix nodded. 'They can't set fire to the neighbourhood when they're surrounded by water like this.'

'Good idea, I suppose,' Simone said.

The bathroom was larger than the bedroom, with a door leading to a spa-sized outside bath.

A kind-faced man in the all-white of house staff appeared and clasped his hands in the Thai greeting.

'This is Kwan,' the Phoenix said. 'He is your personal staff here. He will cook your breakfast to your liking. If you want a massage, just tell him.' She gestured towards Kwan and he gave Simone a mobile phone. 'Press redial and he'll be here for you. There are a couple of bikes out the front for transport, and the beach is about five minutes down that way,' she said, pointing. 'The resort has several restaurants, and it's part of a multi-resort complex as well. If you like, Kwan will take you in the boat across the lagoon to eat at the other hotels in the complex. If you want to go shopping or anything, Patong Beach is about twenty minutes away.' She spread her arms and the red silk of her outfit shimmered. 'Enjoy.'

Simone threw herself into the Phoenix's arms and hugged her. 'Thanks, Auntie Zhu.' She pulled back and greeted the Phoenix the Thai way. 'And sawatdee.'

'Take some time to settle in,' the Phoenix said. She turned to me. 'Emma, a quick word before I leave you to it?'

I followed her back to the villa's main area. 'Just a word of caution,' she said. 'This is a tourist place in one of the world's poorer nations. We do have some difficulty with maintenance of the resort as trained and capable technicians are hard to find. There is crime here, also some underworld activity. I do not interfere — it is not my place as a Celestial unless demons are involved — but be aware that there is a criminal element and they will try to rip you off if you go into town.'

She saw my face and smiled. 'It's not that bad. You and Simone can go into Patong and have a wonderful time and not realise any of it exists. It is a pain in the neck for me, however. Just avoid the bars — not that I think I need to tell you this — and be aware of pickpockets, thieves and rip-off artists who will see you as wealthy tourists and try to take advantage of you. Take Kwan with you; he is a senior member of my demon staff and well-known around town.'

'Thanks, Phoenix,' I said. 'Um ... you've shown us Simone's bedroom; what about Leo and me?'

'One of you will have to sleep on the daybed in the living room, it converts into a third bedroom. The other can take the second floating bedroom, identical to Simone's, on the other side of the villa.'

'By precedence rules, the Immortal Lord Leo should take the other bedroom,' I said.

'Yes, and good luck trying to make him,' the Phoenix said. She nodded to Kwan. 'Make it so.'

Kwan nodded and headed towards the living room area.

She raised her voice and called to Simone. 'I'm coming back tomorrow and you and I are going to spar, young lady. I want to see how you've progressed.'

'We're going to the spa? Can I have a manicure and pedicure?' Simone called back.

'No, spar! With weapons!'

Simone poked her head around the wall. 'I know, I heard you,' she said cheekily. 'But afterwards book me into the spa, I want *everything*.'

'You are spoilt,' I said.

She threw her arms up in the air and jumped. 'I know, and I love it!' She ran back into her bedroom.

'There are DVDs, books and games in the central atrium,' the Phoenix said. 'Kwan will take good care of you; he's probably lighting the incense and essential oils right now.' She shrugged. 'I'll see you tomorrow.'

I sighed and looked around. 'I think this is exactly what Simone needs — some time away from everything, with a large amount of water around her.' I took the Phoenix's hand. 'Thanks, Zhu Que.'

She nodded. 'You are most welcome.' She disappeared.

The next morning I found Simone asleep in the bottom of her wading pool still in her pyjamas. Kwan came and made breakfast for us, leaving Simone's under a serving cover. She slept until lunchtime, shaded from the sun by the courtyard walls.

Leo spent most of the morning doing physical therapy in the pool, trying to make his legs work without using his Celestial skills. In the end he gave up, pulled himself into the spa, turned it on and dozed in the warm bubbles.

Michael had stored the records we'd accessed in the Archives on five or six DVDs and I spent the morning running through them on my laptop, looking for something about my nature. The Archivist had also given me a login and password for the Archive reserves, and I occasionally followed a lead into the main library only to reach a dead end. There was absolutely nothing about the first European settlers in Australia. On Australia itself there was minimal information. There were a few minor mentions of Rainbow Serpents as holding similar characteristics to dragons with their weather and water skills, and some vague references to spirits that existed in the south. I'd learnt more about traditional Australian mythology in primary school. The Asian Shen seemed completely uninterested in the activities of Shen in the other Corners of the World, and it was disturbing to think about the demons making hybrids from the different Centres without the Shen doing much to stop them.

I cross-indexed the town that I had recurring dreams about: it sat on top of a hill, had traditional European-style, thatch-roofed cottages surrounded by low stone walls, hedges and flowering gardens; the other hills around it were steep and the valleys below it were invisible. The landscape reminded me of Wudang Mountain, but the curves were much softer and there was more grass and not as much rock. The cross-index search gave me the same information I'd found on the internet: Wales, Ireland, Spain, Italy. I needed to make another trip to Europe, and this time not indulge Simone by spending the whole time shopping in London, Paris and Milan.

I hadn't mentioned to the Archivist my dream where I was climbing the hill as a snake, the knowledge that there was fresh blood at the top driving me on with a raw hunger. It sounded too much like a Druidic sacrifice ritual, which was very disturbing. Druids had been nature-loving tree-huggers, yes; but they'd also disembowelled people and used their own intestines to tie them, still alive, as sacrifices to the trees they worshipped.

I looked up the Serpent Concubine and watched with horror as the information came up. Well, thank you very much, Miss Concubine. Here I was, trying my best to give Celestial snakes a better reputation, and she'd done the exact opposite. She had been a harsh and merciless mistress, jealous of the Dark Lord and paranoid to the point of schizophrenia. She had beaten her maids, had many of the household demons executed for minor misdemeanours, and the final straw was when she'd *eaten* a couple of human staff who had gone to her to beg for more rest time as they were working seven days a week.

The Dark Lord hadn't been aware of all this as he'd spent most of his time on Wudangshan and trying to deal with the falling Qing dynasty and the Boxer Rebellion — they'd worshipped *him* and he'd been desperately trying to sever his connection with it — and she had been left to sink deeper into loneliness, paranoia and insanity. He'd returned from Wudangshan after the Northern Council had intervened and had her incarcerated for the crime of eating the humans, and he had removed her head himself. After her execution he had her pavilion locked up and his visits to the Northern Heavens became more sporadic; he really only went there when there were serious cases to hear or the energy was low.

The case of the Serpent Concubine was cross-indexed with several similar cases of jealous, power-hungry or just plain insane consorts and concubines on the Celestial Plane. The Phoenix had changed to female after a similar situation had occurred to her male form: two of her wives had fought a duel and killed each other while one of them was pregnant. The Tiger had executed more than twenty of his own wives over the years for jealous palace intrigue. The Dragon hadn't reported any cases to the Celestial administration, despite records of his concubines being executed for 'crimes against Heaven'. I sat looking at the screen, trying to decide whether the fact that many of the other mad concubines had been raised human made the Serpent Concubine any less responsible for her crimes. I decided that it didn't. Damn, I had a lot of PR work ahead of me.

Simone came out of her bathroom, towelling her hair. 'Is there any food? I'm starving.'

I gestured towards the trolley. 'Kwan made you a full English breakfast complete with three different types of muffin, tropical fruit, and scrambled eggs just the way you like them. The whole thing is probably a gluggy mess by now.'

She lifted the cover and wrinkled her nose. 'You're right.' She grabbed a muffin and threw herself onto the couch while she munched on it. 'Leo's asleep in the spa.' She looked over to see what I was doing and I quickly switched back to the European data. 'Working again, Emma? Give it up.'

She went to find the tea-making facilities, shuffling through the different types of tea and putting the kettle on. 'So what are we doing this morning?'

'It's already past midday,' I said. 'We can have some lunch if you like, then the Phoenix said she wanted to see you.'

'What were you going to eat if I was still asleep?' she said.

'I was about to call Kwan and see what we could get delivered.'

'Well, that's not good enough,' Simone said. She leaned towards the outer doors so that Leo could hear her. 'What I really want is a big thick hamburger with lashings of melted cheese and bacon. I wonder if the café makes them.'

Leo turned to look at us and grinned. 'They sure do, and I was just thinking the same thing.'

'Let's go!' Simone said, dropping the teabags.

Leo changed into a black lion and pulled himself out of the spa, treading carefully across the stepping stones back to the villa. He stopped and shook himself, the water cascading everywhere. 'Let me have a quick shower and find some shoes.'

'No taking all day!' Simone said, wagging her finger at him with mock severity.

'That's good coming from you, Miss Sleep-All-Day,' he said.

She tossed back her damp, honey-coloured hair. 'I'm a teenager. I'm allowed.'

He grinned his lion grin. 'I suppose you are.' He walked into the main bathroom and closed the door behind him with his nose.

'Find anything?' Simone said, sitting next to me to finish the muffin.

'Nothing at all. I need to make another trip to Europe,' I said.

Simone jiggled with glee. 'Yay, shopping!'

'Not for shopping.'

'There's always time for shopping.'

The villa phone rang and I answered it. It was the Phoenix. 'Emma, Kwan tells me that Sleeping Beauty is awake. Have you eaten?'

'Not yet,' I said. 'We're going on a hamburger hunt as soon as Leo is in a form that won't scare the other tourists.'

'Emma,' Simone said patiently, 'in human form he's six five, black and ugly as the devil. I really think his lion form is *less* scary.'

'She has a point,' Leo said, coming out of the bathroom in his wheelchair, wearing a designer polo shirt, trim pleated slacks and expensive loafers.

'Well, after you guys have hunted down and

devoured the poor innocent hamburgers, could you meet me at the front of the resort?' the Phoenix said. 'I was serious about sparring with Simone.'

'Will do,' I said, and hung up. 'You heard, Simone?'

Simone grimaced. 'I know what she's going to say.'

'That you're the only human daughter of the God of Martial Arts and the most talented practitioner on any Plane?' Leo said.

'More like I need to go to Celestial High and learn properly,' Simone said, resigned. 'The Masters and the Tiger are always telling me how bad I am.'

'Well, it doesn't matter now because you're going to CH anyway,' I said. I rose. 'Open season on hamburgers. Let's get us a bag of 'em, pardners.'

'Oh wow, you are so lame sometimes, Emma, it hurts.'

I bowed slightly to her. 'I thank you, madam.'

'More like mortal wounds,' Leo said, and wheeled himself to the door. 'Let's go, I'm starving. Sitting in that spa all morning was damn hard work.'

We ate in the hotel's café overlooking the main resort pool. Service was immaculate, right down to the tedious water-glass-and-napkin ceremony. The hamburgers were enormous and exactly the way Simone and Leo liked them, smothered in melted cheese and aioli and served with thick-cut French fries. I had a vegetarian omelette; I needed to watch my weight while I wasn't working out as heavily as I did back home. If I wasn't careful I could balloon out in only a week of slacking.

Leo and I shared a plunger of coffee, and Simone had a huge iced lemon tea.

'I don't know how you can drink something hot,' she said. 'It's so warm and humid here, it's like the middle of summer back home.'

'You get used to drinking hot drinks in hot weather,' I said.

'Especially when you need your caffeine hit,' Leo added.

After we'd let the food settle, the Phoenix met us at the front of the resort in a golf buggy, wearing a pair of red shorts and a yellow polo shirt. She took us around the lagoon and past the resort's private beach. The two-hundred-metre strip of pristine white sand had teak deckchairs with umbrellas and side tables laid out in rows, the clear water of the Andaman Sea glittering in front of them.

'No waves, clear water, I'm going in later,' Simone said with enthusiasm. 'What are the currents like around here?'

'I have no idea,' the Phoenix said. 'I don't like the water, I don't go in.'

'You don't swim at all?' Simone said, curious.

'Not if I can help it,' she said.

'You're not a bird, you're a cat,' Simone said.

'The cat loves his water. I just ... It doesn't do anything for me,' the Phoenix said. 'On the other hand, take me back home to my volcano in Bali, let me swim in the lava and I'm a happy chicken.'

Simone stifled a laugh. 'Roast chicken.'

The Phoenix laughed as well. 'I suppose so.'

After the beach we came to what was obviously the maintenance area of the resort. The buildings were ugly and utilitarian, with ride-on mowers, workbenches and racks of tools under open-sided workshops with plain colourbond roofs. We stopped outside a large barn-type building, about fifty metres long and twenty wide and two storeys high. It had no windows, just a large roller door at the front, which was open.

Inside, the bare interior walls were swathed in silver insulation sheeting and the floor was plain concrete. Large ceiling fans turned above us, not so much cooling as moving the hot, humid air around. I wondered what the building was for, then saw the weapons racks at the far end and the burn marks all over the walls and floor. The insulation sheeting was dull and greenish-grey for the first four metres up from the floor, then the other two metres to the ceiling were as shiny as new.

'I see the burn marks, but did someone flood this building as well?' I said.

'Oh, the staining — that's from the tsunami,' the Phoenix said.

Simone stopped and stared at the walls. 'Oh my ... Oh.' She rested her hand against the wall. 'So much water, so many fragile people ...'

The Phoenix put her arm around Simone's shoulder. 'Nothing you could do about it, Simone. Do not for a minute blame yourself for this. Things like this happen anyway, that is the way nature is, and he *is* nature when it comes to things like this. So put it aside for now and spar with me.' She squeezed Simone. 'You are not responsible.'

Is she saying what I think she's saying? Leo said into my head.

I nodded.

Maybe it wasn't such a good idea bringing Simone here then. If we go into town, there'll still be reminders of the people that died.

I tapped the stone.

What? I was sleeping! it said.

Tell Leo: I think John would want Simone to see what she's capable of when she uses her water power, and how important the training is to help her to control it.

How many people did he kill with this thing? Leo said.

I don't know.

Over 200,000, the stone said.

'Choose a weapon,' the Phoenix said, indicating the racks at the end of the building. 'Or call your own.'

Simone held her hand out and Dark Heavens appeared in it.

'Ah, the Xuan Tian itself, the Dark Lord's most simple and elegant weapon,' the Phoenix said. 'No elaboration, minimal enhancements, a perfectly forged demon killer, the essence of simplicity and deadliness.' She nodded once. 'I am honoured that you choose to wield it here.'

She went to the weapons racks and selected two Malaysian-style kris. The daggers' blades were fifteen centimetres long, and the handles and scabbards were gold and encrusted with precious stones. The blades were curved and obviously very sharp. The Phoenix moved to stand in front of Simone, a dagger in each hand.

Simone and the Phoenix saluted each other with their weapons, then moved into readiness stances. The Phoenix attacked first, moving with impressive speed and agility, pushing Simone back as she blocked the daggers with the sword.

Simone concentrated as she parried the blows, then turned on the Phoenix and attacked. She moved through a series that I recognised from one of the high-level Wudang sword katas and the Phoenix had no difficulty dealing with the blows. I shook my head. Moving through a kata wasn't very clever, particularly when her opponent knew it already and easily blocked each move.

The Phoenix spun, blocked the sword down with one dagger and pressed the other to Simone's throat. Simone quickly raised her hands and conceded defeat and they moved back again.

After the Phoenix had comprehensively bested Simone four times, she stopped and nodded. 'What if I were to pull out a couple of level-seventy demons, Simone? Would you be able to handle them?'

Simone hesitated, then shrugged. 'If I'm facing something really big, I don't bother fighting them with the weapon, I just use a shen or chi blast of energy through the ground or the air, and if it gets really tough, I yin them.'

The Phoenix shook her head. 'You really need more training, little one. I won't even waste a high-level demon from my jar on that.' She turned to me. 'You wouldn't consider replacing some of my stock, would you?'

I raised my hands. 'I can't, Phoenix, I don't know for sure how big they are before they put me at risk. I can do up to about level twenty no problem, but bigger than that and it starts to bother me. I'll learn more about it when the Dark Lord comes back; after all, he's the only one, as far as I know, who can do it.'

The Phoenix gestured towards Leo. 'Can you free yourself from that contraption long enough to spar with me?'

Leo held the arms of the wheelchair and raised himself on his hands, then collapsed back. 'Not right now. I think I'm too full of hamburger.'

The Phoenix nodded. 'Eating meat will reduce your Celestial abilities.'

'If being comfy in my chair here is the price I have to pay for filling my belly with that excellent hamburger, then I think the price is fair,' Leo said.

The Phoenix shook her head. 'Americans.' She smiled at Simone. 'Would you like to try a different weapon?'

'Can you do polearm?' Simone said.

The Phoenix nodded. 'That I can. But how about you use the polearm and I'll use sword? That way you'll have the advantage.'

They began sparring again, and again it wasn't a fair match, with the Phoenix attacking Simone so effectively and pushing her back so hard that she was soon against the wall of the building.

'Simone, lift that arm! You aren't using both hands effectively to counterbalance each other — it should be effortless, with the pole resting balanced in your hands, rather than you clutching it like a drunken bus rider. This is dreadful!' Xuan Wu the Turtle had appeared in the corner of the room. He looked around at us. 'What's going on?'

'Daddy!' Simone dropped the polearm and raced to him. She fell to her knees and clutched him around his neck.

Leo and I went to him as well, the Phoenix behind us.

John studied Simone with his wrinkled turtle eyes. 'How old are you, Simone? You look nearly grown up. I'm missing far too much here.'

'Sixteen,' Simone said into his neck.

John saw me. 'Emma. You don't look a day older.'

'And you're a lying old turtle,' I said.

'What happened to you? Oh ... I remember. One Two Two filled you with demon essence. Have you spoken to Nu Wa?'

'I need a spacesuit to go visit her, John. You didn't mention that she was in *space*.'

'Not in space ...' He hesitated. 'Well, effectively, yes, she is. A minor obstacle that I'm sure you will easily overcome.' He turned to Leo. 'A wheelchair? I vaguely remember a battle where your back was injured. It was permanent?'

Leo nodded, grinning hugely. 'Yes, sir.'

'Wait,' John said. He took a couple of graceful turtle strides to Leo and studied him, his nose level with Leo's knees. 'Immortal.' He ducked his head with triumph. 'I *knew* it.' He butted Leo's knee. 'Congratulations, Lion. I look forward to returning and giving you some training that you'll never forget.'

Leo didn't look away from John. 'Simone, Emma, could I have a moment with the Dark Lord?'

'I don't know how long I'll be able to keep my intelligence, so it had better be quick,' John said.

'Don't bother then, just hug your ladies,' Leo said. 'It can wait.'

'You can ask him silently, Leo,' I said.

Leo concentrated, and John took a small step back. They focused on each other, obviously discussing, then Leo nodded once sharply, wheeled himself around and parked himself next to the wall. 'Your turn, ladies.'

'Simone, go get that polearm,' John said. 'Emma, find a sword, will you? That was *disgraceful*, Simone.'

I summoned the Murasame and it appeared in my hand.

'I hope you didn't spend any time with the Demon King,' John said grimly. 'He won that sword off me about two hundred years ago, and I don't like the idea of you having it.'

'Particularly since I'm part demon,' I said.

'That will just make it more powerful,' John said. 'Okay, let's see a level three. Slowly! You always did that one too fast.'

I nearly bent double with the pain of hearing him say that; I'd completely forgotten that my inability to do the level-three set slowly enough had been one of the most frustrating things that both of us had dealt with when he'd been teaching me. He had constantly reminded me to slow it down.

'Are you all right, Emma?' he said gently.

'Just a rush of memories. Things I'd forgotten, some of the most enjoyable parts of being with you — having you constantly remind me I was doing the level three too fast.'

'We will have many more of those times together,' he said. He nodded his turtle head. 'Let's see it, and *slowly*.' He turned to Simone. 'Level-three polearm.'

Simone looked from John to me. 'Daddy, those are different sets, and both of them move all over the floor. We'll crash into each other. We'll be spending way too much time avoiding each other to concentrate on the sets.'

'You never noticed,' John said with amusement. 'Simone, stand next to Emma, with her on your right. About a metre and a half apart. Good. Now, when I say the word, both of you start the level-three sets. Ready? Commence.'

We both stepped forward at the same time, sweeping our weapons in front of us. Then I turned right and Simone turned left and each of us moved three steps forward.

'Slowly, Emma,' John said, and I couldn't control the huge grin.

We both turned right and were facing away from him. We each took two steps towards each other and we were as close as when we'd started. After ten more moves, it became obvious to both of us that the sets synchronised. We moved in a graceful pattern, sometimes crossing paths, sometimes at opposite ends of the floor, but always performing matching supplementary moves. As we realised, we synchronised our movements even more, sometimes falling into a dance rather than a martial arts set and being pulled up by John about it. We performed the final two moves of the sets, finished up exactly where we'd started, and saluted John.

His turtle mouth was open in a huge grin. 'The two women I love most in the world in perfect deadly harmony. I cannot tell you what a happy turtle I am today.' His voice became more severe. 'Emma, you have been learning and practising, that is obvious. Simone, it is also obvious that you haven't. I'll bet anything you like that if you encounter something big you just shen it.'

Simone grimaced and shrugged.

'Do you have yin?'

She nodded, still grimacing.

'How good is your yin control?'

She dropped her voice, sounding unsure. 'I don't want to use yin; sometimes it gets out of control. They say I could destroy the world.'

'I'm glad there's still a planet here for me to come back to then,' he said. 'How much has the Dragon taught you?'

'Nothing at all. He's finally been ordered by the Jade Emperor to give me some training,' Simone said.

'Good. And while I am here, I will give you some too. I think that is more important than waving a weapon around.'

She was obviously delighted. 'Thanks, Daddy.'

'Emma, Leo,' John said, 'I would give anything to stay with you right now, but I don't know how much time I have and the fate of the world depends on me teaching Simone as quickly as possible to control her yin. We will go somewhere where there is no chance of her harming anything, and I'm afraid neither of you can come.' He dropped his voice. 'I am so sorry, Emma, but this needs to be done.'

'I understand, love,' I said. 'Go, teach her, and help her to control her greatest power.'

'Come and touch my head, Simone,' he said, and she went to him.

'What if you lose control of your intelligence while you're out there?' I said. 'How will Simone get back?'

'I'll show her. I love you,' he said, and they disappeared.

I turned to Leo. 'What did he say? Did he say yes?'

'He said he doesn't want to do it,' Leo said. 'When I pushed him, he said he'd think about it.'

'We'll get there,' I said.

CHAPTER 14

Leo asked for a lift back to the villa, and said he'd meet us at the beach. I stayed on and sparred with the Phoenix for about an hour, and she gave me some valuable tips on using shorter daggers, her preferred weapon.

'They should be returning soon,' she said when we were done. 'Let's head back to your villa; Simone will meet you there.'

As we took the golf buggy back to the villa, I saw a carving of a fierce-faced, half-human bird on the side of the road. I realised the resort was full of them; I hadn't noticed them until now, they were such a part of the scenery.

'That's Garuda, that's *you*,' I said. 'All of southern Asia — Indonesia, Malaysia, Thailand, India — all of them have you as a major god. In the other Centres, Garuda is only a minor deity, or not worshipped at all.'

'I am the Bird Whose Cries Make the World Tremble in Fear,' she said. 'I have pinions of flame and claws of obsidian.' She smiled. 'I'm also a cute little red sparrow.'

'That I can't visualise,' I said. 'The big Garuda bird — easily.'

She bobbed her head. 'I thank you, ma'am. Here we are. Simone is on her way back; she'll be here in about ten minutes.'

I changed into a swimsuit and waited for them in the pool. My days of wearing tiny bikinis were long gone; now I opted for less revealing but still flattering structured two pieces with longer tops. I wasn't overweight, but my body was beginning to succumb to gravity and all help from structured clothing was much appreciated. Louise was already having work done and had suggested I jump on the plastic-surgery merry-go-round too, but I'd strongly resisted. That kind of thing was for glamour hounds.

They appeared in the pool, Simone sitting on top of John's shell. She fell off into the water, and they dived to the bottom together and approached me. I quickly clambered out of the pool.

Simone surfaced. 'I forgot for a moment there, I was so excited about all of this.'

John joined her. 'What's the problem?'

'If Simone touches me, I take Mother form,' I said.

His turtle face fell. 'That explains it. I wondered why you didn't hug me. I thought ... well.'

'You touched him in Guilin with no problems,' Simone said.

I shook my head, silent. I wasn't sure.

His mouth flopped open into his turtle grin. 'I'm not full strength — okay, I'm not even half strength until I find my Serpent. But don't be concerned, Emma, I have much better control than Simone.' He gestured with his head. 'Come and try.'

I reluctantly returned to the pool, stretched one hand out and swept it over his head. Nothing happened, so I rested my hand on his head. Still nothing happened, so I threw my arms around his neck and buried my face against his smooth, cool scales. 'Welcome home, love.'

He butted me with his head. 'I can't stay forever, not until I'm strong enough to take human form. Even then, I don't know. I think this is the longest I've stayed in control of my faculties.' He raised his head to speak to Simone. 'Let's go to the beach, I want to show you something.'

An afternoon breeze had picked up on the shoreline, making the canvas beach umbrellas flap. A few tourists lay on the deckchairs, half asleep, a couple of them receiving massages from roving Thai masseuses. A sarong vendor approached us, the colourful batik fabric strung over her arms; Simone looked through her wares then shook her head.

'I take it they can't see you,' I said to John.

'Nope,' he said. He stopped and ground his feet so his shell rotated in the sand. 'Hot sand feels *so good!*'

Simone shaded her eyes and looked up and down the beach.

'Don't do that, only monkeys do that,' John scolded.

'That's a silly Chinese superstition,' Simone said. 'I can't see Leo, where is he?'

John concentrated and gestured with his head. 'Over to the right, at the end near the rocks. Oh! He's been attacked.'

At the end of the beach a rocky promontory, covered with thick tropical jungle and swarming with insects, jutted out into the water. Leo was on the sand next to the rocks; he had taken black lion form and was facing a humanoid demon that was also black and carrying a large sword.

I rushed to help him but John stopped me. 'Let him fight it.'

'But what if it hurts him?' I said.

'He's *Immortal*, Emma,' John said. 'Good practice for him. Just walk slowly over, he can handle this.'

'This is his first solo battle as an Immortal,' Simone said. She spoke softly so that he couldn't hear her. 'Go, Leo!'

'Can he get out of the wheelchair in human form?' John said. 'If he can't, then he'll need a weapon he can use in human form in the chair. Something like twin daggers, or wakizashi, or something similar ...' He trailed off, musing.

'He can stand and walk just fine when he's under pressure,' I said.

'A sword then,' John said. 'A two-handed claymore type? Or a lighter Western-style blade? An African spear? The Mountain forge knows nothing about them, but they could learn ... No, he's American, not African. The Western-style, I think, and it would have to be black, a good solid guard on it ...' He turned to me and grinned. 'Is the forge up?'

'It is,' I said with dismay. 'I've already ordered a weapon for him; it's nearly done and it's nothing like that. I'll have to get another made.'

'Oh, you're way ahead of me, good,' John said, still strolling towards Leo, who was now clashing with the demon, using claws and teeth to rake it and avoiding its blows. 'What did you order?'

'A long, slender Japanese katana-style, nearly two metres long. The guard is a standard small tsuba with a lion in it, and the end of the handle has a black lion carved into it. At least I have the colour right, it's black.'

John stopped, clumsily turned in the sand and grinned at me. 'That's even more perfect. Why didn't I think of that? The blade will have to be called the Black Lion, that's *ideal* —'

He didn't finish because Simone cried out and ran towards Leo and the demon, summoning Dark Heavens as she went.

The demon had managed to break through Leo's guard and had plunged the sword into his shoulder, between the shoulderblade and the ribcage, and the blade was lodged into his back. Not a mortal wound, but it must have been agony for Leo. The demon swung Leo's body on the sword as he tried to free it, and Leo howled with a combination of anger and pain. The demon finally wrenched the sword free, nearly severing one of Leo's front legs with it. Leo fell heavily, the leg useless, and the demon swung and, with a single blow, took off Leo's head. Leo disappeared.

The demon turned to face Simone. She loaded Dark Heavens with shen energy and blew it up before it could even move towards her. After it exploded, she dropped the sword and fell to kneel in the sand, her head bowed.

'Simone, you really *must* have some training with weapons. Using shen energy like that every single time is going to both shorten your life — in the unlikely event you don't gain Immortality — and weaken your body. You have to stop doing this,' John scolded her.

She turned her tear-streaked face to us as we approached, then buried her head in John's shoulder next to his shell. 'It killed my Leo!'

'Don't be silly, Simone, he'll be back before you know it,' John said. 'Do you know how busy the Courts are at the moment?'

'Not overly busy,' I said.

'Emma, you're as white as a ghost. Come and sit next to me and lean on me with Simone. Both of you are overreacting. He's Immortal. That was a minor inconvenience for him, nothing more. If the Courts aren't too busy he could be back in a couple of weeks.'

'I was planning to give him his new sword in a week,' I said, flopping to sit in the sand and leaning my head on John's shell. 'We were arranging a presentation ceremony and party for him at the Mountain.'

'Well then, let me ask Judge Pao,' John said. He unfocused for a moment, then came back. 'Make the party for about two weeks' time instead, and make it a "welcome back, here's your cool new sword" party.'

I nodded.

Simone wiped her eyes and smiled. 'You're right, Daddy, but I hate to see him hurt like that.'

'Pain is a side effect of being alive,' John said. 'And physical pain is the easiest to bear and the easiest to relieve.'

'I know I'm alive without being stabbed, thank you very much,' she said.

He nodded. 'Good point. Has Leo had much training?'

'He hasn't had any, he's refused it,' I said. 'That's why I made the sword for him, to try and get him to do some training with it.'

'Tell him that I order him to take the training, just as I order Simone to attend CH and learn as well,' John said. 'Both of them should be going to CH together.'

'That's the weirdest idea I've ever heard,' Simone said with wonder.

John bowed his head. 'Thank you. Now.' He turned to the water. 'I wanted to show you two lovely ladies something. Emma, we'll go down to the edge of the water and you can get on my back there; Simone, just follow along.'

He trundled down to where the perfectly clear water hit the smooth sand. The beach was completely wave-free, and the sandy floor made the water appear pale blue-green, transparent and glittering. John seemed only to have two speeds: he could pick his shell up and move lightning-fast, graceful and menacing; or he could lower his shell and move more slowly, appearing clumsy. His slow speed was deceptively comical.

'I wonder why the demon attacked Leo,' Simone said, almost to herself.

'He's Immortal. That's enough for them,' John said. 'What I want to know is why it was up here and not in Hell. It didn't have a master ordering it; it seemed to be on its own. That shouldn't be happening.'

I didn't reply and John looked at me. 'I can hear your brain working, Emma, tell me what's going on.'

'You can hear what I'm thinking?' I said.

'No, but I can hear your brain clicking like a high-speed clockwork machine. There's something you should tell me but you haven't.'

I used the formal tone of an underling reporting to a general. 'The Gates of Hell are not as heavily guarded without you here. Sometimes the Thirty-Six require assistance and the Guards of the Gates are called into battle. When this happens, individual demons escape.'

John was silent for a moment. Then he asked, 'What's it like on Hungry Ghosts Festival?'

'Awful,' Simone said softly. 'It's not just the hungry ghosts that leave Hell and walk the Earth, it's the spirits in Hell as well, the ones that don't have permission to leave, plus thousands more demons. So far the demons have held to the treaty and not harmed anyone, but their presence causes widespread destruction amongst the humans — car accidents, family quarrels, theft, murder.'

'I wish I had never negotiated that,' John said, shaking his turtle head. 'It was such a mistake.'

'At least it's only one day a year,' I said. 'And I'm sure it was worth the price.'

'Sometimes I wonder,' John said. He shook himself. 'All right, hop on, Emma, let's go and have a look.'

He moved into thigh-deep water and I clambered on top of his shell, carefully avoiding the spiked areas.

'When we get into the water, lie across the top and close your eyes; we'll be moving very quickly,' he said. 'You ready, Simone?'

Simone dived into the water ahead of us in reply.

John pulled himself a couple more steps and his feet changed to flippers, his shell turning greener and growing smooth. He'd changed from a land tortoise to a sea turtle. He ducked his head, we lurched under the water and we were off.

I inhaled water and panicked. I coughed and inhaled more, and nearly let go of his shell.

His voice came into my head, reassuring. *Breathe the water, Emma; remember that time in the Japanese bath at the Tiger's palace? One of my fondest memories. You could do it then, it's just a little more pressure now. Relax … good.*

This was different to being carried by the Blue Dragon at Kota Kinabalu; his movement had been smooth and I hadn't felt the water moving past me. John lurched as he thrust with his flippers, and we were moving as fast as a speedboat beneath the water. I could feel the water's drag; the pressure meant that I couldn't open my eyes, and it felt like trying to breathe in a tornado.

I can feel from the way you're holding me that you're finding this uncomfortable, he said. *It's not far, and I assure you that it will be worth it. Just relax, you will not suffocate or be hurt, I promise. Just think of the water that is flowing past you ... as me.*

I nodded, although he probably didn't feel it. I kept my eyes closed and concentrated on holding onto his shell.

The light disappeared from the inside of my eyelids; we were in the shade. The temperature of the water dropped slightly. We travelled like this for a short time then we were in sunlight again. John surfaced and I took a deep breath then coughed up a ridiculous amount of water, nearly vomiting onto the back of his shell as it pumped out of me.

'Don't worry, that's a normal reaction,' John said. 'When I'm able to take human form again, travelling with me underwater will be much easier.'

'I'm glad,' I choked, still coughing up water.

'Wow, this is great,' Simone said with wonder.

I coughed a few more times and managed to look up and around. We were in a natural, hollow limestone chimney; probably the remains of a hundred-metre-wide volcanic plug. The walls were covered in creeping plants and the sky was visible through the top of the rock formation, about fifty metres above us. The sun shone down onto the water, and a small, perfect beach had been created by the current on one side.

John took me to the beach, but didn't climb out of the water. He stayed a sea turtle and lay in the shallows, his eyes closed with bliss. I rolled off him into the water and lay on my back next to him, enjoying the sunshine.

'Go take a look,' he said. 'The cave that leads back outside has glow-worms in the ceiling.'

'Cool,' Simone said, and dived into the water.

The two of us sat together watching the reflections of the ripples on the walls of the chimney, and the tiny blue and yellow glittering fish that flashed past us in schools. The gentle sound of the water hitting the rock echoed around us.

'There are so many things I need to tell you and ask you now you're back,' I said.

'I'm not back for good. As long as I can't take human form, I'll lose my intelligence again,' he said, interrupting. 'I don't know how long I have.'

'I know, I understand. All these things I need to say ... and I can't think of a single one of them.'

'That's all right,' he said. 'You know that words aren't —'

I finished it for him with delight. 'Words aren't necessary! Do you know, Simone teases me mercilessly about that? She makes this serious face and looks me in the eye and says, "Words aren't necessary, Emma, because I love you so much! You are the only one for me!" And then she pretends to put her finger down her throat and makes gagging noises. She says, "Promise me you won't be that mushy when Daddy comes back. I couldn't stand it!"'

'And what do you tell her?'

'To deal.'

He chuckled, the noise vibrating through his shell.

'Do that again,' I said.

'What?'

'That little laugh.' I put my hand on his shell.

He hesitated a moment, then laughed quietly. The vibration ran through my hand and I gasped.

'What, Emma? Are you okay?'

'Uh ... that is ...' I didn't know what to say. 'Your shell *vibrates*.'

He was quiet for a moment, then said, 'Oh my. I didn't know that.' He glanced at me. 'If I know my Emma, you are thinking very evil thoughts right now — and that is one of the reasons I love you.'

I started to laugh and he joined me. We laughed together, and I flopped back to lie on the sand, looking up at the fading blue sky.

'One day, when Simone isn't around ...' he said, then, 'Never mind. I don't want to freak you out.'

'How long before you can take human form?' I said. 'I *really* want that back, John.'

He hesitated. 'There may be an issue when I retake human form, because I am so weak. I hope this doesn't freak you out, but when I become human again ...' He stopped for a moment, gazing at the reflections on the rock face.

'Yes, John?'

He jerked his head slightly. 'Emma?'

I moved closer to him and touched his head. 'You're fading. Call Simone back.'

He nodded, turned away and concentrated.

'What were you going to say about becoming human again?' I said.

Simone surfaced, swam underwater to us, then pulled herself out to lie on the sand on her back.

'Your tummy is very white,' John said. 'You're so fair compared to me. You inherited a lot from your mother.'

Simone grinned. 'I don't get the sun on my tummy much. When I swim ... used to swim in school I wore a one-piece.'

'And stop getting the sun on your face,' he said sternly. 'Treasure your pale complexion, Simone, it shows how noble and refined you are.'

She hissed with derision and rolled onto her stomach.

'What?' he said.

'Welcome to the twenty-first century,' I said. 'Some of her friends go in to have spray-tans.'

'*Chinese* girls get artificial tans?' he said in horror.

'Some do,' Simone said. 'Others get skin bleaching instead, to go in the opposite direction. And artificial nails, and hair extensions, and eyelash extensions, and nose and eye and boob jobs ... Emma wouldn't let me have anything done, even if I asked.'

'You are perfect exactly the way you are,' he said. 'That is so against the essence of the Tao it is scary. The essence of the Tao is to be exactly who you are.'

'Oh, I think they're being exactly who they are,' I said. 'Completely artificial and shallow, focused only on looking good on the outside no matter how hollow they are inside.'

He dropped his head and shook it. 'That is so wrong.'

'What about you becoming human, John?' I asked him again. 'There was something you wanted to say.'

'Was there?' He shook his head again. 'I don't remember. I am fading, I don't know how long I have ...'

He disappeared.

Simone sighed and turned away. 'He didn't even say goodbye.'

'He didn't need to,' I said, 'because it wasn't goodbye; he's coming back.'

'Uh, Emma ...' Simone looked around. 'I can't get you out of here. I can't touch you, and that's a good fifty-metre swim under the rock there through the cave.'

'We have a problem,' I said.

She concentrated. 'The Phoenix is sending a long-tail boat for us, but we have to work out a way to get you through the cave. She wanted to know if you had an open-water licence, and I said no, but she said it's irrelevant anyway because it's not open water. So she'll send a diver here with extra equipment for you, and all you have to do is breathe with the gear and they'll take you through.'

'Before I met your father I thought about getting my licence, but the course was too expensive for me on my kindergarten salary,' I said.

'You should; you could come out with me,' she said.

'I think I'd just slow you down.'

'It would be fun to share that with someone,' she said. 'And I wouldn't ask Leo.'

'Did he ever tell you what happened to make him so terrified of water?' I said.

'No. He never told you?'

'Never. Nobody knows.'

'I hope he comes back soon,' she said wistfully.

The truck engine that propelled the long-tail boat was too loud for us to have any sort of decent conversation, so we sat in silence as it took us back to the resort beach. The boat looked like every other long-tail in the area, with a long spar rising from the bow, decorated with a few brightly coloured silk scarves, and the engine set on top of a long metal pole on the back with a propeller on the end. It was a noisy and uncomfortable way to travel, but also the most traditional way.

The Phoenix met us at the beach. The human diver who had guided me out through the cave lifted us off the boat so that we could wade in to meet her.

'That was such a theme-park ride,' I said as we walked up the beach to where her golf buggy was waiting.

'Was it that exciting?' the Phoenix said.

'No,' I said. 'That fake. We were just talking about fake things, and there we go, riding on a fake long-tail boat.'

'I don't know what you're talking about,' the Phoenix said, confused.

'It's made of *fibreglass*,' I said. 'The real ones are made of beautiful teak, and the older and more loved they are, the more the wood shines. I've seen them. That one,' I waved dismissively at the boat, 'was a fake.'

She shook her head as we boarded the golf buggy. 'You're right. They are passed down from generation to generation, and some of the boats on Phuket have been passed down through many generations. But when the tsunami came, hundreds of the boats were destroyed. We worked out how much timber we would need to rebuild them and it was more forest than the country even owns. So I imported some experts from overseas to build replacement boats for the fishermen and water taxi operators out of fibreglass instead of timber. They're cheaper to build, just as robust, and they have the bonus of not destroying any of our precious forests. The only disadvantage is they do not have the polished beauty of the originals.'

'You're helping replace them?' Simone said.

The Phoenix nodded. 'Nearly all of them are done. In some cases, they were able to salvage the timber off the old boat and rebuild, but many lost their boats altogether. You are right, Emma, they do look like plastic. But they are giving the people of the island their livelihoods back.'

'I don't know how I can apologise enough,' I said. 'I guess I see too much artificiality in Hong Kong, and now see it everywhere.'

'Reality is an illusion anyway,' the Phoenix said. 'All is artificial, all is perception. The truth is a lie. Each of us exists in our own universe.'

'Whoa,' Simone said. 'Zen.'

'Small Wheel, not Zen,' the Phoenix said. 'We follow a more traditional teaching, without the pretentious navel-gazing of the Eastern sects.'

'I can just see the Dragon doing that,' I said.

'Oh, the Dragon is more Zen than anyone,' the Phoenix said. 'He can spend four or five hours performing an elaborate tea ceremony and in the end pass you an exquisitely hand-produced cup full of tea that is cold, extremely bitter and quite revolting — usually with a dead fly in the bottom that he never noticed.'

As we headed back to our villa, the staff were setting up tables and stringing lights along the roofline of the central area of the resort.

'That's for the night market,' the Phoenix said. 'We have one once a week. The locals come in and display their ridiculously overpriced wares for the tourists.'

'Where should we go for wares that aren't ridiculously overpriced?' Simone said.

'Patong — ask Kwan to take you,' the Phoenix said. 'But there are some items in our market that are only available here. There are some craftsmen on the island who are more like studio artists, and I encourage them to display their work here and charge a premium for it. People will be coming from other resorts in the complex to see what's up for sale; it will be fun.'

'What time?' I said.

'Six till nine.'

'Let's have some dinner now — I'm starving — and then go have a look,' Simone said, her face bright with pleasure.

'Would you like to join me for dinner?' the Phoenix said.

'We'd be delighted,' I said.

'Good. Go shower and change, then ask Kwan to bring you to the main lobby. We'll eat in my private room, then have a look at what's happening at the market.'

The tropical sunset flared flaming red and orange in the sky above us, the dark silhouettes of the palm trees providing a colourful contrast. The warm, humid breeze picked up slightly just as the Phoenix dropped us at the front of our villa. It was filled with the fragrance of jasmine and frangipani from the scented candles that Kwan had lit for us. He had turned down each bed, and a colourful sarong wrapped with a ribbon and an orchid lay on each of our pillows.

Simone stopped for a moment to gaze at the spectacular sky, then grinned at me and disappeared into her bathroom.

CHAPTER 15

Simone and I chose to walk back through the gardens together to the central complex, admiring the bobbing purple orchids, birds-of-paradise and hibiscus flowers. Above, the sky faded from its brilliant hues to a pale lilac and then to a dark blue, and stars began to appear.

'The Tiger asked Michael to come and help while Leo's in Hell,' Simone said. 'He'll meet us at the restaurant.'

'We don't really need him, we have you ...' I started, then shrugged. 'Okay, if you're busy in the water or something, he'll come in handy if I'm attacked.'

The lights of the lobby lit up the gardens around it. Michael was waiting there for us, in a pair of expensive pre-ripped jeans and a white-and-yellow horizontal-striped polo shirt. He fell to one knee and saluted us, the movement incongruous in his modern clothing.

'Pity I missed seeing the Dark Lord,' he said. He nodded to us. 'Hope you don't mind me tagging along? My father sent word when he found out Leo got killed. Was he all right? It didn't hurt him too much, did it?'

'It almost took off one of his legs before it killed him,' Simone said, obviously upset. 'I should have moved sooner.'

Michael stepped back and gestured for us to go first. 'That would not be doing him a favour, Princess. You'd wound his pride, and that would hurt more than having a leg taken off. Oh, Emma.' He turned to me. 'Your snake spacesuit is ready — Dad says any time you want to give it a try, hop on up. He'll take you on a ride into the stratosphere so you can see how it goes.'

'I need to be able to move in it, I can't just be carried,' I said.

'His people don't know whether you'll be able to move in it or not. It depends what sort of serpent movement you use.'

'I have no idea,' I said.

'You might have to try being a sidewinder.'

'Now there's a scary thought,' I said. 'What about your job? Are you okay to take some time off?'

'This comes first,' he said.

On the left of the lobby stood the resort's signature Thai restaurant; a hostess dressed in a traditional Thai silk dress of the same rich red as the furnishings waited at the entrance. She clasped her hands, bowed low and touched her hands to her face when she saw us, and gestured for us to go in.

'Suddenly I feel horribly underdressed,' Simone said.

The private room was set up like a Chinese karaoke/dinner/mah-jongg room, with a large-screen TV on one wall and a twelve-seater table. Two of the walls were floor-to-ceiling glass and overlooked the massive pool that was lit with numerous underwater lights, making the water glow. Loi kratongs made of bamboo and shaped like lotus flowers with a candle in the centre floated on the water, completing the entrancing scene.

'And who is this?' the Phoenix said with curiosity, smiling at Michael.

'I am the three hundred and fifteenth son of the White Tiger,' Michael said. 'Not a Horseman, just a friend of the family.'

'Michael!' I said, shocked. 'That is so wrong! Your mother would be horrified to hear you relegating yourself to a number.'

'I know,' he said, grinning at me. He turned back to the Phoenix and saluted her. 'My real name is Michael MacLaren.'

'Your mother was the woman who ...' The Phoenix's voice trailed off.

'Yes, she was the one who was crowned Empress of the West and died when she drank the Elixir of Immortality,' Michael said, his levity disappearing.

The Phoenix's smile warmed. 'I heard she was an exceptional lady. You have certainly gained a lot from her.'

Michael nodded. 'Thank you, ma'am. I've known the Dark Lord's family since I was fifteen, and I was chosen to take Leo's place if he died of AIDS. As that never happened, I spend my time on the Earthly, living as a normal human.'

'I vaguely remember seeing you around the household.' She leaned her chin on her hand and continued to smile at him. 'You should not waste yourself on the Earthly, there is so much to see on the Celestial! How much time do you spend in the south? I'd love to show it to you.'

'Uh ...' Michael began, and Simone rescued him.

'Michael, after dinner could you walk with me through the markets? There are so many cool things we can look at,' she said.

Michael turned with obvious relief. 'We haven't spent nearly enough time together lately, Simone.'

The Phoenix immediately understood and leaned back. 'Check the menus, see what you'd like. How spicy do you like your food? I have a terrible craving for a papaya salad right now, a really *hot* one.'

'I'm not really into terribly hot food,' Simone said, unsure.

'I am. How's the tomyum?' Michael said.

'Might be a little fiery even for your taste, Michael,' I warned. 'This lady swims in lava and sleeps in volcanos, remember.'

'Sounds perfect,' Michael said.

'I'll have a pot of tomyum to share,' the Phoenix said. 'Pineapple rice for the Princess with the spoilt Chinese taste, and some char-grilled beef and chicken. Curry, anyone?'

'Yellow for me, please,' I said. 'Vegetarian.'

'If you can get me a really *hot* red curry with beef in it ...' Michael's face was full of pleasure.

'I like you more and more all the time,' the Phoenix said. She turned to me. 'Where *have* you been hiding him?' She realised what she'd said, raised her hands and laughed. 'That came out the wrong way! I'm sorry, I can't help it sometimes. I just really enjoy being a woman.'

'How long have you been female?' Simone said, curious.

'Only about three hundred years. I did it because I wanted to experience motherhood. It is so rewarding that I never really looked back. I wouldn't try to do it the Western way; I don't know how they cope — trying to raise children and hold down sometimes even a full-time job at the same time, without a domestic helper.' She nodded to me. 'Can't understand why your country doesn't have maids. All of Asia does it; it improves the livelihood of the helper, and frees the employer from being a domestic slave. Maybe Australians like their women to be domestic slaves. Anyway.' She shrugged. 'Maybe I will tire of it in a couple of hundred years or so, but as long as there are young men like Michael around, I don't think I will.'

'Did you like men before?' I said.

'It has a great deal to do with the hormones in the form I take,' she said. 'I really don't understand this business about making a fuss over preference; a beautiful form is a beautiful form. But the female hormones seem to make me appreciate a beautiful male form more. Of course, sometimes there's a girl I'll meet ...' Her expression became wistful, then she snapped back. 'But I haven't yet met anybody that has made me want to change back into a rooster. The feathers are the same, the tail is the same, so there's really no point.'

'But aren't you like ... married to the Dragon or something?' Simone said. 'You two are the matching pair: phoenix and dragon.'

'We are, but it's more like ...' She hesitated, thinking. 'It's more like the marriage of the Emperor and Empress. Full of ritual and symbolism, with very little feeling in it, and both of us pursue our pleasure elsewhere.'

'That's one way you differ from traditional Empresses,' Michael said.

'Oh, not really that much,' she said. 'This Phoenix–Dragon pairing was only introduced in the

Qing anyway. Before that, the Taoists made the Dragon and the Tiger symbolic of yang and yin; quite ironic really.'

'Since they're the Lesser Yang and Yin,' I said.

She nodded. 'Exactly. The Tiger and Dragon wouldn't have anything to do with that, much to the Jade Emperor's annoyance. I can still hear the Tiger shouting, "No way am I taking female form. I am Emperor of the West, not one of that bastard's *women*!" The Heavens are supposed to mirror the Earthly, but in that case there was severe dissonance. Caused some backlash on the Earthly, made things very chaotic.'

'I love how the Greater Yang — the most masculine power of all — is a woman, and the Greater Yin, the most feminine, is a man,' Simone said. 'It's like you two decided together that you were going to rub the Taoist shamans' faces in it.'

'That's just the way it happened,' she said. 'And your father is yang and yin combined in his two-creature form. He is much stranger and more complex than any of us.'

'You have no idea,' I said under my breath, and they heard it and laughed.

After dinner we wandered through the small market together. The stallholders were universally gracious and smiling, presenting their wares and unconcerned if we didn't buy. Simone spent a long time looking at the coloured freshwater pearls, and eventually had a necklace made to order out of pink, coral and peach-coloured pearls in a triple strand.

We arrived at a table that had flat leather cut-outs of elephants and traditional warriors, all painted in brilliant colours. 'What are these?' Simone said.

'Shadow puppets,' the Phoenix said. She held one up for us to see; it was transparent in the light, with the paint adding features to it. 'They hold them up on sticks behind a sheet with a candle behind them and act out the great ancient tales of valour. Sometimes a tale, such as that of Rama, can last all night.'

Simone lifted a thirty-centimetre elephant attached with string to a large piece of card. 'I guess these ones are designed to be framed, not really used.'

'You can frame them against a white background, they look very effective,' the Phoenix said.

Simone bought the elephant. When she placed the baht in the stallholder's hand she gasped. 'I'm sorry! I didn't notice.' She nodded her head. 'Pleased to meet you.'

The stallholder's grin widened. 'No need, ma'am, the Empress warned me you were coming. There are demons around at the moment, and many of us are attempting to hide as much as possible. We are not so powerful as you and we fear them.'

'Shen?' I said. I hadn't picked him.

'He's an elephant,' Simone said with delight. 'First I've ever met.'

The elephant Shen clasped his hands. 'Sawatdee. Welcome.'

We quickly clasped our hands back, and Simone raised the leather elephant shadow puppet with delight. 'A self-portrait!'

'I wish I was as handsome as this one,' the Shen said, 'so that is why I made it. I would appreciate your blessing and wishes of protection, ma'am. The demons come more and more, and we fear them.'

Simone placed both her hands on top of his head and closed her eyes. 'My blessings and protection upon you. May the spirit of Kwan Yin follow you and bring you peace and mercy.'

He bowed his head and clasped his hands again. 'I thank you, ma'am.'

Simone nodded to him and we moved on.

'Well done, Simone, you handled that with true grace,' the Phoenix said.

'It's been happening more and more lately,' Simone said. 'At first I was like ... "I can't bless you, I'm nothing special", but Kwan Yin said that I am lifting their spirits and giving them a gift. And the lingering energy from my touch gives them some small measure of protection from demons, so it's all good.' She shrugged. 'It's sort of fun to do, it makes people so happy.'

I stopped at the next stall, which was covered in bolts of Thai silk. Much of it was shot silk: the main colour had a second thread of a contrasting colour through it that appeared and disappeared as the fabric moved.

'You can buy the silk and have it made at Mr Li's back home, or you can do what Simone did with her necklace and order something made to collect in a couple of days,' the Phoenix said. 'This is first quality, much better than anything you'll find in town.' She dropped her voice. 'The dealer is an ordinary human who grows the worms herself and dyes the fabric up in the hills.'

I hesitated to touch the beautiful fabric. As well as shot silk, there was brocade with colourful flowers and birds woven in silver and gold.

I shook my head. 'It's fabulous, but it's way too fancy for me.'

The Phoenix didn't argue; she'd known me too long.

'Lady Emma!' someone shouted, and we all turned.

Amy raced up to us in human form, with Gold's stone child floating over her shoulder. She saluted us quickly.

'Daddy's dead,' the child said.

'We need you back home, ma'am,' Amy said. She wiped her eyes. 'Gold's been murdered.'

'Is he on the tenth level?' I said quickly, thinking of the stones that had been completely destroyed by Demon Prince Six.

'Yes, he's not been destroyed. He, Zara and the stones that were helping them with the research were all killed, as well as both of our IT guys.'

'They were working in the Academy, they were safe in there,' I said. 'Did they go outside for some reason?'

'Gold went out to buy some food for the IT guys and the demons ran a truck over his car, killing him,' Amy said. 'Then two students who turned out to be demon copies went into the network room where Zara and Calcite were working and killed them and the IT guys. The Masters have locked everything down and are doing a sweep.'

'We have to get home right now,' Simone said to me.

I nodded, and turned to the Phoenix. 'Thank you for the time here, Phoenix, but I think we need to move.'

'I'm sorry, I can't carry you home,' she said. 'I'm pregnant again and I don't want to strain myself. You'll have to fly commercial back to Hong Kong.'

'I understand — and congratulations,' I said. I turned to Michael. 'If you were to take me on a cloud now, would it be faster than taking a flight back first thing tomorrow morning?'

'Let me go up and have a look how far it is,' Michael said, and shot straight into the air, the backwash nearly knocking me off my feet.

'Did you say they wrecked Gold's car?' I asked Amy.

She nodded, some humour appearing through the distress. 'His heart will be broken. I think he loves that car more than he loves me.'

'You might be right,' I said.

'Don't be silly, Amy,' the stone child said. 'Hey, Auntie Emma, Auntie Simone — Daddy and Amy are gonna have *babies*! Amy has them in her tummy, just like an animal mother. Isn't it cool?'

Amy blushed and glanced up at it. 'Do you have to tell *everybody*?'

'Yes!' the child said.

I gave her a quick hug. 'That's wonderful news. When are you due?'

'I'm about three months.' She looked down at herself. 'I think I'm starting to show. We were planning to make an announcement soon.'

Simone hugged her as well. 'That's wonderful, Amy. Take care of yourself, okay? No rushing about too much.' She nodded up at the stone child. 'You look after her.'

'Don't worry, Auntie Simone,' the child said, serious. 'While Daddy's away, I'm looking after Amy real well.'

Amy glanced up at it. 'Yes, you are.'

Michael shot out of the air, slowed and landed gently in front of us.

'I checked the schedule, there's no direct flight to Hong Kong tomorrow,' the stone in my ring said. 'You'd have to go through Bangkok, and the whole trip would take seven hours.'

'I can get you there in three or four,' Michael said.

'Would it be too tiring for you?' the Phoenix said.

'I'll summon a cloud. I can do it,' Michael said.

218

The Phoenix pursed her lips. 'Forgive me for doubting you, young man, but that's an awfully long way and you're not even Immortal.'

'If I get into trouble I'll have someone meet me halfway,' Michael said. 'We just need to get back there.'

We didn't bother to change; we just threw our clothes into our bags and left them in the villa for later collection. Kwan would pack for Leo.

I saluted the Phoenix the Chinese way. 'I appreciate your hospitality, Empress, and hope to return it soon.'

Simone saluted her as well. 'You have kept us in your domicile in ease and comfort, bringing clarity and serenity to our spirits. I thank you.'

The Phoenix saluted us, bowing low. 'I am honoured by your presence.' She dropped the formality and gave me a quick hug. 'Come back soon and have a proper holiday.' She hugged Simone. 'And good job on the protocol.'

Michael summoned a cloud, I stepped onto it and we flew off. The night sky was windier than during the day and occasionally the cloud tossed like a small boat on water. Michael grimaced as he held it in check. I sat kneeling in front of his feet, my hands buried in the cloud in an effort to hold on. Despite this, I fell asleep — but was jarred awake by the cloud bucking beneath me; we'd hit turbulence.

I grabbed at the cloud, but couldn't keep a grip and slid off. Suddenly I was falling through darkness. I concentrated on my energy centres to slow my fall and looked down. I couldn't see anything; there was no moon and the starlight wasn't enough to illuminate below me. I didn't know if we were over ground or water. The ground would be better: I could touch down in a soft landing and wait for Michael to get me. Over water, I could slow my fall but not stop it, and I was going to end up wet. If the waves in the water were strong I'd have to swim against them, and sharks were always a possibility.

'Are we above water?' I asked the stone in my ring.

'Yes. Change to snake, see if you can fly in that form,' the stone said.

I changed, and attempted to use my falling momentum to push my energy centres forward. I felt the movement with a rush of delight; I hadn't thought of flying in serpent form.

'Don't get too pleased with yourself,' the stone said. 'You're still falling, but it's more of a curve, which means Michael will have more trouble finding you. Change back. When we get home you should have a think about doing some training on this in serpent form.'

I changed back, dropped quickly about ten metres, then slowed my fall again.

'Emma, I can't see you!' Michael shouted to my left. 'Stone, glow or something.'

The stone glowed, and I also pressed the illumination button on my wristwatch.

'Got you!' Michael said.

'Slow down, Emma, you're close to the water,' the stone said.

I concentrated and slowed my fall, then crashed flat on my stomach into the water with a jolt of pain. The waves were about a metre high and the current pushed me around. I tried to tread water and keep my head above the surface, but the movement of the waves was unpredictable and I couldn't see further than the next crest. The water continuously broke over my face, making me gasp.

'Keep it up, he's close by,' the stone said, and glowed again.

'Emma!' Michael shouted, but I couldn't tell his direction. I opened my mouth to shout back and inhaled sea water. I coughed, trying to clear it, and inhaled more.

The stone made a loud siren-like sound, going from piercing to garbled as we were pulled above and below the water.

Michael grabbed me by the shoulders and hoisted me out of the water, his grip so tight it was painful. He threw me back onto the cloud, the hard surface jarring me, and we rose again. All the water rushed off me and out of my clothes; Simone was nearby.

'Michael, are you okay?' she said from somewhere in the darkness.

'I don't want to fail you, but I think I've overdone it,' Michael said. 'I can't keep the cloud going much longer, and our relief's another half-hour away.'

'Is there any land nearby?' I said.

Both Simone and Michael were silent for a moment, then Simone said, 'Let me go have a look, there might be something.'

'Be quick,' Michael said. 'I can't hold this much longer.'

'Shrink the cloud,' I said.

'Won't make any difference.'

'How much longer do I have?'

His voice was strained with effort. 'I'm doing the best I can, ma'am.'

I sank into the cloud; it was losing its solidity. Michael's dark shape gently fell to sit next to me.

'I can't believe this,' he said. 'I've completely failed you.'

'Can you summon me a life jacket?' I said.

'I'm too weak.'

'No land anywhere near here,' Simone said, returning. Her voice became fierce. 'If I'd taken the training that everybody told me to, I would be able to summon a cloud too!'

'Humph,' Michael said, his voice fading. 'Damn stupid way to get around anyway.'

'Can you summon me and Michael a boat?' I asked her. 'A life raft?'

'Nothing that big. Put this over your head and tie it around your waist,' she said, handing me a life jacket. I quickly pulled it on, wrapping the tapes around me. The jacket was too big and felt uncomfortable.

'Michael? Michael? Put the jacket on,' Simone said.

The cloud came apart and I fell. I slowed my fall and landed in the water again. The life jacket forced me onto my back, the floats behind my head holding it above the water, but the waves still hit my face, occasionally making me breathe water and cough.

A nearby splash indicated that Michael had fallen in as well.

'Michael!' Simone shouted. Another splash sounded as she hit the water to search for him.

There was silence for a moment, then Simone shouted, 'Don't you dare die on me, Michael MacLaren, I would never forgive myself!'

'I'll do it just to spite you then, squirt,' Michael said.

'I'll hold you up, put the stupid jacket thing on,' she said.

There were some grunts as he struggled with the ties. 'I hope I got it tight enough — drop me, let's see.'

'I should go up higher and drop you,' Simone said. 'Emma, are you okay?'

'She's fine, she just keeps inhaling water,' the stone said.

An arm flailed nearby and hit my shoulder.

'Who is that?' I said.

'Me,' Michael said. 'Grab my hand.'

I took his hand and held it. 'Simone has the other hand,' he said.

'All we have to do now is wait for help,' I said. 'Good job, guys.'

'You are such a dumbass, Michael, you nearly got Emma killed,' Simone said.

'I know,' Michael said ruefully. 'I'm so sorry, Emma. My dad is going to tear my whiskers off.'

'At least we're not in the freezing waters of the North Atlantic,' I said. 'But which one of us is Rose?'

'Me!' the stone shouted, changing its voice to a falsetto. 'Save me, Jack!'

'Oh, shut up,' Michael said.

The water surged beneath us; I was lifted two metres on the swell.

'What was that?' I said.

'I don't know,' Simone said, sounding unsure.

'Any way you can check under us?' Michael said. 'I suddenly went from *Titanic* to *Jaws*.'

The water lifted us again and Michael clutched my hand.

'Just a sec,' Simone said, and there was silence.

'She's gone under to have a look,' Michael said quietly.

The surge lifted us three metres this time and Michael yelped. 'Something touched my foot!'

Something lifted my foot and then both my feet. It slid up my legs and under my behind. It felt like a surfboard running under my body. Then my perception changed and I realised it was a hard, slightly curved object surfacing in the water, and I was sliding down its side on a coating of what felt like oil.

'I think it's Lord Xuan,' Michael said, still clutching my hand. 'His turtle form.'

'John?' I said.

'It's Martin,' Simone said from somewhere above us. 'Hold on to him, he's going to lift you above the water.'

'He's too slippery!' I said, sliding off the edge of his shell and hitting the water again, a metre below.

'Hold on to Michael, I'll lift you both,' Simone said.

Michael's hand yanked mine and I was lifted out of the water by my arm. We floated some distance, then I was gently lowered onto the flat of the turtle's shell.

'Thanks, Martin,' I called.

'You're welcome, Emma,' Martin said, his voice next to my ear. 'I came down because I heard that something had happened to Leo?'

'Leo was attacked by a demon and it killed him,' Simone said.

Martin was silent for a moment, then, 'He's back on the tenth level, where he spent so many years.'

'I know,' Simone said.

'I should go down there,' Martin said.

'Why?' Simone said. 'You never went down last time.'

'Yes, I did,' Martin said. 'I went constantly. He never wanted to speak to me. He still blames me for killing Father.'

'And he's right!' Simone said, her voice fierce.

'I know,' Martin said, almost a moan of pain. 'When the King offered to take me and use me as a toy in return for keeping you safe, I jumped at the chance. It was the punishment I deserved for betraying my family.'

'Emo bullshit,' Simone said, still fierce.

'I deserved it. I wanted to suffer,' Martin said.

'Enough suffering. Enough self-pity. Time to atone by working with us to build a better future for our family,' Simone said, her voice more compassionate.

'Yes,' Martin said. 'So, I am here, and I will shelter you. We are moving extremely slowly towards Hong Kong; I can't move fast without tipping you off. We will meet your relief transport in about twenty minutes.' His voice softened. 'You are wiser than me, Mei Mei.'

'Doesn't take much, Ge Ge.'

CHAPTER 16

About twenty minutes later we saw a light bobbing in the distance, approaching quickly. It was Liu, riding a cloud with dignity, holding his staff beside him and with a light floating next to his shoulder. He dropped down closer to us and his outfit became visible: the traditional brown robes of a Taoist Immortal.

'Why are you all sitting in the dark?' he said as he came within hailing distance. 'Is Simone injured?'

Simone was silent for a moment, then said, 'I completely forgot that nobody else can see in the dark. I am so sorry, guys, you should have told me you couldn't see.'

'Can you fly back unaided?' Liu asked her.

'Yeah, no problem. But Michael's spent and Emma needs a lift.'

'Summon a cloud for Michael to ride on,' he said, then leaned towards her, grinning pointedly. 'Oh, I forgot. You *don't know how*.'

She dropped her head, her grimace visible in his light. 'You don't need to rub it in, Uncle Liu.'

He straightened and nodded. 'Ming Gui, thank you for your assistance. I will take them from here.'

'My honour to serve,' Martin said, and waited patiently while Michael and I stepped onto Liu's cloud.

'We're clear,' I said, and Martin dived under the water.

Liu had much better control of his cloud than Michael had, and we travelled high and smoothly back to Hong Kong. The sun appeared over the horizon as we reached the cityscape, the pollution haze turning its rays orange.

'Where would you like me to drop you?' Liu said.

'I'd like to go straight to the Academy and see what the damage is, then I'll head home and take it easy,' I said. 'Take Michael back to the Folly if you could; he's having trouble staying awake. Simone, what do you want to do? Do you want to go home and rest or come with me?'

'If you don't mind, Emma, I'd just like to go home and take a shower and lie in front of the television for a while,' she said.

'I'll see you at home then. Rest and have something to eat, and I'll be along shortly.'

She nodded and disappeared.

Liu took Michael to the Folly, then took me to Wan Chai and dropped me on the roof of the Academy building. I grimaced when I saw the graffiti next to the entrance.

'Tell Jade to bring some students up here to clean this off, Liu,' I said. 'Na Zha's been at it again.'

'Already done, ma'am, they'll be along shortly,' Liu said. 'It's only 6 am.'

'I forgot,' I said. 'Is anybody in the building?'

'A few of us are trying to get the computers back online.'

'I wouldn't even try, Liu, they aren't really computers. The only resemblance they have to computers is that

227

they're shaped like a box and have standard output ports. Gold showed me inside: he raided every domicile in the Celestial to gather rocks for the engines — ordinary stones that had been on the Celestial for at least five hundred years. All that's inside the boxes are a Celestially tuned stone and a bunch of wires.'

'I'm getting some telepathic messages exactly to that effect,' Liu said.

We went down in the lift to the network hub on the second floor. It looked like a standard IT room: airtight, with a false floor of removable static-free tiles raised about thirty centimetres above the concrete floor to allow for the cables running beneath. Racks like shelving units held stacks of computers with no screens or keyboards — the network servers.

Amy and Edwin were there already. The stone in my ring took human form. It looked at the console, tentatively tapped a couple of keys, and shook its head. 'At least he's using a standard Unix operating system. With a bit of time and intelligence we should have minimal functionality back.'

'Only Gold and the two guys here in IT know how to administer the network,' Amy said. 'Without them, the network's down and nobody knows how to get it back up again.'

Edwin, the Academy doctor, took his glasses off and cleaned them on a cloth from his pocket. 'The demons who did this also erased the data that the stones were working on. We'll have to restore it from backup.'

Amy shrugged. 'Edwin works part-time down here, he likes computers. The demons didn't know that.'

'All the other dragons laugh at me,' Edwin said. 'I can't fix it alone though; I have my medical duties. Could we recruit some local staff?'

'Send messages to the other three Winds, let them know the situation and ask for any extra IT support staff they have,' I said. 'Word it forcefully to the Dragon; I know he always has more staff than he needs. Edwin, go through the backups and see if the data they were processing is there. Liu, with me.'

'My Lord,' Edwin said.

I turned and strode to the lift. 'Stone, stop playing with the computers and get back here. Liu, have any other demon copies been identified?'

'No,' Liu said, hurrying to keep up with me.

'Losing the data is both good and bad. It means they were on to something and the Geek got scared. Having those demon copies get right through our defences isn't; we need to call Ronnie Wong in to help us identify them. Can you handle that and report back?'

'Yes, my Lord.'

I turned and stared at him. 'What?'

He stared back, confused. 'What what?'

The lift opened but I didn't go in. 'Edwin just called me "my Lord" and you just did the same thing. What's going on?'

Liu smiled, embarrassed. 'I'm sorry, my Lor— my Lady, I didn't realise I was doing it.'

'What the hell is going on?' I said loudly, concerned now.

'Calm down, Emma, you're doing it to yourself,' the stone said, back in my ring again. 'In the last couple of minutes everybody's scanned you as the Dark Lord. You don't just sound like him, you *are* him.'

Liu nodded. 'He is here.'

I held my arms out in front of me: my hands looked perfectly normal. 'Do I look like him?'

'No,' Liu said.

'So I sound like him? I have his voice? I hear myself sounding like me.'

'No, ma'am, your appearance and voice are both you. Your essence, however, is him.'

I pointed at Liu, then realised what I was doing and dropped my finger. 'This is *not* going to happen to us.'

'"Us" meaning you and the Dark Lord?' the stone said.

'Simone would kill us!'

'His influence on you will fade over the next twenty-four hours or so,' the stone said. 'Don't be concerned, just enjoy his presence. He's helping you out right now.'

Liu stared at the stone. 'You know what's happening, stone?'

The stone didn't reply.

'He's here with me?' I said.

'Precisely,' the stone said. 'It has something to do with spending time with him. Relax and enjoy it.'

'You know more than you are letting on, my friend,' Liu said grimly.

'Of course,' the stone said.

'Do you know what I am?' I said with force.

'Oh my, I haven't been threatened with the toilet in many a year,' the stone said. 'Here's your answer. *You are an ordinary human being changed by close proximity to the Dark Lord.*'

'Changed to what?'

'Well, the obvious thing is a great big black snake, woman!' the stone said.

Liu stifled a laugh.

'You are such a dick,' I said.

'My human form is male. It comes with the territory,' the stone said.

The corridor shifted under my feet, making me stagger.

Liu took my elbow. 'You okay?'

'She's seen her best friend die, been stranded on a deserted island, dropped in the ocean twice and hasn't slept in twenty-four hours,' the stone said. 'Stupid weak human, she's at the end of her strength. Take her home and put her to bed.'

'I think he just left me,' I said, putting my hand to my forehead, which felt tender and sore. 'I feel a million years old.'

Liu continued to hold my elbow and his eyes unfocused. 'Marcus is bringing students over from the Folly in the bus for morning warm-up ... Michael's passed out ... Oh, whatever.' He linked his arm in mine to continue supporting me. 'I'll drive you home.'

'No *way* am I going in a car with you, Liu Cheng Rong, you are the most suicidal driver I have ever met!' I tried to pull myself free but he was too strong.

'Did you know,' he said conversationally as he led me to the lift, 'that my Merc has a top speed higher than Gold's Boxster? We checked it on the freeway in Guangzhou. Surprised both of us.'

'A Taoist Immortal should be driving something humble like a Mini,' I said.

'A '55 Mercedes sports car *is* humble in this town,' he said. 'Most people laugh at how old it is and wonder why I haven't updated.'

'Rubbish,' I said as he guided me into the lift. 'A lot of people know what a collector's item it is and exactly how much it's worth.'

'That's just a side effect of me never wanting to replace it because it works so well,' he said. 'The monetary value means nothing to me.'

I leaned against the wall of the lift, which seemed to be swaying slightly, as if I was still in the water. 'I'm going in Liu Cheng Rong's car and I'm going to die,' I said softly.

'Geez, you sound like my wife sometimes,' he said as the lift doors opened onto the basement car park.

'There you are, ma'am,' Liu said as he screeched to a halt from a speed of nearly a hundred kilometres an hour in front of the gates of the Black Road building. 'Home and alive.' He concentrated. 'Simone's asleep upstairs, all is well.'

I prised my hands from their death grip on the dash. 'It's all well now we're here.'

'Go on up and rest. Oh,' he added, suddenly remembering, 'don't forget, Simone has an appointment with the principal of Celestial High in three days. Tell her to take it easy until then. I'll see you when you're rested and ready to come back. I should have something for you on those demon copies by then.'

I opened the car door and stepped out. 'Remind me never to go in a car with you ever again.'

The minute I closed the door he did a lightning-fast three-point turn, nearly running over my feet, and tore off down the road, going airborne over the speed hump halfway along.

I took a shower, turned down the noodles Monica offered me, and checked on Simone. She was asleep and her face reminded me of her innocence when she was small.

I went into my own room, pulled back the covers and crawled into bed. It seemed to be swaying slightly.

232

'Am I okay? The bed's rocking,' I said.

'You're fine, it's just exhaustion,' the stone said. 'Sleep first, then eat and drink when you wake up.'

'You know what I am,' I said, struggling to stay awake. 'You've known all along.'

The stone took human form and drifted to sit on the chair next to the bed. 'Emma, believe me, I haven't been holding out on you about what you are. I really don't know.'

'You said most of me isn't here. You said I come and go.'

'That's right. You do.'

'John comes and goes,' I said. 'They saw me as Xuan Wu. I don't want to be his Serpent. If we rejoin, Simone will lose me.'

'Whatever you are, you have no choice in the matter,' the stone said. It crossed its legs and leaned its chin on its hand. 'Trust in yourself and it will all work out in the end.'

'That's what John said.' I gave a huge yawn.

'That's because he was right.'

'I have to stay around for Simone.'

'He said the same thing, Emma. And he's gone.'

'She can't lose all of us!'

'Oh, that's right, I was going to see how long Gold and Leo will be. Just a minute.' It sat more upright and its eyes unfocused. 'They haven't been given priority. Four to six weeks. I speeded things up for you; now it'll be two to three weeks.'

'You can do that? Why didn't you say before?'

The stone grinned ruefully. 'I was using your precedence. As First General, you can do things like that, regardless of your status as a mortal.'

'I'd like a list,' I said.

'A list of what? You'll have to be more specific there, Emma.'

'I can't, I'm falling asleep,' I said, and did.

I slept until lunchtime, then drove myself down to the Academy. I went straight to the server room. Edwin was there, with a couple of demons I'd never seen before: a female and male both appearing in their late teens.

Edwin saluted me. 'The Dragon sent these demons. They're both skilled and should be able to get things back up and running.'

I walked to the console where the demons were busy setting up the restore process. 'How long to recover our data?'

'Twenty-four hours, ma'am,' one of them said. 'Then another twenty-four hours to restore the Shenzhen data to the state it was in when the stones were destroyed.'

'No rush. Gold won't be back for a couple of weeks,' I said.

'The Dragon said we must have this work finished in three days, then return and back up his data,' one of the demons said, and the other one grimaced.

'Take your time; you're staying until I can find new IT staff,' I said. 'It could take weeks.'

The demon opened his mouth to protest.

'And the Dragon won't have anything to say in the matter,' I added. 'Edwin.'

'Ma'am?'

'These demons are to be given a rest cycle. They are not to work twenty-four hours a day. Stone.'

'Ma'am?' the stone said.

'Contact the Blue Dragon and tell him thank you for

these demon staff and I'll be keeping them until I can find replacement IT staff. It could take a while.'

I need them back, the Dragon said into my head.

'Tell the Dragon: no, he doesn't. I'll be keeping them, and thank you.'

The Dragon sighed. *Very well, if you must.*

'I will ensure that you won't be penalised for staying here,' I said to the demons. 'And if you like working for me I'll probably buy you off him.'

The demons shared a look, then turned back to me. 'Did you say a rest cycle?' one of them said.

'At least five hours in every twenty-four, and no cheating,' I said.

The demons shared another glance, then looked at Edwin.

'She means it,' he said. 'You will rest. You will be treated fairly and with compassion here.'

I went up to my office and sagged when I saw Lieutenant Cheung waiting for me next to Yi Hao's desk.

I nodded to him. 'I'll be with you in a moment.'

I waved Yi Hao into my office. When she was inside I closed the door. 'What the *hell* is he doing here?'

'He came to speak to you, ma'am.'

'Did he see anything?'

She stood wide-eyed and didn't reply.

'He's an ordinary human policeman. He has no idea what goes on here. If he finds out anything, we'll be in serious trouble with the Earthly authorities. Get a Celestial up here to act as gatekeeper to stop any weirdness from happening in front of him.' I dropped my handbag behind the desk. 'Okay, let's bring him in and be nice to him.'

Yi Hao opened the office door and nodded to Cheung. 'Miss Donahoe will see you now.'

Cheung came in and sat on the other side of the desk, then leaned on it and glared at me. 'What is going on here? This is supposed to be an office building.'

'It is,' I said.

'I saw a group of people wearing martial arts uniforms and carrying *swords* just five minutes ago in the lift.'

'We provide casting for kung fu movies.'

He leaned back, still impaling me on his glare. 'Exactly what business is this company involved in?'

'No, no, no, you can't go in!' a couple of voices shouted outside.

The door flew open and the Tiger strode in in True Form, so large he filled up the doorway.

'What the *fuck*, Emma! *Nobody* tells me where I can and can't go,' he said, then saw the policeman. 'Hi.'

Cheung bounced to his feet and ran backwards to the wall, where he cowered, his mouth open in a silent scream.

I tapped the stone. 'Damage control.'

'On it,' the stone said. 'Tiger, information coming your way.'

The Tiger changed to human form. 'I see.' He strode to the policeman, who quailed with fear; the Tiger was still twenty centimetres taller than him in human form. The Tiger put his hands on Cheung's face. 'How much do you want wiped?'

'Absolute minimum!' I said. 'The Jade Emperor's forbidden me from wiping people's minds. We were doing it too much when Simone was small.'

'He may have stopped you but he never stopped me,' the Tiger said. 'Wow, this guy has it in for you.

He's convinced you killed Ah Wu and Michelle. Nasty piece of work.' He dropped his head slightly, staring into Cheung's eyes. 'Do you want me to remove his drive to pursue you as well?'

'No. Just remove his memory of your True Form. I'll do the rest; I need to deal with this cleanly. If anyone involved in the case starts showing with amnesia, they're going to suspect we drug them and then we'll *really* have the authorities down on us.'

'Okay,' the Tiger said, concentrating. 'Damn, haven't done anything this fiddly in a while. Human heads are so ugly, so full of shit. Okay, he only saw me as human. He never saw the students with the weapons; as far as he's concerned, this is an ordinary office building.' He glanced up at me, his hands still on the mesmerised Cheung's face. 'Need anything else taken out?'

'I can take it from there,' I said.

'You got it.'

The Tiger released Cheung, who fell to sit in the visitors' chair, his face blank. He shook his head and looked from the Tiger to me. 'Where was I?'

'You were telling Miss Donahoe that you don't have any evidence of foul play on the boat and that it'll be a verdict of death by misadventure,' the Tiger growled. 'And you were about to leave so she can get on with her job of managing her stepdaughter's inheritance, which she happens to be doing extremely well.'

'No,' Cheung said. 'There is more to this case. I wanted the documents relating to the ownership of the boat, please, Miss Donahoe, and all the records of maintenance.'

'They've raised the boat, haven't they?' the Tiger said. 'The gas oven had exploded?'

Tell the Tiger to butt out, I said to the stone, and the Tiger glared at me.

'The boat has been raised. We wish to investigate further,' Cheung said.

Good, that means they haven't found anything and he's just fishing, the Tiger said. *Need some legal assistance? I have a few wives who would tear him to shreds in the courtroom.*

I shook my head without looking away from Cheung.

'Suit yourself,' the Tiger said. 'I'll wait for you out there.'

'I'll provide you with all the documentation as soon as my staff find it,' I said. 'Would you like to wait for it here or have us send it down to you?'

He took a business-card holder out of his jacket pocket, slipped out a card and stood to hold it out to me over the desk with one hand. 'Here's the location of my office; have them send it there by courier, if you could.'

I didn't miss the insult of the single-handed business card. 'I will. Is there anything else?'

He put the card holder away. 'I think we're done here.'

I went around the desk and held the already open door. 'I'll have those documents to you as soon as I can.'

He nodded sharply to me and went out.

The Tiger came back in. 'You need to get this demon stuff out of you so you can move your operations to the Celestial and not have to worry about this bullshit any more.'

'I need a spacesuit so I can go ask Nu Wa to clear it from me. A tiger I know is supposed to be making me one.'

'That's why I'm here,' he said. 'Come and check it out.'

I poked my head out the office door. 'How much really urgent stuff do I have in my in-tray?' I asked Yi Hao.

'Only two or three are of Earth-shattering importance, and they can wait a few hours,' Yi Hao said. 'You were supposed to be gone a week so everybody's holding back until then. You'll have a torrent of life-or-death urgent emails in four days.'

I turned to the Tiger. 'Let's go take a look.'

CHAPTER 17

The Tiger drove us himself in an open-top jeep. In snake form I took up most of the back seat. The road ended and we bumped across the desert, a thick plume of red dust following us.

'This looks like Six's bunker,' I said as we approached a rectangular red building half-buried in the desert gravel. 'Except bigger.'

'Cheapest configuration to build if you're going for a bunker,' the Tiger said loudly over the roar of the engine. 'Easy to secure as well: only one entrance, keep it heavily guarded, you're damn near impregnable.'

'So why did Six have two entrances, with the back one unsecured?' I said.

'What was behind the bunker?'

I remembered the configuration. 'Nothing. Just a blank wall.'

'So you had to go around the front to get to the back?'

'Yeah.'

'Then no need to guard the back — unless people are flying in, in which case you're a fucking idiot.'

'That's how we got in. But he didn't strike me as that stupid,' I said.

'Well, he's dead now, so you'll never know why he left his back door wide open with a "come on in and visit" sign over it. Maybe he just liked it up the ass.'

'You never change, do you?'

'Nope.'

He slid the jeep sideways in the gravel at the front of the bunker, making me lose my grip on the back seat and crash my head painfully into the car door. 'You've never been here before, have you?' He took his hands off the steering wheel and rubbed them together. 'This is going to be fun.'

He opened the door for me and I slithered out, my snout sore. I really wanted to rub it to make it feel better; not having hands was a royal pain sometimes. He led me to the entrance, which was guarded by two of his sons in full desert camouflage commando uniform, carrying automatic weapons and wearing sword belts.

'Guns?' I said.

'Just in case,' the Tiger said, nodding to the guards. 'Guns may not work on demons, but you can never be too careful.'

The bunker was set into the ground so only about a metre of it protruded from the red gravel. The Tiger held out one hand and the wall disappeared, revealing a metre-wide stairway leading down inside the building.

'Have you ever been visited here by anything other than demons?' I said.

'I've been ordered by the Celestial not to share that information.'

'Good God, a Celestial tried to break in,' I said with disbelief.

'I'm sorry, ma'am, not allowed to say.'

'Is what you have in here so damn good that a Celestial would try to break in?' I said.

He smiled and held his hand out towards the stainless-steel door at the end of the narrow corridor. 'Oh, yes.'

The door unlocked with a hiss of escaping air; the building had a positive pressure seal, with filtered air being constantly blown inside it. The pressure build-up meant that air would always travel out rather than in, and dust and gas wouldn't enter the building. The door swung open; in cross-section it was fifteen centimetres thick with three twenty-centimetre-wide bars that slid into the wall.

The Tiger gestured for me to enter. 'Ma'am.'

We walked into a corridor that ran the width of the building and turned a corner at each end. The walls and floor were plain grey concrete with neon lighting above. I stopped and looked left and right. The resemblance was uncanny.

'What?' the Tiger said.

I looked up and down the hallway again. 'Do you have the same architect as Demon Prince Six?'

He raised one hand and gestured along the corridor. 'Large central work areas surrounded by access corridors that are also buffers between the work areas and the outside as an extra precaution. It's just common sense that if you're going to make a building where you're doing the occasional dangerous experiment, you build it like this.'

I thought about it, then nodded. 'I see your point. So what sort of dangerous experiments are you doing?'

He walked left down the corridor and I followed him. 'How about laser weaponry?'

'No such thing,' I said.

'We've done it. Ineffective against demons so we're not pursuing it.'

'Don't you *dare* sell that technology on the Earthly!'

'Of course not.' He grinned over his shoulder at me. 'Wouldn't even sell it to the Dragon — pissed him off most mightily.'

'Good,' I said.

We turned right, walked about ten metres and arrived at double doors with another pair of guards posted on either side. The guards presented their weapons when the Tiger nodded to them, then pushed the doors open for us. The room held benches, stools and large whiteboards. The benches were clear of any apparatus, but the whiteboards were covered in Chinese characters, English words and scribbled diagrams. A group of people sitting on stools in a circle in one corner of the room were having a discussion and making notes on clipboards.

'Emperor present!' one of the guards said loudly behind us.

The workers quickly scrambled off their stools and fell to one knee with their heads bowed.

'You may rise,' the Tiger said, and we approached them. 'This is Lady Emma. Anyone got a snake phobia?'

The staff stared at me wide-eyed, but nobody moved. One woman actually smiled at me.

'Good,' the Tiger said. He pulled himself onto one of the stools. 'This was a brainstorming session?' he said.

The group nodded.

'Result?'

They all shared a look, then shrugged.

An older woman raised her clipboard. 'Can't get the laser to destroy demons. They seem to be completely immune, just as they are to guns. We've tried making

243

the beam hotter, but that just melts the equipment and it's still not hot enough to hurt the demons. It's a dead end, my Lord.'

The Tiger crossed his legs on the stool, relaxed. 'How about we make a laser cannon about three hundred metres long and point it at the Dragon's floating palace? Would it bring it down?'

The woman scribbled some figures on her clipboard, showed it to a colleague and a quiet discussion broke out. The woman nodded. 'Yes, it would go down in flames.'

The Tiger leaned back. 'What a delightful idea.'

'Only if the Dragon's in it, sir,' she said with a small smile.

The Tiger hopped off the stool. 'Clear up the laser, secure-store the records, destroy the weapons and take a two-week vacation, all of you. When you come back you're reassigned. Dismissed.'

The staff fell to one knee again, then set about their work. The Tiger led me out of the room and we turned right. A bank of four industrial-sized lifts, large enough to take a truck, sat in the wall to our left.

'Car park's in the third basement,' the Tiger said. 'Hidden entrance about three hundred metres away.' He pushed the button for the lift and then took us down to basement two. 'Spacesuits are right down the bottom; there's no chance of them exploding and needing to be ejected quickly.'

'How often are things ejected because they're going to explode?' I said.

The Tiger crossed his arms and leaned against the lift wall. 'Oh, once every couple of months.'

'Funny thing,' I said, 'I never need to eject anything that's about to explode from my research facility.'

He grinned down at me. 'That's because your research facility is old-fashioned and boring. Just like its master.'

I nodded my serpent head. 'You have a point.'

The basement had a similar floor plan: a corridor running the circumference of the building and rooms in the middle. The Tiger led me into the first room, which was obviously where the spacesuits were manufactured. Two enormous fabric-cutting tables stood at one end; the robotic arms suspended above them held laser cutting tools. There were three sewing machines on tables to one side, and an arc welder, grinder and a blowtorch in one corner.

The Tiger gestured for me to follow him through double doors to the next room, which was the fitting room. My spacesuit — a long white cloth tube with a glass fishbowl helmet at the front — sat on a work table with staff fussing around it.

When the staff saw us, they fell to one knee then quickly rose. The Tiger guided me over to the table and I raised my head to examine the suit.

'Pleased to meet you, ma'am,' one of the scientists said. 'This is it. The major problem you will have when you're up that high is pressure — well, lack of it. Without the pressure of the air on your body, you'll balloon out, which will kill you.'

'Lack of oxygen will kill me first though,' I said.

'True. We didn't have to worry so much about the issue of you generating heat, because you're cold-blooded. We're really not sure how this will affect the design of the suit. Spacesuits for humans have a cooling system because heat builds up inside and isn't released into the vacuum of space.'

'We have two options,' another scientist said. 'A hard suit, or a soft suit like this one on the table.

Normally, suits for humans have a hard, fibreglass upper-body section that holds all the electricals, and the rest of it is soft. With you, we couldn't make any of it hard, so it's a hundred per cent soft suit.'

'We tried to make something out of the new technology we've been researching,' another said. 'Where only the head part has oxygen sent through it; the rest is pressurised by pressure stockings and no oxygen is sent in.'

'Would being without oxygen damage the body tissue?' I said.

'Doesn't do any damage to be in the water for a reasonable amount of time,' he said. 'Being without air is similar. As long as there's pressure to keep the tissues intact, it should be fine.'

'Beside the point though, because the elastic pressure suit isn't robust enough yet,' a third staff member said. 'So back to this soft suit.'

'It looks like a bunch of arm and leg pieces joined together with metal rings,' I said.

The staff shared a look.

'It is. Making pieces to fit from scratch takes a couple of months,' the Tiger said. 'Putting these together took a couple of days.'

'It has metal ring joints between the soft fabric to allow you to move,' another scientist said. 'Whether or not you will actually be able to move in it is another matter.'

'Would you like to try it on, ma'am?' the first scientist said.

'All right,' I said.

'We'd appreciate it if you could stretch out full-length on the table. That way we can see if we have enough pieces.'

'What about life support?' I said.

'That's an issue we haven't dealt with yet. We may have to add a hard central core to attach it to.'

'I doubt I'll be able to move in something like that,' I said.

'Grow legs,' the Tiger said.

I put my chin on the table, then pushed my head forward so I was able to slither up onto it. I stretched out alongside the suit feeling unpleasantly exposed.

One of the Tiger's staff pulled out a tape measure and measured me. There was a soft discussion, then someone began to shuffle around in the equipment boxes.

'Need a couple more pieces,' the Tiger said. 'Can you make yourself smaller?'

'Not comfortably,' I said.

'Find any?' the Tiger called to the woman who was digging around in the boxes.

'Got a couple, they can go on the tail end,' she called back. She returned with a few more arm pieces. 'Perfect. Let's try it for fit without the under suit.'

They unlatched the pieces and slid them along my body from my tail to my head, locking them together as they went. My body sagged uncomfortably between the rings, but I waited patiently for them to put all the pieces together.

'All the bits except the helmet are in place,' the Tiger said.

'Raise your head, please, ma'am,' one of them said.

I lifted my head, the heavy suit limiting my movement. The rings slid down over my body and clattered together at my tail, leaving me uncovered.

'We need to put the helmet on to make it stay put,' one of the staff said.

The Tiger raised one hand to lift me into the air and I glided off the table onto the floor. One staff member held the helmet while the others gently shifted the rings back up towards my head. I helped them as much as I could. When all the rings were back in place, they put the helmet on my head and locked the rings. I was enclosed in fabric, the helmet just millimetres from the end of my snout.

'This is very claustrophobic,' I said.

Someone attached a hose to the side of the suit and stale-smelling cool air entered the helmet.

'Try to move,' the Tiger said.

The rings and the friction from the fabric made movement possible only with a massive amount of effort. I moved my body from side to side as I normally would, but only every second or third movement gripped the ground enough to push me forward. I managed to cross the room, then stopped to rest, dropping my head and panting.

'Is it that hard?' one of them said.

I nodded.

'Well, she won't be in microgravity so this obviously won't work,' the Tiger said. 'Time for plan B.'

He raised me onto the table again and the staff unlocked the rings, releasing me into the extremely fresh air of the room.

'What's plan B?' I said as I slithered off the table and onto the floor. The rings had bruised me and movement was uncomfortable, but the discomfort would disappear as soon as I changed back to human form.

'A hard suit with wheels, like a mobility chair,' the Tiger said.

I hesitated a moment, then said, 'Make sure it has one of those flags on the back.'

'Oh, don't worry, we'll find a suitable bumper sticker,' he said. He nodded to the staff. 'Good job, but it doesn't work. Back to the drawing board.'

'My Lord,' the staff said, and stood quietly waiting to be dismissed.

'Want to see some of the other stuff happening here?' he asked me. 'Come and check out the lab where we have your blood sample. My kids have been having a field day with it, and they want at least a litre more.'

'Have you cloned me yet?'

'Not for want of trying.' He turned to the staff. 'It's late. Start again tomorrow. I'll make the fibreglass foundry available to you.' He winked at one of the women. 'When are you on next, Doriene?'

She blushed. 'Next week, sir.'

He beckoned her towards him. 'Come here, lovely.'

She approached him shyly and he grabbed her around the waist, pulled her in and kissed her long and hard. He released her and she fell back, breathless and bright-eyed.

He grinned at her. 'See you next week, sweetheart.'

'I cannot believe your own wives call you sir,' I grumbled as we went out the double doors and down the corridor to the next room.

The Tiger stopped and crossed his arms over his chest. 'So when you were training with Ali Wu and he was teaching you the arts, you never called him sir? Student to Master?'

I rose on my coils. 'Once we were out in the open about our feelings, no. If I did, he'd correct me.'

He shook his head and turned away. 'Stupid bastard.'

'Up yours, Devil Tiger.'

He turned back to me and spread his hands, irritated. 'What is this thing with the devil tiger? In the last twelve months it seems everybody's saying that! Where did it come from?'

'Lok talks.'

'That dog needs his balls cut off.'

'So, my friend, do you.'

'Humph,' he said, and opened the next set of doors.

This was a pathology lab, with benches holding rows of glass test tubes and chromatic DNA tests. A centrifuge, loaded with more test tubes, spun in one corner.

'One Twenty-Eight's on your case,' the Tiger said.

The son heard us and came out from behind the barrel of an electron microscope. He appeared to be about twenty, but something about him suggested he was much older. He was Chinese, but with a shock of pure white hair and the tawny eyes of his father. He smiled with the same charismatic roguishness and I shook my head.

'You have been cloning,' I said.

'Nope, just the occasional sapling falling not too far from the tree,' the Tiger said.

One Twenty-Eight strode to his father and clasped his arm around his shoulder; he was about twenty centimetres shorter than the Tiger. They shared a brief embrace then turned to me, both grinning the Tiger's little-boy grin.

'Asshole overload,' I said.

They bowed at exactly the same time, their grins not shifting. One Twenty-Eight fell to one knee to me, then jumped up and returned to the centrifuge, beckoning me to join him.

He pressed a button and the unit stopped. He flipped open the lid of one of the chambers and pulled a test tube out with a long pair of callipers. 'This is your blood,' he said, moving the test tube so I could see it more clearly. 'Normally, when you centrifuge human blood, the platelets sink to the bottom as a red layer and the clear plasma fills the rest of the tube. In your case ... well, see for yourself.'

The top half of the test tube contained plasma, the next quarter held red blood cells, but the bottom quarter was black, oily demon essence.

One Twenty-Eight became serious. 'How do you control that?'

'That was after I'd spent some time on the Celestial as a snake,' I said. 'Usually the demon essence is about half.'

He shook his head and returned the test tube to the centrifuge. 'With that much essence in your blood you should change to demon the minute you return to the Earthly. I don't know how you manage.'

'The stone helps me,' I said. 'I also have help from Kwan Yin.'

'Ah,' One Twenty-Eight said, understanding. 'That explains it.'

I couldn't help it; I smiled even though I knew it wasn't a good look. 'You're a scientist. What she does is so far removed from science it doesn't matter.'

'Exactly,' he said. 'I research what I can, and then just accept wonders like her. I let her be her and don't worry about how she does what she does. That's the essence of the Tao.'

'You've attained the Tao, you're an Immortal,' I said with wonder. 'You should be a single-digit son.'

'No, he shouldn't,' the Tiger said.

One Twenty-Eight shook his head. 'It's a long story, but who cares anyway. What I care about is how we can change you back. How long does it take you to reduce from half to a quarter demon essence?'

'Two weeks.'

'So if you stayed on the Celestial for a month, it would vanish completely?'

'No,' I said. 'The process slows down; it reduces by a fraction of its existing amount. It'll go down by half each week. At the end of six weeks, the amount that it reduces by is negligible.'

'You'll never completely remove it if that's the case,' he said.

'And I'll never walk the Celestial Plane as a human.'

'Can you remove it?' the Tiger asked his son.

One Twenty-Eight paused, thoughtful. He opened the canister on the centrifuge, pulled out the test tube containing my blood and studied it again. Then he put it back and shook his head. 'No. Nobody on the Celestial can fix this. The only one who would have even a remote chance is the Demon King himself. He may be able to manipulate the demon essence and clear her blood.' He turned to us. 'Have you tried to negotiate something with him?'

'He wants to impregnate me in exchange,' I said.

One Twenty-Eight sucked in a quick breath. 'Spawn of you and the King? That would be very bad.'

'How bad?' the Tiger said.

'I'm not even considering it, so it doesn't matter how bad!' I snapped.

'Lady Emma's been taught by the Dark Lord himself; he's given her advanced skills in energy control,' One Twenty-Eight said.

'Lot of good it does me with my blood full of shit,' I said irritably. 'I can't do *anything* with energy while I'm in human form.'

'What about serpent form?' One Twenty-Eight said.

I hesitated, then: 'The energy is different.'

'Beside the point, ma'am. Your cauldrons have been sparked and your gates have been opened; this is near impossible in a normal human. You're a powerful demon, I can see that, and you are one step closer to Celestial than anything the King has access to. Spawn from you and the King would have unique skills and an edge over anything else in Hell.'

'Yep, that sounds bad,' the Tiger said.

'He wouldn't spawn anything more powerful than he is,' I said. 'He'd have to be completely stupid to do that. The minute the spawn were aware of their power they'd try to depose him and take his place.'

'I know. It's an interesting dilemma,' One Twenty-Eight said. 'I'd love to know what he really wants out of this; it's possible he doesn't want your spawn at all. He's always been exceptionally devious in his dealings.'

'His word is good,' I said, protesting.

'Doesn't stop him from being exceptionally devious,' One Twenty-Eight repeated.

'Keep at it, find a way,' the Tiger said. He turned to the DNA tests on the counters. 'Anything show up on these?'

'Nothing at all,' One Twenty-Eight said. 'The technology isn't advanced enough for us to do a general search without knowing specifically what we're looking for. It looks normal. Normal human DNA.'

'Take some now while she's a snake and compare,' the Tiger said.

'I was going to ask that,' One Twenty-Eight said. 'Ma'am, do you mind?'

'If there's any chance of finding out what I am, take as much as you like,' I said; then hesitated when he approached me with a large syringe. 'Whoa, wait a minute — that thing's as big as a milk bottle.'

'You have about three times as much blood in serpent form, ma'am, won't hurt you to take a little more,' he said.

I hissed with pain as he slipped the needle into my skin between the scales then drained me from the back of my neck. 'Hurry up, this hurts.'

He pulled the syringe free, stabbing me with pain again, and wiped the wound with a bandage. 'Thank you, ma'am. If anything shows up I'll be sure to let you know immediately.'

The Tiger spoke without looking at me as we made our way back out. 'If the Demon King is the only one who can fix you, perhaps you should be trying to work something out with him.'

'John said Nu Wa and the Three Purities — remember that,' I said.

'I doubt they'll be able to help you, babe. Nu Wa is an unknown quantity, and the Three Purities are more like an unknowable quantity.'

I stopped and lowered my voice. 'The Demon King offered me a list of possible trades I could make for having the essence cleared.'

'Well, that's a start. What were they?'

I looked around. 'I'll only tell you in a place where nobody can listen in.'

He turned in the other direction and held his hand out. 'This way, ma'am.'

He led me away from the lifts to an empty room at the end of the corridor. It was an operating theatre, complete with a surgery light that, from below, looked like a face.

I turned away. 'I'm not hanging around in here.'

'Wait,' he said, and touched the back of my neck. 'What's the matter?'

'This looks very much like the place where I was injected with demon essence and turned into something that should be destroyed on sight.'

'Well, get over it and tell me what the Demon King offered.'

I struggled with my serpent energy centres to remain calm in that awful place. 'Vow to me you won't pass this information on to anyone. *Anyone*. Understood?'

He hesitated. 'That's awfully dramatic.'

'Promise!'

'I vow I will not share this information with anyone.'

I dropped onto my coils and wound them more comfortably. 'I can't remember all of them, but you'll get the gist of it after only a couple. Your incarceration in a Celestial Jade cage for a thousand years.'

He stepped back slightly. 'Whoa.'

'Either of the other two Winds in a similar situation. The life of Michael MacLaren; actually he asked for his head.'

'Damn!'

'Liu Cheng Rong held on the tenth level for ten thousand years. Or Meredith; either would do.'

'You can stop now —'

'Simone's powers locked out for the rest of her life; reduce her to a normal human girl.'

'That would remove our greatest fighter ...'

'All your wives.'

'No *way*.'

'All the demon armies of the Thirty-Six returned.'

'This is crazy. Are all the options as stupid as that?'

'Yes. And they're all about *other* people suffering to clear me of this. That's why you can't tell anyone; I'm scared someone might actually do what he asks.'

'I'll give him my wives,' the Tiger said, thoughtful. 'Easily done.'

I slithered away and back again. 'And that's exactly why I don't want anyone to know! Do you have any idea what he'll do to them? You can't do that, and that's an order. You are not to offer the Demon King anything in return for my humanity.'

He paused, then: 'Yes, ma'am.'

'Some of your wives are Shen. Some are demons who changed sides. If the Demon King were to get his hands on them — or their children from you — he would have an army to use against us. Don't even think about it.'

'Your words have been trailing my thoughts,' he said, and nodded once, sharply. 'I'll keep it quiet.'

'Good,' I said, and headed towards the lifts again. 'Let's go, I have work to do.'

'Delegate! It will leave you more time for —'

'Eating and screwing. Yes, I know. There are never enough hours in the day for your quota of eating and screwing.'

'You got that one right, baby.'

CHAPTER 18

When I arrived home, I heard a bang from Simone's room then a hissing that sounded as if she was hushing someone. I went to the door and tapped on it. 'Hey, Simone, can I come in?'

'Just a second!' she called urgently, and there was more hushed discussion.

'Do you have a boy in there?' I said. 'Michael, is that you?'

Simone opened the door a crack. 'Nobody here but me.'

'Don't lie to me, Simone, you really suck at it. Who's in there? I'd like to say hello. You don't need to hide anything, sweethear—' I swallowed the word. 'Simone.'

She smiled tightly. 'Nobody here but me. I'm watching a video, that's all.' Then came the sound of water hitting carpet and she squealed. 'No, Freddo, bad boy! Not here on the carpet ...' Her voice changed to a moan. 'Oh damn.'

I opened the door wider and saw the demon foal in the middle of the room, ears back, eyes half-closed, back legs stretched out wide, urinating in a high-pressure stream onto Simone's bedroom carpet. The smell was so strong that my eyes watered.

Simone grabbed Freddo around his middle and they both disappeared.

I went to the kitchen to find Monica. 'You'll never believe what's happened, Monica. Can you get some carpet cleaners up here? We have something of an emergency.'

Fifteen minutes later, Simone returned, cowed and sheepish. She came into the office and sat across the desk from me. 'Sorry, Emma. I'll clean it up, I promise.'

'Him piddling on the carpet was worse than him pooping on it, I swear. The whole flat reeks of it.'

'I'll have the water elementals flush the carpet for me.'

'Carpet cleaners are on their way to steam-clean it.'

She thought for a moment, then concentrated. 'I told Monica to cancel them. I can make the elementals steam.'

'You can't make them soap and deodorise the carpet as well, so tell her to bring the carpet cleaners up,' I said. 'But let your elementals have a try first.'

She grimaced and dropped her head. 'Okay. Sorry, Emma.'

'Why didn't you go to the Celestial to play with him? A Hong Kong flat is not the ideal environment for a young horse.'

'He wanted to see my room.'

I shook my head. 'Can't you find something else to do?'

She swung her chair around in a circle. 'I'm so *bored*! I have nothing else to do!'

'Contact the principal of CH and make an appointment to see him tomorrow with a view to

258

Simone starting school next week,' the stone in my ring said.

'Can I? Will he see me so much earlier than the original appointment?' Simone said.

'Ask him and see,' the stone replied. 'Emma, I've opened a composition email on your desktop with his address in it. Email him and ask him.'

The stone had already written the formal text of the request; all I had to do was fill in the blanks.

> To: Principal, Celestial High
> <RedDragon@CH.com>
> From: Emma Donahoe
> <emmad@newwudang.com.hk>
> Re: Princess Simone Chen of the Northern Heavens
> This honoured servant of the Jade Emperor requests an audience with the honoured Principal of the First Celestial Middle School with regard to the possibility of the early admission of Princess Simone Chen of the Northern Heavens. Your kind consideration of this matter is appreciated.
> Signed and chopped.

'Oh, Emma, you have an appointment next week to collect your chop,' the stone said.

'What?'

'Cool, you'll have your own seal,' Simone said. 'I wonder what they'll put on it.'

'I never ordered this,' I said. 'It's totally unnecessary. As a Westerner I'm not obliged to have one.'

'Too bad,' the stone said. 'Everybody said you should have one, so they had one made and it'll be ready next week.'

Simone leaned on the desk. 'Why do they say "signed and chopped" on emails when there's no signature or chop at all?'

'The words *are* the signature and chop,' the stone said. 'The idea of them.'

Simone leaned back. 'That's stupid.'

I hovered the mouse over the *send* button. 'Are you happy to start at CH earlier?'

She hesitated for a moment, then nodded. 'I have to go anyway. I'm bored as hell here so might as well go sooner.'

'Very well,' I said, and clicked the button.

Simone rose. 'I'll see what I can do about that carpet before the cleaning guys get here. His pee smells *awful*!'

Fifteen minutes later, I received a reply from CH.

To: Emma Donahoe
<emmad@newwudang.com.hk>
   From: Principal, Celestial High
<RedDragon@CH.com>
   Re: Re: Princess Simone Chen of the Northern
Heavens
   This humble servant of the Celestial is gratified
to provide the Princess with an appointment to
discuss the possibility of her early admission into
this institution. If it is suitable for your
Highnesses, a time of nine o'clock Hong Kong
time tomorrow morning has been set aside for you
to put your case to the Principal. This humble
Worthy also requests the attendance of the
Princess's relation Bai Hu, the Esteemed Emperor
of the Western Heavens, to speak on her behalf.
   Signed and chopped.

'Tell Simone,' I said to the stone. 'And ask the Tiger.'

'Tiger says yes,' the stone said. 'Simone says —'

Aww, do I have to wake up early tomorrow? Simone said into my head.

'Back to school, Simone, no more sleeping until lunchtime,' I answered.

I won't be able to sleep at all with this smell in here! I might have to move rooms!

The carpet cleaners showed up early the next morning. Simone had moved into her father's room for the night, and when she came out it was obvious she hadn't slept well. The cleaners shook their heads and tutted at the state of the carpet, then spoke to me with some difficulty in English.

'I understand Cantonese,' Simone said. 'Talk to me, I'll translate.'

The cleaners were obviously relieved. One of them pointed at the floor. 'A steam iron and a hairdryer only made this worse. Is this dog?'

Simone nodded. 'Yes. Big dog.'

They shook their heads. 'We'll try our best, but what you've done to it has made it worse,' the male cleaner said. 'It's gone through to the stuff underneath and dried in there. We may not be able to save it.'

'See what you can do,' I said. They stared at me. 'I can understand, I just can't speak well,' I added.

They nodded, and started plugging in their equipment.

'Uncle Bai's here, it's time to go,' Simone said. She dropped her voice. 'You'll need to change in the living room.'

'Just make sure they don't come out and see me,' I said.

Half an hour later, we materialised on a grassy lawn surrounded by traditional Chinese buildings with green roofs. Students sat on chairs and lounged on the grass around us. A couple of students were battling with swords to one side, a small group of mildly interested spectators watching them.

'Main admin building is this way,' the Tiger said.

A couple of girls rushed over: Sylvie and Precious. They hugged Simone, and Precious jiggled with excitement.

'About time you turned up here,' Sylvie said, swinging Simone's hand with delight. 'I hope we have some classes together.'

'Won't we be in different years?' Simone said.

'No year-grade bullshit at CH,' Precious said in her little-girl voice. 'You work at whatever level you need to. You study until you think you've done enough, then you can go. Most of us are between about twelve and twenty-two or twenty-three, which works out the equivalent of Earthly grades seven to about fourth-year university.' She grinned at Simone. 'Come on, let's show you around.'

'I have to see the principal first,' Simone said with dismay.

'You don't need to sound like that, he's not scary at all,' Sylvie said. 'We'll come too.' She winked at me. 'Nice scales.'

I shook my serpent head and followed them across the lawn to the largest building. Students lounged on the veranda, some of them studying but others working with chi and shen energy. A boy of about sixteen threw a fireball into the ground near a group of girls who were reading on the grass and they squealed and berated him loudly.

We went up onto the veranda, the wood creaking beneath us. The young man who'd thrown the fireball nodded and made way to let us through. The Tiger opened the double doors for us and we went in. There was a standard reception desk inside, with an elderly, scraggly-bearded Chinese man sitting behind it. He grinned when he saw us.

'Oh, the daughter of Xuan Tian, welcome, madam.' He saluted me. 'Heavenly General.' He nodded to the Tiger. 'Emperor. The principal is on his way.'

'Your honoured name, sir?' I said, and added silently to the stone, *This isn't the principal himself trying us out, is it?*

Nah, this is the receptionist, he's been doing this forever, the stone said.

'I am Mr Leung, and I am pleased to make your acquaintance,' the receptionist said. He brightened. 'Ah, here comes Lord Hong now.'

A brilliant red dragon, his fins and tail the same colour as his crimson scales, flew in the door and landed lightly on his back legs just inside. As his feet touched down, he changed to a good-looking young Chinese man of about twenty-five with long red hair, wearing a pair of khaki chino shorts, an olive T-shirt and scruffy sandals. He saluted around us and spread his arms to welcome Simone. 'About time you got here, missy. The Tiger's sons seriously need taking down a peg or two by one of the weakling females that they all despise, and you are the perfect young woman to do it.' He raised his hand to high-five her and she stared at him with wonder.

He changed his hand to a fist. 'Fist bump? No?' He held his hand out for her to shake it. 'How about this?'

She shook his hand. 'Sorry, I'm just a bit ...'

'Shell-shocked. I understand.' He waved us towards the inner door. 'Come on in, let's see what we can do about the removal of shell-shock and the insertion of skills, knowledge and judgement.' He turned to Sylvie and Precious. 'You two troublemakers can leave us now. I'll let you show Simone where the food is later. Does that suit?'

'Sure, Hongie,' Sylvie said, and she and Precious went out.

The principal ushered us into his spacious office. I stopped when I saw it. 'You sure you're a dragon and not a turtle Shen?' I said.

He turned, confused. 'No, I'm one hundred per cent dragon. Why do you ask?'

'Oh, nothing,' I said, and slithered up onto one of the visitors' chairs next to a desk so messy it rivalled John's. Files and open books littered the floor, and a stack of papers on a sideboard appeared precariously close to falling.

Simone pointed at the pile of papers. 'Wouldn't it just be easier to sort them out rather than holding them up by magic?'

'They're not being held up by magic,' the principal said. 'There's no such thing as magic, that's for the realm of fantasy books.'

'Energy then,' Simone said.

'Would you say magic again if someone asked you what was holding them up? Someone other than me?' the principal said.

'Probably,' Simone said, obviously wondering where this was going.

'Then why did you back down?' he said with enthusiasm. 'If you want to use the word "magic", who's going to stop you?'

'You?' Simone said.

'Never,' he said with finality. 'No need to fold up like that if people disagree with you! Stick to your guns, Simone.'

He glanced at the Tiger. 'Tiger, I have been trying to arrange a parent–teacher meeting with you for about six weeks. At least three of your sons are borderline uncontrollable, and two of your daughters are —' He bit off what he was about to say. 'Of a similar nature. Discipline at school is ineffective if it's not backed up at home. You need to do something about these kids!'

The Tiger put his hand on the table. 'And I've been telling you for a hundred and fifty years now that I have nothing to do with the raising of my sons beyond making sure they're fed and housed. If you want to discuss their behaviour, talk to their mothers.'

'They need a strong father figure in their lives,' the principal said with exasperation.

The Tiger leaned over the desk and glared at him. 'I'm Emperor of a quarter of fucking Heaven, boyo. You don't get much stronger than me.'

'Do something about their behaviour or you'll be getting them back.'

The Tiger hesitated for a moment, then said, 'Okay.'

'Oh! I nearly forgot,' the principal said. 'Do you mind if we invite Three One Five in to do some postgraduate honours work? He has an Earthly degree, and I'd really like to top that off with some Celestial polishing.'

'Go right ahead,' the Tiger said. He gestured towards Simone. 'Please accept my beloved niece as a student in your institution. She is brave, smart and talented.'

'I will be honoured to accept her, and will endeavour to do my best to instruct her in the ways of the Celestial,' the principal said. 'Now.' He smiled at Simone. 'Year Ten on the Earthly, right? But no Shen-style training whatsoever?'

'That's right,' Simone said, her voice small.

'Not a problem. You join whichever classes you're interested in. If you have to go off and fight demons or something that's fine. Attend when you can, learn what you want. At the end of it I'll have you back in here and throw you a few really pointless koan to prove that you've either learned wisdom or how to fake it really well.' He spread his hands. 'Any questions?'

'School hours?' I said.

'Whatever Simone chooses. Classes are held between 11 am and 8 pm.'

'That's a late start,' I said.

'Mornings suck and should be banned,' the principal said with feeling. 'Particularly when you've been up gaming all night.'

Simone stared at him.

'There's a kitchen, there's food; I can give you the tour. There are training rooms for combat in both energy and weapons. You can learn maths, languages, science, art, weapons, poisons, equestrian, summoning, dancing, alchemy, calligraphy and advanced demon-handling techniques. We have an extensive library of both fiction and non-fiction, but of course being a dragon I have banned all works by Anne McCaffrey. All you have to do is work out what you want to learn.'

'Equestrian?' Simone said. 'You have horses here?'

'You can bring your own if you want,' he said.

'Even if he's half-demon?'

'Especially if he's half-demon; we can cater for his particular needs.'

'The Red Phoenix said that you have evaluations to see what each student is capable of,' Simone said.

'Yes, it's part of the orientation. We show you around, and use the evaluation to see exactly how scared of you we need to be.'

'Can you tell me if I'm Immortal like my father?'

I looked at Simone. She'd never brought this topic up before.

'No,' the principal said. 'The only way you can find out if you're Immortal is by being examined by a very large Immortal, or getting killed. I think the first option is way preferable, but that's just me.' He grinned at us all. 'Can I show you around now? I love showing off my little school! It's so *cute*!'

They rose and I slid off my chair.

'I hear you expanded the demon-training centre,' the Tiger said as we went out.

'We now do advanced demon-spotting as well as standard binding and controlling,' the principal said. 'As Lady Emma can attest, demon copies are showing up damn near everywhere and we need everybody able to identify them.'

'After this I'm heading down to my own Academy to check the copies that Ronnie Wong has identified,' I said. 'Apparently three demon copies slipped straight through our testing process.'

The principal stopped. 'That is very bad news.' He brightened. 'Can I borrow Ronnie off you for a couple of hours? He can teach the kids how to spot them.'

'No,' I said. 'But I can give you his mobile number and you can ask him yourself. He's a free agent; I don't own him.'

'Wonderful! I've been trying to contact him for a while now and he's been carefully avoiding me. If I have his mobile, I can make his life complete hell until he does what I ask.'

I stopped. 'I'm not so sure I want to give you his number now. Let me talk to him first.'

The principal smiled broadly. 'Go right ahead. I'd love to hear what he has to say.'

I looked around. 'Where's Simone?'

The principal concentrated for a moment. 'Sylvie and Precious are showing her around.' He shrugged. 'Gee, I wanted to do that. I'll have to catch up with them and drag them off her. I *like* showing people around.' He disappeared.

Go back down, I'm fine. I'll see you later, Simone said into my head.

'You sure?' I said, and the Tiger relayed for me.

Yeah, this place is way cool! See you at dinner. Should I do poisons or showjumping?

'Both,' the Tiger said. 'I'd like to see you give my kids a run for their money, and being able to clear any sort of poison from yourself or others is a valuable skill.'

Oh, okay, Simone said. *Talk to you later. I have my phone so you can call me anytime — and they're not banned here! How cool is that?*

'I'll take you back down,' the Tiger said to me. 'Where do you want me to drop you?'

'The Academy. Ronnie's there with the copies.'

'I want to see them too, if I may, ma'am,' he said.

'I think we need as many people as possible to see them,' I said. 'The fact that they made it past the Celestial Masters of Wudang is very disturbing indeed.'

CHAPTER 19

The demon copies were being held in a cell at the far end of the armoury floor, as far from any sensitive areas as possible. They sat side by side on the bed holding each other, obviously terrified. One of them was Apple, my second-year energy student.

'Apple's not a demon; I had a class with her last week,' I said.

Liu pulled me back out of earshot. 'Apple killed one of the human IT guys with a blast of black energy. She has no recollection of doing it.' He dropped his head and shook it. 'I didn't want them to know what they are, but if we're going to have people identifying the demon copies, they have to be instructed on what to look for. That means demonstrating with the demon present. They keep saying that it's a mistake.'

I turned away. 'Those poor kids.'

He didn't let go of my elbow. 'Those poor kids just murdered three of our staff in cold blood. They're demons, Emma. The real Apple, Jeremy and Tanaka are dead, and these things probably killed them.'

Ronnie Wong saw us and approached. 'I'm teaching

as many as possible how to identify them. You'd better come take a look, ma'am.'

'How hard are they to spot?' I said as we drew nearer.

Apple saw me and jumped up to grab the bars. 'Oh, thank God. Lady Emma, please tell everybody that I'm not a demon. You know me, I wouldn't hurt anyone! Please let me out.'

'Apple, please put your hand through the bars,' Ronnie said.

Apple dropped her head, grimaced and put her hand through as asked.

'Don't hurt her!' I said quickly.

'I wouldn't dream of it,' Ronnie said.

He nodded to Liu, who touched Apple's hand. It rippled the same way the demons had when Simone touched them in Paris all that time ago.

'That's the tell. Touch them with shen energy and they do that,' Ronnie said.

'It's an illusion, ma'am, that's not me at all,' Apple said. She moved closer to me, obviously desperate. 'It's a trick! I've been framed. I'm not a demon, I'm Apple, from Chai Wan. You know me!' Her voice changed to sobs. 'Let me out, don't kill me, I'm not a demon, let me *go*!' She reached out to me, her hand waving through the bars, and I stepped back out of her reach. 'Touch me, Emma, see I'm not a demon! Touch me!' She waved her hand desperately at me. 'Touch me!' She screeched the words, higher and more frantic. 'Touch me! Touch me!'

'Back up, Emma, she may be able to shape shift,' Ronnie said, as Apple's hand grew longer towards me. 'I think it would be very bad if she touched you.'

Apple roared with frustration, slammed her hand on the bars, and fell to sit next to the other two. 'All you have to do is touch me and you'll see that I'm not a demon,' she sobbed.

'Is she telling the truth?' I said.

Ronnie grimaced. 'Yes, she's telling the truth. She thinks she's human. They all do.'

'It's a frame-up. You have to find out who did this to us,' Apple said, weeping on the floor. 'You *know* me, ma'am, you know I wouldn't do anything like this. We have to find out who really killed Master Gold.'

Ronnie guided me back down the corridor, followed by Liu. The Tiger remained with the demons, studying them carefully.

'But I had Apple in an energy class last week!' I said. 'She generated chi; I saw it. How could demons do that?'

'It wasn't chi, it was demon essence,' Ronnie said. 'Just like you can generate black chi that looks like demon essence, they can generate gold demon essence that looks like chi. Never seen anything like it; had me completely fooled at first, and stopped me from identifying them for a while.'

'So even if they generate what looks like chi, they could still be demons,' I said. 'That was one of the ways we tested people before.'

'We're in lockdown,' Liu said. 'We've taught five or six of the most senior Masters to check for them, and we're going through the floors one at a time. They have to be Immortals to wield shen on the Earthly, so the testing is taking some time. So far no other demons have turned up.'

'These things are very advanced. Almost undetectable,' Ronnie said. 'I wouldn't be surprised if whoever made them has only made a few.' He turned to me. 'But why reveal them now, and just to damage your computer system? You'll have it backed up again in a few days. Showing his hand for such a small price seems pointless.'

'Gold found something that would give us a lead to where the Geek is making the fake elementals,' I said.

'Oh,' he said, eyes wide. 'And they shut it down and killed Gold. That gave them two weeks' drop on you.'

Liu froze for a moment. 'Found another one. Two more. They're being brought down.' He inhaled sharply. 'Emma, your *secretary* was one of them.'

'Yi Hao?' I said, horrified. 'No! She can't be a copy, she's a demon already. They've made a mistake!'

'Where's the other demon you brought back from One Two Two's nest?' Liu said.

'Uh ...' I hesitated, trying to remember. 'She's been through a lot of jobs, trying to find the one that suited her best. She wanted to be close to me. As soon as something opened up, we were going to move her into my office.'

'A trap was being laid all around you,' Ronnie said. 'I'm surprised they didn't spring it.'

'Contact Lok, tell him about Er Hao. She's in the New Folly,' I said.

Liu grimaced. 'I have to go over there and make sure everyone's safe.' He touched my arm. 'Don't go near them!'

I turned away as he disappeared and looked back at the demon copies. 'They were like a ring closing in on me. A sleeping asset, staying hidden amongst us and waiting for the order to strike. But their masters spent them on Gold instead of me. Whatever Gold had discovered was going to lead us to them. As soon as he's back, we'll have them.'

I strode to the Tiger. 'Contact the Courts for me, tell

them the situation. These demon sleepers have been spent to take Gold out, and we need him, Zara and Calcite back *now* to lead us to the demon that's making the elementals — and probably through that one to the one that made these copies. They're working together. Tell them.'

The Tiger nodded and concentrated. 'They'll be back tomorrow.'

'Get me Michael,' I said.

The stone didn't reply and I tapped it.

'What?'

'Get me Michael, stone.'

'I'll get him,' the Tiger said. 'Why him?'

I gestured around me. 'The Masters are busy isolating the demons; Ronnie's showing everybody how to identify them; you're going to piss off in about two seconds flat, I know you. Simone shouldn't have to see what happens next. And I need a guard because I'm going to the computer room.'

Michael appeared next to his father; he was dressed in a grey business suit. 'Ma'am?'

'Michael, I need you to guard me. Are you free to do it?'

He grimaced. 'I was at work. How long do you need me for?'

'For the rest of the day. Go back, I'll get someone else,' I said.

'No, no, I have nothing on right now.' He pulled out a mobile phone. 'Hello, Doris? This is Michael. I've been called out of the office by one of my clients, he needs advice on his portfolio. Mr Chen. Probably won't be more than a couple of hours, but I'll let you know.' He snapped the phone shut, concentrated and changed his clothes to the white and gold of the Tiger's

Horsemen. He raised one hand and his sword appeared in it. 'What do you need me for?'

'To guard my back. We have a demon infiltration,' I said. 'Apple, stand up. That's an order.'

Apple wiped her nose on her sleeve and rose. 'I'm not a demon, ma'am.'

'Load your hand with shen energy and touch hers,' I said to Michael.

She put her hand through the bars for him and he touched it, then gasped when he saw the way she reacted.

'That is how the demon copies react when touched with shen energy,' I said.

'I'm not a demon copy!' Apple said, becoming desperate again.

I moved slightly closer to the bars, but still out of reach. 'Apple, stay here, and stay calm. I won't let anybody hurt you. I promise. Okay?'

She nodded, and went to sit on the bed and hold the other two demons. 'I trust you, ma'am.'

'With me, Michael, we're going to the computer room,' I said.

'I'll stay here,' the Tiger said. 'Do you mind if I bring some of my people through to have a look?'

'Go right ahead.'

The demons we'd borrowed from the Dragon were working in the server room.

'Test them first,' I said. 'Demons, stay still for a moment.'

Michael touched each of the demons in turn, then shook his head. 'Clear.'

'Drop what you're doing and focus on getting back the data that Gold and the other two stones were working on,' I said to the demons. 'We need that data urgently; the demon will move and we'll lose him otherwise.'

'Understood, ma'am,' one of the demons said, and moved to eject the tape they had in the tape drive and find another to use.

'How long to get that data back up?' I said.

'Forty-eight hours if we work straight through,' the second demon said.

I hesitated for a moment, then: 'I wouldn't normally ask you guys for this, but I'm requesting it now. This isn't an order, you can say no ... Oh, hell.' They couldn't say no, not even to a request. Either I told them or I didn't. 'I need you to work twenty-four hours a day without rest on getting this data back. It's absolutely vital that we find out where this demon's nest is.'

'We were doing that anyway, ma'am,' one of them said.

'I will ensure you are rested when we have this data back,' I said. 'Lord Gold will return in the morning to assist you.'

'Very good, ma'am,' they said in robotic unison, and set to work.

I led Michael back down to the armoury. 'Thanks for helping out on such short notice.'

'Not a problem. Sometimes I miss the excitement.'

'We miss you. I'd love to have you back to guard when Leo's unavailable; and with him attaining Immortality that's more and more of the time.'

'Ma'am. Let me think about it.'

We went out of the lift and to the cells to find three more demons had been added to the three already in there. Two of them were Yi Hao and Er Hao; the third was one of the library staff.

'These are all of them,' Liu said.

I nodded to Michael. 'Thanks, Michael, I appreciate your time. Go back to work.'

Michael hesitated. 'Do you mind if I hang around here for the rest of the day? Suddenly this seems way more fun than watching the market.'

'Sure, make yourself at home, you know where everything is,' I said. 'Pop up to Celestial Wudang — it's looking good.'

He saluted me and disappeared.

I crossed my arms over my chest and studied the six demon copies. 'Now what to do with you?'

'You promised you wouldn't hurt me!' Apple cried, desperate. She fell to her knees next to the bars. 'I'm not a demon! I've been framed!'

'Just destroy them,' the Tiger said. 'They're too dangerous to leave alive; they could escape and blend into the Celestial community.'

Yi Hao and Er Hao broke down into tears. They rose in unison and went to Apple, then sat with her on the floor and held her, the three of them together.

The Tiger changed to my form. 'Come and touch me, Apple.'

I quickly backed up. 'Change back, Tiger, don't do this to her.'

Apple looked from me to the Tiger, then her face went blank. She strode to the Tiger, held out her hand and touched his. I backed up even further as she exploded in a mass of demon essence that spread like oil across the floor before it disappeared.

'Anyone else want to touch me?' the Tiger said, holding his hand out to the other five demons. They all jumped up, ready to do it.

'Back off, Tiger. Take your own form, that's an

order,' I said. 'We need to be able to interrogate them.'
He didn't change, so I went to him and thumped his
shoulder. 'I promised that poor girl I wouldn't hurt her.
You've broken my word and I won't forget it. Now
stand down!'

The Tiger grimaced, changed back and moved away
from the cell. The demons looked confused.

Liu appeared between us. 'What's going on? Why
the faces?'

'He just took my form, touched Apple and she
exploded everywhere,' I said.

Liu sucked in his breath. 'They were going to
convert you.'

'He heard me promise the child she wouldn't be
harmed.'

The Tiger spread his hands and grinned his little-boy
grin. 'I confirmed for you that they were trying to
convert you. I also confirmed that the Apple chick was
definitely demon. I did you a favour.'

Three more demons appeared in the cell; cleaning
staff from the Follies.

'These appear to be the last of them,' Liu said. 'Now
the Celestial needs to sweep for them as well.'

'Can they travel to the Celestial Plane or are they
limited to here?' I said.

'There's only one way to find out,' the Tiger said
gruffly, and he and one of the demons disappeared.

'If he doesn't stop doing this I'll have him executed,'
I said.

The Tiger and the demon reappeared and the Tiger
saluted me. 'They can travel to the Celestial Plane. You
don't want these putting all your students at risk,
ma'am, you need to get rid of them. How about I take
them and put them in my demon-research facility, and

residents of the Celestial can come and check out how to spot them?'

'Stone, summon Martin,' I said.

The Tiger gestured with frustration. 'The last thing you need right now is that clumsy moron. You give them to him and they'll escape before they hit the Celestial.'

Martin appeared and fell to one knee before me. 'This humble Shen greets his Empress.'

'Regent, not Empress, stupid!' the Tiger said.

Martin rose and glared at the Tiger with contempt. 'My Lord Devil Tiger, Emperor of the West,' he said with audible venom.

'Share the info, Tiger,' I said.

The Tiger strode to the other end of the corridor. 'Share it yourself. No way I'm touching minds with *that*.'

I gestured towards the demons. 'Martin, these are extremely advanced demon copies, almost undetectable. They're also unaware of their nature; they think they're the original humans. Do we have somewhere in the Northern Heavens where we could hold and study them?'

'Oh God,' Tanaka gasped, and bent double with pain. 'I really am a demon copy, aren't I?'

'It doesn't matter what you are, it matters who you think you are,' I said. 'And I promise none of you will be hurt.'

'Destroy us,' Jeremy said. 'We killed Lord Gold and the IT guys. Gold looked after us from the day we arrived and we killed him.' He rose and strode to the bars. 'Please, kill me now.'

'I gave you my word, Jeremy,' I said. I turned back to Martin. 'Can we hold them in the North?'

278

Martin grimaced. 'The best place would be the Tiger's facility in the West, ma'am,' he said with obvious distaste. 'He has the most advanced demon-research facility in the Heavens, and his army of Horsemen are there all the time. We only have a skeleton staff of guards up in the Northern Heavens with the Thirty-Six constantly being deployed.' He gestured towards the Tiger. 'Give them to him.'

The Tiger came back. 'Well, look at that, the turtle grew a brain.'

'You can have them only if you promise not to destroy them,' I said. 'Don't hurt them.'

'I promise. Even better, when all this is over, you can order my execution, no trouble at all.'

'Done,' I said. I nodded to him. 'Take them. Take care of them. Spread the word on the Celestial.'

The Tiger fell to one knee, saluted me, and he and the demons disappeared.

'By your leave, ma'am,' Martin said, and I nodded to him. He disappeared too.

I headed up to my office. 'I need a new secretary. Where the hell am I going to find one? I don't want to inflict those long hours on a human; a demon would be best.'

'I'll see if one of my kids wants the job,' the stone said. 'Might be one who lives as a human on the Earthly who wouldn't mind the prestige of the position.'

'Prestige? I don't know about that,' I said. 'And thanks.'

I sat down in Yi Hao's chair to go through the in-tray. Only an hour ago she'd been my trusted right hand and now she was gone. At least I'd made the Tiger promise not to destroy her.

Gold, Zara and Calcite returned early the next morning. I met them in the hub room, and found Gold jumping up and down with the two demons in hysterical delight. He came to me, grinning broadly.

'Please keep these demons, ma'am,' he said. 'I know them from when I was bonded to serving the Dragon all that time ago. They're hard workers and he treats them very poorly. Please let them stay.'

'That's already organised,' I said, to a chorus of whoops from the two demons.

Gold touched my arm. 'I appreciate your compassion, my Lady. These demons will work hard for us.'

'Is the data back up? How close were you to finding the demon we want?' I said.

'Another thirty-six hours, ma'am. I'm sorry but the data transfer from tape takes time; it's not a fast backup method but it is reliable and holds a lot of data,' one of the demons said. 'We have to physically run the tape past the reader and we can't do it too fast.'

'We can help,' Gold said, and Zara and Calcite nodded agreement. 'But it is still a slow process reading the tape, so we won't be able to start processing the data again until at least lunchtime tomorrow.'

'How much more time did you need on the original run-through?'

'A pattern was beginning to emerge,' Gold said. 'Not so much showing people all headed to the same place, but they were being channelled through a number of different agencies to some common locations. We were narrowing it down.'

'The web of companies involved is huge and complex,' Zara said. 'But we were definitely getting there.'

'How much longer?'

'We have about six more hours of crunching to do once we have the data back up, so by midnight tomorrow we should have something.'

'Okay.' I sat at one of the terminals. 'Can I help?'

'Yes,' Gold said. He came to me and leaned on the desk. 'Get out and give us room to work.'

I stared at him for a moment, then rose. 'Suit yourself.'

I went up to my office to find the Tiger lying across the doorway.

He rose and stretched. 'We have to stop meeting like this.'

'Out of the way,' I said, grabbing the documents out of Yi Hao's in-tray and jumping over him to get into my office.

'Whoa,' he said as I sailed over his body. 'That was a good three metres, babe. How far can you jump?'

'Dunno, haven't jumped in human form in a long time,' I said. 'Don't have the room here, and on the Celestial I'm a snake and snakes can't jump.'

'Seems like they do sometimes, they move so damn fast,' he said, sauntering into my office and sitting in the middle of the floor. He licked his paw, carefully running his tongue between his toes. 'Your hard suit is ready.'

I flipped through the documents, then waved one hand at him without looking up. 'Give me twenty minutes, there's some important stuff here.'

'You got it,' he said, and sauntered out again, his tail twitching.

'Wait,' I said, looking up. 'Where are you going?'

He grinned his tiger grin. 'Oh, around.'

I glared at him. 'Stay away from my students, and be back here in twenty. Seduce *anyone* and your tail is mine.'

His grin broadened, revealing his huge canines. 'That's Gold's domain, not mine. I don't seduce anyone, I just have them falling all over themselves to marry me.'

'Not my students,' I said. I waved him away again. 'Be back in twenty.'

He bowed over his front legs. 'Ma'am.'

CHAPTER 20

'**I** want to see the demon-research facility first,' I yelled over the roar of the jeep's engine. 'Then look at the suit after. Is that okay?'

The Tiger hit the handbrake and spun the jeep, skidding on the gravel, then took off again in a different direction. I slipped off the seat and slammed into the back of the front seat, then slid across the floor to hit the door tail-first.

'You nearly tipped me out!' I yelled at him.

'You okay?' he shouted.

I pulled myself back up onto the seat. 'Yeah, I'm fine. Just take it easy.'

'You *sure* you can't wear a seatbelt?'

'Nothing to hold,' I said. 'I just slide through.'

'If you got thrown out it would be bad,' he said, slowing down to about a hundred kilometres an hour.

'Thank you,' I said.

We drove back past the Western Palace complex and onto a paved road without guttering that cut through the desert in a completely straight line.

'How far is it?' I said, leaning my head on the back of the front seat.

'Two hundred li, in the foothills of the mountains.'

'I must come back one day and check out the towns in the mountains,' I said. 'I've heard great things about them.'

'You're heading to Kun Lun later anyway,' he said. 'You can use them as stops on the journey.'

I gazed up at the red mountains, their slopes covered with snow. Behind them even higher mountains soared, their jagged tops decorated with glowing plumes of ice where the high-altitude winds swept it into the sunlight.

'It's a long way up,' I said.

'That's why you have the Snakemobile.'

'No way. They're not calling it that.'

'They wanted to fit an MP3 player and have it cycle the *Inspector Gadget* theme.'

'That would drive me nuts.'

'That's the idea.'

Half an hour later we reached the mountains. There was no gentle incline; they rose like a sheer cliff out of the desert. The road turned right and went up a ramp cut into the cliff face, winding like a switchback up the rock. I turned and looked back as we rose, enjoying the view of the desert. The palace complex spread before us, a darker shade of red than the desert, with the desert landscape stretching as far as the eye could see beyond it. Occasionally water glittered between the buildings: the fountains, watercourses and swimming pools of the complex.

'I didn't realise your palace was so big,' I said. 'It's at least five times the size of John's.'

'Smaller than his real palace,' the Tiger said. 'The complex at Wudang. We measured; Wudangshan is slightly larger in area than the Western Palace.'

I turned to him. 'You *measured*? What an incredibly male thing to do!'

'Not the only thing we've measured,' he said, smiling smugly at the steering wheel.

We seemed to be incredibly high up by the time the Tiger drove inland from the cliff onto a flat area. I turned away from the view below to see where we were. A four-storey complex stood on the thickly snow-covered slope before us, with a large paved circular drive. Balconies skirted each floor, and peaked windows gave glimpses of luxurious hotel rooms inside. An indoor pool was visible on the ground floor of one of the wings, leading further into a health and beauty spa.

'This is a ski resort,' I said.

'That it is,' the Tiger said, driving up to the front door where a white-and-gold-liveried footman opened the jeep's doors for us. 'It's for the wives. Full right now with the snow so good; the girls have to take turns coming up.'

'I see,' I said, slithering out of the jeep and looking around. 'Nice.'

He guided me into the reception area. Polished marble covered the floor, enormous candle-lit chandeliers hung from the ceiling, and a Renaissance-period mural covered one wall. Antique chairs and tables were placed around the lobby, giving it a European feel. The staff behind the reception desk bowed to us, smiling.

A few wives sat in their ski outfits in the bar on the other side of reception, chatting over their drinks. They all rose and kneeled when they saw us.

The Tiger led me up some stairs to where a corridor decorated with antique mirrors and dressers spanned the width of the building. The lift lobby was ahead;

inside the lift, the Tiger put his hand over the panel without pressing a button. The doors closed and the lift went down.

We descended for more than three minutes, and I glanced at him. 'We're going all the way back down again.'

'Buffer zone. Some of the demons can be slightly dangerous,' the Tiger said. 'Don't want them scaring the wives.'

The doors opened and we entered an area about four metres wide and two deep, with no other doors or windows. The Tiger held his hand up at the wall and a pair of massive steel doors, like those of a bank vault, appeared. He waved his hand at the doors, the handles spun and they opened.

'How many of your kids can do that?' I said.

'Sixty-seven,' he said. 'I have sixty-seven Immortal progeny. Oh, but sixty-eight can open the doors; one non-Immortal is exceptional and can manipulate metal like an Immortal.'

'Michael,' I said.

'That's the one.' He gestured towards the corridor. 'This way, ma'am.'

'Am I going to be back in time for dinner? This is taking forever.'

'Nearly there,' he said without looking at me.

We walked down the bare concrete corridor, neon lights the only illumination. Every twenty metres or so, we arrived at a heavy steel gate that the Tiger had to open with his metal-manipulation abilities.

'What happens if someone gets stuck down here?' I said.

'If someone's stuck down here then they're a demon,' he said with finality.

The end of the corridor opened out into a train station, with a cable car suspended in front of us in the tunnel. The doors opened as we approached and we boarded.

'No guards?' I said.

'Guards at the sharp end.'

The doors closed and the cable car started with a jerk that nearly made me slide off the seat again.

'You really weren't made for chairs, were you,' the Tiger said with amusement.

'Only slippery ones give me trouble.'

We ascended through the tunnel, the only break in the monotony being the occasional single neon tube attached to the wall, appearing very close to the sides of the car.

'We're going way further up,' the Tiger said, leaning one arm over the back of the chair and looking up the way we were headed. 'At least twice as high as the resort. The floor beneath us is electrified, and the walls have electrified barriers every ten metres.'

'Did you design this?'

He turned to see me. 'One of the wives did. Used to be French Intelligence, knew all the tricks of the trade.' He turned back towards the tunnel. 'Funny how life is sometimes. She designed all of these safety features and died in a car accident in Paris in 1987.'

'Just like Princess Diana?' I said.

'Just like her. Not her, if that's what you were thinking.' He winked at me. 'It was a close thing though.'

'She turned you down?'

He shook his head. 'Nah, I turned her down. Bit too edgy, too brittle. Not my type.'

'I thought they were all your type.'

'You stick your finger down your throat it's all over,' he said. He rose, holding the pole in the centre of the car. 'Here we are. Let me out first; they'll shoot you on sight.'

Two guards, equipped like those at the Tiger's bunker, stood on duty at the cable-car platform. They pointed their guns at the Tiger as he stepped down.

'Help, I'm in trouble, the demon with me is holding me hostage,' the Tiger said. 'I'm not the real White Tiger, I'm a copy.'

The guards nodded and lowered their weapons.

The Tiger gestured with his head. 'Come on out.'

'They'll shoot me after that little speech,' I said.

'That's the code phrase, ma'am,' one of the guards said. 'A copy or someone being held hostage is very unlikely to say that.'

I hesitated, and the Tiger gestured impatiently. 'Come on out, Emma, it's fine.'

'This is Emma?' one of the guards said, and they shared a look. 'Lady Emma, the Dark Lady?'

I slithered out of the cable car. 'That's me. I'm perfectly harmless, I promise. No need to shoot me.'

The guards fell to one knee, then one of them slipped his gun onto his back and approached, falling to one knee again. 'You're a legend, ma'am,' he said with awe. 'I wish I had a book or something to get your autograph. We've heard the stories, and both of us are honoured to meet you.'

The other guard nodded vigorously, still holding his weapon in ready position.

'You wouldn't be able to get my autograph anyway, I can't write in snake form,' I said.

'My Lord, could you arrange for her to send something up through you?' the guard said.

The Tiger hesitated, his expression conflicted, then he nodded. 'If I have to. Now, to your post, soldier.'

The guard grinned broadly, rose, bowed slightly to me and strode back to his post. He unslung his gun and stood on guard again.

'*I* don't have a fucking fan club,' the Tiger grumbled as he led me down the corridor away from the station.

'Neither do I,' I said, following.

'It's on Facebook,' one of the sons said behind me.

I stopped. 'You're kidding.'

The Tiger gestured for me to keep going. 'I thought you wanted this done by dinnertime. And yeah, it's on Facebook.'

'I don't use Facebook.'

'One of your students created it,' he said. 'It has all your comings and goings.'

'That's a breach of security and is going to be removed,' I said.

'Ah, let them have their fun.' He put his hand out to a blank wall at the end of the corridor.

'What does it say if I'm on the Celestial?' I said, becoming concerned.

Another pair of vault doors appeared and the Tiger opened them. 'It says you're on the Celestial. It's not public viewing, don't worry. You have to be approved before you can see it.'

'Wait a minute, you talk like you've seen it,' I said, following him through the doors.

'Oh, I'm your biggest fan,' he said.

We entered a room about three metres to a side. This one had three guards, all armed and ready, as well as a security desk behind a sheet of bulletproof glass.

'Help, I'm in trouble, the demon with me is holding me hostage,' the Tiger said. 'I'm not the real White Tiger, I'm a copy.'

The guards presented arms. 'Sir!'

'You need to change that phrase,' I said.

'It changes once a week, ma'am,' one of the guards said. 'The wording is slightly different each time.'

I nodded my serpent head.

'And if I might say, ma'am, I'm a huge fan,' the guard added. 'Any chance of getting an autograph?'

'I'll get you one,' the Tiger said, exasperated. He took a step back and gestured with his hand. 'We're nearly there.'

The guard at the security desk unlocked the door and the Tiger opened it for us. The corridor on the other side had a marble floor, large chandeliers hanging from the ceiling, and antique European chairs and dressers along the wall.

I looked around. 'We're back where we started.'

'That's deliberate,' the Tiger said. 'Stick close, the corridors are a maze. Deliberately so. They twist, and have a lot of dead ends, to make escape more difficult.'

'So where are my demons?'

'Do you want to check them first, or look at the labs first?'

'My demons.'

'This way.'

He led me down the corridor, turned right, then took a hard left at a T-intersection. We walked for about five metres, then turned right and then left again. Every corridor we went down appeared to be the same length and was decorated with the same furniture, and all had another corridor branching out halfway along.

After about a hundred metres of twisting identical

passages, we went through a set of double vault doors to another security station that appeared very much like the first one we'd gone through. I tasted the air; we were definitely not in the same room.

'Don't do that, it's creepy,' the Tiger said, and the guards raised their weapons. 'Oh, damn, I have to use the code words first, otherwise they'll shoot us.' He put his hands up. 'Help, I'm in trouble, the demon with me is holding me hostage. I'm not the real White Tiger, I'm a copy.'

'Double confirmation, please, sir,' one of the guards said. The Tiger nodded and raised his hands higher. The guard touched each of us in turn, concentrating. He stepped back. 'All clear. Dad was just talking too much again.'

'Sir,' the guard at the station said, and buzzed us through.

'You don't like seeing me taste the air? What, you don't have any serpent wives?' I said.

'I've never had a serpent wife, they freak me out,' the Tiger said. 'Look what that concubine of Ah Wu's got up to — not going to happen to me, I tell you.'

'I researched that,' I said. 'Do you know a good spin doctor?'

'No way of putting a positive spin on that.'

The room on the other side was identical to the reception area of the hotel. A couple of demons in human form lounged in chairs to one side, talking quietly. They looked up and smiled when they saw us.

The Tiger went to the reception desk. 'Let me see the register.'

The woman behind the desk turned the computer monitor so he could see it, and he held one hand against it. The data scrolled over the screen. 'Round up demons 12,209 to 12,216, send them to the conference room.'

The receptionist nodded. 'My Lord.'

'This way,' the Tiger said, and led me up stairs identical to those in the other lobby. A bank of lifts stood on the left; this time he pressed the button for the first floor.

A simple corridor with rooms on either side, similar to a hotel, led to a set of double doors that opened to another similar corridor, but shorter. A busy restaurant operated on the right, where many demons were sitting at tables and eating from a standard human-style buffet. Two doors opened on the left, and the Tiger led me through the further one into a conference room.

'Drink of water or something?' the Tiger said, pouring a glass for himself from a jug on the sideboard.

'Can you do me a favour and put one of the jugs on the floor for me?' I said.

He obliged and I drank carefully from it.

'This would be a good time to head up to the North and talk to them about eating on the Plane,' the Tiger said.

'I need to arrange something before I actually try it,' I said. 'The whole thing is thoroughly freaking me out.'

'The idea of eating food in snake form is too revolting?'

'No.' I sipped some more water, then raised my snout. 'Too tempting.'

The demons entered, guided by a guard wearing a sword and the livery of a Horseman. They stopped when they saw me.

'It's me, Emma,' I said. 'I wanted to make sure you were okay.'

The Tiger didn't move from the sideboard; he gestured towards the table. 'Sit and tell Lady Emma how you're being treated.'

The demons shared a look and sat at the table. I pulled myself onto a chair to speak to them.

'They're treating you well here? I want to make sure that you're being looked after,' I said.

'I miss you, ma'am,' Yi Hao said. She rose and skittered to the sideboard to grab a napkin and blow her nose into it.

'I miss you too, little one,' I said.

'Is there a chance that we're not the same thing?' Er Hao said. 'We were never humans taken and copied. You knew we were demons right from the start.'

'There is a remote chance that you two aren't demon copies,' the Tiger said. 'We'll hold you until we're sure.'

Yi Hao nodded. 'I'll stay here as long as there's any chance I'll put ma'am at risk.'

'What about you, Jeremy? Tanaka? Sellen, Mercy, Lucia?' I said. 'Are you being treated well?'

'It's like a resort, ma'am,' Jeremy said. 'The only difference between this and a luxurious holiday is the guards and the fact we can't go outside.'

'And the regular demonstrations,' Tanaka said, miserable.

'I'm so sorry, Tanaka, it must be so hard for you.'

'I just wish I could call my family,' he said. 'I miss them, and my friends.'

Jeremy shrugged. 'And I miss my girlfriend.'

'You can never go back, you know that,' the Tiger said.

'I'm trying to remember when the changeover happened, when the real Jeremy died,' Jeremy said. 'I

293

have no idea, I'm sorry.' He shook his head. 'What did you tell my girlfriend? That I died?'

'It's not good to give people false hope,' the Tiger said.

Jeremy nodded. 'I understand.' He stared at me, his gaze intense. 'Ma'am … Emma. Can you do me a favour? Can you promise me something?'

'What, Jeremy?'

'Yes, both of us,' Tanaka said. 'Promise us.'

'I can't let you go; you're programmed to obey your demon masters,' I said.

'I'm not asking for that,' Jeremy said. He took a deep breath. 'Ma'am, when the time comes, and we've outlived our usefulness, and nobody else needs to see how to detect us, could you be the one to end it for us?'

'Please,' Tanaka said.

'Why me?' I said.

'Because I think you understand,' Jeremy said.

'I can't do it. In serpent form I can't perform a clean kill. Particularly on a demon; my venom doesn't work. It would be slow, painful and messy. You don't want that. If we do have to end it I want it to be quick for you.'

'I don't want to die,' one of the other three said. 'Please don't kill me.' The other two demons with her echoed her words. 'We don't want to die!'

'She won't destroy you unless you ask for it,' Jeremy said to them. 'Don't worry, you can trust her.'

The three demons subsided. One of them rushed to the sideboard and grabbed a napkin to blow her nose. When she sat back down, the demon next to her wrapped her arm protectively around her shoulder.

'Don't worry, Lucia, nobody will hurt you. Nobody will destroy you,' I said, and she silently nodded a reply. I glanced at Tanaka. 'Unless you ask for it.'

'I don't care whether it's slow or fast, ma'am,' Tanaka said. 'I want it to be you.'

'Me too,' Jeremy said.

'If the time comes then I'll think about it,' I said.

'No, ma'am, I want your word. Please,' Jeremy said. 'I have nothing to look forward to any more. I'm never going to see sunlight again. I'm dead to everybody who knew me. Please, make it be you. You're the only one I really trust.'

'Give your word, please,' Tanaka said.

I dropped my serpent head. 'I give you my word. Jeremy and Tanaka, I promise that if the time comes to end it for you, I will do it.'

Jeremy and Tanaka shared a relieved smile.

'Is there anything you need?' I said.

They both shrugged. 'We're comfortable and cared for,' Jeremy said. 'Don't worry about us; just make sure there are no more killers like us out there.'

'Whoever did this will *pay*,' the Tiger said. 'There haven't been demons who've been unaware of their nature — and then self-aware — in a very long time. The Demon King himself banned the use of self-destructing demons. Believe me, whoever made you is going to regret that you were ever created.'

'Thank you, sir,' Jeremy said. 'But I'm sure that Lady Emma will find and destroy whoever's done this.' He turned to me. 'I trust you.'

'I wish I could be as confident in my abilities as you are,' I said.

'You're the Dark Lady, ma'am, and we've been privileged to have worked with you,' Jeremy said.

'The privilege has been all mine,' I said. 'Now go back and take it easy. I'm going to see what's happening with the research here.'

'Thank you, ma'am,' Jeremy said; he rose, fell to one knee and saluted me. Tanaka saluted me as well.

'Let's go see this lab,' I said to the Tiger.

He led me to another set of double doors. Once we got through them, the change was dramatic: the luxurious, European-style decor gave way to a bare concrete corridor, with another set of steel doors in front of us. He dropped his head and concentrated, and I heard a hiss of air on the other side of the doors. They opened and he guided me through.

'You have a freaking airlock?' I said. 'That's a waste of time; most demons don't need air.'

'True. But a vacuum blows them up nicely,' he said as we walked down the corridor. 'The shell can't hold in the essence and they explode. Very messy.'

'I didn't know,' I said. 'I'll remember that.'

Another set of airlock doors opened at the other end, and the Tiger closed them behind us; I heard hissing again as the chamber was evacuated. He guided me through the next set of doors to another guard station, where he used the code words. We were buzzed through to a two-storey corridor with cells off walkways on our level and the one below and what seemed to be a bottomless pit in the centre. The cells were completely silent, the only sounds the Tiger's boots and my scales as we moved along the metal walkway.

'How far down does it go?' I said.

Immediately the area erupted with deafening howls and shrieks of pain. The Tiger concentrated, a sound like screaming feedback seared through my head and the demons were silent again.

'About four hundred metres,' the Tiger said. 'There's a lift at the end.'

'Are they in pain?'

'No. They're just missing their mommies.'

'How long do you keep them like this?'

'As long as it takes,' he said grimly, and pressed the button for the lift.

'How long have you had this facility?' I said. 'Did John know about it?'

'We designed it together.' Inside the lift he held his hand over the panel. It changed to his Tiger paw and the lift doors closed and we started down. He changed his hand back again. 'It was his idea to start off with, but I had the kids with the brains, so we agreed to build it here.'

'I wonder if he ever regrets the way he brings up his children,' I said, almost to myself. 'They drop the eggs and leave them.'

'No regrets for being what you are. Ever,' he said. 'That is the Way.'

'But only one in a hundred of his children ever come home,' I said. 'Many of them stay reptiles, never aware of who they are. Some of them take human form, but they *still* don't know what they are. They live human lives, with this terrible secret of being a snake or a turtle, and they're never able to truly fulfil their destiny unless we manage to find them.'

'You have your agents out there,' he said. 'You do your best, which is more than he ever did. If they are destined to be found, you will find them.' He shrugged. 'It's in their nature to study the arts, babe; they get it from their father. I think you'd get most of the ones that are worthwhile by monitoring the martial arts schools.'

'Call me babe again and I'll have you executed.'

'You're already having me executed when we're done here.'

'Twice.'

'Cool.' The lift arrived at the bottom with a jerk and the doors opened. 'This is it.'

A group of five scientists in white lab coats, all of them obviously children of the Tiger, stood at the lift doors wearing huge grins and carrying clipboards. Five guards armed with swords stood around the perimeter of the room behind them. I stopped, frozen. It looked like an operating theatre but was much bigger; about five times the size of an ordinary hospital theatre. There were three tables, each with a light above it and a bank of monitoring equipment next to it, together with an IV unit.

I resisted the urge to turn and flee, concentrating on my energy centres and trying to ground myself. The dark energy from the demons up above definitely wasn't helping; neither was the sight of the ooze demon strapped to one of the tables, its edges flowing outwards as it tried to escape. One of the Tiger's kids said something but I didn't really hear it. There was a rushing in my ears and all I could see was that demon trying to escape. Something inside me wanted to free it; something else wanted to destroy it; and a third powerful, horrible voice wanted to eat it.

I moved slightly towards it, the change coming on me. It felt so *good*. I would finally be free to be what I was, rather than held back in this small, weak serpent form or the even smaller and weaker human form. I glanced around: food everywhere. Finally, I could feed and fill myself and not be so hungry any more.

Control it, Emma, get a handle on it, a voice said into my head.

You can do this, you have the willpower, another voice said.

Fight it down. You need to be here when Xuan Wu — John — returns for you, the first voice said, and I recognised it as the Tiger.

I will help you, the other voice said, and it was John.

Then I was in a glass box, compressed into a tiny space in the back of my mind, with John's presence all around me and engulfing me. I leapt with joy in my tiny enclosure.

'Ah Wu, is that you?' the Tiger said.

I looked around. The Tiger's children were gathered against the back wall, his guards in front of them, their swords ready.

'Of course it's me,' I said. I arched the first third of my length, touched my nose to the floor, spread my body as flat as possible and concentrated. 'Tiger, do me a favour, will you? Feed a small amount of yang — a minimal amount, not enough to hurt me — through the floor under me?'

The floor warmed beneath me, glowing with red energy.

The serpent energy centres were very different from the human ones; although there were still three cauldrons, they were elongated and didn't sit one above the other like they did in the human form. They were long and narrow and stretched out, overlapping through my body, and the gates above each somehow managed to sit at the top without interacting with the cauldrons next to them.

I took deep breaths, turning my consciousness inwards and concentrating on the energy centres. I moved the energy through me, clearing myself of the demon essence.

'Whiter,' I said. 'Stronger.'

The floor didn't become hotter but the energy intensified. I fed it through my energy meridians, lighting up my serpent length and using it to clear more of the demon essence, burning it away.

The Tiger intensified the energy, making it burn white-hot. 'Let's clear that completely!'

'Stop! Stop!' I yelled, as the gateways burned too bright. 'You'll destroy her! Too much.'

The yang became less intense and I relaxed. 'That's a perfect level. Leave it there for a moment.'

I used the yang to clear the essence; it was like burning a black deposit out of the meridians. I couldn't clear it all without killing myself, but it was enough. I took another deep breath. 'Thank you, brother. Release the yang so I can come back.'

The energy snapped off and I was suddenly cold. I raised my snout. 'Okay, let's see what we have here. Is that an ooze demon? Damn, how'd you catch that and what level is it?' I looked around; they were all still standing ready to destroy me. 'I'm not going to hurt you, silly humans,' I said. 'But that ooze demon looks delicious.'

'Ah Wu?' the Tiger said.

'Nice job on the facility, old friend.'

'What about the chick?' he said.

I turned my attention away from the ooze demon. 'What are you talking about?'

'The Emma girl, dumbass. Where is she?'

'No idea what you're talking about,' I said, and slithered towards the demon. I hissed with admiration. 'Damn, that's a big one. How'd you get it?' I turned to look at the Tiger. 'Nobody died picking this up for you, did they?'

'Ah Wu, you're a snake,' he said. 'And you're Emma.'

'What?' I felt myself. I was a snake for the first time in ages, and it felt good. I looked around. 'Did I rejoin? Where's the rest of me?'

I slithered up and down, looking, but I couldn't see the turtle half of me anywhere. The separation hit me like a blow right down my middle, from my head to my tail, knocking me onto my back. Half of me was missing and it *hurt*.

'Where's the rest of me? Tiger? What happened?' I flopped my head back, weakened by the loss, and sensed someone behind a glass wall at the back of my mind, weeping with joy. 'Emma? Where's Emma?' I tried to raise my head but without the other half of me I was barely able to move.

It was Emma sitting at the back of my mind — no, her mind. I was in her head. I was in her body.

I managed to raise my head. 'I've possessed Emma.'

'That you have, my friend,' the Tiger said. 'I didn't know you still had that power in you. I thought you would lose it when you turned.'

'I'm going,' I said. 'Look after her.'

I took down the wall between her and me and ran.

CHAPTER 21

I felt like I'd been hit by a truck.

The Tiger kneeled next to me, his hand on my head, his expression full of concern. 'You back, girlie?'

'Three times,' I said.

'Deal,' he said. I raised my head but he stopped me. 'Do you know what happened?'

'Yes,' I said. 'I don't want to talk about it.' I flipped onto my belly, picked myself up and moved towards the ooze demon. 'Tell me what you're doing with this.'

'But he took you over!'

I turned and glared at him, aware of the power in my serpent eyes. 'I do not want to talk about it.' I gestured with my nose. 'Demon. Now.'

'Damn, girl, he's still in there,' he said with awe.

'Nope, this is one hundred per cent me,' I said. I sharpened my voice. 'Demon!'

'Tell her,' the Tiger said, gesturing towards one of the scientists without looking away from me.

A woman stepped forward holding her clipboard.

'Lower the weapons,' I said. 'I'm no danger to you.'

The guards hesitated.

'Do as she says,' the Tiger said.

The guards lowered their weapons and moved back to their perimeter positions. The scientists gingerly moved around me, trying to be casual and failing. For a quick evil moment I considered smiling at them to completely freak them out, then decided against it.

'We captured the ooze demon in the snow, it was incapacitated by the cold,' the woman said. 'Nobody could touch it, so we called up a couple of sons to levitate it. We've been studying it down here ever since. Cold makes it hibernate; but what we're really interested in is its morphic nature. It can change form.'

'Can it shape shift as well or is it always just goo?' I said, slithering around the table and studying the demon. I ducked out of the way as its tendrils lashed towards me.

'No, it's always goo,' the woman said. 'They tend to hang onto ceilings and drape themselves over their victims. Nasty way to go, they're so toxic.'

'The most difficult thing about them,' one of the male scientists said, 'is that it's impossible to judge their level just by looking at them. We want to find a way to ascertain that.'

I stared at both of them with admiration. 'Any progress?'

'We have a technique using shen energy that works. At the moment, any half-Shen like me can get a rough idea of the level from a distance of about two metres,' the woman said. 'I can judge them to within five levels.'

'What level is this one?' I said, ducking under another lashing tendril. 'It's feisty, isn't it?'

'It's a small one, level forty-five,' she said.

I backed up next to the Tiger and watched it from a safer distance. 'Have you hurt it at all?'

'Morphics don't seem to feel anything; they're not sentient, they're just automated nastiness,' the Tiger said. 'It doesn't even seem to know where it is. All it knows is that it wants us to die.'

'Typical,' I said. 'Any leads on the gold demon essence the demon copies were generating?'

'Uh, they haven't studied them yet,' the Tiger said. 'We need your go-ahead.'

I turned to look at him. 'You can study them but don't cut them up, break them or destroy them. Preferably don't cause them any discomfort either.'

'How about pain equivalent to a hypodermic?' one of the scientists said.

'You're going to stick needles in them?' I said.

The scientists nodded, enthusiastic. 'We want to see inside. We realise we can't cut them up, but sucking out some of their juice would work a treat.'

'Okay, but only if they give you permission after you've fully informed them of everything involved with the procedure.'

'The two students have already told us we can basically do anything we like with them,' the Tiger said. 'They already volunteered.'

'They were good kids,' I said. 'I think some of that has transferred across.'

The Tiger gestured towards the lift. 'It's getting late. We should go back down and take a look at the Snakemobile.'

One of the scientists hissed with laughter, and one of the guards smirked and quietly hummed the theme from *Inspector Gadget*.

'I hate you all,' I said as I followed the Tiger to the lift.

* * *

The Snakemobile was a spherical hard spacesuit set on top of a wheeled propulsion unit powered by an electric motor and three car batteries. Panels sloped down from the sphere, over the motor and batteries to the wheels. I circled the vehicle with curiosity. Two rods stuck out from the front of the lower part.

'What are the rods for?' I said.

'Visibility inside won't be that great so we put them there as antennae to warn you if you're about to hit something,' the Tiger said.

'Not "we", "he",' one of the scientists said. 'It was Dad's idea, don't blame us.'

The Tiger opened the lid of the sphere. 'You sit in here and there are three control sticks for you to move it.'

I curled up inside the hard suit and pushed my snout against the view port. 'This is even more ridiculous.'

'You control it with your tail,' one of the Tiger's children said. 'Can you push it hard enough?'

I touched the lever behind me with my tail; it didn't shift. I gave it a better push and the sphere lurched forward on its wheels and stopped, slamming my snout painfully against the plastic.

'The two levers on either side of the main lever are for steering,' the scientist said. 'We realise you can only push one at a time, so it'll stop, then turn, then you can push it to go forward again.'

'This would be much easier if you just learnt telekinesis,' the Tiger said, his voice muffled by the fibreglass shell around me.

'Can't do it,' I said.

'Seems to be working well enough,' one of the scientists said as I rocked forward, and turned left and right. 'Let's try it outside.'

They moved it outside on a standard box trailer, then rolled it off and opened it for me to climb inside. I slithered in and they closed the top above me. I pushed the lever and the wheels spun in the gravel, then bit into it and I moved forward. I spun to face the Tiger, then spun back again and moved towards the scientists.

'Seems to work well,' a woman scientist said. 'Try it up the hill? You'll be climbing in it.'

'You know what you look like?' the Tiger said. 'Say it for me, babe, go on.'

'Haven't we arranged enough executions for you?' I said.

He waved one hand dismissively. 'Can never be executed enough, you know that.'

I faced the hill and hit the lever to go forward. The unit rattled to the bottom of the hill, then stopped, its wheels spinning in the gravel.

One of the scientists ran forward and fiddled with the settings. 'Ramped it up. Try again.'

'Say the line!' the Tiger said.

'No,' I said, and pushed forward again.

The wheels bit into the gravel and I lurched forward. The vehicle tipped over and I found myself upside down inside the top.

'You okay, Emma?' the Tiger said.

'Yeah,' I said as they righted me. 'What happened?'

'May be top-heavy with your weight in it,' one of them said. 'You're heavier than expected.'

'Fatty,' the Tiger said. 'Say the line!'

I tried the hill again but the vehicle tipped over again.

'Let's try giving you a push up,' one of the women said, righting me. She pushed me slightly up the hill.

'How steep will it be?' I said.

'Fucking steep,' the Tiger said. 'Come on, say it for me. Do it.'

I pushed the lever to move forward and the unit tipped over again.

'Can we weight the bottom?' the Tiger said.

'If we do that it'll wear out the batteries before she gets there,' the woman scientist said. 'How far does it have to go?'

'About fifty k's.'

'We'll be lucky to get that much life out of the batteries we have now. Only way is if we can make the snake smaller.'

'This is as small as I can go for any length of time,' I said.

The Tiger shrugged. 'Back to the drawing board.'

I turned the unit so it was facing down the hill, pushed the lever and it tipped over again, this time rolling down the hill. The Tiger moved quickly to stop me and pushed me upright again.

'We'll have to work something else out, but thanks for your time, everybody,' I said.

The Tiger's expression filled with mischief through the view port. 'Say the line and I'll let you out.'

'Go to hell.'

'Come on, Emma, do it for me,' he said. 'You know you want to!'

'Oh my God, these rods on the front are just for show. They don't do anything, do they?'

'Couldn't resist.'

'Blame Dad. We thought he was being completely lame and tried to stop him,' one of the scientists said.

'Let me out!'

'Just the word! Say the word!'

I took a deep breath and mumbled, 'Exterminate.'

'Yes!' the Tiger yelled, punching the air. He popped the lid so I could climb out. 'Totally worth any number of executions!'

The ringing woke me up. I waved my hand over the bedside table a few times, then hit the alarm button on my clock. It didn't work, so I hit it again, then realised it was the phone. I picked it up and blearily saw the time as I pressed the button: 1:24 am. 'Hello?'

'Lady Emma, my apologies for waking you,' said the demon, 'but Lord Gold said that you would want to know. We've found the common thread in the data. We have the name of the central agency that all the missing people went to.'

I snapped awake. 'Are you still at the office?'

'Yes.'

I threw my legs over the side of the bed. 'I'm on my way.'

'Lord Gold says we'll pick you up, and bring your Hong Kong ID card,' he said, and hung up.

I quickly dressed and went out into the hallway. As I closed my bedroom door, I imagined for a moment that John was asleep in his room and I could give in to the temptation to go visit him.

I turned and headed out the front door.

Gold, Calcite and Zara were waiting in the lobby. The night sky glowed with the lights of Hong Kong, reflected in the low thick clouds that swathed the Peak above us.

Gold gestured for me to follow him to the family car. 'We'll drive you across the border, ma'am, it's in Shenzhen.'

'Who's on duty?' I said.

'Sit and Lee. I notified them and I'll stay in contact.'

'Good job,' I said, climbing into the front passenger seat. 'Let's go.'

'It's a mid-range employment agency, nothing special,' Gold said as he drove us through the deserted Western Harbour Tunnel, the tunnel's blazing lights reflecting on the car's glass. 'They have an office in Dongmen, near the main shops, very central.'

'Do they know we're on our way?'

Gold shrugged. 'Hard to say. I hope not.'

'All the people who disappeared had something in their records that was linked to this agency,' Zara said. 'Even something as minor as a phone number in their call records.'

'Wait, the government had their call records?' I said.

'Yeah,' Calcite said. 'So they can monitor who calls who and track down dissidents.'

'That's a gross invasion of privacy,' I said.

'Uh, this is China,' Gold said. 'Privacy is an interesting theoretical concept.'

'Most people are so accustomed to living crammed in together that they don't have the same level of respect for privacy that you spoiled Westerners do,' Zara said.

'Oh, I don't know,' I said. 'Look at the way people refuse to talk to you on the phone until you identify yourself. And everybody has their phone number withheld on caller display.'

'With the government keeping call records, can you blame them?' Calcite said.

The streets of Shenzhen were nearly deserted, the building fronts lit only by the streetlights and minimal internal shop lights. Tired prostitutes in high heels and huge wigs stared blankly at us as we passed, not seeming to care whether we stopped or not.

Two women were digging a large hole through the paving stones on one side of the road; they stopped and watched us as we drove past. They wore grey thick shirts and pants over their colourful floral clothes and worked under a single electric light bulb.

The agency was in the centre of the shopping district, surrounded by shiny new ultra-modern concrete shopping malls and white-tiled office buildings. Gold stopped the car under one of the office buildings. When we climbed out, he made the car invisible — easier than attempting to find a parking space to avoid being booked by the police. We went to the door of the building and Gold held one hand over it; it unlocked with an audible click. We opened the door, Zara checking behind us to ensure that nobody saw us go in.

We went up to the nineteenth floor, where a number of offices were located along a narrow corridor with white tiles on the walls and floor. The company names were all in Chinese. Gold stopped outside one of the glass doors and concentrated. He nodded, opened the door and we went in. The office floor was covered in shredded paper.

Gold groaned. 'They knew we were coming.'

He went to one of the desks, picked up the monitor from the computer box and dropped it onto the floor. He removed the box's external case, tossed it to one side, then held his hand over the hard disk.

He grinned and shook his head. 'What an idiot. He deleted the data the old-fashioned way.'

'It's not gone?' I said.

Gold yanked the cables from the back of the hard disk, then concentrated and made the screws holding it into the chassis spin out. He pulled it free. 'Take the hard disks, guys, we'll scan them all.'

Zara and Calcite moved through the office pulling the computers apart and extracting the hard disks.

Gold held up the hard disk he'd just removed: a plain silver rectangle with sockets in the back to connect it to the PC. 'They deleted the data, but they didn't know what they were doing. The FAT — the file allocation table — sits at the start of the disk and tells the computer where to look for the data. When you delete a file, it just removes the reference from the FAT; it doesn't delete the actual data. Just like throwing away the index card in a library — the book is still there.' He turned the disk in his hand and focused for a moment. 'All the data is still there. It's fragmented but it shouldn't be too hard for us to put it back together and find out where everybody was being sent.'

Zara and Calcite returned and placed a stack of hard disks on the desk. 'Still a couple to go,' Zara said.

Gold put his hand over the hard disks and concentrated. 'Most of them are full.' He grinned wryly. 'Of either porn or cute pictures of Winnie the Pooh and Disney characters, depending on whether the person using the PC was a man or a woman.'

'Sexist asshole. I happen to like porn, thank you very much,' Zara said, placing a couple more hard disks on the desk.

'And I think Winnie the Pooh is the cutest ever,' Calcite said.

'And how human are you two?' Gold said. 'I never said which was which.'

Calcite and Zara shared a look, then scooped up the hard disks. I helped them, taking about ten myself. We exited the office and stopped in the hallway.

Two fake elementals, one stone and one metal, stood in front of us. The stone one appeared as blocks floating together in a human shape, and the metal one was a smooth human-like form, but their faces were featureless. Their heads brushed the ceiling.

'If we kill one of them and it explodes on me, will it convert me?' I said.

'Yes,' Gold said. 'Stay back. I think it would be a good idea to change to snake, just to be on the safe side.'

'Changing to snake wears me out; I'll just stay back. If I'm far enough away I'll be fine.'

'What do you mean?' Zara said, glancing back at me. 'Convert you to what, ma'am? The serpent is well-known now, there's no need to worry about taking that form.'

'Demon form,' Gold said without looking away from the elementals. They remained unmoving and seemed to be sizing us up.

'But serpents aren't demons,' Calcite said, confused. 'They're always going on about how they're misunderstood and they're really good people — then they wander off and you don't hear about them for years. You know the saying: "Never fall in love with a snake."'

'One Two Two turned me into a Snake Mother,' I said. 'I'm full of demon essence. If I absorb any more, I'll be converted for good.'

'Don't tell anyone,' Gold said. 'It's confidential information; we don't want everybody in the Celestial knowing about this.'

Zara hesitated, then said, 'I think it would be a very good idea for you to get way back and stay there, ma'am. I'd hate to see that happen to you.'

I nodded and moved back, not looking away from the demons. 'I can't gauge them. How big are they?'

'I can't gauge them either,' Gold said. 'Guys?'

'You're bigger than us, Lord Gold,' Zara said. She concentrated and her human form changed to diamond; not faceted like a cut diamond but clear, transparent and smooth, like glass. Calcite changed to pure white, and Gold changed to his stone form: quartz with veins of gold.

'Just stay out of the way, ma'am,' Gold said. 'The Dark Lord would kill me if I was responsible for your death or conversion.'

'I'm responsible for myself,' I said.

'Not while we're guarding!' Gold said, and rushed the stone elemental. He changed form so that his body was egg-shaped and his arms became long, sharp-bladed swords. He ducked under the stone elemental's arms and sliced through its body, then moved back to stand in front of us.

The demon's body slid in half, re-formed, and both demons took a couple of huge strides towards us.

Zara grew and stretched and became even more transparent. Her human form disappeared completely and she became a shapeless clear ooze. She engulfed the stone elemental, then quickly shrank to half her size, then a quarter. She shrank more slowly, rolling back towards us to avoid the metal elemental, until she was the size of a basketball, the remains of the stone elemental, ground to a powder, visible in her centre. She flew into the air, split open into two halves and the dust that was the remains of the stone elemental cascaded out. She hesitated above it, waiting to see what it would do, then retook human form and stood in front of us.

'Metal one left,' Calcite said. 'We need a dragon.'

'Or a serpent,' I said, changing to snake form.

'Wah!' Calcite said. 'I haven't seen your snake form, ma'am. It's huge!'

I rushed the metal elemental, grabbed its faceless head in my mouth, wrapped my coils around it and held it. It struggled, but I was stronger — I was solid muscle. I unlocked my jaw and began to swallow its head. At the same time, I coiled around it to hold its legs and it fell to the ground. We lay locked on the floor, me holding the bound elemental with its head halfway down my throat.

I glanced back at the stones. 'I can't eat this, guys, it would probably fight its way out of me,' I said, my voice muffled by the demon's head.

'Stalemate,' Gold said, still in battle form. 'What do we do now?'

I had a lightning-fast inspiration. 'If we do this quick enough, it won't hurt you too much.' I summoned the Murasame, and it cooperated for a change, appearing on the floor next to me. 'Use this, but be quick.'

Gold reached for the sword.

'Wait!' I said.

He froze.

'I'm telling the sword to let you use it, but it'll still hurt,' I said. 'It'll hurt like mad, but it'll destroy the demon. Cut off its head, Gold.'

'What about you?' he said.

'I'm in snake form. The demon essence won't go into me.'

'Works for me,' Gold said, and grabbed the sword. He howled with pain and dropped it. 'Damn, you weren't joking!'

'The Destroyer,' Calcite said with awe. 'I never thought I'd see it. I'm profoundly honoured.'

'If my arm wasn't ready to drop off, I would be too,' Gold said. He took a deep breath and picked up the sword again. He screamed with agony as he ripped the scabbard off, swung the blade and took the demon's head.

The second the head was gone, Gold dropped the sword and stood panting, staring at it. I waited to see if the demon would re-form; it didn't. I spat out the head and the three of us backed up.

'How about we grab these disks and make a run for the car?' Gold said.

'Teleport,' Zara said.

'Lady Emma can't,' Gold said. 'We have to go down the old-fashioned way.'

'Stairs?' Calcite said.

We looked behind us to the stairwell. I changed back to human form to pick up the disks I'd been carrying. 'Stairs it is.'

'What about the sword?' Zara said.

'It'll find its own way home,' I said. 'And good luck to anybody who tries to steal it.'

'I can vouch for that,' Gold said.

We headed down the stairs back to the car. There were no more demons. Gold stopped when we reached the car. 'Wait,' he said, and changed form, becoming elongated and elastic, his face turning into a twisted caricature of himself. He sent his head under the car. 'Thought I smelled something strange, but there's nothing there. Let's go.'

The trip back to the Peak apartment was uneventful. It was just before dawn as we went up the drive, the rising sun painting the cloudy eastern sky below us a brownish pink. Gold got out of the car to escort me to the front door.

'Leave the disks with us,' he said. 'We'll spend some more time sorting out the data and find out where all the people were sent.'

'How long do you think it'll take?'

He shrugged. 'No idea. Depends how fragmented it is; without the file allocation table it can be a bit of a pain putting it all back together. We should know later today.'

I pressed the button for the lift. 'I was about to say tell Yi Hao that I'll be late in, but she's gone. Just pass the word around, okay?'

'Will do, ma'am,' Gold said, saluted me and walked back to the car.

Just as the lift doors closed, I saw the car dissolve into multiple metallic floating blobs. Zara and Calcite, who had been sitting inside, fell to the ground surrounded by the assorted junk that had been in the car.

I tapped the stone in my ring. 'They replaced the car with metal elementals. Stop the lift and take me back down!'

'Not a good idea,' the stone said. 'Those elementals would kill you.'

'Stop the lift, I have to get back down there,' I said, pressing all the buttons.

'You can't go back down, you'll get killed,' the stone said. 'Stay here where you're safe. Zara is already dead. Gold and Calcite are fighting valiantly but they'll lose. Stay here.'

'I know they're dead, but we need those disks! We have to stop the elementals getting them.'

All the button lights blinked out and the lift stopped.

'What happened?' I said.

'Hold,' the stone said. 'You're right, we need the disks. Give me a moment.'

I summoned the Murasame and stood fidgeting in the lift.

'Fixed,' the stone said, and the lift hurtled towards the ground. 'I suggest you use your energy centres.'

I concentrated and floated slightly above the floor as the lift plummeted. It slowed slightly, then stopped, and the doors opened. I touched down and raced out to see Simone in her pyjamas standing over the pile of junk from the car, Dark Heavens in her hand.

She turned when she heard me. 'Poor stones, they died again! This isn't fair on them.'

I crouched and put my left hand on one of the hard disks in the pile on the ground. 'Are they still good?'

'Yes,' the stone said. 'The Princess destroyed the elementals. Now all we need are the stones back to process the data.'

'Send a request through to Court Ten to expedite the process,' I said.

'Court Ten is closed for the night; they'll reply in the morning,' the stone said.

I rose. 'We need to take these disks upstairs.'

'We need to take all our junk upstairs,' Simone said, staring at the objects on the ground. 'Why did we have twelve boxes of tissues in the boot?'

'No idea,' I said. 'Probably Leo being extra cautious.'

'I can take them. You go back to bed,' Simone said, and disappeared, the pile of stuff vanishing with her.

I went to the lift and pressed the button, then spun as I heard something. Simone had reappeared behind me. 'On second thoughts, I think I'll escort you upstairs.'

I nodded and turned back to the lift. 'We need to buy a new car.'

'Get the latest model, that one was getting so old it was embarrassing,' Simone said.

'You are such a Hong Kong kid.'

'Emma,' she whined, 'I need twelve thousand to buy a new handbag. Can I have an advance on my allowance?'

'Sure,' I said. 'Twelve dollars the minute we're up there.'

She pumped the air. 'Yes! Double what I got last week!'

CHAPTER 22

I went down to the Academy after lunch. The building was quiet without its normal bustle of activity. Even the lunch room was subdued. The students worked their moves in the training rooms silently and with precision as I passed.

I went up to the top floor to my office, and stopped when I saw Chang sitting behind Yi Hao's desk.

He jumped up and saluted me. 'I have been assigned to you, ma'am. I hope I can fulfil your requirements.'

I nodded to him. 'Good. Come into my office.'

He came in and sat across the desk from me, upright in his stiff new Wudang uniform. He obviously wanted to make a good impression.

I flipped through the paperwork on the desk as I spoke to him. 'Your main task is gatekeeper. All the paperwork, phone calls, emails and meetings go through you. I don't have time to look at everything that comes across my desk, so it's your job to go through it and ensure that I never see anything that's going to waste my time.'

He looked concerned. 'How will I know which is which?'

I dropped the papers. 'By learning. You're a smart man, Chang, and that means you're gifted when it comes to learning. I'll tell you which is which from the start and you can take it from there.'

He didn't seem reassured. 'I'll try my best, ma'am.'

'How good are you with email and word processing? Computers? Internet?'

'Basic email, that's all. I've hardly used a computer. It might be better to get someone else, someone experienced with technology.'

'You had a gold-plated Blackberry.'

He grimaced. 'That was easy.'

'Just a second.' I picked up the phone and speed-dialled.

Lok answered. 'What? I'm busy.'

'Lok, arrange for one of the demons from IT to teach Chang how to use the computer; he says he doesn't have much experience. He should pick it up in no time though.'

'Already arranged, ma'am, the demon will be up in an hour or so. They're just tidying up the last of the big backups.'

'Thanks for giving Chang to me.'

'Bah, he smells. Couldn't get rid of him quick enough.'

'When was the last time you had a bath?' I said.

He hung up.

Two hours later, while Chang was learning the email system, the White Tiger rang. 'You lost your fucking stones again?' he said.

'It was really sneaky,' I said. 'They replaced our car with a bunch of metal elementals. They split apart once we got home and attacked us.'

He was silent for a moment, then said, 'Damn, that is sneaky.' His voice brightened. 'Lion back yet?'

'No. I'm expecting him in the next couple of days though.'

'Cool.' His voice filled with triumph. 'I have a solution!'

'What?'

'Demon horses.'

'What?'

'We've created a harness-type thingy big enough to hold you, and it can go on a really big horse's back. The demon should be fine to carry you, and the snow won't bother it too much if we rug it up right and put snowshoes on it. Problem solved.'

'Not solved,' I said. 'Demons can't survive in a vacuum, you said that yourself. And there'll be bugger all air up there.'

'Fuck.' He hung up.

I leaned back in my chair. Leo and the stones wouldn't be back for another day; the paperwork could wait while Chang learnt the ropes; the students were in class; all was well. I picked up the phone.

'Mr Hawkes's office.'

'This is Emma Donahoe. I'd like to speak to Mr Hawkes, please.'

The woman's voice became brisk. 'Would you like to speak to Mr Hawkes's liaison officer? Mr Hawkes doesn't take personal calls. How did you get this number?'

I leaned forward. 'No, this is *Emma Donahoe*. Put me through.'

'I'll put you through to his liaison. Just a moment.'

'No ...' The phone clicked. 'Damn.'

'Roger Davison, can I help you?'

'This is Emma Donahoe and I want to speak to Mr Hawkes. Tell that new secretary who I am.'

'Oh! Sorry, ma'am. Yes, ma'am, give me a moment.'

The phone clicked again, putting me through to the Taipan.

'This is Hawkes. So sorry, Emma, what can I do for you? Demons attacking again?'

'Nothing as major as that, David. My car was destroyed and I need a new one pretty quickly. Do you have a black E-class saloon in any of your dealerships that would be ready to go right now?'

'Let me check the database.' I heard him tapping the keys. 'So really no demons right now? You sure? Because having your car destroyed sounds like fun. I quite enjoy the mayhem you people bring into my life.'

'We destroyed the demons that did it, and we'll be chasing down their masters soon, and *no, you can't come along.* I would have thought you had enough to deal with running an operation like yours.'

'Bah, global financial crisis is small potatoes compared to some of the stuff you people have swirling around you. Ah, here we are. Sorry that took so long, the car dealerships are such a small part of the business that I don't have much to do with them. E-class, black, not fully optioned, just up the street from you in our Wan Chai dealership. Would you like it? If you're willing to wait a few days we can get one with all the bits and pieces for you.'

'No, we don't need all of that. What you have would be perfect.'

'It'll be delivered to your secret headquarters this afternoon. Free for afternoon tea? I can deliver it myself, and you can tell me how the demons destroyed your old one.'

I choked with laughter. 'Secret headquarters? We're hidden right out in the open. No, I have a new secretary, I need to show him around. But I'll get him to arrange something as soon as he's up to speed.'

'Don't be a stranger, crazy lady. Any word from John?'

'Did you ever see his animal form, David?'

'I didn't even know what he was until that business two years ago, Emma. I always thought he was just a local businessman.'

'He appeared to me and Simone a couple of days ago in his animal form; he's slowly coming back.'

'That's good to hear. I look forward to seeing him again. Anything else I can do, please let me know. That business two years ago was the most fun I've ever had in my life and being in the normal world just isn't enough excitement for me any more.'

'I'll keep that in mind.'

I went out of my office to find Chang sitting at Yi Hao's ... his desk, his face screwed up with concentration as he worked through the hundreds of emails in my inbox supervised by the IT demon.

He glanced up when he saw me. 'Would you mind if I reorganised the way the messages are filed? This seems chaotic to me.'

'She was a demon, she was an expert at chaos,' I said. 'Do whatever you think you need to do to get the job done.' I nodded to the IT demon. 'I don't know your name. Do you have one?'

'I'm still deciding, ma'am.'

'Take your time about it, a name is important; but if you choose an English one check the dictionary first. How's everything coming along? I'd like to borrow Chang for half an hour, if possible. I need a break, and I want to evaluate his skills.'

'A break would be good for him, ma'am.'

'Good.' I leaned on Chang's desk. 'Ring Lok, ask him which training room is free right now.'

Chang started frantically rummaging through the documents on his desk looking for the phone book.

I touched his arm. 'Don't rush. Take your time. Do what you need to do.'

He took a deep breath, found the phone book, opened it and called. 'Master Lok. Lady Donahoe would like the use of a training room ... immediately. Yes. Thank you, sir.' He hung up. 'He says training room fifteen.'

I pushed myself off the desk. 'Good. Come with me.'

The training room was two storeys up and we took the stairs. We passed a junior class on the way and I stopped for a moment and poked my head in.

'Master present!' the instructor shouted, and everybody stopped what they were doing, fell to one knee to salute me, and then returned to their work. I leaned on the doorway and watched them, Chang standing uncomfortably next to me.

'How long do you think these guys have been learning, Chang?' I said softly.

'They must have been learning for more than ten years, ma'am. Do you take them into your school when they are children, as Shaolin does?'

'Nobody here is taken unless they are older than eighteen; and sixteen for the Twelve Villages. These are second years.'

He inhaled sharply.

'Having Shen teaching is a huge advantage,' I said, still talking softly. 'We can accelerate the learning process — use special techniques to build strength and flexibility in our students that can't be learnt anywhere else.'

He crossed his arms over his chest. 'That's cheating.'

'No, it isn't, because they need the head start if they're going to face demons, which are ten times harder than any human.' I gestured with my head. 'Room fifteen is this way.'

We went into the training room and I summoned the Murasame. I used it to point towards the weapons rack at the end of the room. 'Pick something you won't hurt yourself with.'

He stared at me. 'Where did that sword come from?'

I dismissed the sword and resummoned it. This time it came back slightly heavier. 'Have you ever heard of a legendary weapon called the Murasame?'

He shook his head, still wide-eyed at the sword's appearance. 'No.'

'Good. Picked something yet?'

'That sword is legendary?'

'A bit, yes,' I said. 'Come on, Chang, we have to get you back in about twenty minutes. Let's not waste time.'

He turned to the weapons rack, appeared confused for a moment, then quickly grabbed a sword, removed the scabbard and tossed it to one side.

I lowered the Murasame and shook my head. 'I said don't waste time. I didn't say rush. Goodness, but you have a lot to learn. Now put that sword back and choose something with care. Don't rush it.'

'Even if I were to choose again, I would choose this weapon,' he said. 'I think it's the most suitable.'

'Very well.' I stepped back and prepared myself. 'Take it very, very slowly. These weapons aren't blunt, they're sharp. I don't want to see you hurt.'

'I treat all weapons as if they were sharp, ma'am,' he said with pride and stepped forward to engage me.

I put my sword up and guarded as he made some tidy strikes at me, moving slowly and with elegant precision. He ramped up the speed slightly and I continued to guard, following his moves and backing up to give him room.

When I was close to the back wall I said, 'Stop.'

He halted immediately in mid-strike.

'Good. Now guard.'

He nodded and lowered the sword and I moved through the attacks. He blocked with impressive style, and I ramped it up a bit faster, with him continuing to block effortlessly. His face went rigid with concentration and he changed from guard to attack, performing a fast horizontal waist-high swing at me. I blocked it easily, pushing his blade down, but his own momentum worked against him. His sword sliced over the top of his knee and he fell. He watched with horror as a small fountain of blood spewed out of him and spiralled into the Murasame. The sword continued to siphon the blood even after I'd tossed it to one side.

The sweet fragrance of his fresh, warm blood filled the room and my eyes clouded over as the need hit me. It would be so good to change and share the sword's feasting ...

I put my hand over the wound to stop the sword from draining him. When the Murasame had eased its pull, I took my hand away and tore the fabric of his pants where they'd been cut to have a closer look at the wound. It was deep but hadn't hit any major blood vessels. It looked like his blade had gone underneath his kneecap and torn all the ligaments holding it in place — a small, neat wound that could easily make him limp on that leg for the rest of his life. His face was white with shock and he panted as I put pressure on the wound.

'Stay still,' I said. 'Don't move.' I raised my voice to be heard in the next room. 'Sit, I need you in here, please.'

Sit came in, followed by five or six of his students.

'Students out, wait in the next room,' I called. 'Just Master Sit.'

Sit came and crouched next to us. 'What happened?'

'Bad guard, hit his kneecap with the sword,' I said. 'Murasame nearly finished him off for me.'

Sit glanced at the dark blade. 'Not surprised.'

I leaned in to speak into Chang's face. 'Chang, can you hear me?'

He nodded, his face rigid with pain.

'It'll save a great deal of time if I heal this up now rather than passing you on to Edwin,' I said. 'There's a lot of tendon damage here; it will take multiple operations to fix it.'

'Does he know?' Sit said.

'No,' I said.

'I'll hold him if you like.'

I nodded, and Sit went behind Chang and held his arms.

'What are you doing?' Chang said. 'Why are you holding me?'

I spoke into Chang's face again. 'We're holding you to keep you still because this isn't going to be fun. Chang, I can heal this wound as if it never happened, but to do that I'm going to have to change form.'

He stared at me.

I put my hand on his shoulder and gazed into his eyes. 'Don't panic. I won't hurt you.'

327

I rose, took two steps back, concentrated and took my snake form. Chang went berserk, making guttural snarls of terror and trying to free himself from Sit's grasp. I concentrated on his knee, touched my nose to it and healed it while Sit easily held Chang's writhing body.

I changed back and crouched in front of Chang again. 'All fixed. The snake is gone.'

'I should sedate him,' Sit said.

'He'll be working closely with me,' I said, putting my hand on Chang's arm to steady him. He went rigid and stared at me with horror. 'If he can't deal with the fact that I'm a snake then we might have to find someone else.'

I tapped his cheek. 'Chang. Chang, it's me. You don't need to be afraid. If you want to work with me, you have to accept that I'm a snake. If you can't deal with it, we'll put you back with Lok.'

'She will never hurt you,' Sit said into Chang's ear. 'Trust her. The snake won't hurt you.' He dropped his head and shook it, loosening his hold on Chang. 'Phobia. This is bad.'

I rose and turned away from his expression. So close.

'Deep breaths, deep breaths,' Sit said softly. 'Breathe.'

Chang grunted and I turned back to see that Sit had released him. Chang was pulling himself to his feet without his usual grace, clumsy with shock. He stood staring at me, panting.

I spread my arms. 'I'm sorry, Chang. I did it to heal you.'

He took more deep breaths, but didn't move. 'Change again.'

'That wouldn't be a good idea. I can see how I affect you.'

He took a quick step forward, then his face froze as he realised that he was closer to me. He gestured towards me. 'Change again. I can handle it.'

'Are you sure?'

'You healed me. You didn't hurt me. You're right: I need to get used to it,' he said.

I changed to snake again and he bellowed with terror and jumped back.

'Hold, Chang,' Sit said from behind him. 'It's her.'

I stayed very still.

'Say something,' Sit said.

'It's me,' I said gently. 'I know it's strange, but it's really me. The Dark Lord himself, Xuan Tian, is a snake too, Chang. You'll have to get used to us.'

'That's right, he's a turtle snake thing,' Chang said with wonder. 'I remember him from the temple. He's so strange.' He gestured towards me. 'But not as strange as you, ma'am.'

'You are quite correct,' Sit said with quiet amusement.

Chang took a couple of deep breaths and sidled towards me. 'Will you hurt me if I touch you?'

'No,' I said. I dropped my head slightly so he could reach. 'Feel free.'

'What is that on your head?'

'It's her crown,' Sit said with pride. 'She is Empress of the Northern Heavens.'

'It's not and I'm not, but I'll let that slide for now,' I said. 'You okay? Do you want to continue working with me?'

Chang took one large stride towards me, shoved out his hand and swiped me on the snout. I dropped my

329

head and hissed with pain, and he leapt back again with another yell.

'It's okay, it's okay,' I said. 'You just smacked me on the snout and it hurt.'

He moved forward again and touched my nose more lightly. 'I'm sorry, ma'am. I didn't mean to.'

'I know that,' I said. 'What do I feel like? Move your hand over the top of my head and down my neck.'

He did as I said, feeling the scales. 'You're not slimy at all!'

'Of course not,' I said. 'Only Snake Mothers have slime.'

'What's a Snake Mother?'

'Uh ...' I hesitated. 'Right now I don't think knowing about them is a good idea.'

He nodded and ran his hand down the side of my neck, a surprisingly pleasant feeling.

'You are dry and warm and soft,' he said. 'Nothing like I expected.'

'Thank you,' I said. 'Serpents are healers. When someone is injured and I can help, I will take this form to heal them.'

'You healed my leg,' he said with wonder.

'That I did,' I said. 'I would not have changed otherwise.'

He dropped his hand and grinned. 'I think we need to get back to work now; they'll be waiting for me upstairs.'

I changed back to human form. 'You are one of the bravest humans I have ever seen, Chang. I saw what that took. You're right, let's head back to the office. Sit, could you take over his weapons training? He needs a lot of work.'

'I'll work out a schedule, ma'am,' Sit said. He nodded to Chang. 'You are very brave. I'll be in touch with you about lessons.'

'I want to learn with Lady Emma,' Chang said.

'You were just injured in a lesson with me, which means I'm not good enough to teach you,' I said. 'You need a better teacher, one who can control your impatience.'

His face fell. 'Once again I've ruined it for myself with my own impatience.'

I turned to go and he stopped me. 'Ma'am?'

I turned back. 'Yes?'

'You are going to leave the sword on the floor in the middle of the room? That blade is evil, it drank blood!'

'It's not evil, it's just yin,' I said. 'And it will find its own way home, don't worry about it.'

He shrugged. 'If you say so.'

'Thanks for the help, Sit,' I said.

'Not a problem at all, ma'am, he is a remarkable human. What do you have him doing?'

'He's my new secretary.'

'But he's a man.'

'Oh, Sit, you disappoint me.'

Sit shook his head. 'I disappoint myself sometimes, ma'am. My apologies, Chang. I'll see you later.' He disappeared.

Chang started with shock. 'He is an Immortal?'

'That he is; most of the Masters are,' I said. I went out to the lobby and pressed the button for the lift. 'Let's go.'

Michael was waiting outside my office when we returned, in his work suit. Chang stopped when he saw him and glanced at me.

'This is Michael,' I said. 'He's part of the family and free to come and go as he pleases. He will occasionally take the form of a bloody great tiger as well; just ignore that.'

Michael nodded to me. 'Can we talk, ma'am?'

'Come on in, Michael.'

Chang gingerly took his seat behind the desk and started flipping through paperwork.

'Round up anything you have questions on and we'll go through them when I'm done with Michael,' I said. 'Also, contact Master Meredith Liu — her number's in the Academy phone directory — and ask her to check with the Courts of the tenth level of Hell about how long it'll be before we get the stones and the Black Lion returned. We need them as quickly as possible if we're to raid this nest before I see Nu Wa.'

Chang's mouth dropped open and his eyes went wide.

'Chang, get a piece of paper, write it down,' I said, and he scrabbled around the desk, then picked up a pencil and notebook.

I repeated the instructions for him and he shook his head. 'Nu Wa — tenth level of Hell — are you *serious*, ma'am?'

'Normal day in New Wudang, my friend,' Michael said with amusement. 'Hang around long enough and things will get really weird.'

Chang stared at him for a moment, then grinned broadly. 'This was definitely the right decision.'

'Way to go blowing up all preconceptions about what a secretary should be,' Michael said with admiration as he closed my office door behind him. 'He's just an ordinary human though; you sure he'll be able to do it?'

I shrugged. 'He's smart as anything and has some Shaolin. He'll be great.'

Michael frowned as he sat. 'Does he know the risk?'

I hesitated for a moment, then sobered. 'No. I'll talk to him. I just got caught up in settling him in; I didn't make that clear.'

'Does he know about you?'

'He knows I'm a snake.'

'And the other stuff?'

'What did you want to see me about, Michael?'

He leaned back. 'Apparently, you've ordered me to go to Celestial High. I'm twenty-four years old, I have a Master's degree, I have a full-time job and I'm not going back to high school.'

'Okay,' I said. 'I didn't order it, I just gave permission, but your choice. No problem at all.'

'Thanks,' he said, and rose. 'What was I supposed to be studying at CH anyway? Year Twelve math?'

'Poison administration and clearance, advanced Shen energy manipulation, up to level seventy-five demon binding and taming,' I said. 'Stuff you'd get from a senior class here anyway, so it's much the same whether you go there or here.'

'Why there then?'

'They asked.'

'Yeah, I got an über-formal email from them. Sound like a stuffy bunch of old-fashioned teachers — just what I don't need.'

'You've never been up there?'

'I don't need to repeat high school.'

'Tell you what,' I said, and rose to open the door for him. 'Go up and say hello to Lord Hong for me. After that, the decision is yours.'

He saluted me, 'Ma'am,' and went out.

'Any word from Court Ten?' I asked Chang.

'You didn't tell me it was Judge Pao!' Chang said, raising his hands. 'He's a legend. He's real! He's really down there!'

'He's a royal pain in the ass,' I said. 'Never met anybody quite so inflexible in my entire life. So any word?'

'The Lion will be back by dinnertime today. The stones will be back in three days, on Thursday. What happened to them?'

'Nothing much. Call my house, tell Monica that Leo will be home for dinner. Invite Michael, his number's there too. Family reunion. Clear my appointments for Thursday, I'm going demon hunting. Contact the following Masters — write this down.'

He raised the pencil he was already holding.

'Meredith Liu — you already talked to her. Her husband, Liu Cheng Rong —'

'Wait, wait,' he said. 'Wait. Immortals are married? They're supposed to be celibate and have no emotional attachments.'

'Don't confuse bodhisattvas with Immortals, particularly Raised Immortals. Immortals can succumb to the pleasures of the Earthly as much as anybody. Their nature once they're Raised depends entirely upon the way they were Raised — and there's a number of different ways of going about it. This doesn't include nature Shen like Xuan Tian, who are a class unto themselves. It's extremely complicated, and I'll give you a full explanation later, but right now I need you to contact them for me. Both Lius, the Blue Dragon, the White Tiger; not the Red Phoenix, she has enough on her plate ...'

'These gods are *real*?'

'You acknowledge the Xuan Wu is real and are surprised at the existence of the other three? Also Na Zha — no, don't bother with Na Zha; I don't care how good a demon killer he is, he's too much trouble. Monkey King ... nah. Similar. Contact General Ma, Vanguard of the Thirty-Six, ask him how busy the Thirty-Six are right now and if they can spare any of the generals. You getting this?'

'All those gods are *real*?'

'Chang.' I leaned on the door. 'I've yet to find a mythological creature that *isn't* real.'

'I'm not real,' the White Tiger said from the other doorway.

'I wish you weren't,' I said, and gestured towards my office.

'Who is this, ma'am?' Chang said. 'Does he have free passage as well?'

'This is Michael's father, the White Tiger of the West.'

'Emperor to you, human,' the Tiger said, his tawny eyes focused on Chang. 'Don't get in my way.'

'He's a devil!' Chang said, pointing at the Tiger. 'He eats unborn children and brings bad luck!'

The Tiger leaned on Chang's desk and grinned maliciously. 'You bet your pasty human ass I do. So stay out of my way.'

'Ignore him, Chang, he's really a big pussycat.' I gestured with my head. 'In here, pussycat.'

'I eat humans like him for breakfast,' the Tiger growled as he followed me into my office, closing the door behind him. He spread his arms wide as I sat at my desk. 'You love me.'

'Of course I do,' I said, checking my email. Chang had missed a few, but overall it was a good job. 'I even give you a cat toy at Christmas.'

He sat in a visitors' chair. 'I solved the problem! I got it wrong — the harness wasn't for demon horses. *I'm* going to carry you. Me and the other two cats.'

I turned to see him. 'What other two cats?'

'Michael and Leo. We'll take turns carrying you.'

'Michael's not Immortal; he can't survive in a vacuum. Hell, I'm not even sure Leo and Simone can.'

'They can! And I've checked Michael, he's good.' He leaned on my desk. 'So when's the Lion back? We can head out as soon as he returns. The sooner the better.'

'He's back this evening,' I said.

He slapped the table. 'Tomorrow morning then, first thing. By nightfall tomorrow, you'll be talking to Nu Wa.' He leaned back and put his hands behind his head. 'Fixed.'

'The stones will be back soon and we need to move on the Geek as quickly as possible.'

'When are they back?'

'Three days. Thursday.'

'See? It works out perfectly. Tomorrow, Nu Wa; day after, regroup and prepare; Thursday, Geek; Friday, come to the palace and lounge beside the pool with me. I'll throw a celebration dinner: Geek gone; Emma able to walk the Celestial on two legs.'

'I'll talk to Michael and Leo about it over dinner. I'm not sure this is a good time to be rushing off when we're so close to finding the Geek's nest.'

He waved one hand dismissively. 'It's a perfect time; you have nothing to do for the next two days otherwise. I'll come and share dinner with you; thanks for the invite. See you at seven at your little flat.'

'It's not that little,' I said, protesting, but he'd already disappeared.

Chang tapped on the door.

'Enter,' I said, still checking the emails.

He came in and put a mug of Ceylon tea on the desk in front of me, then a bundle of papers. 'You said to bring these in when the Tiger had gone.'

'How did you know he'd gone?'

'I didn't. The tea was an excuse to check.'

I sipped it. 'How did you know how I like it?'

'Lok told me.'

I nodded. 'Let's go through these papers.'

CHAPTER 23

I opened the front door of the apartment to find Michael standing there with a young human girl, a slim Chinese, in her early twenties.

'What's going on?' I said.

'This is Clarissa. I think it's about time she learned the truth,' Michael said. 'I'm going on a dangerous trek tomorrow and it's only right that she's aware of the whole deal.'

'Are you sure?' I said.

He nodded grimly and gestured for her to enter.

I held my hand out to her. 'Hi, Clarissa, I'm Emma.'

She shook my hand, her face full of delight, and spoke with a charming American accent. 'Nice to finally meet you.'

'You're American too?' I said as I closed the door behind them.

She nodded. 'I work in the same place as Michael.'

Simone came down the hall and stopped when she saw them. 'Oh,' she said. 'I wondered why you used the front door.' She nodded to Clarissa. 'Hi, I'm Simone, Michael's ... sort of ... cousin. But not really.'

'Does Michael normally use the servants' entrance?'

Clarissa said with a laugh.

'Uh, yeah. That's part of the explanation,' Michael said. He rubbed the back of his head. 'Come on through and meet the family.'

'I've been wanting to meet you all for a while,' Clarissa said. 'Michael's made up this whole mysterious business about his family, you know? Totally unnecessary.' She turned to me. 'Are you his aunt or something?'

'I'm not a blood relative; it's very complicated,' I said. 'Come into the dining room and we'll talk about tomorrow.'

Michael shook his head. 'I want to explain everything,' he said. 'All of it.' He turned to Clarissa. 'They haven't had any priming; this is the family straight up, the way they come. Right, Emma?'

'Michael never told us you were coming,' I said. 'Michael, are you *sure* this is a good idea?'

'This is starting to sound very interesting,' Clarissa said, smiling. 'I can't begin to imagine what the big secret is.'

'This is a very bad idea, Michael,' Simone said, her voice mild. She shrugged. 'Your dad and Leo are in the dining room already.'

'I get to meet your mysterious father too; this gets better all the time,' Clarissa said.

Michael took her arm and guided her towards the dining room; Simone and I followed. As we went in Bai Hu was shouting at Leo, who was glaring at him.

'You are worse than useless against anything that attacks you unless you get yourself trained again, man! Have a sword or a polearm or something made and get some training! Your lion form is very pretty, but fucking useless if a big demon attacks.' He saw us and waved for us to sit. 'Get this damn lion some training, Emma; he's fucking useless as a guard with the damage that's been done to his memory.'

Leo raised his hands. 'I'm getting some training, so leave it already!'

'Well, it's about time,' the Tiger growled, then broke into a huge boyish grin when he saw Clarissa. 'And who's this lovely one?'

'This is my girlfriend,' Michael said stiffly. 'Clarissa, this is my father.'

The Tiger rose and held his hand out to her. 'Barry Hu. Lovely to meet you.'

'Clarissa,' she said, smiling. 'You don't look old enough to be Michael's father.'

The Tiger sat and waved one hand airily. 'They all say that. I was young and stupid when we had Michael.' He gestured for her to sit. 'So take a seat and tell us all about yourself.'

She sat next to him, wide-eyed and enraptured. 'I work with Michael. We went to Harvard together, and took up cadetships at the financial house at the same time.'

The Tiger changed his appearance so that he was older and less attractive, but she didn't seem to notice. 'How much has he told you about us?'

'Nothing,' Michael said, obviously unhappy. 'But since we're going on a dangerous trek tomorrow, I thought it only fair that she knows everything.'

'That's not really necessary —' the Tiger began.

'Everything,' Michael said firmly. 'The whole thing. You, Leo, Emma, Simone, everything.'

The Tiger put one hand on the table. 'Usually we wait until they've said yes to a marriage proposal.'

'I want her to know before it gets too serious.'

'What *is* the big secret anyway?' Clarissa said, looking around at us, delighted. 'All of you are spies or something?'

'Why does everybody always assume that?' I said.

'Because spies deal in secrets as much as we do,' the Tiger said.

'Not spies then? Aliens?' she said, amused.

'I wish we were,' I said, leaning my chin on my hand. 'It would be easier to explain.'

'Try gods,' Michael said.

'Gods?' she repeated, still amused and playing along with the joke.

'Actually, Michael's father is a god,' Simone said. 'My father is too. Michael and I are demi-gods. Leo is a Taoist Immortal.'

'No, that doesn't work, he's black,' she said. 'Taoist Immortals are definitely Chinese. Try again.'

'It's the twenty-first century and people are travelling around,' Leo said. 'So even though I was originally American, technically speaking I'm a Taoist Immortal.' He shook his head. 'Damn, that really does sound strange, doesn't it?'

'What about you, Emma?' she said, turning her attention to me. 'You sound Australian. You're a ... a ... what are they called? Binyip?'

'Bunyip!' Simone said, delighted. 'Thanks, Clarissa, that clears everything up for me.'

'So let me get this straight,' Clarissa said. She pointed at Bai Hu. 'God.' She gestured around the table. 'Demi-gods, Taoist Immortal, Bunyip. Is that right? So ...' She leaned on the table and smiled at Michael. 'What's the big trek tomorrow? Going to Bunyipland to take some tourist shots?'

'Visiting the goddess Nu Wa in Heaven,' he said.

She clapped her hands. 'Wonderful! Can I come?'

'Told you this was a bad idea,' Simone said.

'What can we do to prove to you that we're everything we say we are?' Michael said.

'Oh, I don't know, something really impressive,' she said. 'Change into gods and fly through the heavens?'

'A hundred says that if we change she'll be a screamer,' the Tiger said.

'I'm not taking that bet, I happen to agree with you,' I said.

'That is so rude!' Simone said.

'Michael, we should call this off now and just have dinner normally,' I said. 'Anything we do to prove all of this to Clarissa will freak her out completely, and you'll probably lose her.'

'I'm right here,' Clarissa said pointedly.

'Sorry,' I said. 'But I don't want to risk what you and Michael have together.'

'She can take it,' Michael said.

'You're drug dealers!' Clarissa said, eyes wide. 'You're criminals!' She rose and put her hands on the table. 'I don't believe this of you, Michael!'

'She's smart and brave and hot as all damn, Three One Five,' the Tiger said. 'Wipe her memory and let it go.'

'No!' Michael said. He slammed one hand on the table. 'I want to come back to the Celestial, dammit! I want to be Emma's Retainer again. I want to go to CH and Wudangshan and learn some really advanced stuff. And if I do, she needs to know what I'm involved in.'

'There's a senior place among the Horsemen if you want to come back,' the Tiger said.

'Wudangshan,' Michael said.

'Sit down, Clarissa, we're not criminals,' Simone

said, sounding tired. 'Believe it or not we really are gods. Nobody's going to hurt you, but we may have to scare the living daylights out of you to prove what we're saying.' She turned to Michael. 'You'll lose her, Mike. Don't do this to her.'

Clarissa sat back down and clutched at Michael's hand. 'What the hell is going on?' she said weakly.

'If I return to the Celestial she has to know,' Michael said. 'I won't be able to pretend that I'm living a normal life. Weirdness follows us around like a stray dog. Hell, look at Lok. We're talking about moving in together, and if she moves into my place — which is the obvious choice if I return to the Celestial — then she's gonna have to meet that ugly rude mutt. She has to know.'

'When we tell the students, we just introduce them to Gold,' I said. 'That's much easier. What you have here is a whole roomful of teeth and claws. This is *not* a good idea.'

'Teeth and claws?' Clarissa said. She clutched Michael's hand tighter and he put one arm protectively around her shoulder.

'Nobody will hurt you here,' he said gently. 'This is my family. They may look a bit scary sometimes, but they're humanity's greatest champions.'

'Champions?'

'Sworn to protect all humans from the demon horde,' the Tiger said, his tawny eyes focused on her.

'Demons?'

'At least she's starting to take it seriously,' Simone said.

Michael leaned into her and spoke softly. 'We can prove that we're gods. We can change. My father's a tiger god, and so am I. Simone's a human god. Leo's human as well.'

She thought about it, then smiled broadly. 'Okay, joke's gone far enough.' She took a deep breath, still smiling. 'I'm starving. Where's the food?'

'Two hundred she's a screamer,' the Tiger said.

'Show her the photo in the hallway to start with,' Leo said.

'Show her real life,' I said. 'Just Bai Hu's True Form.'

'Not enough room in here,' the Tiger said, looking around. 'Living room or training room.'

Michael rose without letting go of Clarissa's hand. 'Come with me, we'll go to the training room.' He took her other hand and gazed intensely down at her. 'Whatever happens, you are in no danger, you understand? Nobody will hurt you here.'

She rose and studied his face, obviously beginning to wonder.

'He's right, nobody will hurt you,' I said. 'Let's go.'

She walked out into the hallway, then stopped and wrinkled her nose. It had begun to rain outside and the humidity had made the smell rise out of the carpet.

'Sorry about the smell,' Simone said, embarrassed. 'I brought my horse home to see my room and he piddled all over the carpet. We'll probably have to replace it, the smell just won't come out.'

'You brought your *horse* in here?' Clarissa said.

'He was only little,' Simone said.

'Move out for a week or so and replace all the carpet, it's filthy,' the Tiger said.

'That's a good idea,' Simone said.

We went into the training room and Clarissa took two alarmed steps back when she saw the weapons.

'Simone's father is the God of Martial Arts,' I said. 'This is his practice room.'

'Don't worry, none of those weapons are ever used on humans like you,' Michael said, still holding both her hands in his. 'You're perfectly safe.'

I went to stand on the other side of her. 'We'll leave the door open; if you want to walk out you can. Take it slowly. Nobody is holding you here. Michael, let her go.'

Michael released her and she grabbed one of his hands and held it anyway.

'Let me explain what's happening,' I said. 'Michael's father is Bai Hu, the White Tiger God of the West. Have you heard of him?'

'No,' Clarissa said.

'It's your own mythology, girl!' the Tiger said, standing on the other side of the room.

'My parents never talk about that stuff. They say it's old people's superstition.'

'Makes our life easier,' the Tiger said. 'And harder at the same time, when we have situations like this.'

Michael raised Clarissa's hand in his. 'My father is going to change into a tiger.'

Clarissa stared at Bai Hu.

'I won't hurt you,' Bai Hu said. 'The tiger form is just a shape. I'm still the same person.'

'This is such a bad idea,' Simone said softly.

'You are very brave, Clarissa,' I said. 'I'll tell you what. You heard Michael's dad bet me two hundred dollars that you'll scream? I'll take that bet, Tiger.'

'Done,' the Tiger said.

'If you don't scream, I win two hundred dollars and it's all yours,' I said.

'If you don't scream, I'll be prouder of you than I've ever been of anyone,' Michael said to her. He squeezed her hand. 'Are you ready?'

'Oh!' she said, obviously relieved. 'You're all magicians? A family of illusionists? This looks so real though!' She looked around. 'Where are the mirrors and stuff? I see mirrors on that wall, but it doesn't look like there's anything behind them.'

'I'm not using the mirrors, this is real,' Bai Hu said. 'I'll change to tiger, then change back, then come close to you and change again, and you can see that it's real.'

'Is your pet tiger safe?' she said, unsure. 'Those magicians in Las Vegas got mauled!' She backed towards the door and Michael didn't stop her. 'I don't want to see the tricks, thanks. Can we just leave it there?'

Bai Hu changed to his tiger form and she squealed.

'That counts,' the Tiger said.

'No, it doesn't,' I said. 'That was more a squeal.'

'Full-on scream, Tiger wins,' Simone said.

Clarissa pointed at Bai Hu, her finger trembling. 'That was very good. It even looked like it talked.'

Bai Hu shook his shaggy head. 'This gets harder all the time with advances in technology.'

'Oh, I dunno,' Michael said. 'People don't believe photos of dragons in the sky, they just say they're photoshopped. Makes life a lot easier for them.'

'Yeah,' Simone said. 'Nobody believes their own eyes any more.'

'Is it tame?' Clarissa said.

'It's my father,' Michael said. 'I can change too.'

She laughed, and it had a slightly hysterical edge. 'A family of illusionists. How come I never hear about your shows?'

Bai Hu changed back and put his hands on his hips. 'This is a total waste of time.'

'We need to get this done and start planning the trip,' I said. 'Any suggestions?'

'Leave it there. She'll ask about it later and Michael can show her again,' the Tiger said. 'That's usually what happens with these modern girls. No rush, you have all the time in the world.' He rubbed his hands together. 'What's for dinner? Your housekeeper always does something good for me.'

'Change into a snake, Emma,' Michael said.

The Tiger stopped halfway to the door. 'That would work.'

'No,' I said, and went out.

'A snake?' Clarissa said behind me.

'She's a really big black snake. Like, really big. Three or four metres long at her biggest,' Simone said. 'And I agree with her. Not a good idea.'

I went into the dining room and sat at the table. Monica nodded to me as she placed the plates in the middle.

Everybody else came in, Clarissa still holding Michael's hand. They sat at the table in silence.

'I hope you're okay for Chinese family style,' I said. 'Everything in the middle and shared.'

'Yeah, that's the way we have it at home,' Clarissa said. 'Mom and Dad are originally from Hong Kong.'

'Do you speak any Cantonese?' I said.

'Not really. I can understand, but not really speak that much.'

'Enough to get by at yum cha,' Michael said, smiling at her as he served her from the plates in the middle.

She smiled back at him, then around the table. 'So you guys are stage magicians? When are you performing?'

'We're not stage magicians, we're gods,' Simone said patiently.

'Let's leave the discussion of what we are and move on to tomorrow,' the Tiger said. He served himself some soup from the tureen in the centre of the table. 'Early start at the Western Palace. Emma, you'll be in serpent form of course. Michael and Leo, cat form. We'll be going the first few thousand feet by cloud and then meet the cars and travel the rest of the way by jeep, stopping to walk when we can't drive any higher. So wear something warm on your human forms.'

'I'm staying human for this?' Simone said.

'Yes, and change to Celestial if the going gets too rough,' Bai Hu said.

'Do we need to go armed?' Michael said. 'Any chance of facing demons on the way up?'

'Not in my dominion,' the Tiger growled. 'No need for weaponry.'

'Are you absolutely positive about that?' Simone said.

'Yes,' the Tiger said. 'Besides, we don't want to take weapons into Nu Wa's valley, it could be seen as an insult.'

Clarissa ate quietly, eyeing us as we spoke.

'Are you *sure* my spacesuit will work?' I said. 'We haven't even tested it.'

'It'll work,' the Tiger said. 'It's proven technology. I've done suits like this before for my wives who like to dive —'

'Wives?' Clarissa said. She looked from Michael to the Tiger. '*Wives?*'

'Dad has more than one wife and makes no secret of it,' Michael said. 'All the wives know and none of them care.'

The Tiger put down his bowl and spread his hands, still holding his chopsticks. 'Hey, I'm good.'

'What about your mother?' Clarissa asked Michael.

'My mother's dead, you know that,' Michael said, not looking up from his food.

'But didn't she care?' Clarissa said. She glanced around the table again. 'Having more than one wife is illegal. You can't do that.'

'You can do whatever you like when you're a god,' the Tiger said. 'Which I just happen to be, so it works out well. Eat up.'

Clarissa rose and put her chopsticks down firmly. 'Michael, I think I'll go now.'

Michael got up too and moved to take her hand but she shook him away. 'No, I'll find my own way, thanks.'

She left the dining room and he followed her. Their voices could be heard arguing all the way to the front door until it slammed.

'He lost her,' the Tiger said. 'I hope he still comes tomorrow; we need him.' He tasted the soup. 'Waste of time giving *me* watercress soup. You can never cool my blood; I'm yang itself.'

A couple of minutes later, Michael materialised in his seat. He leaned his elbows on the table and put his head in his hands. 'I teleported her straight home. She accused me of drugging her and said she never wants to see me again. I changed to a tiger in front of her and she went inside and locked the door in my face.'

'If she loves you enough, she'll give you a second chance,' the Tiger said. 'If she doesn't trust you about this, then she isn't worth worrying about.'

'That's easy for you to say, Mister Hundred Wives,' Michael said, his head still in his hands.

'Are you still coming tomorrow? We need you,' the Tiger said.

Michael sighed loudly and dropped his hands. 'Yeah, I'll come. I meant it about rejoining the Celestial.'

'Is it worth losing Clarissa for?' I said.

'If she can't handle it then I don't have much choice.'

'Go back and talk to her when you return from the West,' the Tiger said. 'Let her think about it. She'll come round. They always do.'

'I hope you're right, Uncle Bai,' Simone said.

'Now eat up, you need your strength for tomorrow,' the Tiger said. 'And Michael, if you need any help at all with her, let me know. I'll give you a hand.'

'I saw the way she looked at you, Dad. It would be better if you just kept away.'

The Tiger raised his hands. 'Whatever you want.'

CHAPTER 24

The final outpost before we began the long walk was a wooden two-storey house clinging to the steep, rocky, snow-covered hillside. The two SUVs and the truck full of gear that had been sent up earlier were parked outside. The family who lived there — all dragon Shen — offered us their hospitality while we put together our equipment for the next stage. We sat on the wooden floor around their primitive fireplace while the Tiger explained how my spacesuit worked.

'You told them the most comfortable position was curled up, so they made it round with a lump on top for your head. It opens up completely and you coil inside it like rope. Can you do that?'

'I would have liked some practice,' I said.

'No time like the present,' the Tiger said. He glanced around at Michael and Leo, who were still in human form while we prepared. 'We have six oxygen bottles. Two will be attached to Emma's suit; and two for each of the cats not carrying Emma. As we empty them we destroy them.'

'How long will each bottle last?' Michael said,

studying the cylinders in their large leather and aluminium harness.

'We're hoping that with Emma in a low life-sign trance, each will last at least two hours. Twelve hours altogether, plenty of time.' He studied me carefully. 'How low can you take it?'

'We really should have done a dry run!' I said. 'I don't know. I'm cold-blooded; if you keep me chilled and I go into a good trance, it should be next to nothing. We reptiles can do that.'

He nodded sharply. 'Sounds good.' He looked around again. 'Once the atmosphere gets too thin to breathe, it won't transmit sound, so switch to telepathy. Keep comms to a minimum anyway; we'll need every scrap of energy we have to get to the top.'

Michael hefted his harness. 'Let's do this. Time's wasting.'

'Uh ...' Simone winced. 'Can I use the bathroom first?'

'Of course,' our dragon host said. He gestured towards the small, smoke-stained kitchen. 'Through there.'

'Emma,' the Tiger said, 'you go into a trance; every hour we'll change your carrier and I'll rap on the outside of your pod to bring you out of it so we can move you. Does that work?'

'Yes,' I said.

'Let's go outside and set up while Simone puts on fresh make-up,' the Tiger said with amusement. He sighed theatrically. 'Girls — always have to do it properly. Me, I'll just write my name in the snow.'

'You can't do that in tiger form,' Michael said as he carried his harness down the stairs and out into the snow.

'Oh, yes I can,' the Tiger said. 'In *both* languages.'

Leo grinned at him. 'Now that I'd like to see.'

'Not right now!' I said.

'Deal,' the Tiger said. 'Okay. You two cats change; Simone stays human. I'll do the buckles and pod and shit for everybody except me, and she'll do me after I change.'

'She's had no practice at this,' I said.

'Doesn't need it; it's very straightforward, much like a saddle — you just cinch it up,' he said. 'Drop your bottles and change and I'll harness you up.'

Michael and Leo placed their harnesses on the ground and changed. Leo's lion form was slightly larger than Michael's tiger; about the same size as the Tiger's True Form.

The Tiger stood back and put his hands on his hips. 'Damn, Lion, you're a big bastard.'

'That's what all the guys say,' Leo said, his voice a throaty growl.

The Tiger picked up a pair of gas bottles in their harness and fitted them to Leo's back. He pushed them to make sure the harness was firm and stepped back. 'How's that?'

Leo walked up and down, then leapt, testing it. 'Tighten it around my shoulders.'

The Tiger pulled one of the straps tighter and Leo nodded. 'Good.'

Simone came out as the Tiger was fitting Michael's harness. 'All working?'

'Watch how this goes,' the Tiger said. 'This strap under the front, that one under the back. This one has to be tighter, it's the main secure. With Emma in the pod, it has to be centred, and this strap here has to be really, really firm. See?'

Simone nodded. 'Got it.'

'Okay.' The Tiger opened my pod. 'In you hop, Emma.'

I curled up inside the circular suit; it was the perfect size for me, but incredibly claustrophobic when he closed it. It had been made from a plaster mould they'd taken of my snake body and fitted with almost no room to spare.

'Stay awake while Simone puts you on top,' the Tiger said. 'Just the way you like it.'

'I haven't executed you in a while,' I said.

'Can't hear you.'

As Simone lifted me in the harness and placed me on the Tiger's back, it quickly became apparent that they'd forgotten to turn on the life support. I couldn't open the pod from the inside and I was suffocating. I banged my head on the top, but Simone and the Tiger were focused on getting the straps correct.

The stone yelped with the third strike. 'No air!'

'Oh God, sorry, Emma,' Simone said, and a wash of ice-cold oxygen entered the pod.

'Now you've put too much in, you're making her dizzy,' the stone said.

'Turn it down slightly, Simone. Stone, you have to stay awake,' the Tiger said. 'She won't be able to communicate once we get past the atmosphere.'

'Damn,' the stone said. 'She'll be asleep and I'll be awake — this is not a good idea.'

'I think I've been saying this for a while,' I said.

'Don't be such an old woman about it — oh, you are an old woman. So keep quiet,' the Tiger said. 'Let's get this over with, get you on two legs on the Celestial, and stop everybody whining about having a snake for a boss.'

'Oh, is that why you're rushing this?' I said, as Simone gave the pod a final check.

'Of course it is,' the Tiger said. 'Are we all good to go?'

'Just let me get my pack on,' Simone said. 'Okay.'

'If you need to take Celestial Form to make it easier, don't hesitate,' the Tiger said. 'Emma, you can power down now. I'll rap your pod when it's time for the changeover.'

I'm counting on you to help me stay alive, I said to the stone.

A responsibility I wish I did not have, the stone said.

'I'm going down,' I said out loud.

'We got you, baby,' the Tiger said.

He started walking, swaying me from side to side. I couldn't see anything. I cycled the energy through my serpent centres and went down.

'Emma!' someone shouted and I came back. The lid of the pod popped open and Simone peered inside. 'Are you still there, Emma?'

'I'm here,' I said, raising my head into blinding sunlight. I looked around; we were high on a snowy ridge with steep drops on either side. 'Geez, I wish I hadn't looked now.'

'We're moving you to Leo,' Simone said. 'This is proving tougher than we expected. The Tiger thought he could carry you for a couple of hours but he's only managed an hour.'

'How's my oxygen?' I said.

'Your first bottle is at fifty per cent,' the Tiger said. 'Right on plan. You're doing great.'

'Where's Kun Lun?'

The Tiger pointed behind me. I turned to see and nearly fell out of the pod. We were up so high that the red plains were a misty blur a huge distance below us. Behind me were the mountains, each with a jagged, pyramid-shaped peak. They shone brightly against the dark, high-altitude sky.

'How high are we?' I said. 'Damn, all those mountains look like the top of Everest.'

'About six thousand metres,' the Tiger said. 'We have to go through those mountains to get to the valley where Nu Wa lives. Higher than this, we can't open the pod so it'll make the changeover harder. Just try to stay still when we move you, and rap your nose twice against the top if you're in trouble. Do you need anything? Because we need to get you on Leo and keep moving.'

'I'm good,' I said, and they nodded and put the lid back on me. I lurched as they lifted me and put me onto Leo, then we moved off again.

Simone tapped the top of the pod. 'Got air, Emma?' she said, muffled through the fibreglass.

Told them yes, the stone said.

'Good,' Simone said. 'Then go down again, please, to save your oxygen.'

I was jerked awake by the pod lurching as they transferred me again.

'How's it going, stone?' I said.

'The Tiger was supposed to tap you to wake you up, but he's concentrating. Let me give you a view outside. I can make the pod invisible for you,' the stone said.

The sides of the pod disappeared and I was on a steep hillside, dark, sharp rocks jutting out from the snowdrifts. Michael was looking back over his shoulder as the Tiger and Leo, both in human form, transferred me onto his back. Simone was sitting on the ground looking concerned.

'We're doing just fine, right on time,' the Tiger said, grunting as he lifted me. 'Air's nearly run out, but we're all coping very well.' He patted Michael on the shoulder and they did up the straps. 'First gas bottle's done, right on schedule. Open your mouth to empty your lungs while I do the changeover. Absolutely nothing to worry about.'

Simone took a big drink from a sports bottle, then slipped the bottle into the side of her pack. She grimaced as she pulled herself to her feet and hitched her pack onto her back. 'Onwards and upwards.'

'That's damn steep,' I said. 'You handling it okay?'

'I told you it would be fucking steep,' the Tiger said. 'No way could the Snakemobile handle this.'

'Let's go,' Michael said, staggering slightly as he adjusted to my weight. 'My paws are already killing me.'

'Soft, soft, soft, you need to spend way more time like this,' the Tiger said, changing to True Form and waiting as Simone fitted him with the spare gas bottle harness. 'Go down as quickly as you can, Emma, save your oxygen.'

'Okay.'

I was jarred awake by them moving me again. The Tiger rapped the top of the pod and I tapped it once in reply.

Your stone seems to have fallen asleep, the Tiger said.

'No, I'm here, I'm here,' the stone said. 'Sorry, just ... dozing.'

The sides of the pod disappeared again and I saw the Tiger's hand in front of my face. He was lifting me off Michael, who collapsed onto the ground as soon as I was pulled free. The Tiger carefully tilted my pod and lowered it onto the snow. I looked around: we were on a snowy ledge with a rock overhang above us. Simone was sitting on the ground again, but she'd changed to Celestial Form, her tawny hair flowing around her and her brown eyes huge. Instead of her usual robes of dark space and glittering stars, she wore a black Mountain uniform, cotton jacket and pants; nevertheless, her hands were blue with cold.

She jerked as someone spoke to her, and nodded. She came to me and lifted my pod, struggling to get it onto the Tiger's back.

They're tiring more than they expected, the stone said. *It's hard doing this in zero oxygen. They can manage without it by burning energy, but it's not ideal.*

Simone tightened the straps around the Tiger, patted him on the shoulder, then turned and put her own pack on. She smiled at me as if she could see me, then gestured with her head. The Tiger turned the way we were going and the almost vertical black stone mountainside became visible, with a narrow path passing around a steep gorge.

Go down, Emma, the stone said, and I did.

I hit the ground with a jar that went right through my body.

Sorry, Simone said.

The pod is slippery with ice, the stone said.

It made the walls of the pod disappear again and the view was breathtaking. We were impossibly high, on the ridge of one of the peaks, the black rock jagged and steep below us on both sides. The sky was as dark as night, with stars visible. I could see the curve of the Earth and the faint outline of the Western Heavens below, the red desert faded to a dusty brown. The horizon had a glowing blue aura — the atmosphere.

Let all your breath out, I need to change your bottle, Simone said.

I exhaled as hard as I could while the oxygen escaped from the pod; it gave me a strange feeling of bloatedness. Simone hooked up another bottle and the pod filled with air again.

Tap once to say you're okay, she said.

I tapped the top of the pod with my head.

We have some small issues, the Tiger said.

That sounds like major problems to me, I said to the stone.

Leo is dying, and Michael can't make it much further, the Tiger said. *Simone can't carry you, so it's just me. We'll have to slow down, but we're fine; we have four bottles left and we're about three-quarters of the way there.*

Leo's dying?

He's absolutely no fucking good in zero oxygen, has no training whatsoever, the Tiger said. *Neither has Missy Princess here, but she's so powerful it doesn't make any difference. Michael has the training, but he's only a mortal and we'll probably have to make him go back real soon.*

Send him back now, I said.

No, no, I can do at least another hour, I'm good, Michael said.

Don't you dare kill yourself for this! I said. *Tiger, keep an eye on him!*

Don't worry, babe, I am.

Simone tapped the top of the pod and the walls went opaque. *Downtime, Emma. Save your oxygen.*

How did the Shang king make this journey all those years ago? I asked the stone. *He was just an ordinary human.*

Nu Wa was on the Earthly Plane then, in the Kun Lun Mountains, the stone said. *After the Shang/Zhou thing she moved up here and hasn't spoken to anybody since.*

Down, Emma, Simone said again.

I took a deep breath of the sweet, ice-cold oxygen and went down.

I hit the ground upside down and skidded down a hill for a long, terrifying moment until I stopped with a crack against the fibreglass skin of the pod.

'Stone?' I said. The stone didn't reply so I tapped my crown on the lid of the pod. 'Stone! Wake up!'

'Sorry, Emma, it's just so damn *cold*. We stones like it much warmer,' the stone said.

'So do we reptiles, I'm struggling to stay awake,' I said. 'What happened? I'm upside down.'

The walls of the pod disappeared and I tried to look around. Simone was holding my pod with one hand and gripping onto rock with the other, her blue hands lined with white and red from the effort. I had a moment of vertigo as I realised we were both hanging over a ledge, Simone's hand the only thing stopping my pod from falling. Her face was rigid with concentration.

The world spun as I was lifted free, and then I was jarred again as the pod hit the ground the right way up. My field of vision was limited to black rock in front of me.

'Don't disturb them, he's pulling her up,' the stone said. 'She fumbled while she was freeing you from the harness to give him a break and you slid down the side of the mountain. She flew after you, threw herself over the edge and stopped you from falling off.'

'Tell them I want to stop this now,' I said. 'Where are Leo and Michael?'

'Let them get somewhere safe before we ask them,' the stone said.

I was roughly lifted again, and the world became white and gold as the Tiger, in human form, held me close to his chest and took a couple of huge strides. He fell onto his knees, dropping me onto the rock, and changed back to True Form. Simone fell to sit beside him, her face as blue as her hands. She closed her eyes and raised one hand, seeming to be taking deep breaths of the non-existent air.

Her voice gasped in my head. *The Tiger sent Michael back — God, I hope he makes it back down okay. Leo died about ten minutes ago. I have one of your gas bottles in my pack, it's all I can carry, so you have the two on you and one on me. We'll be fine, we're very close now, I can see the summit. Don't worry, Emma, we'll get you there!*

'I have one and a half on the pod, if I've been awake through all the transfers,' I said. 'Simone has one. I've already used two and half bottles to get up here, and we still have some way to go ...'

'You'll make it back down, don't worry,' the stone said. 'Leo had one on him, and it's still there on the way back.'

We'll get you there! the Tiger said. *If it kills us!*

Not if it kills Simone, I said.

It's too far to go back now, Emma, Simone said.

'This was such a bad idea,' I said.

'Whose idea was it?' the stone said.

'Mine,' I said, full of misery.

No, it wasn't, it was Daddy's! Simone said. *Trust him. Take a deep breath and go down. We're only about another hour from the very top. Oh! Take a look around first.*

The rocks fell away as Simone lifted the pod to put me onto the Tiger's back. She struggled with the straps and had to stop, panting, every couple of minutes to rest. When she was done, the Tiger walked to the edge of the rocky platform to show me the view.

Highest point in the Western Heavens, he said.

The red desert was invisible; all I could see was the blue haze of the atmosphere and the curve of the Earth even more pronounced. The stars blazed in the night sky.

Simone stood next to us, still in her Wudang uniform, but her Celestial Form had grown and she was nearly three metres tall. *So beautiful*, she said, *well worth the trip. I should have taken Uncle Bai up on his offer to come into space a long time ago.*

Still have to make a field trip to the Apollo landing sites, the Tiger said. *We can take Emma along with us in her little spacesuit here.*

I hope all the tourists aren't disturbing it too much, Simone said.

Not too many of us can make that trip, the Tiger said. *Only the very, very largest Shen. Like me and you — the best of them.* He turned left onto a small ledge leading down off the platform. *We head down from here, along that ledge, through the pass. So close. We'll get you there, babe!*

I fell asleep without going down; it was just too damn cold.

* * *

We stopped moving but I didn't really notice. It was just so cold.

'Stone?' I said.

No reply.

Stone? Tiger? Simone?

Nothing.

I tapped my head on the top of the pod. Nothing happened.

I tapped twice. I was in trouble: it was unbelievably cold and we weren't moving.

Simone?

Nothing.

John?

I'm sorry, Emma, someone said. I tried to move my head but it was stuck. I was enclosed; the walls were all around me, holding me in, and I panicked. I tried to free myself but I was held tight. It was difficult to breathe. I was stuck in a freezing, airless container of some sort and I was dying. I tried to concentrate but it was cold and I couldn't clear my mind.

Stone? I said.

No reply.

I made myself larger, trying to free myself, but the enclosure didn't break. The air was stale. I panted, trying to get enough into me. It was obvious that I was suffocating, and if I didn't free myself soon I would die.

Don't, the stone said.

I'll die if I don't, I said. *I can't breathe!*

I concentrated, made a huge effort and expanded, pushing myself against the walls of the container. I hoped I could break it; if I couldn't, it would break me. The pressure was enormous — but not as bad as the suffocation. I used my last scraps of energy, made myself suddenly huge and the container broke. I was free. I raised my head and tried to take a breath, but nothing happened. There was nothing to breathe in.

Simone lay on the ground in the snow next to me, her eyes wide and glazed, her hand touching the broken wall of my container. The Tiger was behind her, in True Form, open-mouthed and panting.

Oh, now you've done it, babe, the Tiger said. He made some feeble, scrabbling attempts to move, his paws making small piles in the snow, then stopped. He moved his head so he could see me better. *You were right. We should have done a dry run.*

This suffocation was even worse; the heat drained out of me and the silence was complete. I thought I saw Simone's eye flicker for a moment, then there was a blinding white flash and nothing else.

CHAPTER 25

'She's coming around,' the stone said, its accent making it sound like a doctor in a British soap opera.

'Emma, don't panic, you're safe,' Simone said.

I raised my head slightly; my vision was blurred. I shifted under the silken sheets and had a moment of panic — I had legs; I was in human form; I'd die. I tried to change to snake but couldn't do it.

'Help me!' I said. 'I need to be snake!'

'You're safe, you can stay human,' Simone said, clasping my hand.

I ripped my hand away. 'Don't touch me!'

'I can touch you. You can be human. This is a special place,' Simone said. Her voice filled with amusement. 'We all nearly died because we listened to the Tiger. Last time we do that, eh?'

'Should have known better,' I said. I rubbed my eyes; I felt hot and ached all over. 'Where are we?'

'Oh, she said the line and I never even asked for it,' the stone said. 'She's dehydrated, give her a drink. Here, Emma, let me lift you.'

The stone was sitting next to the bed in human form. It wore a dark green Chinese robe but still retained its European appearance. It slipped one arm behind my back and helped me upright.

I was in a traditional Chinese rosewood four-poster bed hung with translucent embroidered pink silk curtains on three sides and open on the fourth. I couldn't see much of the room but it appeared to be full of rosewood furniture and flowers, all the fabric and fittings in variations of pink and red. I was wearing pink silk pyjamas to match.

'This looks like a wedding suite,' I said.

'I think it is,' Simone said. 'But it isn't the sort of thing you go into detail about.'

The stone handed me a tall glass glistening with condensation. 'Drink it slowly, you're very weak.'

I took a sip and nearly choked. The stone helped me, holding the glass still so I didn't spill it.

'I had the same reaction the first time,' Simone said.

I took a couple of deep breaths, then another sip. The drink was ice-cold and tasted like a mountain spring, full of sparkling minerals, but at the same time lightly sweet and fresh, full of the flavours of mown grass and sunshine, with the bite of alcohol but somehow not. I took a huge gulp and it rang through me like crystal vibrating. I pulled the glass away from my face and stared at it.

A woman appeared in the doorway. She was small and round, with a matronly figure and a kind, plain face. She wore a traditional Tang-style robe of floating pink sheer silk with an apron over it in a darker pink held with a wide, elaborately embroidered pink and gold belt. Her hair was styled in twisted raised braids decorated with gold and cloisonné pins, some of them with pearls hanging from them. She smiled and somehow I felt a million times better.

John, in human form, was standing next to her, smiling his turtle smile. I shoved the glass at the stone, leapt out of bed and charged to him. I came to a halt in front of him, hesitating. Could I touch him?

He answered my question by scooping me up, holding me tight and kissing me so hard it hurt. I lost myself in him, unable to let him go, wanting to climb inside him and hold him, and this moment, forever.

He pulled back, smiled at me and his eyes wrinkled up. 'You have to breathe sometime, Emma.'

'No, I don't,' I said, and I kissed him again. He loosened his hold on me so I slid down him to touch the floor, but we didn't let go of each other.

He looked into my eyes, his own eyes intense. *This woman next to me is Nu Wa. You need to show her a great deal of respect.*

I quickly fell to one knee in front of Nu Wa and bowed my head. 'I thank you for your generous hospitality in our time of need, my Lady.'

She took my hand and raised me. 'You are more than welcome, Dark Lady.'

I smiled up into John's face but his severe expression didn't change.

I know what you're thinking, because I'm thinking the same thing. Yes, this is a honeymoon suite, but no, we can't do anything. This is Nu Wa's palace and we must show the lady proper respect. She would not like it. What's the expression? Not under my roof. So no more kissing in front of her; that spontaneous demonstration was amusing but if we continue she'll become extremely upset with us. He smiled slightly.

Decorum, my Lady, hard as it is. Treat her like your elderly and old-fashioned grandmother.

I lost my balance and stumbled backwards. He caught me, lifted me easily and carried me gently back to the bed. 'You're very weak. You need to rest. All of you nearly died.'

'The Tiger and Leo did die,' Simone said. 'Daddy and Kwan Yin were too late.'

The bed was gently spinning, the top of the canopy whirling above me, and I watched it with interest until it went dark.

I had a moment of disorientation as I saw the silk curtains, then remembered where I was and pulled myself upright. I took a huge drink from the glass beside the table and immediately felt better. My own jeans, T-shirt and my underwear — or very good copies of them all, down to the holes — were on the chair next to the bed.

Simone tapped on the door. 'Can I come in?'

'Can you wait till I'm dressed?' I said.

'Might be better if I come in and talk before you go anywhere, if you don't mind.'

'Come on in then,' I said.

She sat on the chair, moving the clothes onto the bed out of the way. 'Daddy and Nu Wa are talking about your case. He asked me to warn you about a few things before you come out.'

I settled more comfortably onto the bed. 'Go right ahead.'

'First, don't kill any insect demons. All her servants are insects.'

I stared at her. 'Her servants are insect demons?'

'She says they're the only things that could make it

up this high. Second, Daddy asks if you remember his warning from before.'

'I do.'

'Okay. Phew, I don't have to tell you that — you have no idea what a relief that is. Third, take very special care with drinking this stuff she gives you; it's horribly addictive.'

I picked up the empty glass and studied it. 'It's some sort of drug?'

'No. Not a drug, not alcohol; it's addictive because it's just so good. Daddy says, if you can, choose to drink water or tea instead.'

'I understand. What's she like?'

'She's absolutely lovely. Sad and lonely though. Apparently, last night was the first time she's left her pavilion and come into her palace since the Shang/Zhou wars. Can you tell me the story? Daddy says to ask you, because you're better at this sort of thing than he is.'

'What sort of thing?'

'Storytelling.'

'Oh, I see.' I put the story together in my head. 'The Shang king came to Nu Wa's palace, saw her, was mesmerised by her beauty and wrote a pornographic poem about what a hottie she was on the wall of her temple. She got mightily pissed with him and sent one of her servants, a fox spirit called Daji, to take over his favourite concubine and distract him into neglecting his kingdom. Instead of running the country, he spent all his time with her making out, and anyone who drew his attention to this was chained to a hollow pillar of iron with a fire lit inside it and tortured to death.'

Simone winced.

'A few brave generals who didn't agree with this went off, raised an army and brought him down, but not before the entire empire was torn apart by civil war.'

'That explains everything,' she said. 'Thanks.'

'You're welcome. Anything else?'

'No, just come on out when you're ready.'

'Any special protocols?'

'Daddy says just treat her like a grandmother.'

I bent to speak softly to her. 'Where's the bathroom?'

'Out the door, turn left, first on the right,' she said. 'There's a little pile of toiletries and stuff on the long bench for you. Go for your life.'

'You have no idea how much I need to.' I waved her away. 'Out.'

I stepped out of the bathroom, unsure of where to go. The hallway had a polished dark wooden floor, and the walls were wood panelling along the bottom with lighter plaster on the top half bordered by more dark wood — just like a traditional Chinese house. A couple of doors stood further along the corridor; probably other guest rooms. The bathroom's window was frosted so I hadn't been able see out, but the traditional red silk lanterns hanging from the ceiling weren't illuminated and I assumed it must be daytime.

A cockroach demon, about a metre long with a thick brown carapace, came down the hallway towards me and stopped, its feelers moving uncertainly.

'Can you tell me the way to the Lady Nu Wa?' I said.

It spun on its six legs and scurried back the way it had come. I sighed. Great, this place could be huge and I had to find my own way.

The cockroach stopped at the end of the corridor, turned back to see me and waved its feelers. Oh.

'Sorry, I'm coming,' I said, and followed it.

The corridor ended in a pair of double doors. The cockroach raised itself on its four hindmost legs and used the front two to open the doors for me, then stood back to one side to let me through.

'Thank you,' I said.

I walked through the doors and stopped. I was standing on bare, snowy ground, with a simple wooden pavilion ahead of me in the darkness, light shining from its windows. John, Nu Wa and Simone were sitting on cushions on the pavilion floor, and John gestured for me to join them. I walked across the snow, shivering as a blast of impossibly cold air hit me. The sky was completely black and the stars blazed bright without twinkling; no atmosphere up there. A ring of black, jagged mountain peaks circled the snow-filled valley.

I entered the pavilion to find the temperature only a few degrees warmer. The pavilion was small, about three metres by four, and had tatami-style woven rice mats on the floor along with cushions to sit on. There was a low coffee table set with tea things, and a large statue of the Buddha with incense burning in front of it.

I fell to one knee in front of Nu Wa and bowed my head. 'My Lady. I thank you for the comfort of your hospitality and the warmth of your home. Your care has eased my body and raised my spirit.'

Nu Wa smiled a grandmotherly smile and raised one hand, gesturing for me to approach. I went to her and she took my hand.

'Move back, Simone,' John said, and Simone spun on her cushion out of the way.

'Why does she need to make room?' I said, and was flattened. I hit the floor hard, only just managing to fall correctly and not injure my head. A cold, dark emptiness rushed through me like a flood of water, sweeping my consciousness with it. I drowned, my awareness submerged, tossed and beaten, with nothing to cling to.

The rushing water stopped and I took a huge breath, then gasped a few times.

Nu Wa took my other hand, holding both. 'I am sorry, child, I did not expect my examination to have such an effect on you. If you were Shen, demon or human, that would not have happened.'

'I'm not any of them?' I said.

'Nothing I have seen before,' she said.

I struggled to sit upright, nodded to Nu Wa and she released me.

'John, you knew that would happen. You told Simone to move back,' I said.

'I suspected,' he said. 'Drink some tea, and take some deep breaths. Ground and centre, cycle your energy.'

I did as he said, taking a few sips of tea and centring the energy at the same time.

'Oh, you are well trained, the Dark Lord has taught you well,' Nu Wa said. She touched my arm. 'Again, I apologise. I did not expect such a reaction.'

'Do you know why that happened?' John said.

'No.' Nu Wa kept her hand on my arm and her eyes unfocused. 'This one is full of riddles! So many layers, so much buried. So much potential for preservation and for destruction, for love and hate, and so much that isn't even there.' Her voice became fierce and full of command. 'Jade Building Block.'

'I am here to serve, my Lady,' the stone said, full of deference.

'Wow,' Simone said softly.

'What say you?' Nu Wa asked the stone.

'What you have said yourself already, Goddess. Layers, some buried, and love, and hate, and much of it not even there. And power, my Lady, dark power that roils at the heart of her. Dark, destructive power that she keeps firmly in check.'

Nu Wa came back. 'Go to the home of your ancestors,' she told me. 'Follow your family's history back to whence they came. That is the key.'

'My dad's doing that right now,' I said.

She nodded once. 'Good.'

'She has been filled with demon essence by a Prince of Demons,' John said.

'Nobody should be able to do that,' Nu Wa said. 'Nobody should have that done to them. And nobody should survive having that done to them.'

'I was the only one who survived it,' I said.

'Find your ancestors,' Nu Wa said. 'Your heritage betrays you.'

Simone inhaled sharply.

'Can you clear it, Honoured Lady?' I said.

'No,' Nu Wa said. 'I suspect that the Dark Lord was aware of this, and brought you anyway in the hope that even if I could not clear it I could identify what you are.'

'And you can do neither,' I said. I dropped my head. 'I killed two of my friends and nearly killed a third coming up here for nothing.'

'I'm sure Nu Wa has tried her best, Emma,' John began.

'No, I don't mean it like that,' I said, interrupting. 'I don't blame you, my Lady. I blame myself for the vanity of forcing others to make this journey when there was very little chance of a positive outcome. I've made them suffer for nothing.'

'It was my idea, Emma,' John said softly.

'He's right. Do not blame yourself; blame the silly turtle for this extremely bad idea,' Nu Wa said with amusement. 'If you wish to clear this demon essence from you, there are two paths you may take. First, talk to the Three Pure Ones. If they cannot help, then talk to the King of the Demons. I know he is a last resort, but it is within his power to aid you in this. If one more demon explodes on you, it will be the end.'

'I do not negotiate with demons,' I said.

'Why does she sound so much like Daddy sometimes?' Simone said.

'It is up to your father to explain his demonic side to you, little one,' Nu Wa said, 'and how that makes it possible for him to possess the bodies of others.'

'He's *possessed* someone?' Simone said.

'Me,' I said.

'It won't happen again. I am so sorry, Emma,' John said. 'You were losing it and the Turtle just wanted to help. I think, more than anything, I was desperate to find my Serpent and you just happened to be there.'

'When did this happen?' Simone said.

'A couple of days ago in the Western Palace,' I said.

'Just how much demon are you, Xuan Wu?' Simone said fiercely.

John stared at her, his face rigid and his dark eyes full of conflict.

'That much?' she said.

He nodded once sharply.

'I'm half demon?'

John gestured towards me. 'Do you love Emma?'

Simone glanced at me, then back at her father. 'Like my own mother.'

'She is more than half demon.'

'But she controls it ...' Simone stopped and looked down. 'I see.' She looked back up at him. 'What if *I* lose control?'

'There is no control for you to lose,' he said. 'I fathered you as Shen, not demon.'

'So I'm half-Shen, not half-demon at all,' she said.

He hesitated, then said, 'You have a heritage, just as Emma does. Yours is known, hers is not. If you chose, Simone, you could take your place in Hell amongst the mightiest of the demon horde. You could, if you wished, be Queen.'

'Not right now; you took my yin.'

'Even with your yin locked, you could still destroy the King.' He swept his hand towards us. 'Both of you could destroy him: Simone with your shen; Emma with your Destroyer. Either of you could be Queen.'

'Like either of us would want that,' I said.

He leaned back and put his hands on his knees. 'Which is why I love you both.'

'Were you ever Demon King?' Simone said.

'No,' John said. 'I am too much a force of chaos to hunger for power. Even now I have no wish to rule, but the Celestial chooses me because I am skilled.'

'And the Celestial feels your loss,' I said. 'The demons move against us all the more, the spirits leak from the gates of Hell, and evil walks the world because its greatest protector destroyed himself for the love of a woman.'

He nodded, solemn.

'He should join me in penitence,' Nu Wa said.

'You have atoned,' John said. 'Do not continue to punish yourself, Lady. It was an aeon ago and long forgotten. Remember some of the evil that I am responsible for; the Celestial will forgive and welcome you back, just as it has me.'

'I do not seek the Celestial's forgiveness,' Nu Wa said sadly. 'I seek my own. And it is not yet forthcoming.' She raised both hands, palms up. 'Now return to the palace and say your farewells, and I will send you back down to the Earthly Plane no wiser than you are now, with my apologies.'

Back inside the palace, Simone, John and I shared a vegetarian meal prepared and served by cockroaches and weevils. Nu Wa had refused to join us and stayed in her pavilion.

'Can't we just stay here?' Simone said. 'All three of us together, a family?'

'She wouldn't let us, even if that was what we truly wished,' John said. 'She has given us this time to share and talk and be a family as a gift.'

I touched his arm. 'The best gift in the world.'

He smiled back, took my hand and held it tight.

'So what next, Emma?' Simone said.

'We have a day, then we're Geek hunting,' I said.

'Geek?' John said.

Simone concentrated on him and they shared the information.

'God, I wish I could do that,' I said softly.

'You will be able to eventually,' Simone said. 'It's just a skill.'

They snapped out of it, and John nodded. 'These demons need to be taken down.' He looked from

Simone to me. 'But you should take some time and rest before facing them.'

'We can't afford to,' I said, running my hands through my hair and retying my ponytail. 'He's one step ahead of us. Every time we hit a nest, he's already cleared it out and set a bundle of lovely traps for us. Last one destroyed the car and killed all three stones.'

'When are the stones back?' John said.

'Should be today, if my watch is right,' I said.

He dropped his head. 'I wish I could be there to help you. With me there, they would not be able to stand against us.'

Simone leaned over the table and held his arm. 'What's happening with you? I'm just getting glimpses.' She choked on the words. 'When will you be *back*, Daddy?'

He raised his head to see into her eyes, his own full of misery. She took a deep, shuddering breath and pulled back. 'I see.'

'What?' I said.

Simone glanced at me, her eyes full of tears. 'He has no idea. He's in little pieces all over the place, a scattered consciousness, brought together for a short time by the power of the Goddess.' She looked from him to me. 'And it hurts, Emma. It hurts him so much!' She broke down and ran out of the room.

'And I did this,' I said.

'I did it to myself,' he said. He took my hand again and held it tight. 'Just remember my promise to you: I will find you.'

'You shouldn't have to find me! I'll always be here waiting for you. Does that mean I'll be lost?'

He released my hand, leaned on the table and put his hand on his forehead.

'I see,' I said. I took a deep breath and sat up straighter. 'Well, whatever happens, we know how it ends, so we just have to survive until we get there.'

He didn't reply and I was back at home in my room.

I was about halfway around the Lugard Road Peak walk a couple of hours later when my phone rang in my pocket. For a moment I considered not answering it, but too many people relied on me. I flipped it open. 'Emma.'

It was Chang. 'Red box, ma'am. They said if one appears you have to be informed immediately.'

I wanted to punch something. 'Dammit!'

'Ma'am?'

I took a deep breath. 'Sorry, Chang. Bring it up to the Peak for me, please. I'll look at it in the apartment.'

'Uh ...' He hesitated. 'What is it, ma'am? Why is it so important?'

'It's an edict from the Jade Emperor.'

He inhaled sharply. 'Seriously?'

'Yes. That's why I have to be informed immediately. It'll be either from His JEness himself or one of the other Real Higher-Ups.'

'His JEness? Does he know you call him that, ma'am?'

'Probably. Anything else?'

'No, ma'am. Everything here is reasonably under control. About ten people want to talk to you about assorted non-urgent things but I told them to wait until tomorrow.'

'Good man. I'll be down there later to go through things with you.'

'Thank you, ma'am.'

'Oh, and Chang ...'

378

'Ma'am?'

'You're doing a fine job.'

He was silent for a moment, then said in a small voice, 'Thank you, ma'am.'

I arrived back at the Peak apartment in time to see Chang pulling up at the front gate in the new Mercedes.

'A gentleman whose face I've seen before said this car was for you,' he said. 'The Masters said to bring it up with the box.'

I pointed at car spot number one. 'Park it there and bring the box up.'

Upstairs, I guided him into my office and sat at the desk. I waved for him to give me the red box, and he jumped as he remembered he had it and put it on the desk in front of me.

'I have come a long way since the last time I was here,' he said. 'And my heart is full of joy at the journey I've made.'

'Me too,' I said.

I thumbed the clasp on the front of the box and it opened. There were two scrolls inside, neither of them bound with red ribbon. One was bound with green; the other with white.

'Nothing from the Jade Emperor,' I said. 'Let's see what we have here.'

I opened the scroll bound with the green ribbon, read it and slammed it on the table. 'Shit.'

Chang jumped again. 'Ma'am?'

'Er Lang's demanded an evaluation in five days. Bastard! None of the students are ready for this. We have to prepare them, move them to Guangzhou, put them in the House on the Hill, and then he tests them.'

'Tests them?'

'If they pass they're selected to join the Jade Emperor's own private guard. It's prestigious and I love doing it for them, but he's asked for seniors and they're really not ready for this with only five days' prep. God, but that man hates me! Stone.'

The stone didn't reply so I tapped it.

'Hm?'

'Read this scroll and pass the information on to the Academy. We have to start preparing the students — and the House on the Hill — now.'

'Oh my. One has to wonder what you did to piss him off, Emma, really. This is just harassment.'

I grumbled quietly as I took out the white-ribboned scroll and rolled it open. 'Shit!'

'What now?' Chang said, beginning to be amused by my theatrics.

'I have to go to freaking *Hell* and answer to Judge Pao *this afternoon* on why I keep getting my Retainers killed.'

'Do you want me to tell him to piss off?' the stone said.

'Can I?' I said. 'It's none of his business.'

'Not really,' the stone said. 'It's worth a try but it could annoy him even more.'

'It shouldn't take long. Says here the boat'll be ready for me at 3 pm; all I have to do is go down to the dock, go to Hell, talk to him, and probably be back well in time for dinner.'

'I love this job more and more every day,' Chang said with wonder. He checked his watch. 'It's two now, ma'am, which dock do you have to go to?'

'Shum Wan,' I said. 'Where you go for the boats across to the floating restaurants.'

'Really?' he said, grinning broadly.

'Yeah. Let me get changed. You're fine like that — you can take me down in the new Merc and wait for me there.'

'Ma'am ...' Chang's face became intense. 'Any chance ...'

'Sorry, no humans allowed,' I said. 'You go into Hell, you never come out again.'

'But you're human,' he said.

'That is where you are very mistaken, my friend,' the stone said. 'She has never been human; she's always been a cold-hearted, evil demon snake.'

'My stone knows me better than the one I am promised to marry,' I said. 'Give me ten minutes to make myself all pretty and we'll go down to Shum Wan.'

I put on my traditional black robe with the armour over it, pulled my hair up into a bun held with the ebony spike, and slipped the Murasame onto my back. I even put on some make-up to seal the deal. This was one meeting where I didn't want to mess around.

Chang's eyes went wide when he saw me. 'You look like a scarier version of the Entombed Warriors,' he said.

I bowed slightly. 'Thank you. Let's go.'

'I like this human,' the stone said as we went out to the lift. 'He really has you picked.'

'Who is that talking anyway?' Chang said.

'My engagement ring.'

'Oh.' His face cleared as he understood. 'I was warned about it.'

'Good,' the stone said.

'I'll need a Retainer,' I said in the car. 'Stone, find Michael. Have him meet me at Shum Wan.'

'Michael's in hospital, ma'am,' Chang said.

That stopped me. 'What?'

'Dehydration and exposure,' the stone said. 'Frostbite as well, but he won't lose any fingers or toes. He'll be fine, he's just resting.'

'I should have been informed of this immediately.'

'Please forgive me, my Lady,' Chang said.

'Why didn't you tell me, Chang?'

Chang was silent.

'In future, I must know immediately of any injuries sustained by my Retainers. Understood?'

I opened my mobile phone to call Michael.

Why didn't he tell me? Why didn't anyone tell me? I asked the stone.

He was supposed to tell you, the stone said.

Why didn't he then? I took a deep breath. *Okay, one mistake. I'll let it pass.*

He's jealous, ma'am.

Any more of that and he'll be back with Lok on garbage patrol, and you can tell him that silently. Make it a private warning.

I watched Chang's face change as Michael answered his phone. 'Hi, Emma.'

'Are you okay?'

'I'm fine. I want to leave but they won't let me. I should be out tomorrow.'

'This won't slow down your getting rid of that limp, will it?'

'Nah, hasn't made any difference.'

'What about Clarissa?'

'She's here.'

'Does she believe you yet?'

He hesitated, then, 'We'll get there.'

'I'm glad she cares enough to put up with this, Michael.'

'We're not there yet.'

CHAPTER 26

Chang stopped at the lay-by next to the Shum Wan piers. I hopped out, pulled the Murasame out of the back of the car, then leaned in to speak to him.

'I need you to wait for me; I could be up to a couple of hours. I'll need you right here when I return, so don't go anywhere. The car's too new to have the invisibility charm put on it —'

His face lit up.

'Yes, we have invisibility charms, but there isn't one on you right now.' I pulled my head out of the car and looked around; no police nearby. I stuck my head back in to speak to him. 'If the police show, pull away, go around the hill a few times, then come back. Just don't go too far away, okay?'

He nodded. 'Understood, ma'am. I will be here when you return.'

I closed the door, rapped on the roof, then clipped the sword to my back — and turned to find a group of elderly European tourists staring at me.

'Excuse me,' one woman said in a strong London accent. 'Can you tell us which is the right jetty for the floating restaurant?'

'Uh ...' I looked around. 'Which one?'

'Jumbo?'

I pointed. 'The middle one.'

She nodded. 'Thank you.' She looked me up and down. 'Are you going there?'

'No, I'm going to a ...' I thought frantically. 'A fancy dress party on a junk out in the harbour.'

'Oh.' She smiled politely. 'Have fun then. Thank you.'

One of the men in the group piped up. 'Where did you get that costume? My son would give anything for an Entombed Warrior costume. Can you buy them here?'

'No,' I said. 'It was custom-made.' The boat to Hell pulled into the unused pier. 'There's my ride, have fun at the floating restaurant.'

'Is that a real sword?' the man said.

'No, just plastic,' I said, and the Murasame jabbed me in the back with the end of the scabbard, making me jump.

'Are you all right?' the woman said, moving closer, concerned.

'I'm just fine,' I said. I gestured towards the pier. 'There's the Jumbo boat — you'd better hurry if you want to catch it.'

Most of them scurried off down the hill, leaving the curious man and woman behind.

'What do you have on under the robe?' the woman said.

I lifted the hem. 'Just a pair of jeans.'

'Are those Doc Martens?' the man said.

I nodded. 'Completely everything-proof. Only problem is that the air cushions in the soles wear out just when you have them worn in.' I gestured with my head towards the pier. 'Your boat's about to leave.'

384

'Oh!' the woman said, and took his arm. 'Let's go.'

He let her pull him down the hill and waved to me. 'Have fun at your party.'

I waved back. 'Thanks. Have fun at the restaurant.'

I shook my head and walked down to the pier where the demons were tying up the boat to Hell.

An official was waiting for me on the roof of the administration building as I stepped out of the lift. His eyes went wide when he saw the way I was dressed, then he composed himself and gestured for me to follow him.

I raised my hand to make him wait a moment, closed my eyes, took a deep breath and told the Murasame to *shut the hell up*. The sword couldn't speak aloud but inside my head it was screaming for blood. It really, *really* liked being in Hell and wanted something to cut up — *now*. Its demands didn't help my control over my demon nature, which wanted me to transform and rush to the Pits to share in a feeding frenzy. The voices roared around me, spiralling me into darkness. I took another deep breath, touched the serpent within me, drew upon my yang nature and silenced them. I opened my eyes again, saluted the official and turned to follow him down the stairs to Court Ten.

'Are you well, ma'am?' he said.

'I am well. My Retainer has been injured and cannot attend me; please inform the Court that I will attend alone.'

'That's the reason you're here, ma'am.'

'Humph.'

We went down the stairs and along the path that skirted the lake that separated the Celestial and

Demonic parts of Hell. Court Ten was first on the left, at the end of one of the causeways that led to the Pits on the other side of the lake. I strode up to it, trying to appear as confident as possible, with the official scurrying behind me.

The Court building was a traditional Chinese two-storey house, with pillars and brackets holding up the green tiled roof and a balcony on the second level. Two demons stood guard at the entrance, one on either side. They opened the doors as I approached, and I took a deep breath and walked into the hall.

The entrance was deserted. A pair of red double doors stood in front of me, again flanked by a pair of demons. They bowed to me and opened the doors.

I took long, confident steps into the courtroom, stopped in the middle of the room, fell to one knee and saluted as a warrior. 'I am Lady Emma Donahoe, Acting First Heavenly General, Regent of the Northern Heavens, Administrator of Wudangshan. I have been summoned.'

I remained on one knee with my head bowed as Judge Pao replied. He wore a traditional plain black robe and his dark-skinned face was fierce.

'You have been summoned here, madam, to answer to the Courts as to the reckless endangerment of your army, Retainers and servants. These Shen,' he gestured towards the benches at the side of the room, where Gold, Jade, Zara and Calcite sat together with the Tiger and Leo, 'have all died multiple times recently in your service. The Lord Leo was only a day back on the Earthly before he was killed again — following you.'

I rose to reply but Gold got there first. 'If I may, my Lord,' he said, standing. 'I represent the Lady Emma in legal matters.'

'You are dead!' Judge Pao said.

Gold raised his hands. 'I may be dead, my Lord, but I can still speak on my Lady's behalf.'

Judge Pao had a whispered discussion with an official behind him, then waved Gold forward. 'You may speak.'

Gold bowed to me. 'My Lady. Permission to speak on your behalf.'

Stone, quick. If I let him speak on my behalf does that weaken my image and make me look like a helpless woman?

Only if you act like a helpless woman, the stone said. *It's all up to the amount of bravado you throw around here.*

Testosterone ahoy!

I stomped backwards and forwards a few times, head down, then waved one hand airily at Gold without looking at him. 'You may speak on my behalf, despite the fact that you spoke out of turn. Speak well, stone, because I do not have time to be wasting with this.'

Oh, well done, ma'am, Gold said with admiration.

I stood with my hands on my hips and glared around the courtroom. I desperately wanted to wink at Leo, who was staring at me.

Gold stepped forward to stand next to me and put his hands behind his back. 'Lady Emma is one of the Celestial's finest, but when people go to their deaths she does not lead them there.'

'If she's not leading then her role is undermined and she should step down,' Judge Pao said.

'Jade Building Block,' Gold said.

'Present,' the stone said.

'Master Leo and myself, Calcite and Zara have died twice in the last week following Lady Emma. The White Tiger of the West has died once. Is this true?'

'This is true.'

There was a murmur of consternation around the court.

'Did she order us to die for her?'

'No,' the stone said. 'Unlike many Celestials, she will not throw Immortals to their deaths.'

'No, that can't be true,' Gold said, feigning disbelief. 'We're Immortal, death means nothing to us, our Master is within his ... or her ...' He bowed to me, acknowledging the difference, and I nodded back, trying to keep my expression stern. '... his or her rights to order us to our deaths. They all do it. It is only when we are ordered to our deaths with little forethought for our comfort and needs, or too many times in a short period, that there is a problem.'

'That is the problem here,' Judge Pao said.

'The problem then, as I see it, is that we have been ordered to our deaths too many times in too short a time by Lady Emma.'

'That is the case being heard here,' Judge Pao said. 'You are proving the case against her, stone.'

'Jade Building Block, how many times has Lady Emma ordered an Immortal — any Immortal — to their death?'

'Never,' the stone said.

'Not once?'

'I am checking my memory matrix now. I am correct. Lady Emma Donahoe, the Dark Lady, has never ordered a Shen to die.'

'But we die anyway,' Gold said. 'I've died twice in the last few days.'

'You die following her. She does not lead you. It is your choice,' the stone said.

Your turn, Gold said.

I stepped forward and glared at Judge Pao. 'You accuse me of leading my Shen to their deaths too many times.' I turned and gestured towards the Immortals sitting to one side. 'I never lead anyone to their death; they follow me by choice themselves. Your case has no valid basis.' I fell to one knee and saluted. 'By your leave, I will withdraw. There are demons out there who are duplicating elementals and humans; they must be stopped, and I will be the one to stop them.' I rose. 'My staff, my soldiers and my Retainers will follow me to fight; and if they follow me to fight and die it is their choice.'

I didn't wait for a reply, I just spun on my heel and walked out of the courtroom.

'What of those who are not Immortal and follow you to their deaths?' Judge Pao shouted behind me.

That stopped me for a moment, then I took a deep breath and continued walking.

Are you sure he's not possessing you right now? the stone said.

Oh no, he'd have been much less arrogant. He's way better at being soft and kind and getting his own way by scaring the shit out of everybody with just a look.

I think you just did exactly the same thing, ma'am.

I waited a couple of minutes outside the courtroom, and sagged with relief when the stones, Jade, Leo and Bai Hu all filed out towards me.

Bai Hu slapped me on the back. 'Magnificent. Ah Wu couldn't have done better. Pao is choking on his rice wine.'

'I don't know,' Gold said. 'It was a bit messy; we could have stated our case with more precision.'

'It was pretty good considering it was all made up on the run,' I said.

'Are my children all right, ma'am?' Jade said, grasping my hand.

'I think you should ask their father,' I said. 'He has them.'

She nodded and turned away.

'I think we should leave before Pao changes his mind about letting us go,' the Tiger said. 'Let's get out of here.'

We took the lift back up from Hell, then the boat to the pier. Chang, as promised, was waiting for us at the lay-by.

Leo wheeled himself up to the car and looked suspiciously inside. 'Who's this?'

'That's Chang, my new secretary,' I said. 'We lost the car; we'll have to get this one fixed up for you.' I opened the back door. 'In you hop.'

'I'll take myself, if you don't mind,' Leo said. 'I'll meet you back at the shop.' He disappeared.

I turned back to see the Tiger and the stones. 'Anybody want a lift?'

'We're fine, ma'am, we want to head back to the Academy and get stuck into that data as quickly as possible. Time is wasting,' Gold said. He saluted me. 'By your leave.'

'Go,' I said, and he and the two other stones disappeared.

The Tiger spread his arms, strode up to me and enveloped me in a huge hug. 'That was totally incredible,' he said into my ear. 'One of the hottest things I've ever seen, and I've got wives who are warriors.'

He hugged me tighter and thrust his pelvis into me. I dropped my weight slightly, pushed one shoulder into him and tossed him over my shoulder onto his back. He grinned at me from the ground and disappeared.

I unclipped the Murasame and dismissed it, then climbed into the front passenger side of the car. 'Let's go.'

Back at the Academy I went straight to the IT hub. Gold, Zara and Calcite were sitting in a circle around the stack of disks piled haphazardly on the floor.

'They can't talk, they're down. Let me link in,' the stone said. 'Done.'

'How long?' I said.

'They've processed about seventy-five per cent,' the stone said. 'They're doing well. The data was mostly unfragmented. They'll have it put back together later tonight.'

'Not another late-night phone call,' I said. 'What's the rock next to the disks for?'

'Storage. That holds the data from the Department of Statistics.'

'Is there anything I can do?'

'No. Leave them to it and have an early night.' I turned to go out but it stopped me. 'Wait. My mistake. They are seventy-five per cent through the contents of the disks. They will then need to finish processing the data from the Department of Statistics. Then they will need to cross-reference.' It was silent for another moment. 'My apologies, ma'am, my child says at least twelve hours.'

'Damn,' I said. 'Plenty of time for the demon to get ahead of us.'

'They apologise and say that they are working as fast as they can.'

'No need to apologise,' I said.

When I arrived back at my office, Leo was there, in his wheelchair across the desk from Chang.

'I don't know where you found this one, Emma,' he said without looking away from Chang. 'But I think you should send him back.'

'What did you say to him, Chang? Leo is one of the most senior and respected Masters in the Academy.'

Chang gestured towards Leo. 'How can he be a Master in a wheelchair? Why do you keep him around when he's lost the use of his legs? Surely the best for all concerned would be for him to retire.'

'Let me handle this, Emma,' Leo said through his teeth and wheeled himself to the doorway. He concentrated for a moment then snapped back. 'Training room fourteen is free. You and me, little Chinese boy. Let's see what you got.'

Chang rose, his face fierce with restrained anger. 'I cannot believe a black man would call anyone "boy". I will not go easy on you because you are a cripple.'

Leo appeared shocked, then his face went hard again. 'Somebody warned you about insulting me, eh? Too bad you didn't learn anything.' He wheeled himself through the door. 'Follow me.'

Aren't you going to stop them, Emma? the stone said as I followed Chang out the door.

Nah, I said. *This will be interesting.*

'There is no honour to be gained in defeating a cripple, but in this case he has more than asked for it,' Chang said, still glaring at Leo as we arrived at the lifts.

I didn't reply, I just crossed my arms over my chest.

'Nice outfit, Emma,' Leo said as the lift doors opened.

'Yeah, someone at the pier asked me where they could buy one.'

'We should branch out into the costume business,' Leo said. He wheeled himself out of the lift two floors higher and headed towards room fourteen. He stopped and glanced up at me. 'You don't need to come along for this. I can handle myself.'

'I know that,' I said. 'Humour an old woman.'

'Laugh a minute,' Leo said grimly.

We entered room fourteen and I closed the door. Leo took one side of the room and Chang stood on the other.

'If you choose you can use a weapon,' Chang said. 'It will make this fairer.'

'Oh, that's funny,' Leo said. 'Because I was about to say the same thing.'

Chang sensibly moved into a low guard, standing slightly side-on to Leo with his right hand in front of his pelvis and his left at waist-level. Leo didn't move, then his face screwed up with concentration and he rose and stepped out of the wheelchair, pushing it away behind him.

Wow, the Lion really is pissed, the stone said.

Chang moved to a higher guard, looking Leo in the eye. Leo moved into a standard long defensive stance and both of them remained completely still for a good sixty seconds. Leo was slightly taller than Chang, but they were close on the same size and build otherwise.

Oh, this is a good match, the stone said. *Leo is terribly out of practice, you know that, ma'am.*

I nodded almost imperceptibly and the movement was enough to set them off. They both took two huge strides forward to each other. Leo dropped to perform a roundhouse kick to take Chang's feet out from under him; Chang went for Leo's head with a straight right.

Leo's kick worked and Chang hit the floor, rolling and springing upright. Leo didn't attack again, he took two steps back and stood waiting with his guard up.

'Is the wheelchair a ruse?' Chang said. 'Do you deal in lies?'

'No,' Leo said. 'My spine is destroyed. Ninety-nine per cent of the time I can't walk when I'm in human form.'

Chang straightened slightly. 'Human form? You are a Shen?'

Leo's face went blank and he dropped his guard. 'Well, how about that. I guess I am.'

Chang took the opportunity to rush Leo, attacking with both left and right. Leo blocked him easily, striking him in the abdomen and knocking him back but not moving in to finish it. He took another defensive stance and waited for Chang.

Chang moved sideways a couple of steps, measuring Leo, and Leo followed the movement, turning without lowering his guard. Chang went in again, this time using a close-in hold and attempting to floor Leo. Leo was overbalanced for a second, then turned his weight around and used it to drop Chang heavily onto his back.

Chang flipped up and took a couple of steps back. He didn't hesitate; he went for Leo again before Leo was fully ready, with a flurry of blows at his head, faster than the eye could see. Leo blocked all of them easily, took one on the forearm, twisted it down and used it to unbalance Chang. He spun Chang so he was facing away from him and pushed him away, nearly tipping him over again.

Leo moved into a long defensive stance.

Chang dropped to one knee and lowered his head. 'I apologise for insulting you, my Lord. I concede.'

Leo straightened, bewildered, then collapsed as his legs gave way. Chang jumped up to help him and Leo dazedly accepted his assistance into the wheelchair.

'Good,' I said. 'Back to my office, we have work to do.'

I discussed plans for the raid with Leo and Chang as I went through the papers in my in-tray. 'Tomorrow we're going into Shenzhen to nail this Geek demon that's been making the fake elementals. How'd it go with rounding up help, Chang?'

Chang jumped up and ran out of my office, then returned with a notepad. 'The Masters Liu request your indulgence in permitting them to stay here and "mind the shop". Marshal Ma says that three generals — Marshal Guang Ze of the Wind Wheel, Marshal Bi Tian Hua of the Rolling Thunder, and Marshal Zhu Bo Niang of the Heavenly Sword — can attend you. He says,' he checked the paper, '"these three losers can cover most elemental attacks if we can keep them sober long enough".' His eyes went wide and he looked up at me. 'Is he *serious*?'

'Nah, they're about the most sober of the generals we have,' I said. 'You should see Liang Tien out on the town though. He's an animal.'

'With four legs, the body of a dragon and the head of a monster,' Leo said.

'That's the one,' I said. 'Three generals, Leo, me, the Tiger said he'd show, a couple of stones to lead the way — oh, and Simone. That should be plenty to take this little Geek down.'

'Me too, ma'am,' Chang said.

I leaned back. 'You haven't sworn allegiance yet.'

Chang rose out of his chair and fell to one knee in front of me. I stood up; this was a big step and it was right to acknowledge it.

'I swear allegiance to you, my Lady,' Chang said. 'I will follow you to the ends of the Earth; I will obey your every order without question; I will protect you with my life. This I swear.'

I sat down again, and so did he.

'You're ordered to stay behind,' I said. 'You're not coming with us.'

Chang opened his mouth and closed it. Leo hid his smile.

'Did Marshal Ma say when and where we're meeting?' I said.

'Nine o'clock tomorrow morning,' Chang said. 'Here at the Academy.'

'That works,' I said. 'Let's run through this, then call it a night.'

'I'll see you back at home, Emma,' Leo said. He patted Chang on the back as he wheeled himself out. 'Look after her.'

When Chang and I were done, I called Simone on the way down in the elevator.

'And he *peed* on the carpet in my room and now it has to be replaced! Hello?'

'It's me. Are you coming home for dinner?'

'Let me check my timetable.' She made some weird noises as she rummaged around in her bag, obviously with her phone jammed under her chin. 'Can you use something a little less mundane to call me so I don't have to bother with the handset?'

'The stone has to use one of its children to relay all the time — not worth it.'

'That makes sense. I have a demon essence class in thirty minutes, then that's all for tonight. I'll be home about eight. Is that okay?'

'We're all having dinner at home tonight to welcome Michael out of hospital. He's bringing Clarissa. Can you make it a bit earlier?'

'Can someone use a stone or something to record the lesson on demon essences?' she said.

'I'll do it for you, Simone,' a girl said.

'Thanks.' She came back to me. 'I'll see you there.'

I put my phone back in my bag and turned to Chang, who was with me in the lift. 'I'll drive you to the New Folly then take the car up to the Peak. Take the bus to the Academy tomorrow morning.'

'I can drive you home, ma'am,' he said.

'How are you supposed to get home after that?' I said. 'The car has to stay at the Peak tonight, for the meeting tomorrow morning. No, I'll drop you.'

'So tonight's dinner is family only?' he said.

'That's right.'

'And Lord Leo is family?'

'More than you know.'

Michael gently guided Clarissa to a seat at the table. She sat down looking uncomfortable.

'It's nice to see you again,' I said, trying to break the tension.

'You all look so normal,' she said.

'We can be completely normal when we want to be,' Simone said. 'Come shopping with us sometime. Leo takes ages trying stuff on, and Emma hates the whole business and doesn't stop complaining.'

'Well, it's boring,' I said.

'I do not!' Leo said.

Clarissa relaxed slightly, smiling.

'That's more like it,' I said. 'Do you have anything you want to ask us? Michael's probably told you a lot of stuff, but you must have some questions.'

Monica brought in a tray holding the dinner dishes, smiled around the table and went out.

'You forgot the rice again!' Leo called.

She poked her head around the door. 'No, I didn't, sir, it's coming with the soup.' She waved one hand at him, smiling with mischief. 'So impatient. Aren't you supposed to be serene and calm and mystical?'

He made a soft sound of amusement and shook his head. 'She gets cheekier every day. I blame Marcus.'

Clarissa studied Leo. 'You really are an Immortal? I've heard the stories — she's right.'

'There are two types of Immortals,' Leo said, enjoying her attention. 'Those that achieve the Tao — the Way — and attune themselves to the Universe through a process of mystical bull— nonsense.'

Simone nearly spat out her tea.

'And then there are the Immortals like me, who were Raised as a sort of Celestial promotion — I was given the Elixir of Immortality by the Jade Emperor himself. I don't have the purity of spirit that those other Immortals do. I eat meat, I hook up with —' He stopped. 'Anyway, I'm more like a super-powered ordinary mortal-type guy.'

'And then there are the ones like Michael's dad,' I said. 'Nature spirits, who are elemental and powerful and completely inhuman. They can choose to attain the Tao if they wish, but they're Immortal anyway, and they retain their animal nature whatever they do.'

'Which explains the hundred wives,' Michael said.

'I met some of them,' Clarissa said. 'How do they put up with it?'

'Michael's mother didn't,' Simone said. 'She left him.'

'The only one who did,' Michael said thoughtfully. 'And when she went back to him, it killed her.'

Monica brought in the rice and soup. 'Master Leo's rice.'

'Emma, you're Michael's boss, right?' Clarissa said.

'Until Lord Xuan Wu returns, yes, I am.'

'How much danger will he be in if he returns to work for you?'

I put my chopsticks down and sat back. 'You'll never be in danger.'

'That's not what I'm asking,' she said. 'We're talking about moving in together. That dog is great fun, by the way. But if we're living together, and he's working for you, how often will I be sitting there waiting for him to come home and not having any idea where he is?'

'You never asked this before,' Michael said.

'I want to ask her, not you,' Clarissa said. 'She's the one you'll be guarding — the one you'll be taking a bullet for if need be.'

I nodded. 'I understand.' I tapped the stone. 'Hey, wake up.'

'Who is this?' the stone said.

'Michael's girlfriend.'

'Bah, ordinary human,' the stone said. 'You woke me up for this?'

'Who's that speaking?' Clarissa said.

'It's the stone in my engagement ring, a piece of sentient jade,' I said. 'It's rude, arrogant and abusive.'

'You forgot lazy,' the stone said.

'Yeah, that too. Anyway, stone, ask Zara if she'd like to do a job for me when she's free from everything else. I need someone to act as a link between Clarissa and Michael while he's working on the Celestial.'

'Zara belongs to my dad,' Michael said.

'Precisely,' I said. 'Is it okay with you?'

'It's a great idea,' he said.

I would be honoured, Zara said.

All yours, the Tiger said.

'Okay, Clarissa, here's what we'll do. We're going to give you a stone — a diamond — that talks just like my engagement ring. You can use it to talk to Michael anytime you like and keep in touch with him regardless of where he is. Right now, the stone is busy doing a computing job for me, but when she's free, she's all yours. Her name is Zara.'

'A diamond?' Clarissa said, turning to Michael, her eyes wide.

'You'll love her when you meet her,' he said. He turned back to the food. 'Dinner's getting cold. Let me get you some of this chicken, Monica does amazing things with it.'

Clarissa opened her mouth to say something, then changed her mind, her disappointment evident.

I don't know who's more stupid, you or Michael, the stone said.

Me, I said.

Michael smiled at Clarissa, completely unaware.

CHAPTER 27

I arrived at the Academy the next morning to find a bunch of people in front of Chang's desk and him sitting bewildered behind it.

'Chang, escort our honoured guests to meeting room nine, the conference room on this floor, and have the demons serve them tea,' I said. 'I'll be along shortly, everyone.'

'Come with me,' Simone said. 'Chang, stay here. I'll look after them.'

I went into my office and quickly checked the email. Nothing important. 'Are they done?' I asked the stone.

'No,' it said. 'They're still cross-indexing.'

'Computers ... always takes longer than they say.'

'Call any of the stones "computers" to their faces ...'

'I know, I know, mortal insult, et cetera, et cetera. Nothing important here, I might as well go join the generals in room nine,' I said. 'Where's that goddamn Tiger?'

'No reply,' the stone said.

'I know what he's doing,' I said. 'Oversexed bastard.'

'Ma'am, sometimes ...' the stone said, and its voice trailed off.

'Yes?'

'Never mind.'

'I sound like John. Yes, I'm hearing it myself now.' I headed out to meeting room nine. 'And it's freaking me out as well.'

The generals rose and saluted me as I entered, then we all sat. Zhu Bo Niang's usual form was a girl of fifteen, but for this meeting she'd aged to about thirty, and wore an elegant pink twin set and cream tailored slacks. The two male generals wore no-nonsense robes and armour.

'The stones are still working on it,' I said. 'We should have a result soon.'

'You can tell us about Nu Wa while we're waiting,' Zhu Bo Niang said. 'I hear she was nothing as expected.'

'She's sad and lonely and won't leave her pavilion,' Simone said. 'I wish the Celestial would send her a message to say she can come back.'

'We do,' Guang Ze said. 'We've been sending her messages for thousands of years, and she hasn't replied.'

'Tell us about this demon we're hunting,' Bi Tian Hua said. 'Sounds fun.'

'Stone, put up a couple of pictures of the fake elementals he's made,' I said, and a collection of three-dimensional images of the various types of elementals appeared over the table. 'He's part of the original trio that was assisting One Two Two nine years ago; they were controlling stones, making fake elementals and making demonic copies of humans that are close to undetectable.'

'I've heard about that,' Guang Ze said. 'Very disturbing.' He leaned on the table. 'Any word on the return of the Dark Lord? His presence would be extremely reassuring.'

'Daddy doesn't know when. Nobody knows,' Simone said. 'He's in pieces.'

'We should search for him, bring him back together,' Guang Ze said. 'Why hasn't Ma suggested this?'

'Ma himself went out into the world looking for him and found nothing,' I said. 'He's still too wild and elemental to be found.'

'If Ma can't do it, nobody can,' Bi Tian Hua said. 'Ma can go places none of us are able to. We just have to cultivate patience.'

'When he is strong enough to be found, we may be able to join forces — all thirty-six of us — and bring him back,' Bo Niang said.

'That would incapacitate all of us for a considerable time,' Guang Ze said.

Bo Niang shrugged. 'It's an option if things become desperate. He's more powerful than all of us put together — if needed, we can be sacrificed to ensure his return.'

'Just one of us could sacrifice themselves completely, as well,' Bi Tian Hua said.

Bo Niang nodded agreement. 'That would work, and the other thirty-five would remain at full strength.'

'What do you mean completely?' Simone said.

'You're talking about total absorption and destruction to bring him back?' I said.

Bi Tian Hua nodded. 'It is an option.'

'No it isn't!' I said.

'They're done,' the stone said. 'Gold is on his way.'

Gold appeared at the end of the table. 'Turn the freak show off, Dad, I need the space,' he said.

The elementals disappeared, and a map of Shenzhen took their place floating above the table.

'Everything comes together at this point,' Gold said. The map zoomed in to a compound on the north side of the city, far from the Hong Kong border. 'Shenzhen Ming Dian Electronics Company. They have three factory buildings and dorms as well. Every single person we processed has some sort of link with this company.' He smiled, triumphant. 'That's where the Geek is.'

The Tiger appeared at the end of the table, tucking his shirt in. 'What are we waiting for? Let's go.'

The rest of the group rose and I stopped them. 'Wait, wait, wait. What did the company specialise in?'

'Just computers.'

'No,' I said. 'Video cards, motherboards, what?'

'Ironically enough, storage,' Gold said. 'Hard disks, disk controllers, RAID controllers —'

'Raid?' Guang Ze said.

'Not that sort of raid. It means Random Array of Independent Disks; it's a way of storing —'

'I see,' Guang Ze said. 'Computer stuff.'

'Yes. How is this relevant, ma'am? If you don't mind me saying so, we need to move.'

'No,' I said. 'He's been one step ahead of us all the way, and he's had three days to move his operation. Find all the *other* computer companies in Shenzhen that are producing the same stuff, because one of them will be where he's moved to.'

'He could still be in the same place,' Gold said, protesting.

'Simone and Tiger, work together and send some

elementals to Ming Dian and see if there are any demons there,' I said. 'I bet you ten dollars it's been cleared out.'

'I need to be about fifty metres away to send in elementals,' Simone said.

'Then hurry up and teleport!' I said. 'Come back with an answer for us. Keep your head down and stay invisible, don't let them know you're there.'

'Come on, Simone, let me show you how it's done,' the Tiger said, and he and Simone disappeared.

'Let me hook up with Calcite and Zara,' Gold said. He disappeared as well.

'You'd better be right, Emma, otherwise you'll never live this down,' Bo Niang said with humour.

'Either way, he's there or he's not,' I said. 'My bet is that he's moved on, but he needs the same sort of equipment to keep making the elementals.'

The Tiger and Simone reappeared.

'She's right,' Simone said. 'All cleared out, nothing there.'

'Ma was right,' Guang Ze said.

'Damn straight,' Bi said.

'About what?' I said.

'You,' Bo Niang said.

'Scares the living shit out of me,' the Tiger said. He sat at the table. 'No beer? What sort of hospitality is this, woman?' He summoned a can of beer and popped it open. 'Tell those stones to hurry up. I got three women on the boil and I want something to dig my claws into.'

Gold reappeared, Calcite and Zara with him.

'How many?' I said.

The map zoomed out over the table and five red dots appeared, three close to each other and two on the other side of town. 'Five that specialise in storage,' Gold said. Several green dots appeared, most of them in a cluster with two or three in separate locations. 'Plus ten more that do it as well as other types of technology.'

I studied the map and pointed. 'Tiger and Simone, see that one? That's the specialty producer that's furthest from Hong Kong, and it's not clustered with the others.' I turned to Simone. 'This teleporting isn't wearing you out, is it? We need you strong when we find it.'

'Let's go,' Simone said, and she and the Tiger disappeared again, the Tiger's beer left forgotten on the table.

Not here, Simone said. *It's closed up. Financial crisis, probably. The signs out the front say that it's a joint venture with an American firm.*

Passing on the location of the next furthest one away, Gold said.

On our way, Simone said.

'So many firms folded up and blamed the GFC,' Guang Ze said, 'when in fact the owners just siphoned off all the funds and left. It's disgusting.'

'Corruption is a problem you just have to deal with,' Bo Niang said.

'How do you deal with it when you encounter it?' Bi Tian Hua said, leaning forward with interest.

'It depends on the situation,' Bo Niang said. 'If it's a government official —'

Found it! the Tiger roared in my head. *Holy fucking SHIT but this place is full of demons. Get your asses down here right now, there's some serious fun brewing! Oh — I forgot.* His beer disappeared off the table.

Simone reappeared. 'Change to snake, Emma, I'll carry you down. Everybody else can teleport.'

'This is wearing you out too much,' I said.

406

'I'm fine,' Simone said. 'Change. If we don't get down there right now the Tiger'll go in solo and mess it all up.'

I changed to serpent, she touched my head, and we arrived in Shenzhen. The rest of the group appeared behind me; Bo Niang had changed to robes and armour, the same as Bi and Guang. Leo appeared in his wheelchair then changed to lion form and leapt out of it, tipping it over. Gold appeared as well, in battle form: his human shape made of stone.

The Tiger grinned when he saw us. 'Good job.'

I changed back to human form and summoned the Murasame.

'Waste of time,' Simone said. 'You kill anything with that, you're converted. Better to come as snake.'

'If I change again I'll be weak; give me a chance to get my breath,' I said.

'Let's go,' the Tiger said, and walked up to the gates.

The complex was a set of rectangular concrete buildings in the modern Stalinist Chinese style: utilitarian and unrelentingly ugly. The only greenery was a few large pots containing nondescript plants heavily coated in dust and yellowed from the pollution. There was a single driveway entrance to the complex off the road, blocked by wire gates under a larger concrete gate structure in the wall. The gates were chained and padlocked, with an armed security guard on either side. The guards hadn't seen us — one of the Shen must have made us invisible — but they appeared uneasy, glancing around.

'Demon or human?' I said.

'Demon,' the Tiger said. 'Stand back.'

The guards crumpled to the ground and demon goo splattered everywhere.

'Oh, good job letting them know we're here,' Bo Niang said.

'They wouldn't have had a chance to report back,' the Tiger said. He raised one hand and the gates sprang open.

'Camera,' Gold said, and pointed at the CCTV camera above the gate. 'Fixed. I'm in the network. I can see the other security cameras; not showing anything unusual. Not surprising, I suppose. If you have something nasty going on you don't want anybody to see it.'

We went through the gates and they closed and locked behind us. A large sign just inside showed a map of the different buildings in the complex.

'Four buildings,' the Tiger said. 'One dormitory. One administration. Two manufacturing.' He turned to me. 'Which one?'

'Administration,' I said.

He pointed at the four-storey building next to us. 'That's it.'

I changed to serpent. 'Time to move. Zara and Calcite, stay here and guard the exits. Let us know if he tries to get out.'

'Ma'am,' they said, and shrank to tiny stones.

We charged into the reception area of the administration block entrance. Two demons in the form of pretty young women jumped up when they saw us, and Simone destroyed them with blasts of chi. We raced past the reception desk and crashed through the doors on the other side — which led into a large room with manufacturing assembly lines stretching away from us all the way to the other end of the building. We stopped to check whether the workers seated in the cheap student chairs at the assembly line were demons, and they all turned to look at us at the same time — all women with exactly the same face.

Simone gasped. 'That is *freaky*.'

The women jumped up and came for us, arms outstretched. They weren't armed and they weren't high level, but their sheer force of numbers would slow us down.

Bo Niang summoned her slender jade sword, raised it horizontally above her head, held her other hand out in front of her and concentrated. The sword made a single pinging sound and all the demons froze.

'How long will that last?' the Tiger said.

'Forever,' Bo Niang said. 'They are frozen in time. They can only be freed if I release them or if they are destroyed.' She turned to see us. 'Come back and destroy them later, it is the kindest thing.'

'Deal,' the Tiger said.

We ran to the other end of the building, through the rows of frozen identical demons. The stairwell was on the right, padlocked to stop the staff from escaping or passing free merchandise to outsiders. The Tiger broke the lock and we went up to the next floor. It was filled with cubicles, each one staffed by another identical demon. The cubicles had wide corridors between them, and a pole in the centre of each group of four cubicles that contained the electricals.

'I can't freeze these; it's line of sight,' Bo Niang said.

'My turn,' Guang Ze said.

He floated a metre off the floor and summoned his wind wheel beneath him. It spun, producing a blast of titanic air that blew the cubicle walls, desks, computers, everything into the walls. The demons hit the walls as well and splattered into demon essence.

When all the demons were destroyed, Guang released the wheel and returned to the floor.

'You should have kept it out, just in case,' the Tiger said.

Four elementals crashed through the double doors at the other end of the building and stomped towards us: one water, one metal, one wood and one stone. They were all about the same size and roughly human-shaped, their heads brushing the high ceiling.

Bi Tian Hua raised both arms, his face went fierce and a bolt of lightning seared up through the pillars that had held the power conduits, across the ceiling and straight down through the tops of the elementals' heads.

The wood elemental exploded in flames. The metal one changed into what appeared to be mercury and disintegrated outwards, coating everything around it with silvery goo. The water one swayed back slightly, but when the lightning ceased it moved towards us again. The stone one was completely unaffected.

'Water is me,' Simone said.

She stepped forward, raised one hand, dropped her head slightly and concentrated on the water elemental, her hazel eyes blazing. It stopped, seeming to stare at her with its featureless face, then took another hesitant step towards her.

'Oh no, you don't, you are *mine*,' she said through her teeth. She clenched her fist and jerked it downwards. The elemental disintegrated into water and splashed over the floor.

'Good job, little one,' the Tiger said. 'Where'd you learn that?'

'CH, of course,' she said. 'One more that doesn't seem to be bothered by any of us, and I'm weak to earth.'

'On the contrary, ma'am, I don't believe you're weak to anything,' Guang Ze said. 'To arms, I think.'

The three generals summoned their swords and prepared to rush the stone elemental.

'Let me,' Gold said, and grew so that his stone form became as big as the stone elemental. He changed his arms to hammers, which grew impossibly long, swung out to the sides and crashed into the demon, crushing it. It fell to pieces.

'Keep moving!' the Tiger shouted. 'We still have two more floors and it knows we're here!'

'We should teleport straight to the top floor,' Leo said as we raced up the stairs.

'Haven't you tried already?' the Tiger said.

Leo was silent a moment, then said, 'I see.'

'If enough of us work together we can stop others from teleporting in the vicinity,' Guang Ze said. 'But we can't hold it forever.'

The stairs didn't go up to the top floor so we entered the third floor instead. It was occupied by six polished-metal, high-technology machines, each about three metres cubed, their top half glassed in on three sides and holding a robot arm.

'They look a bit like futuristic claw machines,' Simone said. 'All they need is a bunch of plushy Pokemon inside.'

'Silicon wafer inscribers?' Gold said. He went closer and studied one. 'Aluminium platter etchers? No.' He walked around it and peered at the control panel and screen. 'I have no idea.'

'I do,' I said without moving. 'Fake-elemental generators.'

Gold inhaled sharply. 'Oh my.'

Simone squeaked and ran to one machine and grabbed the handle of the glass door, trying to pull it open. It wouldn't budge and she pulled harder. Eventually the whole thing gave way and the glass shattered, falling in pieces around her. She reached inside the machine to pull out a blob of green liquid the size of a basketball and swirling with ribbons of creamy opaqueness.

She fell to her knees, ignoring the glass. 'This is one of mine, and it's dead,' she said, desolate. 'It killed one of my elementals.'

'So that's how it made them,' I said. 'It must have captured real ones and converted them into the fake ones.'

The Tiger stopped and concentrated. 'Holy fuck, I never counted mine.' He clenched his fists to his sides, then strode to one of the machines and punched it, making a huge dent in its metalwork. 'This bastard is going to *die*!'

'Why didn't the elementals tell you?' I said.

'They can't count!' the Tiger and Simone said together.

'Numbers mean nothing to them,' the Tiger said, flexing the hand that had punched the machine. 'They were unaware that their own numbers were disappearing. They have very little sense of self or individuality, and absolutely no idea how numbers work.' He raised his head. 'It's up there waiting for us, and I really hope that it's shitted its pants in terror.' He grinned with malice. 'Because this is not going to be quick.'

Simone strode to stand next to him. 'Tell the others.'

'I already have. The Phoenix says to do some serious damage on her behalf.'

'And the Dragon?'

The Tiger made a hissing sound of distaste. 'He doesn't give a fuck, the heartless bastard.'

'The Jade Emperor will be just as pissed and he doesn't have the freedom to rush down here and do what we can do,' Simone said. She glanced up at the Tiger. 'So, right now, it's you and me, Bai Hu. Let's show this demon exactly what happens to assholes who mess with our treasures.'

The Tiger dropped his head and concentrated, his tawny eyes wide, and raised his hands slightly. The machines melted around him, turning into steaming heaps of slag mixed with melted glass. 'That's what happens to them.' He shook himself out. 'Let's go up.'

They both headed towards the other end of the room where a pair of lifts were set into the wall. We followed them. The Tiger put his hand over the button, then shook his head and went to the doors and wrenched them open. He stuck his head into the shaft and looked down and up.

'Can't move them,' he said. 'Power's gone and the automatic braking system's engaged.'

'We can fly up,' Simone said. 'Easy.'

'What about the Lion and the serpent?' the Tiger said.

'I can fly,' Leo said.

Simone glanced at me. 'I'll carry you, Emma.'

'She's too big, don't be stupid,' the Tiger said, his head still in the lift shaft.

'I can climb up the wires,' I said.

The Tiger glanced back at me. 'Seriously?'

I grew until I was about four metres long, stuck my head into the shaft and wrapped myself around the set of cables. 'Seriously.'

I didn't wait for them to reply; I slithered easily up the cables to the top and waited at the door. The Tiger floated up, raised one hand and blew the doors out. I stuck my head out and slithered onto the floor, everybody else following.

This floor was mostly offices and conference rooms around the edge of the building, with some cubicles in the centre. It was deserted.

The Tiger strode into the middle of the central space. 'Come on out, my friend. If you turn, we will take you in.'

The demon appeared in the doorway of one of the offices. He looked about twenty-five and was overweight with a short ponytail. 'If I turn, my sister will hunt me down and kill me.'

'We will protect you,' I said.

He grimaced. 'Empty words. Weren't you just in Hell answering for having so many die in your service?'

I was silent at that.

'I have a place where you would be perfectly safe,' the Tiger said.

'Prison,' the demon said.

'Would you prefer destruction?' Guang Ze said.

The demon shrugged. 'I'd prefer to win and walk away from this, but I don't think it's going to happen.' He stuck his chin out at us. 'How'd you find me anyway? I thought I destroyed all the links. The demons here are all copies of a single template. There's nothing here that could possibly indicate my presence. I even put a manufacturing floor on the first floor of the administration building, like so many other computer companies here that are short of space.'

'Lady Emma's too fucking smart for her own good,' the Tiger said.

414

The demon focused on me. 'The serpent. My sister will enjoy meeting you, ma'am.'

I dropped my head slightly. 'I look forward to it. If you turn, we could put you in Wudangshan, or in the West; either way you will be safe.'

'Safe and imprisoned.' He raised his hands. 'You see all of this? I'm rich. I'm a wealthy Chinese entrepreneur. I have a mansion on five qing of land, beautiful gardens, artificial lake, only a few li north of here. I have a house on the Peak, just up from you, Emma, that I bought for over a hundred million Hong Kong, and a helicopter to take me there when I don't feel like taking myself. I have a collection of supercars. I have four wives — one of them is even human.' He lowered his hands. 'Why would I give that up for a prison cell?'

'Because life is better than nothing? And if you turn, you could try for humanity,' I said.

'Demon, human, so much work to reach Immortality and join the Celestial, when I have it all here already,' the demon said. 'Can we just skip —'

A Snake Mother — the Death Mother — appeared next to him. 'Are they annoying you, honey?'

'I thought you said nothing could teleport in here!' Leo said.

'Nothing can, this whole area is locked,' Bo Niang said. 'She didn't teleport within here, she teleported from somewhere else *to* here.'

The Death Mother grabbed the Geek around the throat with one hand, hoisted him easily and kissed him. He struggled, kicking and pulling at her hand, then punching at her. She ignored it, lingering on the kiss for a long time, then held him away from her and dropped him. He fell to the floor, choking, then rose.

415

'I think I've had second thoughts!' he shouted. He raced towards us, hands raised. 'Get me away from her!' He grabbed the Tiger's arm. 'Protect me, I am yours.' He glanced around at us. 'Whoever wants me can have me; just don't let *her* get me.'

The Death Mother raised herself on her coils. She was one of the biggest Snake Mothers I'd ever seen — more than four metres long, high level eighties or low nineties — and clear venom oozed from between her scales. She grinned menacingly. 'Oh, come on, Thirty-three, this could be fun.'

Simone took Celestial Form. She grew to more than two metres tall, and her jeans and T-shirt changed to blue-black robes dotted with pinpoints of light. She summoned Seven Stars and removed it from its scabbard. 'Finally, a challenge,' she said.

The Death Mother's expression changed from amusement to ferocity. She hesitated, then slithered backwards, turned and leapt out the window.

'Calcite, Zara, get her!' Gold yelled, running to the window. 'Pin her down! Don't approach too close ...' He leaned on the window frame. 'No! Zara, don't *fight* her ...' He dropped his head and shook it. 'Damn.' He leapt over the frame and out.

We ran to the window. Gold splattered like goo as he hit the ground, then re-formed and kneeled next to Zara's body. Calcite lay dead nearby. Both of the stones disappeared. Gold rose and turned to face the Death Mother. She raced towards the compound exit, made a huge leap over the concrete gate into the street and disappeared.

'Judge Pao is going to be so pissed with you,' Simone said, her voice the same as it always was.

'Yeah,' I said. 'I wonder where I can hide.'

'You can come and hide with me, ma'am,' the Geek said. He glanced around. 'Who has the safest hiding place?'

'By your leave, ma'am,' the Tiger said. 'I'll take him.'

'Your choice, Thirty-three,' I said. 'Wudangshan or the West?'

'Which is more secure?' the Geek said.

'Probably the West,' I said. 'Never seen anything quite like it. Like something out of James Bond.'

The Geek smiled slightly. 'Sounds exactly what I need.'

'The teleport block is down, we can go,' Simone said.

'I'll send a clean-up team for those machines,' the Tiger said.

'I'll take responsibility for the demons downstairs; my students can practise on them,' I said.

'We're not too far from one of my hotels here, you know,' the Tiger said. 'It has an excellent Japanese restaurant.' He grinned around at us. 'Who wants sushi for lunch?'

CHAPTER 28

Simone tapped on my office door later that afternoon and came in.

I saw her face. 'Are you okay?'

She sat across the desk from me and sighed heavily. 'I'm supposed to be doing advanced weapons right now, but I really don't want to.'

'Then don't.'

'It's not that easy.' She swivelled her chair so she was side-on to me. 'That Geek demon, it destroyed my elementals, Emma. They're a part of me, and it used them and twisted them.' She spun back to face me. 'I hate it so much.'

'I can understand that.'

'I want to destroy it!' She ran her hands through her hair. 'I want it to suffer, Emma, I want to make it scream forever.' She looked into my eyes. 'Maybe I'm more demon than Daddy says I am. I've killed ...' She dropped her head, then looked back up at me. 'I killed someone, and I got *commended* for it! I'm a murderer, and look at me now. This demon has asked for protection and there's nothing I'd like better than to go in and tear it into very small pieces. I think I'm changing, and I don't like what I'm changing into.'

I rose. 'Come with me.' I took her into the training room. 'Choose a weapon, any weapon, and wait for me here.'

I went out to the storage room and found the demon jar. It was almost empty, with only a few smaller demons left in the bottom. I wasn't about to risk my humanity refilling it. I returned to the training room with the jar, popped the lid and pulled out the tiniest demon, only a level three. I stood across from Simone holding the demon bead in my hand. 'Choose a weapon.'

Simone shook her head. 'I don't want to handle anything destructive right now.'

'You are the most destructive thing in this room.'

'Daddy locked my yin.'

'Even without it.' I gestured towards the rack of weapons at the short end of the room. 'Choose a weapon. Or summon Dark Heavens, or even Seven Stars.'

She summoned Dark Heavens and held the sword as if it were toxic.

I stood beside her and threw the demon onto the floor. It formed into an ordinary-looking young man.

'This reminds me of your first time,' she said. 'Daddy beat himself up for ages because you were injured. He said, "How could the God of Martial Arts make such a mistake? I must hand in my godhood." We've come so far, Emma.'

'We still have a long way to go as well,' I said.

'Are you going to unbind it so I can destroy it?' Simone said.

'Imagine it's the Geek,' I said. 'Picture it in your mind as the Geek. Prince Thirty-three.'

She stared at it and the demon changed form into the Geek.

'I didn't know I could do that,' she said. 'I guess it's because I'm so close in nature to them.'

'Do you want to destroy it?' I said.

She shook her head. 'No.'

'If it was the Geek, would you want to destroy it?'

'Yes, I would. But it's not, so I don't.'

'Then don't,' I said, and unbound the demon. It leapt for me and immediately disintegrated. She'd turned her Third Eye on it and destroyed it anyway.

'I didn't want to do that,' she said desperately.

'That's the point, Simone: you didn't want to, but you had to. It couldn't be returned to the jar, and I couldn't destroy it. It had to be you, even though you didn't want to do it. If you truly wanted the Geek dead despite the fact that it turned, you would be out there now carving a swathe of destruction through demonkind, purely out of a need for revenge.'

'I don't want to destroy anything more,' she said.

I nodded, and closed the jar. 'Have you ever been on a demon hunt?' I said.

'No! Those things are pointless and stupid. I don't find chasing things down and killing them fun at all.'

'You're not a killer, Simone,' I said. 'You may be a fighter, defending yourself and those you love, but you're not someone who will ever kill for fun. That's the difference between you and a demon. You may want to chase that Geek down and kill it, but you're never going to do it.' I went out with the jar, and stopped in the doorway. 'And sometimes I am so proud of you it hurts.'

*　*　*

Ma was waiting for me outside my office when I arrived at the Academy the next morning.

He rose. 'You need to tell your new secretary who I am, Emma.'

'My apologies,' I said. 'Chang, this is Marshal Ma Hua Guang, Magistrate of the Only True Power, Vanguard of the Thirty-Six —'

'I told him that,' Ma said. 'He didn't believe me. He said you weren't here and asked me to wait. He even made me tea.'

'I do believe you, sir, but Lady Emma wasn't here,' Chang said.

'Next time a god wanders in, page me on my mobile,' I said.

'That's everybody!' Chang said, spreading his arms in protest. 'You've yet to have an ordinary mortal come into your office, ma'am.'

'Your secretary has a point,' Ma said. 'You did the right thing, Chang. Now let's go into your office and talk about the First Platform, Emma.'

Chang saluted Ma and returned to his desk.

Inside my office, I checked my diary. Chang's writing was all upper case and large and spidery, nothing like Yi Hao's tiny scribbled scrawl. My diary looked entirely different. 'He even pencilled you in,' I said. 'He's good.'

'If you ever let him go, let me know,' Ma said. 'A good personal assistant is worth their weight in gold.'

I sat behind the desk. 'How long will it take to go to the First Platform? I have a full schedule. Er Lang's asked for an evaluation in four days and my students aren't ready.'

He sat across from me. 'That's a difficult question to answer. It could be seconds on this Plane, it could be weeks. It's so detached from our reality that time means nothing there. And we must pass through the Second, which is a trial in itself.'

'Then I think I should hold off until after the evaluation,' I said. I looked down at my diary. 'How about a week from now?'

'Let me check.' He pulled an electronic organiser out of his suit jacket pocket and tapped it with the stylus, concentrating on it. He raised it. 'You should get one of these, they're very handy.'

'Screen isn't big enough for me to see everything that's happening. And I have my stone, which is inherently intelligent,' I said.

'I think the word is "belligerent" rather than "intelligent",' he said. 'Yes, I'm free.' He put the organiser away. 'Booked in for first thing next Friday. See you then.'

Kwan Yin materialised next to him. 'You must not delay. You must go now.'

'Very well,' Ma said. 'Emma, change into something warmer — no weapons. A tracksuit would be best.'

'Are the jeans and T-shirt okay if I add a sweater?'

'Yes, that will be fine. Can you come and help me escort her through the Second, my Lady?'

Kwan Yin nodded. 'I will assist you.'

I rose. 'I'll be right back.'

'Hurry, Emma,' Kwan Yin said. 'You must do this now.'

I went out and leaned on Chang's desk. 'I'm going to the First Platform now. I may be gone for a couple of weeks; I may be gone for minutes. Got a pencil? Good. Inform the Lius. Have them pass the message on to the generals. Let Simone know.'

Simone appeared next to me. 'I'm coming with you.'

Her face went strange. 'I want to come!' She disappeared, and I heard her talking to Kwan Yin in my office.

'She's arguing with a bodhisattva,' Chang said with wonder.

'Teenagers,' I said. 'Pass the message on; have my energy classes reassigned; let the Northern Heavens know. Tell Monica. Tell Leo. I have to find a jumper; I'll be right back with more stuff for you to do as I remember it.' I headed out towards the top-floor changing room.

When I came back, pulling the sweater over my head, Chang raised his eyebrows. 'Is that cashmere?'

'Yeah,' I said. 'It was a gift, a long time ago.'

He turned away and grinned at his computer. 'Must have been a long time ago to have so many holes. You should look after your clothes better, ma'am.'

I stopped and pointed at him. 'I am going to tell the Jade Purity you said that.'

His grin widened. 'I can't believe you're actually going there.'

I turned away. 'Neither can I.'

Ma and Kwan Yin were standing together behind my desk with Simone next to them.

'Why did I need to get a jumper?' I said. 'I should be doing this as snake.'

'We will bypass the Third,' Kwan Yin said. 'You may remain in human form; your demonic nature will not be an issue on the Second and First.' She added, without looking away from me, 'Simone, I am sorry. Leave us.'

Simone looked as if she was going to argue, then she raised her hands. 'Good luck, Emma. Come back whole.' She went out and slammed the door behind her.

'Clear your mind,' Kwan Yin said. 'You must go with your thoughts completely empty. You are an expert at this, and you must use all of your expertise. Go into the highest level, the clearest, purest and most formless mindset you are capable of. You must make the demon nature so small and quiet that it is almost not there.'

'Good thing I've been snake so much lately,' I said.

'Less talking, more mystical bullshit,' Ma said with amusement.

'He is correct,' Kwan Yin said.

I moved into a horse stance, took a deep breath and did what I could to still the movement of the chi through me. I slipped into the deepest trance I could manage, resting my feet on the earth and my head in the sky, my mind clear and my thoughts empty.

'Try to stay as clear and empty as you are now,' Ma said gently. 'We are on the Second.'

I opened my eyes and nearly lost it. We were standing high on a hill, a valley spread before us. The land was green with grass for as far as I could see, with a forest along the mountainside to my left. The land appeared deserted; no houses or roads. The sky was a pale, pure, almost crystalline blue, without a single cloud. The air seemed somehow fresher than even on the Celestial Plane; it was like breathing clarity.

A deep, resonating sense of peace ran through me, like a huge bell in the centre of me. It nearly knocked me down with the force of its joy and majesty.

'Do not lose yourself in it,' Kwan Yin said, her gentle voice urgent. 'Stay here, stay yourself. This is not yet your time.'

'I need to gather my strength for the next leg of the journey,' Ma said. 'This means that I need about half an hour while I go into the correct trance state. You *must* keep your mind clear and your thoughts pure, Emma, otherwise you will be destroyed.'

'I will help you,' Kwan Yin said.

'This air is like the pure oxygen I was breathing in my spacesuit,' I said.

'Don't breathe too deeply, it will make you dizzy,' Ma said. He took Celestial Form and gracefully sat on the grass. He crossed his legs and closed his eyes. 'I'm going deep. I suggest you do the same.'

'Come, Emma, sit,' Kwan Yin said, and pulled me down to sit on the grass next to her. She held my hand and I felt her serene presence assisting me with the demon nature. 'Keep your mind clear.'

I couldn't speak, I just concentrated on the purity and clarity of my thoughts.

'You are doing well,' she said. 'One day this will all be yours.'

I opened my mouth to reply.

'Do not speak!' she said. 'Do not think of that. Do not think of anything. Breathe, and release, and let your thoughts become as still as deep water.'

I felt a gathering around me; other consciousnesses, as gentle and harmonious as Kwan Yin's. A hand took my free one and I opened my eyes.

They sat in a circle with us, holding hands and forming a chain from Ma to me. They all wore white robes similar to Kwan Yin's. Some of them were male, some were female, and they seemed to be a mix of all ages and races, but I found it difficult to focus on them.

'Thank you,' Ma said softly, his voice full of reverence.

'You are welcome,' they replied in unison, their voices creating a gentle harmony.

'Why?' I said.

'Because the Dark Lord is needed,' they said, almost in a whisper. 'Now it is time to rise.'

Pieces of my head went left and right at the same time; my brain was shattered into tiny motes, all flying horizontally away from me. My body disappeared.

'Hold,' Ma said. 'Hold my hand.'

I grasped Ma's hand and tried to breathe, but the air was both there and nonexistent.

'Don't panic!' he said, softly urgent. 'If you panic you are lost. Hold the calmness, clasp it tightly within you.'

'Think of the Dark Lord,' another voice said.

'Think of me,' John said.

'John?'

'Think of me.'

I held his image in my head — his noble features, wild hair and ancient eyes — and the shattered feeling lessened.

'Now,' Ma said, his voice serene. 'It's hard enough to retain your consciousness and awareness here, but you also have to use them.'

I opened my eyes to nothing. We were hanging in midair, but the air didn't exist either; there was nothing to see, just greyness. There was no depth and no texture.

'Do you have it?' Ma said, his brilliantly crimson robes somehow muted by the greyness.

I locked the image of John — from the family photo hanging in the hallway back at the Peak — into my mind. 'I have it.'

'I use his image too,' Ma said with quiet amusement, and I glanced up at him. His face was serene but his eyes were full of untold tales.

'I don't think we should let go of one another's hand,' he said. 'Otherwise we might be separated in the nothingness. So now we wait for the Celestial Worthy of Mysterious Harmony to become aware of our presence. That's taken up to twenty-four hours in the past.'

'This is easier than the Second,' I said.

'Nah,' he said, looking around. 'It's like Hong Kong's weather. You step outside and think, oh, it's not too hot and humid, I'll be fine. Then half an hour later, you're drenched by the humidity and weak from the heat. It sneaks up on you. So rest your mind as much as you can. It's an effort just staying aware.'

'Where's John? I heard him.'

'Nowhere.'

A figure appeared in the mist, dark against the grey. 'Who has entered the Heaven of the Three Purities?'

'I am Marshal Ma Hua Guang, Vanguard of the Thirty-Six, right hand of the Dark Lord, the Xuan Wu. This is his Lady Emma, Regent of the Northern Heavens.'

'This is highly unusual,' the dark shape said. 'She is demon ... she is mortal ... she is nothing I have seen before ... What is she?'

'That's why we're here,' I said.

Solidity coalesced around my feet and I was standing. The greyness didn't become clearer though and the figure who was talking to us, presumably the Celestial Worthy of Mysterious Harmony, remained barely visible.

'We request an audience with the Three Purities, as directed by Xuan Tian himself,' Ma said.

'What is the purpose of this visit?' the Worthy said. 'Is the Dark Lord in trouble again? It seems only a minute ago you were here asking for our assistance with the demon horde.'

'That was three thousand years ago,' I said with wonder.

'Yes, a minute,' the Worthy said.

'The Dark Lady, promised consort of the Dark Lord, has been filled with demon essence by a master of the cruel arts,' Ma said. 'She cannot join him in her proper place in the Heavens while she is like this. We seek the indulgence of the Purities in restoring her to her correct nature and freeing her to take her place on the Celestial.'

'Jade Building Block!' the Worthy said. 'How dare you show your blunt and backwards facets on this Plane, worthless stone! I should cast you down now.'

'This isn't about me, it's about the Lady who carries me,' the stone said.

'Worthless stone, you fail to show respect,' the Worthy said. 'I reject you! I expel you! Go back to whence you came.'

'Emma, remove me and drop me,' the stone said.

Removing the stone would involve ... something to do with fingers. I rallied my awareness. 'I don't think so. John gave you to me, you represent ...' I tried to remember. 'You represent something important to me.'

'She is unable to retain her awareness here, Majesty,' Ma said. 'If we cannot see the Purities soon, she will be lost.'

Suddenly I was thinking more clearly than I'd ever thought before. The solution to the problem with the demon essence was obvious. 'Oh, I know how to fix it. Just let me back down to the Earthly, no need to bother anybody now. It's an interesting mix of traditional alchemical principles —'

'That you will lose the minute you touch the Earthly,' Ma said. 'He's cleared your mind so you can tell him what you want.'

'And made me more intelligent as a side effect,' I said.

'No,' the Worthy said. 'Just clearer. Now what is it that you seek, madam?'

I fell to one knee and bowed my head. 'I seek the assistance of the Three Pure Ones. I have been filled with demon essence and they may have the power to clear it. Also, I would love to hear any thoughts they have on what I am.'

'I will return directly,' the Worthy said, and his dark shape disappeared.

My mind immediately went blank and I tried to focus.

'Don't force it,' Ma said. 'They'll give your mind back when they return.'

'I had the solution,' I said softly. 'It was so clear.'

'Nothing will ever be as clear again. When you return, it will be gone.'

I wanted to be angry for some reason but I couldn't remember why.

A building moved towards us through the greyness. It had no walls, just pillars holding up the traditional roof, and was constructed of dark polished wood. The floor was of woven rice mats — tatami mats.

Ma inhaled sharply. 'All three.'

Three elderly gentlemen sat in the centre of the building side by side. Their faces were impossible to make out. I was aware that their robes were complex but I couldn't see them. I couldn't see anything. I couldn't think anything. What was I doing?

Ma held my hand tighter. 'Focus, Emma. For John.'

'John?' I said. 'Who's John?'

Someone slid into view next to us, still almost invisible in the grey. 'You may approach.'

'Where am I?' I said.

Emma, focus, you're on the First Platform and about to address the Three Purities. Don't lose it, dear one, keep yourself together, for your love, an English voice said.

'That's funny, you sound English,' I said.

'I beg your indulgence, Celestial Worthy, my mistress's mind is failing,' the stone said. 'Please assist her, or her journey here will be for nothing.'

'Silence, worthless stone!' the dark shape said.

'The stone speaks the truth, Majesty,' Ma said. 'The world below needs the Dark Lord's power. Once again the demon horde has risen —'

'We just helped you with that!' the Worthy said.

'And the Dark Lord needs the love of this woman to assist him —'

'Of all the Celestials, the Dark Lord should know that love is an Earthly emotion that ties you to the World of Ruin,' the Worthy said. 'Do you have anything worthwhile to bring to the attention of the Purities, or are you as worthless as the stone you have brought here with you?'

Emma! the stone said, its voice fierce. *Emma, if you want their help, you have to snap out of it now and talk to them!*

Someone took my free hand; another dark shape that I couldn't make out. Its grip was cold as ice and I shivered, trying to free myself.

'Don't,' John said. 'Let me help you.'

'My Lord,' Ma said with awe.

A rush of ice-cold clarity gave me an instant brain freeze and I bent double at the pain.

The cold grip disappeared. I straightened, pulled Ma with me to the building, stepped up onto the platform, then fell to one knee. 'Please, help me.'

'Approach,' the middle man said, still sitting cross-legged on the floor.

I released Ma's hand, rose and took a couple of steps so that I was in front of the Purity, then kneeled again, this time on both knees. He was still almost impossible to make out.

He reached inside his robes and took out something white and circular. He placed it on the matting in front of me. 'Take this. This will assist you in the time of need that fast approaches.'

I picked it up; it was a circular piece of white jade, about ten centimetres across, carved with the image of the Xuan Wu in animal form — the snake and turtle intertwined.

'Will this remove the demon essence from me?' I said.

'What demon essence?' the Upper Purity said.

'I am full of demon essence, Pure One. It interferes with ... with ... with everything.'

'And why have you come to us?'

'To ask you to help me. To clear me of the demon essence so that I can walk the Celestial once again.'

'You can walk the Celestial now, just not with your legs.'

'I fear that I will change, Pure One. The demon essence will take control of me and I will hurt the ones I love.'

'We always hurt the ones we love; that is the nature of the World of Ruin. Love is but a selfish fallacy that leads to suffering.'

'I beg of you, Majesties, please clear this demon essence from me.'

'We will not change your essence. You must be what you are; that is the Way.'

I took a deep breath and tried a different tack. 'I do not know what I am, and I ask your assistance in helping me to find out.'

'Do you live?' the Jade Purity on my left said.

I bowed my head. 'Yes. I live.'

'What do you know?'

'I know nothing.'

'Good. A beginning. Do you sleep?'

'Yes, Majesty.'

'When you wake, what is your first thought?'

'Uh ...' The clarity was leaving me. 'That my family is safe.'

'Your first thought is not "what am I"?'

'No, Majesty, the ones I love come first.'

'You are a small mote of wisdom, little one. Well met.'

'Can you help me?'

'You do not need our help,' the Great Purity on my right said, and they disappeared.

'You are free to go. You have been given a gift of mighty power; treasure it,' the Celestial Worthy said, and his dark shape disappeared as well.

I wanted to feel frustrated but I had trouble feeling anything.

'This is unusual,' Ma said from somewhere nearby. 'Usually when they're done with me they return me to the Earthly. Looks like we have to find our own way down.'

I was lost. Everything was grey and I didn't really care. I was dissolving and it was peaceful.

'Emma, say something,' Ma said.

'Over here,' the English voice said.

'I'm trying to get to you,' Ma said. 'It's starting to affect me, I won't be able to keep it up much longer ...'

'I think you're close,' the voice said.

Something dark sliced through the greyness next to me: a bolt of black, icy coldness. It gripped me, holding me immobile, but I didn't really care.

'Ma,' it said.

'Here,' Ma said, somewhere to my left and fading away.

I was ripped sideways and then jarred to a halt, the momentum flinging my nonexistent limbs around. The cold blackness began to hurt me, like ice on bare skin, but I was so tired that I didn't really care. My mind was numb.

'You're killing her,' Ma said.

'Everything's killing her,' the darkness said. 'Hold on tight.'

I shot upright to sitting position and took a huge gasping breath. Someone held my hand. 'Hold on, Emma, you're safe.'

I fell back and someone caught me. The light was blinding and I screwed up my eyes, trying to focus. I put my hand to my swollen, tender head and the world spun around me. I shot upright again, unable to control myself, and vomited to one side.

'Oh, charming,' Simone said.

'All over the cashmere,' Leo said. 'Ruined.'

I retched a few times, and tried to open my eyes. Someone gave me some tissues and I wiped my mouth, then ineffectually mopped my saturated jumper.

'What's this?' Leo said.

'It's jade,' Chang said. 'White jade — the Xuan Wu — it must be priceless.'

'She won't let go of it,' Leo said.

'Leave it then,' Simone said. 'Should we drop her at the infirmary or just take her home?'

'How long have I been gone?' I said.

'Two days.'

I snapped open my eyes. 'But that means the evaluation is in two days and we're not nearly ready!' The light seared through my head, frying my brain, and I hissed with pain and closed my eyes again.

I heard footsteps. A fourth person had entered. I prised open my eyelids and saw a blurry version of Edwin, the Academy doctor.

'Vomiting, sensitivity to light — I didn't know Lady Emma suffered from migraine headaches,' he said.

'I don't,' I said.

'Well, that's what this is,' Edwin said. 'Take her home and put her to bed in a dark room with ... I was about to say powerful painkillers but they won't work on you. So, Emma, take serpent form at home and curl up in a beanbag. You'll be fine.'

'We have an evaluation ...' I said.

'Yes, we do, and it's all under control,' Simone said. 'Leo, can you get out of the chair to carry her?'

'No,' Leo said. 'Chang, you do it. Take her down to the car and drive her home. I'll meet you there.'

'Yes, sir,' Chang said, and I felt myself lifted by strong arms.

CHAPTER 29

The hot water felt so good against my skin, helping the pain to subside. Strong arms held me and I relaxed and enjoyed ...

'Wait,' I said, and forced open my eyes. 'Leo?'

'You got some in your hair,' he said. 'Stay still.'

'Nice boxers.'

'Yeah, I wish I could say the same for you, sweetheart. I need to go shopping for you again.'

'You don't know what size I am.'

He turned the water off. 'All clean. And yes, I do, although it's obvious that you don't.'

'A girl can dream,' I said as he wrapped me in a huge fluffy towel like a child. 'Your chair okay with the water on it?'

'Yeah, it's aluminum,' he said. 'It won't rust.'

'Aluminium.'

'Aluminum! We had that fight and I won!'

He popped me into his lap and wheeled into my room.

'I can dress myself now,' I said.

'I'm not leaving till I see you stand up by yourself.'

I pulled myself off his lap, clutched the towel around me, slid my feet onto the floor and forced myself upright. The world had other ideas, however, tipping me over so that I fell back into his lap.

'Looks like I have to dry you and dress you myself.' He roughly rubbed me with the towel, making me giggle.

'That's what I like to hear,' he said. 'I hardly ever hear you laugh any more.'

'We'll have more laughs together when John comes back.'

He hesitated, then, 'I hope we do.'

I gasped. 'Where's the jade they gave me?'

He reached for my pyjamas and passed them to me. 'Here, on the bed, don't panic. What does it do?'

'I have no idea,' I said as I pulled the pyjama top over my head. 'They just said it would help me in my time of need.'

'Touch it to me,' the stone said.

'Wait till I have pants on,' I said.

'Overrated,' the stone said.

'If I were you I would be locking this dirty old man out of your room, Emma,' Leo said.

'Does nothing for me, same as you,' the stone said.

'Emma told me about you,' Leo said.

The stone was silent at that.

I pulled my pants on and touched the jade to the stone.

'This is a demon destroyer,' the stone said. 'Touch it and order it, and it will destroy every demon within two hundred metres or so. All of them.'

'Wait,' I said, and fell to sit on the bed. 'Will it destroy *me*?'

The stone was silent for a moment, then said, 'Yes.'

'Then don't use it; give it to someone else,' Leo said.

'It can't be used by anyone else,' the stone said.

'They didn't happen to clear the demon essence out of me when I wasn't looking, did they?'

'No. This jade will destroy you.'

'And they said I would need to use it,' I said.

'Well, that's good news,' Leo said. 'It means that you'll be cleared of the demon nature before you need to use it.'

I tossed the jade in my hand. 'Kwan Yin said I had to go to the First Platform immediately. The only thing I got out of it ... was this.'

'You use that thing and none of us will ever forgive you,' Leo said.

'If she uses that thing then there won't be anyone to forgive,' the stone said.

Leo pulled the covers back and lifted my legs to slip them between the sheets. 'Rest now. If you want to change to snake and lie on the beanbags, give me a shout and I'll carry you across.'

'I have to get to Guangzhou,' I said. 'Are the students there yet? We need to be ready —'

'Rest! That's an order, Miss Mortal, from a Shen. Me. Shut up and rest. It's all under control.'

'Leo the Shen.'

'Damn straight, lady. The Lius have it under control, the students are at the house, Chang will drive you there tomorrow —'

'The car isn't registered in China. It can't go over.'

Leo started to wheel himself out of my room. 'It has the old plates on it, which'll do until we get new plates. Don't *worry*, Emma, it's all taken care of. Rest.'

'The Second Platform is so beautiful, Leo.'

He stopped and turned back. 'The place where the Buddhas live?'

'Yes. The air is like ... The sky is ... It's wonderful.'

'I thought it would be kind of like ... emptiness. Nothing. That's what they say Nirvana is.'

'That was her mortal and unenlightened mind trying to make sense of it,' the stone said.

'What was the highest platform like?' Leo said.

'Grey.'

'It nearly killed her,' the stone said.

'Not a place you want to go back to,' I said.

Leo wheeled himself towards the door again. 'This supernatural stuff completely freaks me out.'

'Thank you, Mr Shen.'

'You're welcome, Miss Mortal.'

I made myself more comfortable under the quilt. 'Bastard,' I said under my breath.

I heard that.

When I opened my bedroom door the next morning, Leo, Monica and Simone were standing in the hall waiting for me.

'See, told you she was awake. You sure you're strong enough, Emma?' Simone said. 'Ma told me what you went through.'

'I'm fine,' I said, gesturing for her to move out of the way so I could pass.

'I've made you some breakfast, ma'am; fresh peanut butter on the table,' Monica said.

I walked past them down the hall towards the living room. 'I'll eat something on the way, thanks, Monica.'

'You don't need to rush over there,' Leo said. 'It's all under control; the Lius are giving the students some last-minute tips, it's fine! At least eat something; you didn't eat anything last night.'

'Edwin said you must eat, Emma, otherwise that migraine will come back,' Simone said.

'Wholemeal toast, just the way you like it, still hot,' Monica said. 'And a nice cup of tea.'

I turned to her. 'Could you put it in a thermos so I can take it with me?'

'What's a thermos?' Monica said, turning to Leo and Simone.

'A vacuum flask,' Simone said. She saw Monica's still-confused face. 'One of those things you use to keep drinks hot.'

'Oh, the Japanese thing the Master bought,' she said. 'I thought that was just for Chinese tea. You can put Western drinks in it too?'

'Yes, you can, so hurry up. Where's Chang?' I said.

Chang was waiting for me in the living room, holding the car keys. 'I'm here, ready to take you, ma'am.'

'At last! Someone who'll listen to me,' I said. I opened the shoe cupboard and pulled out my loafers. 'Straight to the house in Guangzhou. I have my passport; do you have your ID card?'

'Yes, ma'am, all ready to go,' Chang said, his face bright with pride.

'You are not going without eating something!' Leo said, pointing at me. He dropped his hand. 'Chang, you are not to take her anywhere until I tell you that you can.'

Chang looked from Leo to me. 'Lady Emma hasn't eaten anything? After yesterday?'

'Just take five minutes and eat something, Emma, please,' Simone said. 'It won't make any difference to the students if you arrive five minutes later. They're all set and ready to go.'

'Chang, you are ordered to stay here until Lady Emma has eaten,' Leo said, his deep voice full of command.

Chang crossed his arms over his chest and sat down on the couch. 'I'm sorry, ma'am, but I agree with them. Eat something and then I'll take you.'

I spun on the spot and saw all their faces full of determination. Simone had her hands on her hips and was glaring at me. Monica was wringing her hands. Leo had his hands on the arms of his wheelchair, ready to leap out and stop me. And Chang was sitting on the couch, his arms crossed over his chest, his face rigid with stubbornness.

I flipped my shoes off. 'Oh, okay, but I hope you have a copy of the *Post* there. If I have to sit there I want to catch up on the news as well.'

'Heaven forbid you should talk to us,' Leo said.

'I'll read you the latest and we can talk about it,' Simone said.

I turned to her. 'Actually, that sounds like the best suggestion I've heard so far today.' I gestured towards Leo and Chang. 'Would you gentlemen care to join us ladies for breakfast and a chat?'

'Me too?' Chang said.

'Yes, you too,' I said. 'Since you're here, you might as well join us.'

'Is that all right with you, sir?'

Leo waved him into the dining room. 'Come on in.'

Chang followed the directions on the GPS that Gold had installed in the car. The village that we passed through to get to the House on the Hill had become a housing estate now: a series of rectangular twelve-storey buildings lined up side by side, bare concrete and dirt between them. The hill behind the estate had been reinforced with ugly sprayed concrete to stop the slope from failing when it rained heavily, but from the layers of repairs it hadn't worked very well.

After we'd wound our way past the estate, the road narrowed and became steeper, passing through bamboo groves and then through the front gate of our property. We topped out onto the hill and the house was visible below us: a white concrete mansion with a green tiled roof. The fish ponds on the land below the hill were gone now, and a brown pollution haze obscured the rows of apartment blocks and multistorey factory buildings of Guangzhou in the distance.

The new cinder-block barracks stood near the house; we'd thrown them up in a hurry for the students who came to study here. The barracks offered minimal comfort, but the students never stayed more than a couple of days and said the accommodation was more than sufficient.

The tennis court had been extended to a training practice field; the court surface was ideal for this purpose, providing just enough spring to ensure the students' joints weren't stressed too much. A group of students were on the field now, practising Wudang staff in perfect synchronicity.

'Wait, is that Leo leading the students?' I said.

'Appears to be, ma'am,' Chang said as he guided the car down the hill to the front of the house.

'Well, it's about damn time!' I said.

I hopped out of the car and went to the edge of the field to watch

'He's been practising,' the stone said.

'Good for him,' I said, and went inside the house and up the stairs.

'Where are you, ma'am?' Chang called from downstairs.

I leaned over the balustrade. 'Bring my bags up to the first room on the left, Chang.'

I rubbed my fingers along some scorch marks on the wood, left by the demon dogs when they'd nearly killed Leo all that time ago.

Chang stopped at the top of the stairs and let out his breath. 'Damn.'

Simone had converted the play area at the top of the stairs into a gaming room; it held one of every type of console and a couple of stone-powered computers hooked up to a massive plasma screen that covered the whole wall.

'When Simone chills out, she doesn't mess around,' I said.

'She's a lucky girl,' Chang said.

'No, she isn't. She has no father, no mother, and I can't give her a hug when she needs to feel better.'

I guided Chang to my room with its white wicker furniture and comfortable bed. 'Leave the bags here, then go down and present yourself to Master Leo. Tell him to find you a spot in the barracks and to allocate you a place in the training regime. We need to work hard to be ready for tomorrow.'

Chang hesitated for a moment, then saluted. 'Ma'am.'

I went into the room and sat on one of the chairs. I'd yelled at John here. He'd told me the truth here.

Any chance of you sparing some of your army? the Tiger said cheerfully into my head.

'Demon attack?' I said.

This is ... His voice changed from light-hearted to serious. *Okay, this is real bad. I got a hundred and fifty wives up here in the resort and the fucking Geek somehow managed to bring a whole shitload of fake fire elementals into my facility. I dunno how he did it, it's supposed to be impregnable, but ...* His voice faded out.

'What?' I said.

Shit, they're out of the lab into the cells and they're letting the caged demons out. Fuck, I hope the airlock holds them in because that's all that's between them and the tame demons in the demon hotel on the other side ... Oh, fuck.

'Stone, tell Simone.'

On my way, Simone said.

Not Simone, the Tiger said. *She's not Immortal, and the whole place is on fire. It's all burning.*

I'm going up anyway, Simone said.

Emma, do me a favour, honey? the Tiger said. *I'm stuck at the far end. Nobody can get in or out without walking through all the security. I need someone with brains and guts to sort out my fucktarded wives and get them evacuated. Simone, if you're going to come up here, please go to the other end and help out with the wives. You can't come directly into this part anyway, it's all sealed, and the wives are the most important thing.*

'Can Simone give me a lift?' I said.

Leo appeared in the doorway. 'I will. Change to snake.'

'Do you know where to go?'

He held his hand out. 'Show me. Take my hand and think hard about where it is. I can find it from there.'

'You have been practising, sir,' the stone said.

'Damn straight,' Leo said.

I took his hand and conjured a diagram in my head of where the facility was.

'Holy ... and there are fire elementals at the far end of that? This is nasty,' Leo said. 'Change.'

I changed to snake, and the ground slammed me on the chin, knocking my head back and then down again.

'You okay?' Leo said. He was on his back on the floor next to me.

'More practice, eh?' I said.

'Getting there.' He changed to lion form and pulled himself to his feet. 'How are we supposed to get them out of here? We're miles from anywhere.'

I raised my head and looked around. We were in the forecourt of the ski resort. The wives were standing in groups in the snow, talking quietly, obviously confused. Some of them saw Leo and me and hurried away to join others further back.

Cars are on the way up. Keep them back where they're safe, the Tiger said. *The elementals haven't made it through to the demon hotel*. His voice changed slightly from ferocity to sadness. *Ma'am, I am so sorry.*

'My demons,' I whispered. I raised my head and raced into the hotel. 'My demons!'

'Emma, stay out here!' Leo shouted, loping after me.

Simone was standing in the lobby, looking around. 'How do we get through?'

'Michael.' I looked around. 'We need Michael. Michael, or one of the Immortal sons.'

Simone concentrated and Michael appeared next to her. 'What's going on?' he said.

Simone grabbed his hand and stared fiercely at him, transferring the information. His expression changed and he dragged her to the lifts. 'Come on!'

Mind my wives! the Tiger roared in my head.

'Mind your own damn wives. My demons are in there and they may not be copies!' I shouted.

Leave them, they're copies, he said more calmly.

'Over my dead body,' I said.

We arrived at the lifts and Michael opened them with a glance. We went in and he manipulated the control panel to take us down.

'Wow, this is a long way,' Simone said.

We arrived at the bottom and the doors opened to the blank room. Michael raised one hand and the vault doors appeared. He gestured and the gears spun, opening the doors. We ran through to the first gate. Michael concentrated and it opened. We moved through the five gates, with Michael opening each one as we arrived. We hit the bottom of the cable-car tunnel.

Michael stuck his head into the tunnel. 'No cars. It's been shut down. We have to walk.' He looked down. 'The floor's electrified.'

Simone took Celestial Form, in her Wudang uniform, and floated above the ground. She slid effortlessly into the tunnel. 'I can go.'

Michael took Celestial Form as well; he didn't appear to age, but his clothing changed to white-and-gold jacket and pants, and his hair grew longer and gold, all the way down his back. 'You don't need to; I can do it.'

'Is there a way to turn off the electricity?' I said. 'Stone! Relay!'

'The switch is at the other end,' Michael said. 'I'll just float up and turn it off for you. Let me do it, I'm stronger.'

'Michael.' Simone touched his arm. 'Are you really stronger than me?'

He settled to stand on the floor of the cable-car station and stared at her, then looked away. 'No. You were always five times stronger than anybody.'

'And I'm more likely to survive if I do touch it.'

He grabbed her hand, pulled her down and kissed her quickly, then released her. She floated back up, both of them looking surprised. He stepped back. 'Just be careful, okay, squirt?'

She nodded and turned to the tunnel and floated into it.

'Do that again and I will tear you into very small pieces,' Leo growled at Michael.

'Shut up, Leo,' Simone said, her calm voice echoing through the tunnel.

A spark jumped and she squeaked. We peered up the tunnel to see.

'I'm okay. It was something like static, I just got too close,' Simone said. 'Probably because of my nature.'

'Nature?' Leo said.

'Water,' I said. 'Both of them are weak to electricity — she's water and he's metal.'

'Metal is weaker,' she said, her voice floating down the corridor.

'Concentrate. Don't talk. Just concentrate,' Michael said.

There was another spark and she squeaked again.

'She should come back down,' Leo said.

'I'm nearly there,' she said. Her feet tapped on the floor at the other end. 'I am there. Where's the switch?'

'No idea,' Michael said. 'Let me see ...'

'Ask the Tiger,' I said.

'He won't say,' Simone said.

Stay down that end, you stupid people, the Tiger said. *It's bad up here.*

'Sounds like he needs help,' I said.

'All in favour of ignoring the Tiger say "aye",' Simone said.

We all chorused 'Aye'.

'I think this is it,' she said. 'Let me see.'

'That worked. I can sense it's off,' Michael said.

'You sure?' Leo said suspiciously. 'Isn't there supposed to be a powering-down sound, or a light going off, or sparks or something?'

'Do you get that when you turn the iron off?' Michael said. He jumped into the corridor, turned and grinned at us, revealing big cat canines. 'All off. Thank you, madam.'

'Just hurry up!' Simone called.

We ran to the end of the tunnel. The guards stood there frozen, their eyes wide.

Simone gestured towards them. 'I didn't want guns pointed at me so I bound them.'

You can let them go, they won't stop you, the Tiger said.

The guards sagged and took deep breaths, then pointed the guns at us.

'My apologies,' one of them said. 'We've been ordered to keep you here.' They moved into position so that all four of us were covered. 'Raise your hands, please.'

Now stay there! the Tiger said.

'Do as they say,' I said, and we all raised our hands.

Simone concentrated. 'They're bound again. Let's go.'

'Liar!' I said to the Tiger.

Only for you, baby.

Simone pointed at the blank wall. 'The vault door's there. Michael?'

'Got it,' Michael said, and the door appeared. The wheels turned and it opened.

'If I remember right, there's a corridor, then a guard station with three guards in it,' I said. 'Tiger, if you can hear me, please tell them to stand down. I really don't want to mess with any ridiculous code words, I just want to get to my demons.'

They won't stand down on telepathic command, the Tiger said. *The code phrase is: 'Help, I'm being held hostage by this evil snake demon.'*

'Bastard!'

Thank you.

'Did you get that, Simone?'

Simone was silent for a moment, then she replied, her voice full of suppressed laughter. 'Yeah, I got it.'

Michael opened the doors for us and the guards stood waiting with their weapons pointed at us.

'Help, I'm being held hostage by this evil snake demon,' Simone said. 'Now please don't point those at my family.'

The soldiers lowered their weapons and stepped back.

'Thank you,' I said.

You're welcome.

'I wasn't talking to you.'

'I'm glad you're here, ma'am,' one of the soldiers said to Simone. 'These things are nasty. Some of our brothers have died, and our mothers are outside at the other end. We're counting on you.' They saluted her, raising their weapons to her. 'Ma'am.'

Simone was silent for a moment, then said, 'I'll do my best.'

'That's all we can ask for, ma'am,' he said, and they stepped back.

'There's a maze on the other side,' I said.

'I can see it,' Simone said. 'Don't worry, I can see it all.'

'The path through the maze is the character for

Tiger,' Michael said as he made the doors materialise and open. 'Pretty stupid and obvious, really.'

'Oh, it is too!' Simone said with wonder. She turned to Michael. 'You're right!'

'About it being stupid and obvious?' he said as we went down the first path in the maze.

'Well, it is your dad we're talking about.'

As we wound through the corridors, the air became warmer. I tasted it. 'The air tastes of ash and burning,' I said. 'Not a good sign.'

Simone raised both arms to the side as we reached the end of the maze and a group of ten water elementals, each of them a sphere of water about the size of a basketball, materialised around her. 'These will help.'

Michael opened the final door for us and the two guards stood with their weapons ready on the other side.

'Don't bother with the code words, ma'am,' one of them said to Simone. 'Just please go and help. My mother is outside.'

Michael opened the doors and we entered the lobby of the demon hotel. The hotel staff wore standard uniforms, but all of them carried swords and had the demons gathered in groups in the lobby, sitting on the floor with their hands behind their heads. I saw my demons and slithered to them.

'Yi Hao, Er Hao,' I said.

They jumped up and ran to me, and the guard raised her sword to attack them.

'Stand down,' Simone said. 'This is Lady Emma, and they are her demons.'

The guard subsided. Yi Hao and Er Hao fell to their knees in front of me.

'They won't tell us what is happening, ma'am,' Er Hao said. 'Are they going to destroy us? We've done nothing.'

'You are in danger,' I said. 'There are fake fire elementals on the other side.' I tasted the air: stronger ash and burning, a raw taste that seared my throat.

'They should let us go then,' one of the other demons called.

'No,' Jeremy said loudly. 'We're demons, and we can't be trusted.' He rose and took a few steps towards me. 'Princess Simone is here. Lady Emma is here. They can take down anything that attacks.' He turned back to the demons. 'We'll be fine, we just have to stay put and wait.'

I glanced back at Simone and we shared a look.

We can't let them go, she said. *They're controlled by the Geek or the Death Mother.*

I know.

'Stay here,' I said. I touched my nose to Yi Hao and Er Hao and they nodded, tears flowing down their faces. 'We'll fix this.'

'We trust you, ma'am,' Yi Hao said. She raised one hand and touched my nose. 'Who's looking after you? Your diary must be a mess, and you had some urgent business in your in-tray —'

'Don't worry about that,' I said. I raised myself on my coils to talk to all of them. 'Go to the far end of the building and stay there. If the fire elementals come in and get past us, try fire extinguishers on them, and run.'

Yi Hao nodded. 'We trust you.' She touched Er Hao on the arm and they rejoined their group.

'Come on,' the guards said, and guided the demons to the other end of the building. This version of the

450

hotel had no indoor swimming pool, just a large hall under the building, and they all sat on the ground there.

'I would really, really like to see a turtle here right now,' Simone said.

'So would I,' I said. 'But we have to assume that it isn't going to happen.'

CHAPTER 30

We took the lift up to where the restaurant and conference rooms were located. The smoke was visible in the air.

'This is very bad,' I said, looking around.

Simone pointed to the airlock entrance. 'Do we go through there?'

'Yes,' I said. 'And it's supposed to be a vacuum seal.'

'But there's smoke here,' Michael said.

'That means the seal is down,' Simone said.

'There's nothing but a couple of doors between this area and all those demons,' I said.

'What did your dad have in there?' Simone asked Michael.

'All the nastiest things he caught. At least three or four real big Snake Mothers. A couple of oozes, a buttload of really big humanoids. He even caught two or three dinosaur shape changers — raptor types — and they're in there too.'

'All of that and a group of fire elementals,' Simone said, facing the door with her water elementals floating around her. She took a deep breath. 'A turtle right now would be really, really good.'

Something hit the door, denting it, and we all took a step back. The smell of burning intensified.

'Emma, move back,' Simone said without looking away from the door. 'In fact, I think it might be best if you went all the way back to the hotel.'

'You can't fight these, they're too big even for your snake,' Michael said.

'You kids should both go back, you're not Immortal,' Leo said. 'And take Emma with you.'

'We can fight,' Michael said, and summoned his sword, the White Tiger.

Simone raised one hand and Seven Stars appeared in it, the blade bare. 'Emma can't fight. Emma, go back.'

Leo changed from lion to human form, wearing a Wudang uniform, and stood without difficulty. He concentrated and grew even taller, becoming darker and wider and deeper. He remained big, black and bald, but he was nearly three metres tall. His face lost its late-forties appearance and became younger and full of intensity.

'I didn't know you had a Celestial Form, old man,' Michael said.

'I didn't either,' Leo said. 'How about that.'

Something hit the doors again, and a hole appeared in the centre. The edges of the hole changed from grey to glowing red.

Leo glanced at me. 'I think they're right, Emma. Go back.'

'I'll stand at the rear. Don't forget what I am,' I said.

'You're just a snake,' Simone said. 'You're just your ordinary snake self, not the super-powered version — and you can't fight these.'

'I'm not here to fight,' I said. 'I'm a healer.'

The middle of the door began to melt and we all moved back at the intensity of the heat.

'Just stay back and don't try to help then,' Simone said.

'The demons on the other side of the door are holding back as well,' Michael said. 'The heat from the melting metal will be as intense for them as it is for us.'

A two-metre-long, tentacle-shaped flame poked through the hole in the door and lashed around. It touched the floor and the flames oozed to the end of it, forming themselves into a human-shaped demon made of flame.

We all took another step back.

Simone raised one arm and gestured and one of the water elementals flew towards the fire elemental. The water elemental grew to a sphere of three metres across and encased the fire elemental. The water touching the fire boiled, the bubbles visible within the water, and the water around the edges froze.

'Compensate, compensate!' Simone said, concentrating on the elemental. 'Colder!'

A floating mist of condensation appeared around the water. Crystals appeared in its structure and the boiling within it eased.

Simone gasped and sagged. 'I have it. It's contained.' She turned to look at us. 'But I can't hold it forever.'

Another flame tentacle came through the door and Simone turned back to face it.

'How many of those things are there?' I said.

'Five,' Michael said. He backed up again. 'That's why we never saw any fire elementals when we were attacked before. Always the other elements, but not fire. He was saving them for this.'

This tentacle turned into two fire elementals, which stopped when they saw us. They merged into one, and it wrapped its arms around the fire elemental held inside the ice bubble.

Simone raised one hand and three of her water elementals joined together, grew into a larger sphere and engulfed both of the fire elementals and their frozen brother. The sphere froze with an audible crack.

'This is not a good time for me to be without my yin,' Simone said, her voice strained with effort.

'You don't have yin?' Michael said.

'Daddy locked it out of me. He said I might destroy the world.'

'Makes sense.' Michael readied himself. 'The other demons are approaching.'

We're fighting the demons from the other side but it's not looking good, the Tiger said. *We've taken down the raptors and most of the humanoids, but the Mothers are too big, and we have two more fires back here that we can't even get close to.*

A siren went off over the intercom system.

Evacuate, the Tiger said. *Destroy the demons and run. Everybody out.*

'No!' I shouted, slithering quickly back to the demons being held in the demon hotel. The staff had already started to slice them up. They ran around in terror and cowered in the corners.

'I am Emma Donahoe, First Heavenly General, and I order you to stop this!' I roared.

The staff ignored me.

I went to one of them and stood between him and the demons. 'That is an order!' I looked around. 'Stop destroying these demons now. Stand down! Tiger,

455

order your staff to stand down right now, that is an order!'

Do it, the Tiger said.

The guards looked at each other, then lowered their weapons.

'I am First Heavenly General and you obey my orders above all others,' I hissed at the guards. 'The Tiger should not have had to confirm that. Do not for a moment forget who I am.'

You pulling rank on me, girlie? the Tiger said.

'Damn straight,' I said. I focused on the guards. 'Evacuate these demons under guard. Take them to the lobby of the other hotel down the bottom and keep them under guard and separate from the wives. The reason they're in this part of the facility is because they've turned, and demons that have turned must be protected.'

I moved to face the demons. 'Go with the guards. I've made sure they won't hurt you. Follow orders, go quietly and behave.'

I turned back to the guards. 'If any of them disobey you, even for a second, destroy them without hesitation.' I couldn't slither backwards so I turned and moved out of the way. 'Now go.'

'Thank you, ma'am,' Jeremy said.

'Watch those ones particularly carefully,' I said, indicating Jeremy's group with my nose. 'They haven't turned; they're demon copies of humans.'

Jeremy's expression darkened and he dropped his head as he walked past.

'Just be yourself, Jeremy, and nobody will hurt you,' I said more gently.

He smiled slightly at me, dropped his head again and went out.

I rejoined Simone, Michael and Leo at the top of the stairs. The fire elementals remained frozen inside the water, but another fire elemental had come through the door. Simone was in the process of freezing it. Something struck the door again, and hands appeared in the hole, trying to make it bigger. The hands disappeared and a sword poked through; an armed demon was attempting to widen the hole.

'I can't hold these fire elementals forever,' Simone said. She loaded Seven Stars with her own chakra energy, each chakra forming a different-coloured ball of light in one of the seven indentations in the sword. 'Michael, help them through the door so we can destroy them and then leave.'

'What's happening on your side, Tiger?' I said.

There was no reply.

'Nobody's left alive, it's just us. It's a good thing we came up,' Michael said.

He raised one hand towards the door and it shattered. He readied himself with his sword. 'Come on in, demons, we can take you.'

Two armed humanoids came through, followed by three enormous Snake Mothers.

'Permission to use Dark Heavens, ma'am,' Leo said.

'Granted,' Simone and I said in unison.

'I need to talk to the forge about getting something made for me,' Leo said as he raised the sword. His voice changed to surprise. 'Well, how about that.' Dark Heavens had grown in his hands to match the size of his Celestial Form.

Simone raised Seven Stars above her head, the point towards the two humanoid demons. A flash of bright white light shot from the end of the sword and destroyed both of them.

'Don't do that, you'll wear yourself out before we get to the hard ones!' Michael shouted.

'We are at the hard ones,' Simone said. Her voice changed to menacing. 'And I'm not nearly worn out yet.'

Martin strode into the room and stopped in front of me. He was in Celestial Form, with green and tan robes, his long brown hair held in a topknot by a jade green ribbon that flowed down to his feet. He carried the Silver Serpent.

'Sorry I took so long,' he said. 'The Tiger was asking for help with his wives without telling anybody what was really going on.'

'Are the Northern Heavens guarded sufficiently?' I said.

'Ma'am. All is secure.'

'Good,' I said.

The Snake Mothers waited at the doorway without attacking.

'Is this everything?' I said.

The Geek, the Death Mother and Kitty Kwok stepped through the doorway and stood just inside it.

'That's everything,' Simone said grimly.

'Oh, look, Emma's a snake again,' Kitty said. 'But not as strong as last time. I wonder why? Might have something to do with all that demon essence I pumped into her.'

The Death Mother moved up to stand next to the three armed demons; she held a massive machine gun with one hand. 'I'll take the Princess,' she said.

'Black Lion,' one of the Mothers said. 'You three take the remaining ones.'

'I'm a thinker, not a fighter,' the Geek said, his voice wavering. He moved to stand behind Kitty. 'Just kill them all.'

'I want Emma alive!' Kitty shouted. 'The King'll trade anything for her!'

'Simone alive would be handy as well,' the Death Mother said. 'But I think it's too dangerous to try to capture her; we should just take her head off.'

One of the other Mothers rose on her coils. 'Sounds like a plan.'

I turned and moved back to the wall; I wasn't big enough in serpent form to take these on. I lowered my nose to the ground, concentrated and the white jade disk appeared. I raised my head and turned back. The demons and Celestials were facing off, and the water encasing the fire elementals was beginning to boil again.

'The fire elementals are escaping,' Simone said.

Martin raised one hand and concentrated and the demons stopped moving. He'd bound them all. 'I can't hold this for long, and there are too many of them for us to fight,' he said.

'We can do it,' Simone said.

'Too risky,' Martin said. 'Ten of them, three of us — we can't all survive that. The Bai Hu's army is at the bottom waiting, they can help. We can't do this alone.'

'Can they move faster than us?' Simone said.

'Yes. But I can hold them. Run!' Martin said, and pushed Simone behind him.

Leo grabbed Simone's hand and pulled her towards the lift. Michael followed. I picked up the jade disk in my mouth and followed them.

'Cowards!' the Death Mother shouted. 'When I can move, you are all dead!'

'Go!' Martin said, staring at the demons.

'Shut the doors behind us,' I said to Michael, my voice muffled by the disk in my mouth.

We went down in the lift to the guard room leading to the maze. The two guards were standing there uncertainly, holding their weapons.

'Follow us,' I said.

They nodded and stood on either side of the door. Michael opened it and we ran through the maze. The room at the other end held another three guards and I ordered them to follow us as well.

Michael opened the vault doors, we went through, and he closed them again. We were in the blank corridor where the Tiger and I had discussed my fan club.

'That will hold them for a while,' Michael said as the vault doors disappeared behind us. 'No way will they get that open. They probably can't even see it.'

A white-hot point of heat and light, so bright it burned into my retinas, appeared in the middle of the wall where the door was.

'They can't get it open?' Leo said.

'I'm not sure it's a good idea taking them down to the hotel,' I said. 'I should just use this jade disk and be done with it.'

'Only as a last resort,' Simone said. 'It'll destroy the tame demons and the demon wives as well.'

'And Emma!' Leo shouted.

Simone glared at him. 'You think I don't know that? But she doesn't give a damn about herself; she has as much of a death wish as you do.' She slashed one hand through the air. 'I want both of you alive, so only as a last resort!'

I dropped my serpent head. 'Okay.' I turned to the tunnel. 'Is the electricity still off?'

'Yes,' Michael said.

'You go,' one of the guards said. 'When you're at the bottom, I'll turn it back on.'

'Don't you dare,' Leo said. 'If anyone stays, it should be me. I'm the only Immortal here.'

The air filled with acrid, metallic smoke.

'Don't argue with me, just go!' the guard said. 'My mother's down there, and you are three times more powerful than anything we have. Losing you now would put my mother at risk. There's an army at the bottom to help you. So go!'

The stone in my ring took human form. 'Lovely sentiment, little man, but absolutely no need for it.' He turned to us. 'Off you go. I'll do it.'

'I'll shout when we're at the end,' Simone said, and jumped off the edge into the tunnel.

We followed her.

'Through!' Simone shouted, and the stone floated through the air behind us and returned to the ring.

All of the doors were still open, and Michael closed them behind us as we went through. We reached the final vault doors to the lifts and Michael closed these as well. The lift doors hung open and we went in.

'Be nice if that held them in,' Simone said.

'Where's the limit of the teleportation lock?' I asked one of the guards.

Michael concentrated. 'Here. Once they're here, they can teleport.'

'I suppose it's too much to ask that they'll take what they came for and leave,' Simone said.

The lift doors opened and we entered the lobby of the ski resort. Michael melted the lift doors open, effectively stopping the lifts from working.

'I think they came for us,' he said.

'No, the Death Mother came for the Geek,' I said as we went out to the forecourt. 'She gave him something when she kissed him — something that allowed them all to get in here.'

Simone inhaled sharply. 'There are demons back there in the labs, looking at all your dad's research,' she said to Michael.

About half the wives had been evacuated, but half remained; they were sitting in the snow with fifty or so guards standing over them. The demons and their guards were visible next to the swimming pool on the ground floor of the residential wing of the resort.

'This isn't an army, there's only ten or so guards here. What happened?' I said.

Michael went to one of the guards and quickly embraced him. They slapped each other on the back. 'We have a group of big demons following us,' Michael told him when they released each other. 'Where's everybody else? When are the buses coming back up?'

'Demons attacked us,' the guard said. 'A group of six or seven out of the lot that came down from the hotel. Never seen anything like it. They ran to us, and when they were close, they exploded. Like high-end incendiaries.' He gestured with his head. 'There's fifty of us lying dead over there.'

'I told them to watch those demons more carefully!' I said.

'They were tiny; how were we to know they'd do that?' the guard said.

I slithered backwards and forwards with frustration. 'I warned them. Why didn't they listen?'

The guard glared at me. 'We did listen. We watched them. But we've never seen a demon explode like that before. Where the *fuck* did that come from?'

'It's something they did in the past, but the current Demon King has outlawed it,' I said.

'Looks like the current King is on the way out then,' the guard said, his face grim.

'How soon can you get the wives out?' Michael said.

'The second transfer just left; we have a good hour before it's back, and it can only take about forty of them,' the guard said. 'We'll teleport the remainder while the bus returns for the rest of the tame demons.'

I dropped the jade disk in the forecourt and went into the swimming pool area. 'Start walking now,' I said to the demons. 'Head down the hill. Walk on the road. Get at least two hundred metres away from here.'

'You are *not* using that thing!' Simone said behind me.

'Not right now, no,' I said, and returned to the forecourt.

She barked with frustration. 'Smartass!'

'Thank you,' I said.

Michael had already instructed the guards to move the wives to the back of the building where they would be safer. I joined him there after the demons had started the march down the hill.

'How many demon wives here? They should move away as well,' I said.

They don't want to identify themselves, Michael said. *They'd rather die.*

A huge crash resounded through the building.

'That was the demons blowing up one of the elevator cars,' Michael said. He shifted his grip on his sword and turned to the guards. 'Mark, Andy, Ross, stay with the wives.' He gestured with his sword. 'Everybody else, with me.'

We went back around to the forecourt.

'Me at point,' Leo said. 'Simone, Michael. Emma, guards, to the rear.'

We moved into the defensive formation with Leo at the front.

Leo readied himself. 'Me on point — feels kinda weird.'

'It shouldn't, it's where you belong,' Michael said. 'Here we go,' he added as the demons came out of the building.

The three Snake Mothers approached us, with the Death Mother at the front.

'I'll take the big one,' Leo said.

'Left,' Michael said.

'Centre,' Simone said. 'You guards take the right. Emma, stay back, and don't, whatever you do, use that stone.'

The fire elementals didn't come out; they stayed in the hotel and ignited everything — furniture, carpets, curtains. Heat and smoke billowed out of the building and we were forced to move back. The wives screamed and ran, the guards guiding them down the hill.

The Death Mother slithered towards Simone, raising the gun. Simone concentrated with Seven Stars in one hand. The Mother shook the gun a few times, checked the load mechanism and dropped it. Simone had made it useless.

Leo attacked the Death Mother with Dark Heavens, swinging at her, but she avoided his blows, moving with disturbing speed. She lashed out at him and struck him across the throat and he reeled back. He wiped his face and readied himself.

Michael was an even match with the Mother he was facing. He had loaded his sword with shen energy and moved as fast as she did, but neither of them could break through each other's guard.

The second Snake Mother attacked the guards, sweeping five of them away in one hit. She grabbed a sixth with a hand at each end of his torso, broke his spine with an audible crack and tossed him aside. She turned to the other five guards and killed them with relish, breaking their bodies and tearing out their throats.

Simone swung Seven Stars at the Mother she'd called and cut it in two, ducking under its arms as they flailed towards her. The demon exploded and she rushed to attack the Mother that had killed the guards. She didn't load the sword with energy; she was obviously tiring.

I went to the injured guard, took his arm in my mouth and dragged him back away from the fight. I touched my nose to him; the damage was severe and I couldn't fix him. I did what I could to relieve his pain then raised my head to check the battle.

Leo was losing. The Death Mother had broken his left arm and he was blocking her blows with difficulty.

Michael kept checking on Leo and Simone, which proved his undoing. The Snake Mother he was facing saw him look away and hit him squarely on the side of the head, knocking him down. She moved to assist the Mother attacking Simone.

Leo fell to one knee, keeping the Death Mother away by sheer stubbornness. It was only a matter of time before she finished him or he lost the use of his legs from exhaustion.

Simone was now facing two Mothers at once, and they were working together to get through her guard. They had already drawn blood — her uniform was torn on one side and wet with it. She raised the sword, concentrated and sent a blast of shen energy out of the sword and through both of them, dissipating them. She rushed to help Leo with the Death Mother.

I dragged Michael back to where the crippled guard was lying. He wasn't severely injured this time; only concussion — his brain had hit the inside of his skull and there was bruising but not a major haemorrhage like the last time. He'd be fine.

The Death Mother backed up when faced with both Leo and Simone. Simone sent a blast of shen at the Mother and she deflected it into the ground, then grimaced with satisfaction. The fire elementals strode out of the building towards her. I could feel their heat from fifty metres away, and they melted the snow in a ten-metre radius around them. These were much bigger than the ones we'd faced back in Europe.

Simone and Leo hesitated. The Death Mother backed up — carefully keeping a good distance — to allow the elementals to come to the front. The Geek appeared in the entrance of the burning hotel and crossed his arms over his chest.

Simone threw a ball of shen energy at one of the elementals but it travelled straight through it. She summoned a group of water elementals, which tried to surround the fire, but they were vaporised as they touched it.

She's weakened by exhaustion and blood loss, the stone said.

The stone didn't need to tell me that. Simone was in mortal danger and the damn turtle wasn't showing up to help her.

I think he used everything he had to get you off the First Platform, the stone said. *That would be enough to flatten anybody for weeks. Ma was usually out of action for a month after going to the First.*

Wonderful. I looked behind me for the jade disk and picked it up.

Last resort, the stone said.

I held the disk in my mouth and watched.

Simone took two huge strides forward and swung Seven Stars at a fire elemental. It went straight through the demon without damaging it. The fake elementals raised their arms and a burst of flame jetted from the ends, like a flamethrower, completely encasing Simone and Leo. Simone reeled back out of the inferno coughing, her clothes and hair smouldering.

The demons stopped the fire blast and Leo's scorched body lay on the ground in front of them. He disappeared.

The demons blasted Simone again, and this time she ran back out of the flames. They seemed to be enjoying it, taking their time about moving closer to her.

The stupid girl's drained from using too much shen energy, the stone said.

'Don't use it!' Simone shouted.

A cluster of water elementals appeared around her and threw themselves at the fire elementals. They concentrated their water attack on one, destroying it, but were vaporised in the process. The cloud of steam threw itself at another fire elemental but disappeared before touching it.

Ma'am, the stone said. *It has been my honour to serve you. I hope I am destroyed with you.*

'Simone!' I shouted.

'Don't use it!'

'I love you.'

'No!'

'Don't use it,' a male voice said behind me, and I turned with a leap of joy.

The joy turned to dismay as I saw the Demon King standing there with a satisfied smile.

'I can't stop them, they're not mine,' the King said. 'But these demons need to be taken down. I really wanted something good in return, Emma, but I'll do it for free, just this once.' He raised his hand. 'Quick. Come to me and I'll remove the demon essence.'

Simone screamed and I turned to see her. She was crouched on the ground with her hands over her head and the demons were enveloping her with white-hot fire.

'I swear that's all I'll do,' the King said. 'I'll remove the essence and you can use the stone. No payment required.'

I slithered over to him and he touched the top of my head. 'I've saved both your lives,' he whispered as the demon essence spiralled out of me into him. 'It would be very, very nice to receive something in return.' He took his hand away from my head. 'I give you my word, Lady Emma, that you can change to human form right now and use that stone without injury. This I swear.' He disappeared.

Simone's screams tore at me. I didn't bother changing to human form. Either the stone would destroy me or it wouldn't, but either way it would destroy the demons. I hurried towards her to ensure that all the demons would be in the field of the jade.

The Death Mother saw what I had in my mouth, grimaced and disappeared. The Geek ran back into the hotel yelling something.

I told the stone to destroy the demons.

A pressure wave threw me into the air; it spread out from me, making a visible ripple in the smoke. The fire elementals disintegrated as the wave hit them. Simone was thrown into the air too. She was limp when she hit the ground again, the dust and ash flying around her.

The jade disk disappeared and I hit the ground hard.

CHAPTER 31

I came around to find a huge, grinning, brightly lit face right above me. I realised what it was with a bolt of panic: a hospital examination light. I was strapped to a hospital bed, and the light was above me, and someone was talking — a male voice, high-pitched with fear.

'Isn't that enough?' he said. 'More than that and you'll kill her.'

'I want to see how far I can go,' a female voice said, and I recognised it — Kitty Kwok.

My vision cleared but I couldn't see much. Each eye saw something different; one of the disadvantages of being a snake with an eye either side of my head. The Geek was tied down on another hospital bed to my left, a tube coming out of his arm. To my right, I could just make out Kitty's pink cashmere twin set and the end of her arm and hand next to my head. I flicked my tongue, tasting the air, and immediately regretted it. It tasted of demon.

Kitty's face moved into view of my right eye. 'Don't change to human or you'll die. Stay snake. Let's see how far we can go.'

'You're killing me!' the Geek said.

470

'And?' Kitty said.

'You need me!'

'Your pretty machines are gone. The elementals did what I wanted them to do — they got us into here, and I have all the information I was looking for. I don't need you any more — except to do this.'

'Bitch!'

'Oh, whatever.' Her hands moved and the IV tube swayed. 'Your snake is much harder to fill up, Emma, you know that? It'll take Thirty-three forever to die at this rate.' Her voice filled with satisfaction. 'So much more fun.'

My Inner Eye still worked; she hadn't filled me with enough demon essence to block it yet. I used it to check around me. I was in the Tiger's demon laboratory; they hadn't taken me far. I quickly looked for Simone and Michael, and saw them at the bottom of the complex in the snow: unconscious but okay.

'So how does it feel not being able to walk the Earth?' I said. 'Stuck in Hell?'

'I quite like Hell,' Kitty said. 'No laws, no rules, you can do what you like. Simon had the right idea — but he went through his toys much too fast. I prefer to take my time with them. I come out occasionally, you know. I go shopping, kidnap some prostitutes — it's all good.'

'Do you know what I am?' I said.

'No. The King keeps boasting that he knows, and that he'll use you one day. But he's always boasting about all kinds of stupid shit.'

'Use me for what?'

She put her hand on my head; my crown containing the stone was gone. 'Hush. It won't be long before I'll be using you, not him.'

'Kitty ...' the Geek moaned.

'I wish I could see how much has gone into you,' Kitty said. 'A direct transfusion like this is so inaccurate. It's like breastfeeding instead of the bottle — the bottle is so much better, you can see how much the baby has had.' She patted my head. 'My baby.'

'Are you sure you'll be able to control her once she's converted?' another voice said.

'No,' Kitty said. 'If we can't control her, I'm counting on you to take her out. Can you do it?'

There was a wet slithering sound that I recognised: a Snake Mother. Probably the Death Mother. 'What level Mother is she?'

'I think about eighty-five from the intel,' Kitty said.

The Death Mother hissed. 'Easy. I'm at least five levels above that.'

'It's dark,' the Geek said. 'It's so dark. It's cold.'

'She's not even feeling it,' Kitty said. 'We may have to pull in some smaller stuff and top her up.'

Power grew inside me, full of rage and hate and destruction.

'Something's happening,' the Mother said. 'She smells different.'

Kitty took her hand off my head. 'What does she smell like?'

'Demon.'

The change was coming upon me. Fighting it would only make it stronger. I remained calm, touching my serpent yang, thinking of the ones I loved. I had to remain in touch with the deep well of tranquillity within me, because the anger would destroy me. I had to concentrate on the love, not the hate.

'She's fighting it,' the Death Mother said.

'Let her fight,' Kitty said. 'The more she fights it, the stronger it'll get.'

'She's fighting it by not fighting it,' the Mother said.

'You creatures and your mystical bullshit,' Kitty said. 'Whatever. She won't be able to do anything once her blood's full of demon essence. Either it'll kill her or convert her.'

I didn't really hear them; I concentrated on my family, my little girl, my turtle, my lion friend. The feeling eased.

I heard a pinging sound, like a ceramic vase being hit.

'Hey, he's empty,' the Death Mother said. 'Whoops.' The ceramic shattered and she laughed. 'Nothing but a shell left. We should have videoed that, it was great.'

'Go find some others to put into her,' Kitty said. 'How big was he?'

'Tiny. Level sixty-something. Couldn't even sire spawn on the smallest Mother.'

'We need another couple to top her up. She's not converted, and we need to get her there.'

'Come and give me a hand then. You open the cage, I'll hold the demon.'

'Bah.' Kitty slapped my bed and left.

I checked the Geek. His essence had been drained completely and his shell had cracked. He looked like a smashed Easter egg.

A green sleeve and white hand appeared on my right. The drip was pulled out of my back with a lance of pain.

Quiet, the stone said. *I'm unhooking you, then I want you to hide. I'll hold them off as long as I can.*

'How?' I whispered.

I said, quiet!

Screams erupted at the top of the complex as Kitty and the Death Mother grabbed another demon.

The bonds slid from me and I slithered off the table. I looked around. The lab was completely trashed; only the two beds holding me and the Geek were still in one piece, and his only had three legs. The walls were covered with scorch marks from the fire elementals. The only way out was the lift back up to where Kitty and the Mother were. I was trapped.

I'll distract them, the stone said. *Wait behind a cabinet close to the lift, and as soon as they're out make a run for it. You have to get into the lift before the doors close. Hurry, Emma, I can't hold this form for long; you only have a couple of minutes at the most.*

I nodded my serpent head. There were cabinets for holding surgical tools and monitoring equipment lined up against the wall, most of them dented and hanging open. I slithered behind the one closest to the lift, pressing myself between its back and the wall. I peered out of the gap; the stone had taken my serpent form and was hiding underneath a cabinet on the other side of the room, its tail hanging out.

If you can make yourself smaller it would be a very good thing, the stone said.

I did my best.

The lift doors opened and the room filled with the screams and wails of the captured demon.

'Shit, she's loose!' the Death Mother said. 'Hold this!' She threw the demon at Kitty, who held it with difficulty, and raced towards the stone.

'Get away from me, you bitch!' the stone shouted in my voice, slithering further under the cabinet. It made itself smaller and moved lightning fast, the Mother trying to grab it.

Kitty was wrestling with the demon, which had

474

nearly got away from her. She held it with difficulty as it dragged her across the room.

Now, the stone said.

I made myself as small as possible, moved as fast as I could, and slithered to the lift. I made it just before the doors closed by themselves — and they hadn't seen me. I pressed the button for the top floor, and moved backwards and forwards in the lift as it carried me. When the doors opened again, I headed through the cell block to the rooms on the other side.

I heard the demon screaming down below and Kitty yelling at the Death Mother to catch me.

They still think I'm you, the stone said. *Get out. I can't hold it.*

When I arrived back at the forecourt of the hotel, Simone ran to me and grabbed me around the neck. 'Oh God, Emma, I thought I'd lost you. What happened to you? I came around and only a couple of guards were left, and Michael couldn't remember anything. Where's Leo?'

'Leo died,' I said.

'What was that explosion thing? Did you use the jade? Why didn't it kill you?'

'The Demon King wants me alive,' I said. 'Probably to do his dirty work. He took the demon essence out of me so I could use the jade without being destroyed. Are the tame demons okay?'

'They were out of range, they're fine. Those other demons exploded?'

'Yes. We have to warn the Celestial.' I looked around. 'Right now, I need a lift home.'

'Emma.' She touched my head. 'You said the Demon King took the essence out of you. He lied.'

'No, he didn't,' I said. 'Kitty and the Death Mother took me to the Tiger's lab and filled me up again.'

'What about the Geek?'

'That's what they filled me up with. Look at me.'

She inhaled sharply. 'No way. It's worse than ever. You're so on the edge — Emma, that's scary. How did you get away? I didn't even know where you were.'

'My stone helped me. I have no idea where it is.'

'Everybody's in the Courts; there's just you, me and Michael left, and Michael's got a bump on his head the size of a grapefruit,' she said. 'Just what he needed after that last injury. He's on the bus being taken back down.' She fell to sit in the snow. 'I'm wrecked. Give me a couple of minutes to get my breath, then we'll go inside and finish them off.'

'Leave them,' I said. 'We'll chase them down later.'

'We have them right here!' she protested.

'And nobody else but us,' I said. 'And you're, as you say, wrecked. Let's leave the stone to do its job and find out where they're going.'

'You sure it'll do that for us?'

'It'll do its best. That's all we can ask for.'

She bent her head over her legs, wrapped her arms around her knees and held them tight, rocking backwards and forwards. 'I nearly lost, Emma. I'm not supposed to lose!' She looked up at me, her face streaked with tears, and I moved closer to put my head on her shoulder. 'I'm not supposed to lose!'

Her head shot up. 'The Tiger's Number One is coming. Let me go, Emma, I have to fix myself up.'

She wiped her eyes and I moved back. She stood, concentrated and a dark glow blossomed around her. Her Wudang uniform changed to her Celestial robes and the redness disappeared from her eyes. She took a deep breath and shook herself out.

The Tiger's Number One Son in Celestial Form, wearing a white silk robe embossed with gold tiger stripes, appeared in front of us and saluted. 'Regent. Princess.'

'Hi, Greg,' Simone said.

He waved. 'Hi. We need you out; I'm going to yang the whole thing. Right down to bedrock.'

'Emma's stone is down there!' Simone said.

'It can't be destroyed by anything as mundane as yang,' I said. 'In fact, I don't think there's anything that can destroy it at all.'

'Time,' Greg said. 'Which is something you guys don't have. You need to go down to the palace; the other sons will be there providing protection from the radiation. I have to do this now, and it'll be hot.'

'Can you take me, Simone?' I said.

'As far as the palace, sure,' she said. 'After that I'll need a break before I can take you home.'

'That's fine,' I said.

She put her hand on my head and we were in the gardens of the palace, next to a stream flowing through a series of stepped channels.

'Look away from the mountains,' Simone said, and covered my eyes just as a blinding flash filled the air. There was nothing for ten seconds, then the ground shook beneath us with a shockwave that felt like it lifted us and dropped us again.

'Two in one day; we're doing well,' Simone said. 'At least this one didn't knock us out.'

'Are you all right?' my mother said, clutching both of us when we arrived at their villa. 'I heard there was a fight, some demons — something happened. And there was a huge explosion — someone just blew up the ski resort.'

'We're okay, just kinda exhausted,' Simone said. 'Do you mind if I use your shower?'

'I'll get Jen to bring you something to wear,' my mother said. 'All your clothes are scorched, sweetheart — what happened?'

'I'd prefer not to go into it,' Simone said, and headed for the bathroom.

'Will she eat something when she comes out?' my father said.

'It would probably be a good idea,' I said. 'Some tea too. I think it's shock.'

'You have to wonder how all of this builds up in her,' my mother said as she checked the fridge. 'I don't have anything, we'll send out.' She turned to me and leaned on the fridge. 'It has to have an effect on her after a while, Emma. All she does is fight.'

'Yeah, hamburger,' my father said into the phone. 'It's for Princess Simone. Yes, thick-cut. Extra aioli. Strawberry.' He put the phone down. 'I wish you'd eat something too, Emma.'

Louise tapped on the door, then opened it and poked her head through to talk to me. 'Come out here into the garden.'

'What for?' I said suspiciously.

'Just come on out. I have something for you. Where's Simone?'

'Having a shower.'

'Hey, that's a good question,' she said. 'When you're snake, do you still take baths and stuff?'

'Yeah,' I said. 'I can't tolerate soap or chlorine, and if I bathe too much I get a horrible scale rot — God, that's a bitch to get rid of. But I like lying in warm water now and then.'

'Sounds more like swimming than washing,' she said.

'Well, I'm not a greasy, stinky, fur-covered mammal,' I said, 'all matted and oily and covered in shit. I never really get that dirty.' I raised my head. 'Damn, where did that come from?'

'You sound like Daddy again; he used to be rude about mammals sometimes,' Simone said. She pulled the fluffy bathrobe she was wearing tighter around her. 'Could you stop doing that?' She leaned against the wall and her voice broke. 'Just ... stop it?'

My mother ran to her and bundled her into a huge hug. She led her to sit on the couch and held her, letting her cry.

'I'm sorry, Nanna,' Simone said into my mother's shoulder.

'That's what nannas are for, sweetheart,' my mother said, rocking Simone. 'Let it out.'

I went to Simone and curled up next to her. She pulled me in and held me as my mother rocked her.

'Come out to the garden,' Louise said to me. 'I've been wanting to see if this will work.'

'Go away,' I said. 'We're having a family crisis.'

There was the sound of frantic flapping outside. 'Shit!' Louise said. 'It nearly got away. Come on, Emma, it's a present for you.'

'What do you have there?' I said.

'Come and see.'

'Just tell me.'

'No, come and have a look.'

I pushed the door open with my snout to see what she was talking about. Louise stood in my parents' tiny garden holding a live, flapping chicken upside down by its legs.

She held it out to me. 'Takeaway.'

'Thank you. Take it away,' I said.

'Come on, I want to see you eating. Do it for me.'

I turned away. 'No.'

'Whoops!' she said, and I turned back. She'd dropped the chicken and it ran away from her. It ran. It moved. It ran away.

I pursued it with relish, moving faster than it did and pinning it in a corner of the garden against the high wall. It stared at me with its mindless eyes and I lunged towards it, grabbed it in my mouth and wrapped my coils around it. I squeezed it, enjoying the feeling of its struggles becoming weaker. When it stopped moving, I released my coils and started to eat it whole, using my throat to crush it as I swallowed. I wiggled my mouth from side to side, pushing it further in, relishing the sensation of feathers filling my mouth and juices running down my throat.

'What does it taste like?' Louise said, wide-eyed and fascinated.

'Just blood,' I said. 'It's the textures that are the fun part. That and the twitches. Add the taste of the warm blood and the whole thing is raw enjoyment.'

She crouched to watch. 'Way cool.'

I stopped. 'Oh my *God*, what am I doing?'

My father came out and closed the door behind him. 'You're eating. This is a good thing, Emma. Don't worry, Simone didn't see. Louise, honey, go to the front gate and make sure nobody else comes into the garden while she finishes up, please?'

'Oh look, it moved again,' Louise said.

'You are a little ghoul,' my father said.

'I'm sorry, Dad. Please don't watch.'

'I'm not talking to you, Emma. You need to eat, and if this is what you have to do, it's what you have to do. I'm talking to that little ghoul Louise. She said she'd do this and I didn't believe her.'

'Oh! I forgot.' Louise pulled out a mobile phone and held it up in front of me. 'I need to take a video.'

My father snatched the phone out of her hand. 'I thought you were Emma's friend. Watch the gate.'

Louise hesitated, then turned and walked to the front gate. 'What you said though. She needed to eat.'

'Finish it, Emma,' my father said. 'Don't think about it, just eat.'

I worked my mouth around the chicken, trying not to enjoy the feeling and failing. The texture, the taste and the movement — all worked together in a harmony of sensation that was unlike anything I'd experienced before. I closed my mouth; the chicken was down. I writhed a few times, pushing it further into me, the bones in my throat crushing its body and squeezing out its goodness.

'You're done,' my father said. 'Let's go back inside.'

'At least let me take a photo of the lump!' Louise said.

I raised my head. 'There's a lump?'

'Don't worry about it, Emma, just come inside,' my father said.

'I need to sleep and digest now,' I said ruefully.

'Stay here overnight and rest,' my father said. 'You and Simone.'

I felt a jolt of dismay. 'I can't, Dad, I have an evaluation tomorrow. I have to be there.'

'Let them do it without you,' he said as we went inside.

'You ate something,' Simone said, still in my mother's arms. 'About time.' She glanced up at my mother. 'Any chance of me getting something? Just some ramen would be okay if you have some.'

The doorbell rang, and a second later Louise came in with a steaming plate of hamburger and chips in one hand and a strawberry milkshake in the other. 'How about this?' she said.

Simone grinned and jumped up. 'That's perfect. Thanks, everybody.'

She grabbed the food off Louise and sat at the table. My mother turned the kettle on in the kitchen, and she and Louise sat to join her.

'I have to be there,' I said. 'It's an evaluation.'

'Sounds like just a test,' Louise said, munching on one of Simone's chips. 'You don't really have to be there, do you? Just tell them. Damn, Emma, you have freaking gods and Immortals and the whole shebang working for you — can't they look after it themselves?'

'It's Er Lang,' I said.

Her eyes went wide. 'Oh. That weirdo. I heard about him. He has it in for you.'

'As soon as Simone is strong enough, she has to take me back down,' I said. 'I'm sorry.'

'It's okay, Emma,' Simone said, waving a chip at me. 'I'll take you first thing tomorrow morning, is that all right? Can I come back up and stay here for a while though? It's kinda relaxing with Nan and Pop.'

My mother threw her arm around Simone's shoulders. 'That sounds like a great idea.'

'Sure,' I said.

'So tell me, Simone,' Louise said, stealing another chip. 'Can you beat Emma up?'

Simone stopped with the hamburger halfway to her

mouth. 'Uh ...' She looked from Louise to me, then shook her head. 'Fact is, I've been slacking off on the martial arts, and she's way better than me. Hand to hand or weapons, straight up with no special abilities, and Emma's got me down cold.'

'What sort of special abilities?' Louise said eagerly. She pointed at Simone with the chip. 'Like, what can you do?'

'Well, up until about two weeks ago, destroy the world,' Simone said softly. 'I could pull out raw yin and make everything cease to exist.'

'Really?' Louise said. She grinned. 'Cool.'

'You are such a nut, Auntie Louise,' Simone said, dipping a chip in the aioli. 'Have another chip; you might as well steal them all.'

I went to the fireplace, which had a small, comforting fire burning in it, and curled up to digest the chicken. I tried not to think about the consequences of having all this raw meat inside me when we went back down to the Earthly Plane the next morning and I returned to human form.

Something touched my head and I heard a soft male voice say, 'Emma.'

I raised my head, still drowsy from the warmth and the food. It was the stone, crouched in human form in front of me. It sat down cross-legged in front of the fire.

'Where'd they go?' I said.

'I couldn't follow them all the way,' it said. 'South. A long way south. But if they went in a straight line, then it was east of Thailand, in Cambodia, Laos or Vietnam.'

'That can't be right; Six said Thailand.'

'And who did he say that to?'

I hesitated. 'Me.'

'Your crown was yanged,' the stone said sadly. It touched the top of my head. 'We need to get you a new one.'

My father came out of the bedroom in pyjamas, pulling on a scruffy dark blue dressing gown. 'Is everything all right, Emma?' He saw the stone. 'Who is this?'

The stone rose and bowed slightly, saluting my father. 'Sir. I'm the Jade Building Block.'

'You're the stone?'

The stone nodded.

My father shrugged. 'Okay, then. Keep it down, you two, you'll wake Barbie.' He returned to the bedroom then turned at the doorway. 'And let Emma sleep, she's got a belly full of chicken.'

The stone sat cross-legged again and I curled up next to it. It folded up into its stone form. 'Sorry, I'm drained from taking human form again. I can't hold it.'

'How is everybody in the Courts?' I said.

'Let me check,' the stone said. 'They're shut down for the night. You pissed off Judge Pao, ma'am, he's going to make you wait before he lets them out.'

I dropped my head on the floor again. I wanted to sigh but reptiles don't.

'You have a couple of demons you need to sort out,' the stone said.

'Who?'

'Yi Hao and Er Hao. They survived.'

I raised my head again and smiled with delight, not caring how it looked. 'They didn't explode?'

'No; they got far enough away before you used the jade. They weren't the same thing as the copies either;

you were right. They want to go home, ma'am. And Er Hao requests a position closer to you again.'

'That's wonderful news,' I said. 'But I still don't trust them. I'll put them to work in Wudangshan until I'm sure that they're clear. These copies have been very sneaky.'

'Good idea.'

'I wish John was here.'

'So do I.'

We sat in silence until I went back to sleep.

CHAPTER 32

We landed on the lawn in front of the House on the Hill. The seniors were practising on the tennis court, led by Liu. When they saw me, they stopped to kneel — most of them anyway. Some just stared.

Liu walked briskly over to me. 'Ma'am. I heard what happened. Thank the Heavens you made it down here. Why are you still in serpent form though?'

'Do you still need me?' Simone said.

I turned to her. 'No. You go back and take it easy.'

She kissed the top of my head and disappeared.

I turned back to Liu. 'I ate as a snake, and if I change back to human I'm concerned that I'll have a stomach full of raw meat, all the bits and everything. That's not a risk I'm willing to take.'

Liu's face went grim. 'Greeting Er Lang as a serpent isn't a good idea, ma'am. The traditional greeting is the salute, and you can't do it.'

'Are there any snake Shen around that I could ask?'

He shook his head.

I slithered towards the students who were still kneeling on the practice field. 'How long do we have before he arrives?'

'He's due at nine, in an hour, but he'll probably be at least half an hour late.'

'To gain face by making us wait.' I studied the students. 'Up you get, guys.' They rose and saluted me in unison. 'You all look terrific. I'm sure we'll do just great.'

I turned back to Liu. 'Which other Masters are here?'

'Meredith's around; she has the senior energy experts meditating to control their nerves. Weapons Master Chen is here, as well as Sit and Park.'

'And poor Leo's back in Court Ten. He'll have to buy a flat down there.'

'Chang tells me there are a couple of pissy missives from Judge Pao in your email, ma'am.'

'Where is Chang? Is he okay?'

'He's down at the Academy, minding your desk.'

'Good,' I said. 'Pass this information on to the Celestial Masters: the Geek, Thirty-three, was destroyed by the Death Mother and Kitty Kwok. The Tiger's Number One yanged the entire facility, but they got out in time and headed south and east, probably to Laos or Vietnam. I don't want anything done about it until we get past this evaluation though.'

'We can do it, ma'am,' Liu said. 'It's just disappointing for us that it's at such short notice. The students really aren't ready and won't be able to give their best.'

'As long as we survive,' I said. I moved closer to Liu to speak quietly to him. 'How visible is the lump inside me?'

'Absolutely bleeding obvious,' Liu said. 'What did you eat? A dog or something?'

'Chicken,' I said.

'What did it taste like?'

I was about to answer when I saw the mischief on his face. I tapped him with my snout. 'It's making me drowsy; my crown's gone and the stone has to sit inside the muscles of my back; and I look like something out of a zoo. This evaluation is going to be a disaster.'

'We'll manage,' he said. 'Go upstairs and curl up somewhere warm while I keep these kids occupied. I'll call you when it's time.'

'Make sure we're all in position at least half an hour before he's due to arrive. *Due* to arrive, not when we expect him — so about thirty minutes from now.'

'Don't worry, we'll be *fine*,' Liu said. He patted the top of my head. 'Go digest some more and make that damn dog lump smaller.'

'Dog!' I said. 'The dog!'

'Don't worry, Lok is here.'

I dropped my head. 'Phew.'

'Go inside. It's all under control.'

I curled up on my bed and tried to clear my thoughts ready for the trial to come. The door burst open and John, in human form, charged in. 'Simone's not here! Where's Simone?'

'She's in the Western Heavens,' I said. 'She's safe, don't worry.'

'She can't travel to the Celestial yet, she has to be under the protection of her mother ...' His voice trailed off. 'Michelle is alive?' His face filled with joy. 'Michelle's alive!'

'Michelle is dead. Simone is sixteen years old and can travel to the Celestial herself,' I said.

He fell to sit in one of the chairs and put his head in his hands. 'What's happening?'

'John,' I said. 'It's me, Emma.'

He dropped his hands and studied me, confused. 'Emma?'

I slithered across the bed so I was closer to him, but didn't touch him. 'You've lost your memory. You've been through some trauma. You're spending most of your time in True Form, and somehow you've found your way back here. Everybody is safe.'

He leaned back. 'As long as everybody is safe.' He focused on me. 'Who are you?' His face went grim. 'Peony.' He rose, raised one hand and summoned Dark Heavens. 'Peony, you have broken the laws of the Celestial —'

'I'm not Peony, I'm Emma,' I said.

'I don't know any snakes called Emma. The name is familiar, but I don't know any snakes called that.'

'I used to be human. I'm *not* Peony, John, put the sword away. Peony is dead. I'm Emma, and I used to be human.'

'A human called Emma,' he said as if from a million miles away. The joy filled him again. 'Emma!' He dismissed Dark Heavens, grabbed my serpent neck and held me close. 'Emma.' He pulled away slightly and looked into my eyes. 'What the hell happened to you?'

'Do you have any idea how many times you've asked me that?' I said. 'It seems to be taking forever for you to come back.'

'How long is it now? Simone's sixteen? Damn, nine years?'

'Nearly ten. The Lady said ten.'

'At a minimum, and that would have to be with some help.' His eyes unfocused. 'I wonder if I'm getting help. I'm already in human form, this is strange.' He concentrated on me again. 'Who cares. I'm here, I'm with you, and you are gorgeous.' He kissed the top of my head. 'Can you take human form?'

I dropped my head and leaned on him. 'I have a belly full of raw chicken. Bones and all.'

'And?'

'I don't want to make my human form sick.'

'That won't happen. The food is in the snake, not the human. When you change, it'll be gone.'

I concentrated and took human form, and stood up next to him. The demon essence rushed through me and I pushed it down. 'How does that work?'

'Something to do with the different Planes. There are people out there who have made a study of it, but I never cared enough to worry about it.' He wrapped his arms around me and smiled down at me. 'My Emma. You haven't changed at all.'

I put my hands around the back of his neck and pulled him down to kiss him. His arms around me tightened and his breathing quickened. He released me and pulled back to look into my eyes. 'Oh, yes.'

Thirty minutes, ma'am, Liu said into my head. *Time to prepare.*

'Prepare for what?' John said.

'Er Lang's coming to do an evaluation. He wants five recruits for the Jade Emperor's Elite Guard.'

He moved away. 'Good. Let's go see what our Disciples can do.'

'Always work first; always putting your duty before yourself.' I pulled him back in and pressed myself against him. 'How about we just stay here?'

His face became intense. 'That's a very good idea.'

He gently pushed me down so I was sitting on the bed and he sat next to me, still with his hands around the back of my neck. His eyes unfocused for a moment and all our clothes were gone.

I moved my face closer to his. 'How close are you to full strength again? That was impressive.'

'Still a long way to go. You've yet to see really impressive,' he said. He leaned back to study me. 'Magnificent.'

I ran my hands over his chest, revelling in the golden, silken skin. 'Yes, you are.'

I pushed myself into him and ran my fingers up and down his muscular back and felt him tremble in response.

I ran my mouth over his chest and along his collarbone, enjoying the salty musky taste of him. He leaned down so that I could reach his throat, and I nibbled on his ear, making him gasp. He buried his face in the side of my neck, then pulled back to study me, his eyes warm and dark. He put his hands either side of my face, his eyes roving over my features.

I pulled him in again for a long, lingering kiss and his grip on me tightened. I ran my hands along the muscles of his back again, then loaded them with what little chi I had left and ran them down over the base of his spine.

A low sound of pleasure escaped him. 'You know exactly what to do.'

'That's because I'm a reptile too,' I whispered into his ear, and he completely lost it.

We lay side by side on the covers, holding each other close. 'How long do we have before it starts?' he said into the side of my head.

'I don't know and I don't really care.'

'How is Simone doing?'

'She's studying at Celestial High now; she's made friends and is enjoying it.'

He shifted slightly next to me. 'I suppose things have changed now. When it was Michelle, the focus would have been on the Earthly. Now, with you, she can live fully on the Celestial.'

'I need to clear this demon essence from me.'

'Did you see the Pure Ones?'

'They didn't help.'

'There's only one option then.'

'I know.' I looked into his eyes. 'All of the trades he wants are too costly.'

'I can imagine. Just stay as you are, Emma, do your best to control it, and when I return for good, I'll fix it for you. I'm powerful enough. I can do it.'

I looked up into his face. 'You don't sound too sure, John.'

'You always could read me.'

I pulled him tighter. 'You're not here for good yet? Please stay.'

He sighed gently. 'I wish I could. I really do. But I'm not there yet. I could disappear any moment. So hold this time tight and treasure it. I don't know how long it will be before I return.'

'You should see Simone.'

He stiffened and gasped. 'I put my own pleasure before my child. What sort of father am I?'

I moved my face closer to his and grinned. 'A turtle.'

'That I am, Lady Emma.' He sat up, and was fully dressed again. 'I think you should be preparing for this evaluation. I'll go up to the West and say hello to her. I need to move fast, because somehow I have been drained of ching energy.' His grin turned wry. 'No idea how that happened.'

'John.' I sat up and put my hand on his cheek. 'Thank you for this time.'

He took my hand and kissed it. 'There will be plenty more times. I will return for you.' He disappeared.

I pulled on a fresh Wudang uniform and went downstairs and out to the front of the house. The students had gathered there in neat, unmoving lines. I went to join the Masters at the front of the group.

'About time. I thought you two would be forever,' Liu said.

'There's this thing called privacy ...' I said.

'Interesting theoretical concept,' he said with amusement. 'Don't worry, I wasn't looking; I could sense his presence, and I'm not completely stupid. Next time tell him hello for me. We still have at least forty-five minutes before Er Lang arrives —' His expression changed. 'His entourage is here. Twenty minutes early.' He stared at me. 'Damn, Emma, what the *hell* did you do to piss him off? That's unprecedented.'

I didn't look away from the drive. 'We're ready for him.'

He straightened. 'Yes, we are.'

Er Lang, in human form, rode over the crest of the hill on a heavily muscled black horse. A polearm was attached to the saddle, and his large black dog walked next to the horse's shoulder.

Liu whistled softly between his teeth. 'Alone. No entourage.' He switched to silent speech. *Completely unprecedented. He heaps insult on top of insult.*

The two of us stepped forward to greet him. He stopped his horse, dropped the reins and saluted us. 'Lady Emma. Master Liu.'

We saluted back. 'Lord Er Lang.'

He didn't dismount; he spoke to us from the back of the horse, another huge breach of protocol. 'There is a hearing in two weeks, Lady Emma. It must be ascertained whether or not you are competent to hold the role of First Heavenly General.'

'The Jade Emperor told me just last week that I am doing a good job,' I said.

He gracefully dismounted from the horse. 'The Jade Emperor cannot be aware of all that takes place within his dominion, particularly now that his right hand, the Dark Arts of War, is missing.'

One of the house demons came forward to take the reins of Er Lang's horse, and Er Lang raised one hand. 'Wind Spirit must not be tended by demons. He must be tended by humans or Shen.'

I spoke to the Disciples without turning around. 'Any humans or Shen here good with ponies?'

Karen stepped forward from the student ranks. 'I'll do it, ma'am, I like horses. I had one back in England.'

'Go right ahead, Karen.'

Er Lang eyed her with disdain. 'I am not sure your students are capable of caring for such a nobly bred animal. On second thought, I will release him to return to the Celestial.' He waved one hand and the horse disappeared.

Karen glanced at me. I nodded to her and she returned to the ranks of students, her expression rigid with restraint.

'Please come with me, my Lord, and let me show you our hospitality,' I said.

Er Lang nodded and took a step forward, then stopped. 'What of my companion?'

Lok came forward and bowed his shaggy head over his forelegs to Er Lang's dog. 'My Lord. Please allow me to show you the hospitality of New Wudang. The Lady Emma has provided accommodation that is eminently suitable for such as we.'

Er Lang's dog studied Lok with disdain. 'You are not a dog by true nature, I can see this.'

'That is correct, my Lord. This form has been forced upon me against my will.'

Er Lang's dog tilted his head slightly. 'Against your will? So if you had a choice, you would choose not to be a dog?' His voice gained an edge of malice. 'Being a dog is something that you abhor?'

Er Lang watched the exchange with satisfaction.

Lok looked Er Lang's dog in the eye. 'I pursue the Tao. The Tao is the true nature of all. Being a dog, although it is enjoyable and satisfying, is not my true nature, so I hope that one day I will be able to leave this form and return to my true form, to be closer to the Tao.'

Er Lang's dog nodded. 'Pursuit of the Tao is always noble and should never be discouraged.' The corners of his mouth turned up slightly, the dog equivalent of a smile. 'Show me the way.'

After Liu and I had shown Er Lang his room, we went into the downstairs office. Er Lang sat across the desk from me and Liu stood behind me.

'We will begin the evaluations this afternoon,' Er Lang said. 'The Celestial One has five vacancies in the Elite Guard.'

'May I once again recommend junior Masters rather than senior students?' Liu said. 'Most of these Disciples have been studying the arts for less than ten years. I doubt that any would qualify.'

Er Lang glared at Liu, as if about to say something, then changed his mind. 'I will rest until the evaluation.

The accommodation is basic, but I do not intend to be here long.' He rose and saluted me. 'We will begin at two. Ensure that your students are ready. I will see the physically trained ones today, then those who have aptitude with energy tomorrow morning, then those who are talented with both tomorrow afternoon. Final selection will follow the day after.' He nodded to us. 'I will see you at two. Have something sent to my room.' He walked out.

I sagged over the desk.

'Sexist pig,' Liu said. 'You should hear Meredith carry on about him. She wants to call him out.'

'Could she take him?'

Liu smiled slightly. 'It would be a close thing, but he would probably win and that would make him even more insufferable.'

'Is that possible?'

'You didn't see him after the Monkey King beat him. According to the guys, that was totally insufferable.'

I shook my head. 'Let's get these students fed and organised for this afternoon.'

'Humph,' he said. 'As if any of them will eat. Want to join me for lunch?'

'I'm not really hungry. The chicken is gone, but I still feel like I ate it.'

'Oh yeah,' he said, opening the door to go out. 'And it tasted like chicken.'

I didn't have anything on the desk in front of me to throw at him.

When Ah Yat took Er Lang his lunch, I followed her into his room. He was sitting in one of the chairs next to the window, going through the printouts of the students' records. He gestured for Ah Yat to place the tray on the table in front of him, moving the papers out of the way, and ignored me. I waited until she had gone out and closed the door. Er Lang continued to ignore me, slurping the soup that came with his Hainan chicken.

'Is it because I'm a chick?' I said.

'I do not have an issue with your gender.'

'Is it because I'm a snake then?' I moved closer to him. 'What *is* your issue with me? Can we sort this out before my students get hurt?'

'All Disciples of the Dark Lord are aware of the risk.'

I paced back and forth across his room. 'Whatever your issue with me is, please don't take it out on my students.'

'Worried they'll be damaged and no use to you later?'

I stopped and stared at him. 'What is that supposed to mean?'

He put the spoon down. 'I know what you are. You can stop pretending. You've kept it a secret, but you can't keep secrets from me. I will show all of Creation exactly what sort of monster you are.'

'I'm not a monster!'

He turned back to his chicken. 'What would happen if I were to turn my Third Eye on you? Particularly since my Third Eye isn't hidden away under flesh and bone, it is on the *outside* of my body? I had my Third Eye open when you came to the Celestial Palace, madam, and I saw you for what you are.'

I took a deep breath. 'I have control of the demon essence.'

'No, madam,' he said. 'The demon essence has control of you. Run back to Hell, because I know what you are and I will do everything in my power to stop you from destroying the Celestial.'

'I don't want to destroy anything!'

'You are a demon. It is your nature. Stop hiding, I know your secret. Run now, because your students will suffer if you don't.'

'What does this have to do with the students?'

He put his chopsticks down and glared at me. 'The Jade Emperor himself has ordered me not to destroy you. But I will find a way to show the world what you are, and a way to stop you.'

'The Jade Emperor knows what he's doing.'

'He is too distracted, and too busy, and too trusting. I see you for what you are.' An expression of fury filled his face. 'Now go back to Hell!'

'This is between you and me,' I said. 'All I ask is that you not bring my students into it. Don't hurt them. Take me to the Celestial and tell the Jade Emperor your doubts.'

'I don't need to,' he said. He picked his chopsticks up again. 'Today all the world will see what you are, and you will be destroyed.'

I turned and opened the door, then turned back to him. 'All I ask is that you don't hurt my students,' I repeated.

'What must be done must be done,' he said. 'And you must be stopped.'

I went out and pulled the door closed behind me. I headed for the barracks and the mess hall.

'Liu,' I said at the doorway. 'With me for a moment.'

Liu put his chopsticks down and accompanied me out to the garden.

'He knows about my demon nature, and he wants to show the world,' I said.

'Whatever you do, whatever happens, stay back from any demons.'

'Look inside me,' I said.

He put his hand on my forehead and gasped. 'What the *hell*?'

'The Demon King took the demon essence out so I could use the jade disk. That *bitch* Kitty Kwok grabbed me while I was unconscious and filled me back up again. With even more. All of the Geek.'

'Stay well back from anything. You should take serpent form, but even in serpent form you could lose it at any time.' He walked briskly away then came back again, obviously agitated. 'You should have told me! You need to spend time on the Celestial in serpent form *right now* if you're not to change.' He shook his head. 'This is insane.'

Meredith appeared next to him. 'Really?' She put her hand on my forehead, and jerked it away as if it had been burned. 'You should go up to the Celestial *now* and cycle down for at least three days to reduce this. How are you staying human?' She looked me in the eyes. 'Whatever you do, don't get angry, or get any demon essence on you. You'll lose it immediately.'

'*And* she just ate meat. Alive. Whole,' Liu said.

'Well, that is just the icing on the biscuit, isn't it?' she said.

'And the time she spent with the Dark Lord is the coloured sprinkles,' he said.

Meredith sighed and shook her head. 'Turtles.'

'What time is it?' I said.

Meredith checked her watch. 'We have about twenty minutes.'

Liu nodded. 'Time to line them up. Whatever you do, stay calm. Stone?'

The stone didn't reply.

'It helped me get out of the demon lab,' I said. 'It copied my snake form and then used human form, which seems to wear it out.'

Liu nodded. 'Nothing we can do to bring it around right now to help you. Looks like you're on your own. Stay calm, stay chilled, stay focused. And whatever you do, stay well back. Even in snake form you could still be turned.' He straightened. 'We can do this.'

The students lined up nervously on the practice field. Er Lang strode out of the house, stood in front of them and put his hands behind his back. He nodded and three young men appeared behind him, as aloof and unemotional as he was. Two were holding a demon jar by large handles; they placed the jar on the ground next to Er Lang. The third carried a folder of documents and passed a sheet of paper to him.

'Scott Walker,' Er Lang said.

Our weakest student, Liu said. *This is deliberate.*

Scott stepped forward and stood in front of the group facing Er Lang. Er Lang checked the document he was holding. 'Chain whip.'

His weakest weapon.

One of the young men assisting Er Lang concentrated and a metal-linked whip with five sharpened barbs on the end appeared in his hands. The chain whip was one of the most difficult weapons to master, and the slightest error in the use of it could cause nasty damage to the practitioner. Fortunately this one didn't have barbs all the way along its length; but it was longer than standard, making it even more difficult to wield.

Scott stepped up to the assistant, took the coiled chain whip and walked back to face Er Lang. He saluted with the weapon in his right hand.

Er Lang went to the demon jar, opened the lid and pulled out a demon bead. He tossed it onto the ground in front of Scott and it formed into a Snake Mother. Some of the students in the group made quiet sounds of horror. Scott took a step back, then gathered himself and stepped forward again, squaring his shoulders to face it.

'Ready yourself,' Er Lang said.

Keep calm, don't lose it, Liu said to me.

'Hold,' I said. 'That is too large for this student.'

Er Lang raised one hand and the Mother went for Scott.

Scott uncoiled the whip, swung it at the Mother and it wrapped around her torso, the barbs on the end digging into her flesh. She hissed with pain, pulled them out and used the whip to jerk him off his feet. He released the whip and she tossed it to one side. She slithered up to him, picked him up by the throat and brought his face up to eye level with hers. He fought her, first by kicking at her abdomen and then by making a double-handed blow to her neck, but she ignored him. His struggles weakened, his breath coming in choked gasps.

'Don't lose it!' Liu shouted.

Liu summoned his staff and made for the demon but Tymen, Scott's friend, got there first. 'Come on, guys, help him!' He fell to one knee, concentrated and sent a blast of chi at the Mother. It didn't do much; Tymen wasn't competent with energy, he was more proficient at physical. The Snake Mother absorbed it, then threw a ball of black demon essence at Tymen, knocking him flat.

The other students advanced on the Mother, but Liu shouted at them: 'Get back. Hand to hand will do nothing. Let me.'

He swung his staff at the demon's head and she blocked it. He went with the movement, letting her carry the staff downwards, then swung it again at her snake end. The staff knocked her sideways and she dropped Scott.

I changed to snake and raced forward to pull Scott away, but the Mother was faster. She grabbed me by the throat and raised me to eye level, studying me carefully.

'Is this the one?' she said.

'It is,' Er Lang said.

'This is wrong!' Liu shouted, and swung at the Mother again. 'If Emma absorbs any more demon essence she'll be turned completely. You have to get her away from it. Stop this!'

Er Lang crossed his arms over his chest, his face grim with satisfaction.

The Mother avoided Liu's blows, then wrenched his staff from his hands and tossed it aside. She grinned, flicking her forked tongue, and gestured a come-on to him.

Liu held out one hand and a sword appeared in it. 'Drop the snake and I'll let you live.'

'Try me,' she said, sounding like a cat yowling.

Liu unfocused a moment. 'How many?' he said. He hesitated. 'I don't think they'll hurt you, honey, just stay put. Don't fight them.' He glanced at Er Lang. 'You have demons menacing my wife and her students. Whose side are you on? Hurt Meredith and all of the Celestial will be down on you.'

Er Lang gestured with one hand. 'Just do it. Let the world see the truth.'

'No!' Liu shouted, and lowered the sword. He turned to the Mother. 'Drop her! Whatever this Celestial has offered you, he lied! He plans to destroy you. If you free the snake now I'll give you safe passage.'

The Mother didn't reply. Her hand closed on my neck, throttling me. I tried to wrap my coils around her arms to stop her, but she was much stronger than me. I sucked the air in, but it didn't come.

Leo and Martin appeared to my right, both in Celestial Form and armed with their swords. Martin made the Silver Serpent sing and the Mother froze, her grip loosening on me. I took huge sucking breaths and the world became clearer.

'Don't kill it!' Liu shouted, but it was too late. Leo stepped forward and swung at the Mother with Dark Heavens, cutting her in two. She exploded in demon goo and I fell through a rain of foul-smelling blackness, landing with a splash in the venom.

'No, no, no, no, no,' Liu moaned. 'Oh, Emma, no.'

There was nothing I could do. A quiet sucking sounded in my ears as I filled with the essence. I willed myself into a trance, visualising the faces of those I loved. My man, my child, my friends, my students — I had to stay human for them. The demon essence siphoned into me and there was nothing I could do to stop it. I touched the yang inside me but it was at the bottom of a well full of demon blackness. The blackness filled me from the bottom to the top and I drowned in it. I slid into the change as though down a slope covered in oil, scrabbling to stop myself. Then I fell into blackness.

CHAPTER 33

Something was holding me. I cast around, fighting the binding. Whoever had me was good. There were lovely young trained humans nearby, and some Celestials. If I could free myself from this binding I could feast, and I was so hungry.

'I thought she couldn't be changed as snake,' the black one said. 'I thought it would be all right.'

'Kitty filled her so full that it didn't take anything to send her over the edge,' the old one said, and I recognised him as the one that was binding me. I tried to attack him, hissing with frustration.

'Oh, Emma, what have they done to you?' the child said, approaching me.

I held back and watched her as she drew near; she was big enough to destroy me, but hadn't yet. I had a chance at her, and if I could kill her the King would reward me — I might even be able to join his harem. The thought made me itch with need.

'Stay back, I think she's completely turned,' the old one said.

'What's your name?' I asked the child.

'Simone. Emma, it's me, Simone. You're like a mother to me ...'

I dropped on my coils and held my arms out. 'Simone. Come give me a hug.'

She strode towards me with her arms out. The minute she was within reach I grabbed her shoulder and pulled her into me, facing her away from me with my hand around her throat. 'Let me go and I'll let her live.'

The child became limp in my grasp, then glowed with white burning energy that scorched me. I hissed with pain and released her and she moved out of reach again.

'She's turned.' She fell to her knees on the grass. 'She's turned. She's gone.' She stood up again, wiped her forearm across her eyes and faced me. 'What are we going to do?'

The Dark Lord of the North, the Xuan Wu, the most feared of all the Celestials, appeared next to the child.

'Can you fix her, Daddy?' the child said.

'No,' he said. 'I think it would be best if you all left while I see what I can do. We need to be very quick, I don't have much time.'

'The Demon King,' the child said.

I hissed. The Demon King wouldn't help me; he would destroy me for the mistake of being captured like this. His retribution was swift and merciless.

'I'm not leaving,' the child said.

'Neither am I,' the black one said. 'This is my fault.'

'It's just as much my fault,' the green and brown Celestial said. 'I should have checked.'

'I'll guard while you sort this out,' the old one said.

'Liu, clear the students,' the Dark Lord said, his eyes intense and fearsome. 'Get them out of here. If you have a bus, put them on it. Move quickly. If I lose it before they're gone, she'll be unbound. Don't worry, I have her now.'

Liu saluted the Dark Lord, and carefully walked past me out of reach of my talons. He raised his arms. 'Okay, kids, you're with me. Meredith, bring yours too, we'll get them out of here.'

The Dark Lord spoke to the Green General without looking away from me. 'Er Lang, for a very smart man sometimes you are very stupid. The Jade Emperor knew all about this.'

'She's a demon!' Er Lang shouted, pointing at me, and I hissed at him.

'Only because of what you did to her,' the Dark Lord said.

Er Lang crossed his arms over his chest. 'She was already turned.'

The Dark Lord spun and glared at Er Lang. 'No, she wasn't. She was in complete control. We could have cleared it from her, and now we can't. You've destroyed any chance she had of being human, being a Celestial and being my wife.'

'You can fix her, Daddy, please say you can fix her,' the child said, her voice small.

'We'll have to find some way of holding her until I'm strong enough to deal with this,' the Dark Lord said. 'I will probably disappear at anytime, this has severely drained me.'

Wife? The Dark Lord. Wife? Something leapt within me and I knew what I had to do. I lowered myself on my coils. 'Protect me, I am yours.'

'No,' the Dark Lord said softly.

'There's the solution,' the black one said. 'Just tame her.'

'She will lose all free will!' the Dark Lord said. 'She

will be free to move anywhere, Earthly or Celestial, but she will be worse than a slave.'

'I am yours,' I said to the Dark Lord. 'I will serve you and obey you. Protect me.'

'No,' the Dark Lord said. 'Anything but this.'

'Finish it,' Er Lang said grimly. 'Give her the Fire Essence Pill and be done with it.'

'You have just cost me the love of my life,' the Dark Lord said to Er Lang. 'You have turned her from my partner and my love into less than a slave. It will take me a very long time to forgive you for this.'

'I did what I had to do,' Er Lang said.

The Dark Lord came to me. 'Take my hand.'

I rose and quickly took his hand and the tiny ball of fire passed into me, into the centre of my being. If I ever disobeyed him, it would destroy me. I dropped on my coils again and lowered my head. 'Order me, my Lord, and I will obey.'

'Oh God, Emma,' the child said, and turned away. The black one bundled her into his arms and held her.

'Take human form,' the Dark Lord said, and I did.

'She looks the same,' the black one said. 'Emma, can you hear me?'

I didn't reply. I only answered the Dark Lord, my master.

'Do you have any memory of who you were?' the Dark Lord said.

I kneeled in front of him. 'I only know you and your orders. I exist to obey.'

'After a while they grow out of it a bit, don't they?' the black one said. 'The old Emma will come back, won't she?'

'There is a small possibility of that, but I wouldn't count on it,' the Dark Lord said. 'Too much too soon.

She was changed and then she was tamed, one after the other. I don't think she will ever remember who she was.' His voice broke. 'She's gone. And I can't hold it. I'm going too. Demon Emma, obey the child Simone while I am gone.'

'Can the Demon King fix her?' the child said. 'Daddy? Daddy?'

The Dark Lord was gone and I felt empty. I needed him to direct me; without him I was nothing. I bowed my head, still on my knees. I obeyed the child now.

'Rise,' Simone said.

I stood and waited patiently for my next order.

'What do you want to do, Emma?' she said.

'I want to obey the Dark Lord,' I said. 'He has told me to obey you. I will obey you.'

'You know, I should be thrilled to bits,' Simone said. 'I can do whatever I want now.'

'Not thrilled to bits?' the black one said.

'No,' she said, and held his hand. 'I feel awful.' She wiped her eyes with her other hand. 'We will fix you, Emma. We'll work something out. Let's go home.'

'You can't, you still have the evaluation,' the green and brown one said.

'You don't seriously want to continue with that,' Simone said to Er Lang.

'I achieved my goal. I showed her for what she is. And I think I have done nobody a favour,' Er Lang said. He raised his head. 'I have been summoned. The Celestial wishes to discuss this matter with me. I think I am to be disciplined.'

He saluted around the group. 'This matter is concluded.' He stood for a moment, his hands still in the salute, then fell to one knee in front of Simone. 'And I sincerely apologise for this. It was not my intention to cause grief to you, Princess. If I had known, I would not have done this.'

'If you'd asked, you'd have known,' the black one said gruffly. 'You've cost us dearly here today, General.'

Er Lang dropped his head. 'I know.' He disappeared.

'Let's go home,' Simone said.

They put me in the back of the car with Simone and a big human drove us. I sat quietly, attentive and eager to do the child's bidding. I felt secure; this was the Dark Lord's own vehicle and that brought me closer to him.

'Emma,' Simone said, 'do you remember any martial arts?'

'No, ma'am.'

'Do you remember your students?'

'No, ma'am.'

'You sound like a robot!'

'My apologies, my Lady. It is the way I sound, I have no control over it.'

'What would you like to do when you get home? Are you hungry? Do you want to rest? How about heading down to the Academy and checking what's happening?'

'Whatever you wish for me to do, I will do to the best of my ability.'

'Would you like to be human, Emma?'

That stopped me. If I was human, I would have free will. I didn't answer immediately; I thought about it for a moment.

'Yes,' Simone said softly.

'Yes, I would like free will,' I said. 'I would like to be able to make my own decisions. That would be ...' I hesitated as I imagined the brilliant shining concept of being able to choose my own life. 'That would be greater than a dream.'

'Well, that's a start,' Simone said.

They took me to a luxurious apartment high on a mountain in a city. They took me into a well-appointed room scattered with the belongings of its female owner.

'This is your room, Emma,' Simone said.

I looked around; it needed tidying.

I turned to Simone. 'Is this your house?'

'Yes,' she said. 'This is your room.'

'If this is your house, then it needs to be neater,' I said, and began tidying the belongings.

She came to me and put her hand on my arm. 'Stop.'

I immediately ceased what I was doing and stood waiting for the next order.

'Do you recognise anything here, Emma? This is your room,' the black one said.

I looked around. 'Yes. I recognise these items.'

'They're yours.'

I was silent. The concept of ownership was beyond my comprehension.

A middle-aged, round-faced woman came in, busy and excited. 'Simone, little one, welcome home.' She hugged Simone and touched the black one on the arm. She turned to me and nodded. 'Would you like something to eat, ma'am? You're home early.'

I stood waiting for an order.

'Monica, something's happened to Emma,' Simone said. 'Her head is kind of ... broken. She won't do anything unless I tell her to.'

'Like one of those demon servants?' Monica said.

'That's exactly what she is,' the black one said.

'They changed her to a demon and she became a demon servant. She's lost her will. She lives to obey.'

Monica stared at me, eyes wide. 'What a horrible thing to happen. Can you fix it?'

'I dread to think of the price for fixing this,' Simone said, her voice weak. 'But whatever it is, we'll find a way to pay it.' She turned to Monica. 'I don't think she's even aware of whether she's hungry or not. Make her some noodles, please; we'll have to ensure she's fed and cared for properly.'

'I will care for you, ma'am,' I said. 'Tell me what to do.'

'Go with Leo and Monica and eat some noodles,' Simone said. 'I want you to stay strong, so make sure you eat, okay?'

I bowed to her. 'I will. I will be strong for you.'

'This is awful,' Monica whispered. 'It's like she's gone.'

'I just hope Daddy comes back soon,' Simone said as I let them lead me to the dining room.

A group of people entered the dining room while I was eating: the old one from before, a European woman, and a large white cat. I moved to take my bowl out so they could have the table, but the black one, Leo, stopped me.

'You stay; this is about you,' he said.

I nodded and sat.

The big white cat came to me and put his paw on my head, then shook his own. 'Shit.'

'And Er Lang did this?' the European woman said as they sat around the table.

'He converted her. Daddy was there, so she chose to be tamed,' Simone said.

'I'm going to damn well write to the Jade Emperor and complain about that,' the cat said. 'Not good enough. Who does Er Lang think he is?'

'The Jade Emperor summoned him right after it had been done,' Simone said.

'Good,' the cat said. 'I hope he's demoted, useless piece of shit.'

'Mind your language in front of the Princess,' Leo said.

The cat stared at Leo for a moment, then grinned broadly. 'Yes, *sir*.'

'I mean it,' Leo said.

'Does anyone have any ideas on how we can fix this?' Simone said.

'Just keep her here until the Dark Lord has enough strength to come back,' the old one said.

I sat straighter at the mention of the Dark Lord. Now they had my attention.

'He can't fix this,' the cat said. 'Only the Demon King can fix this.'

'Daddy said he might be able to,' Simone said.

'He's a damn fool,' the cat said. 'Just keep her safe, and keep her close to you. When Ah Wu shows up again, he'll go straight to find either her or you, and if you're together he'll go for both of you.'

'No,' Simone said. 'I can't take her with me to school; she'll act like a servant in front of everybody. I can't humiliate her like that.'

'She has a point,' the old one said. 'Leave her here, and have someone stay close by her and contact you if he shows.'

Simone ran her hands through her hair. 'It could be months. He just visited her in human form ...'

'We know,' the European woman said. 'You don't need to tell us.'

'Perfect timing, as usual,' the cat said. 'Damn turtle.'

'You can talk,' Simone said.

The cat grinned and shrugged.

'There's this thing called privacy ...' Leo said.

'Interesting theoretical concept; ask Ming Gui for further exposition,' the old one said. 'We have to keep doing our jobs until we find a solution for this.'

'Can you guys run the Academy?' Simone said.

'I guess we have to,' the European woman said, sharing a look with the old one. 'It'll mean slowing down the training as we concentrate on the administration side that Emma was handling, but hopefully it'll just be temporary.'

'Temporary?' Simone said, her face full of hope. 'You can see what lies ahead?'

The Immortals at the table all shared a look.

'The future is never fixed, Simone,' the old one said.

'Weirdest damn thing you ever saw,' Leo said. 'You would not believe how it moves, how fluid it is. It's like watching a fast-running stream with rocks being constantly thrown into it. Big rocks.'

'You can see it, Leo?' Simone said, wide-eyed.

'Imagine trying to see a painting three metres down at the bottom of a stream,' Leo said. 'In the dark. And the painting's changing all the time, and it's some sort of abstract nonsense. That's what it's like.'

'That is a very apt way of describing it,' the old one said.

'You just see the rough shapes, and they constantly change,' the woman said. 'The clarity of your vision depends upon your alignment to the Tao.'

'I was Raised by the Elixir, I never got the Tao, so I don't see much,' Leo said ruefully.

'So what shape do you see here?' Simone asked the old one.

'Darkness,' he said.

'But that's Daddy.'

'So we wait until he shows.'

By day I worked, when they let me. I cleaned and tidied. By night I stood silent, listening to them sleep, and listening for the Dark Lord. He would come. Shadows of his echoes reverberated through the apartment, rippling through time. Snatches of laughter and music and screams of terror and pain. I ate when they reminded me to. Simone and Leo talked to me, and tried to make me more than I was. I wanted to be more for them, but it wasn't there. I was incapable of being more and it hurt me as much as it hurt them.

I dreamed of free will.

Leo appeared in front of me one day while I was parked against the wall doing nothing. He put his hand out to me. 'Come with me.'

I took his hand and followed him.

We landed in the Academy, a place I wasn't permitted to visit any more. I couldn't control the smile.

'Happy?' Leo said, smiling as well.

'I love this place so much,' I said. 'It's full of all my favourite things and people.'

'What are your favourite things?' he said.

'The arts,' I said. 'The arts, and the students, and the Masters, and my family.'

'Who are your family?' he said, becoming excited.

I stopped. 'I have family? Demons don't have family.'

He sighed. 'Lost you. I really thought we were

bringing you back.' He straightened. 'Whatever. Lord Xuan is here and wants to see you.'

'Lord Xuan?' I cast around, searching for him, and found him on the top floor of the building. 'He's here!' I transported myself directly to him and fell to one knee in front of him. 'My Lord. I am here to do your bidding.'

Lord Xuan rubbed one hand over his face. 'This is very hard.'

'Try living with it,' Simone said. 'She doesn't even sleep, she just stands there. And when I ask her what she's doing, she says she's listening for you.'

Leo and the green and brown one appeared.

'What are you doing here, Martin?' Simone said.

'I want to give myself to the King again,' Martin said. 'He may take me as a trade.' His face went grim. 'The Mothers loved me.'

'That will not be an option,' the Dark Lord said.

'I think you should explore every option, my Lord,' Leo said. 'Is he coming?'

'We'll have to take down the seals to let him in,' the Dark Lord said.

'I've already arranged for Ronnie Wong to come in and fix them once we're done,' Simone said.

'Good,' the Dark Lord said. He glanced down at Simone. 'I'm not sure I want you around when I talk to him. This could get ugly.'

She met his gaze. 'One day, we'll be working together, Dad. One day, I'll be close to your equal and Princess of the Northern Heavens in more than just name. I'll be fighting demons beside you and facing the forces of Hell.'

'You have a point,' he said, his voice full of affection. 'Trying to protect you from ugly is a complete waste of time. It's what we do.'

'Damn straight,' she said, looking back at me. 'Let's do this.'

The Dark Lord called the Demon King. I heard it but I did not fear. My master would protect me.

The Demon King appeared, and smiled at the Dark Lord. 'About time. Let's talk business.' He crossed his arms over his chest. 'Damn, she's fine. Just look at her. Such a waste to change her back.' He pulled out a sheet of paper. 'I gave Emma a list of options, but you probably haven't seen it, so let's go through them.'

'Take me,' Martin said.

'I don't want you,' the Demon King said. 'You are entirely too much trouble, regardless of how the girls feel about you. And don't even think it,' he added, pointing at Leo. 'I don't want you either.' He looked at the sheet of paper. 'Let's start with you, Ah Wu. How about you in a jade cage for ... oh ...' He made a show of thinking about it. 'About a thousand years?'

'No,' the Dark Lord said.

'Five hundred?'

'Try something else. You're not having me.'

The Demon King grinned at the Dark Lord. 'But I've wanted you for so long! Every kid I've spawned has gone after your head. All this time, every single one of them, out there after you. Do you realise exactly how much of a royal pain in the ass you are?'

'That's why the answer is no.'

The King spun and pointed. 'Him.'

The cat had appeared on the other side of the room and he took a step back. 'How long for?'

'Five thousand years.'

'No,' the Dark Lord said.

'A thousand? Or how about one of the others? How about that ugly blue dragon, the bastard? He's such a selfish piece of shit it would do him good to sit in a cage for a while.'

'Now *that's* a tempting offer,' the cat said.

'You are not having any of the Four Winds,' the Dark Lord said. 'We are too important to the safety of too many. Each of our dominions is spread too thin when one of us is gone. The hundred years I could be gone is already far too long. The answer is no. Not me, not them. Try again.'

'Another day out of Hell,' the King said.

The Dark Lord went still, his expression full of restraint.

'The humans are accustomed to it now, Ah Wu,' the King said. 'They leave offerings everywhere on Hungry Ghosts Day; the spirits are well fed. Another day added to that, they won't even notice.'

'Is that doable?' the cat said.

'If I give them another day every year, their power will grow while they are out,' the Dark Lord said. 'As it is, they grow stronger every year and we must constantly work to reduce their power. If they had two days, they would be four times stronger — then eight — they would begin to have physical effects on the population of the Earthly.'

'The Hungry Ghosts could actually hurt people directly?' Simone said.

'Yes,' the Dark Lord said. 'As it is, they influence people with dark ambition. With two days, they would be able to act on those ambitions themselves.'

'I guess that's a no then,' the King said. 'Shame.' He shrugged. 'I'm out of ideas.'

'Take my wives,' the cat said. 'You can have them.'

'Oh, now that's a tempting offer,' the King said.

'No,' the Dark Lord said. 'That is not an option.'

'They're *my* wives!' the cat shouted.

'And I'm your Lord and I say no!' the Dark Lord said.

'Pulling rank?'

The Dark Lord nodded once sharply.

'Twice in a hundred years,' the cat said. 'What is it with you and women? They're always getting you into trouble.'

The Demon King grinned broadly. 'The Tiger has a point.'

The Tiger turned away. 'Always falling for the wrong damn females. That snake concubine bitch, then that Michelle bitch, now this Emma bitch. Always the wrong chick.'

'The Death Mother plotted against you,' I said. 'The Geek, the Death Mother, Prince Six and his consort — they all plotted against you. Only the Death Mother is left. We can bring her to you in exchange. In exchange for my free will.'

They all stared at me.

'Oh, Emma,' Simone said softly. 'It's about time.'

The Dark Lord glanced sharply at the Demon King. 'That we can do.'

The Demon King raised one hand and grinned. 'Oh, I don't think so. You'll destroy her anyway. But how about this?' His grin widened. 'Kitty Kwok. She's the one behind it all. She's the one who financed Simon, and who gathered those other four together to go after me. I want her, and she's human. I can't touch her, by the terms of an agreement that I have with *you*.' He leaned towards the Dark Lord. 'But you can. You can bring her to me and put her in a cage of Celestial Jade for me.'

'Why Celestial Jade?' the Tiger said. 'This stinks of a trap for the Dark Lord.'

518

'She's been using some sort of twisted energy manipulation, draining children to give her Immortality,' the Demon King said. 'If I'm to hold her, I need something that'll hold an Immortal.'

'We can give you Kitty Kwok,' I said. 'But don't torture or kill her. Just hold her.'

'This is a trap!' the Tiger shouted.

'No, no, no,' the Demon King said. 'I promise. I give my word.' He paused, and chose his words carefully, and the air grew silent around us as power gathered. 'Xuan Wu, promise to bring me Kitty Kwok and put her in a cage of Celestial Jade for me. I vow I will not torture or kill her. I will not hold you, Turtle, that I swear. Promise you will do this thing for me, and I will free your Lady from the demon essence.' He waved one hand at me. 'Make me this promise and I will free her right now. She will be free from the demon essence, she will walk the Celestial whole, and she can be yours again when you return, which, from the looks of you, won't take much longer. This I swear by all the forces of Hell.'

'Emma, do you agree to giving him Kitty Kwok?' the Dark Lord said.

'She doesn't have enough free will to decide,' Simone said.

'Yes, I do,' I said. 'I would do anything to be by his side and to be human. I will give Kitty Kwok to the Demon King under these terms.'

'This absolutely fucking reeks of a trap,' the Tiger said.

'I know,' the Dark Lord said. 'But it is the only way we can free Emma.'

'I vow I will not hold the Turtle in the Celestial Jade,' the Demon King said. 'I will release him immediately.'

'And Emma,' the Dark Lord said. 'You will release Emma.'

'I will release Emma. I do not want Emma, this I promise. I don't want either of you. What I want is for you to put Kitty Kwok in a cage of jade for me.'

The Tiger turned away. 'I really don't like this.'

'Neither do I,' the Dark Lord said. 'But right now I cannot fault it.' He stood straighter and looked the Demon King in the eye. 'I will do it.'

'We have an agreement?'

The Dark Lord nodded, his eyes fierce. 'We have an agreement.'

'Make the vow. I have already made mine. I give you my word by the Ten Levels of Hell.'

The air grew thicker and more silent around us. It was as if the whole world held its breath.

'I vow that I will capture Kitty Kwok, take her to Hell and place her in a cage of Celestial Jade for you. This I swear as Xuan Wu, Xuan Tian Shang Di.'

A blast of wind blew through the room, and was gone.

'Kneel, Emma,' the Demon King said kindly. 'Everybody move back. This might get messy.'

'Don't hurt her!' Simone said.

Xuan Wu took Simone by the shoulders and pulled her back slightly. 'Stay back, Simone.'

'When you did this the last time, it was easy,' I said to the Demon King. 'Why do you need them to move back now?'

'Because last time you weren't fully demon,' the King said. 'Down, Emma, this is going to hurt.'

I kneeled, and focused on Xuan Wu's dark eyes. They were full of pain. 'Everybody back,' he said. 'The King is right. This may get messy.'

The Demon King kneeled behind me, so close I could feel his body against my back. He put his hands on my shoulders and I felt his breath on the back of my neck as he spoke. 'Whatever happens, don't touch her until I'm done. Nobody move until I say I'm done. I'm not going to hurt her — well, okay, I am going to hurt her, but this is what you want. I'm not going to do any permanent damage to her. Just stay away, because if you interfere through any of this, you'll kill her.'

'Do as he says,' the Dark Lord said.

'Are you ready, Emma?' the Demon King said to the back of my neck.

I nodded. 'I'm ready.'

It started as a prickle on the back of my neck and spread through my shoulders, gaining heat quickly. The heat grew inside me, becoming unbearable, and I pulled away.

'Stay,' he said into my ear. 'Don't fight it. You have to keep still and let me burn this out of you.'

I held myself still, trembling, with his hands on my shoulders and molten fire running through me. The burning flared within me and I couldn't bear it. I had to let something out.

I heard screaming, and then realised it was me.

Focus on me.

I concentrated on his dark eyes that reflected the pain I felt within me. I couldn't breathe; my lungs were full of fire. I gasped in air and every breath filled me with more burning. My skin peeled from me and my raw, bleeding flesh screamed as it touched the air.

I burned, and I looked into his eyes, and the floor spiralled up to meet me.

I coughed, and moaned at the pain. Every single centimetre of me felt as if it had been scorched raw. I tried to move to make myself more comfortable, and moaned again.

Strong hands grabbed me and lifted me to sit and I screamed at the roughness of the movement. Someone put their hands on my face and I took deep, heaving, grunting breaths. I couldn't hold it any more; I let it out as another scream, but it didn't make me feel better.

'What do we do ... what do we do?' Simone was saying.

I tried to tell her that I was all right but I couldn't speak. Every breath felt like sharp metal piercing through me. The hands touched me on my raw skin and caused me even more searing pain. Every place I was touched was another lance into me. My eyes were open but I was blind. My tongue was gone, my skin was gone, everything was gone.

'Get her to the infirmary,' John said. His voice moved closer. 'Emma, you will survive this. You must survive this. I can't hold it any longer ...'

'No!' Simone shouted, hoarse with effort. 'Don't leave me now! Don't leave us now!'

'He'll be back,' Leo said.

A sharp pain stabbed me in the thigh. I wanted to ask if it was a painkiller, I wanted to beg that it was a painkiller. Painkillers would work now, wouldn't they? Drugs would work?

The drowsiness flooded through me and I became detached. The pain went away, and I went away from the pain. I breathed more easily. Painkillers worked. Thank the Heavens.

CHAPTER 34

'She can't survive this,' Edwin said. 'She has third-degree burns to ... well, to one hundred per cent of her. She's been burnt down to the lowest dermal layer all over, some parts even further. Inside as well — I don't know how she's breathing. She should be dead now, and she will be dead soon. All I can do is ease her pain.'

'No, Edwin, the Demon King burned the demon essence out of her,' Simone said. 'We made a pact with him. She'll survive.'

'She can't survive.'

'She will!'

I wanted to ask for more pain relief but I couldn't speak because my tongue was gone. I cycled down, moving my new, clean chi energy through me. The outside was a shredded mass of agony, but the inside was clean. I wanted to scream with joy and pain at the same time.

'Can you change to serpent, Emma?' Simone said, holding my hand, causing me sharp pain. It was bearable with the drugs but it was still there.

I shook my head. I didn't have the focus to change, not with this amount of drugs and pain and bleeding.

Strong hands held my left arm at the elbow. I recognised the feeling of having a drip inserted and nearly panicked at the flashback of the demon essence going into me.

'No, Emma, it's Edwin, it's saline,' Simone said. 'Saline and more painkillers.'

I relaxed and she sighed.

To my vast relief, I floated above the bed, no longer touching it. Now I didn't have anything except Simone's hand against my raw skin. I relaxed even more.

'Thanks, Leo,' Simone said softly.

'The stone said to do it,' Leo said. 'It says every touch is agony for her.' His voice broke. 'Why did it have to be like this?'

Simone tried to release my hand, but I held it. She tried to shake herself free and I had to let go; the pain was too much. 'If being touched hurts then it's not worth it,' she said.

I flailed around, looking for her hand, and she took it again.

There were noises and protests, then the Tiger spoke. 'Holy fucking shit.'

'Mind your language,' Leo said.

'I agree with him,' Simone said, her voice weary. 'Oh God, she's bleeding on me. There's blood and goo coming out of her skin everywhere.'

I wanted to push her away, she shouldn't have to see this.

'No, Emma,' she said. 'I'm here for you. I'll always be here for you.'

'She says she'll be here for you as well, Simone,' the stone said.

'You can relay?'

'She's in a hazy state and her mind is muddled with the pain,' the stone said. 'Her tongue is gone, her eyes are burnt out of her head, and she's absolutely thrilled to be free of the demon essence, the silly human. She's dying of burns and happy.'

'She won't die. She can't die.'

'She thinks the same thing.'

'We *asked* for this,' Simone said, desperate. 'We *paid* for this.'

'Ma'am,' Edwin said, 'she has twelve hours at the most with these sorts of burns. That's twelve hours using her advanced energy skills to keep her alive. I will do my best to keep her comfortable, and you can stay with her.'

'I'll stay with her until the end,' Simone said. 'Whatever happens, I'll be here.'

'Me too,' Leo said.

'She says thank you,' the stone said.

I floated up from the quiet place into the pain again. Someone had wrapped me in cool, damp cloth and it eased the agony slightly.

I'm here, we're here, the stone said. *Emma, it doesn't look good for you. It's been six hours and you're just as bad. The burns are poisoning you, you're dying. If you have anything you want to say to them, now would be a good time, because very soon Edwin will to have to overdose you just to keep you on the sane side of pain relief.*

No, the Demon King vowed to fix me. *We made a deal.*

He may have made a mistake, Emma. None of the Celestials know for sure, this has never happened before — a human filled with demon essence and then cleared again.

Okay. It was time.

'She says she loves you,' the stone relayed. 'She loves you all. And Simone, if you could call your father to say goodbye, she would appreciate it.'

'I have been calling him, stone. He's not replying. I think he'll be gone for a while.' Simone's voice was full of tears. 'We'll have to tell him when he comes back.'

'She'll be fine, she'll heal,' Leo said. 'The Demon King made a deal with them. It won't end like this, it can't.' His voice became strained and thick. 'This isn't happening!'

He went out, he couldn't take it, the stone said.

There was silence as they sat with me. I did my best to stay conscious through the pain and dullness spreading through me. Every remaining minute with them counted. I was leaving Simone alone. I couldn't leave Simone alone!

'Tell her that it's okay for her to go, please, Simone,' the stone said. 'She's beating herself up because you'll be left alone.'

'I won't be left alone, and I will manage,' Simone said. 'Daddy's coming back for me, and I have Leo, and my brother and sister, and Monica. You don't have to feel bad, Emma. I'll miss you, but I understand.'

They were silent again, and Simone quietly wept.

'How is she?' Meredith said softly.

'Please help,' Simone said.

'Emma,' Meredith said, her voice calm and cool. 'Emma, I'm going to come into your mind and try to help you change to snake. Changing to snake might fix this. Do you understand?'

'She says yes,' the stone said.

'I don't know what the King was thinking,' Meredith said as she took my hand and established the link. 'This isn't a cure, this is murder. His pride and arrogance and greed have killed her.'

She sent tendrils of her consciousness through my mind, blue and serene. I relaxed into the feeling; her mind was like deep water, still and clear and with a calmness that helped me.

'I'm glad I could help,' she said. 'Now, stone, if you would: show me what she does when she changes to snake.'

The stone laid it out like a blueprint plotted on graph paper, disassembled and clinical.

'Right,' Meredith said, her voice brisk. 'Do me a favour, guys, nobody touch me while I try to bring this about. And warn the other telepathic Shen around the place to keep quiet?'

'Word's gone out,' Leo said. He'd come in with Meredith.

'For the first time in Wudang's history, we have complete telepathic silence,' Simone said.

I heard the silence too. I hadn't been aware of the telepathic background buzz before, but now it was as if every insect and bird in a forest had stopped.

'You were always sensitive to it,' Meredith said. 'Try to gather your energy for this, Emma. From what the stone says, the change does take it out of you.'

I did what I could but the drugs and the pain and the bleeding made it difficult.

'All right,' Meredith said. Her voice changed; she sounded like she was about to lift something heavy. 'Here we go.'

She forced the change on me and it pushed me into a smaller place. I didn't fit, I was squeezed into a shape that wasn't me, and I tried to help by changing myself to fit it. I couldn't; my body didn't want to move. The squeezing added to the pain and I lost control, spiralling into chaos. My mind filled with a jumble of images and light and I fought for breath. I'd changed but I couldn't change. I let my breath out in a long, agonising gasp that tore a scream out of me, and the change stopped.

'Stay away!' Meredith shouted.

Her consciousness sharply changed direction: she stopped forcing me into the wrong shape and instead moved to my heart, my lungs, my brain, and kept me alive. She fed my aching insides, slapped them to make them work again, and furiously knitted up the damage she'd done.

'Don't leave me now, don't leave me now!' she said through her teeth.

My heart took a huge leap and I breathed again. I panted, and wanted to cry from the pain.

'Edwin,' the stone said. 'I don't care how much she has, give her more. I'll tell you when she's close to the edge.'

Numbing drowsiness flooded through me. They'd topped up the painkillers.

'I just shortened her life by at least six hours,' Meredith said, her voice bereft. 'She's gone under, she's close to unconscious. You won't get anything coherent out of her any more.'

Emma, do you hear me? the stone said. *Your mind is slowing down.*

It was all too hard. Time to slip away ... so easy. So easy.

'I think she probably has an hour or so at the most,' Meredith said. 'I'm sorry, dear, but it would have killed her. We can't save her.'

'I understand,' Simone said. 'You did your best, and I appreciate it. Just leave us now.'

'She's nearly gone,' the stone said. 'She's not really conscious any more. It's just a matter of time. She says, "Stay with me."'

'I will,' Simone said.

A bolt of icy flames seared through me and I screamed. My skin was on fire, burning with blue ice, and I screamed. My brain exploded, shooting sparks into the air. I turned as I floated, my vision full of black and blue and ice and more fire, but this fire was cold.

The essence of the Xuan Wu was with me. This wasn't my John, this was the creature that was the cold and winter, the direction North, yang and yin joined together to make yin, blacker than any black. It was death and destruction and cold, and it absorbed me, sucking me into the icy blackness. It flooded around me, filling me, filling the air, filling my body until my blood ran with darkness and I screamed.

I fell onto the bed and I could breathe. I raised my hand and touched scales. I opened my eyes and saw scales and dark eyes full of the nothingness of pure yin and the wisdom of millennia and the grief of a million deaths.

The Xuan Wu Serpent touched its nose to me, as gentle as a feather, and its consciousness touched mine. My own serpent rose to meet it, kindred in spirit and nature and in love. It loved me, and I loved it, and we were one.

Then it was gone and I lay on the bed sucking in air, trying to focus with my new eyes and feeling more alive than I ever had. I was free of the demon essence and I was alive.

I shivered; I was suddenly cold. My whole body shook with the cold. Someone pulled blankets over me, but it didn't help. I felt like I'd never be warm again.

'Just rest,' Simone said. 'Just sleep.'

'Everything will be all right,' Leo said with wonder.

'Yes, it will,' the stone said.

I opened my eyes. Simone was sitting on one side of me, Leo was on the other, and both of them were leaning on the bed asleep. Michael was in a corner, in Tiger form, also asleep. Martin was in human form, slumped against the wall.

I touched Simone's head and stroked her honey-coloured hair. She roused and blinked at me blearily, then threw herself at me and held me.

'Whoa, gently, you're hurting her,' the stone said, and she held me more carefully.

Leo woke, sat up and ran his hand over his bald head. He saw us and took my hand.

'She's awake,' Simone said. 'Look at her now. How is she? Edwin said he can't find anything wrong with her.'

'Physically, he's right,' the stone said. 'But her body's in shock from what she's been through. The snake might have healed her, but her body remembers what happened and it's still shaken up.'

'Can you speak, Emma?' Simone said. 'Your tongue was burnt out.'

'Yes,' I whispered. I tried to say more but the words wouldn't come.

'She can't speak much, she's kind of broken,' the stone said. 'All of her is broken and it will take time to heal, but she'll be fine. Just let her rest, and she'll come back together and be here for you.'

'And we'll be here for you, Emma,' Leo said.

'Yes, we will,' Simone said.

Edwin must have heard us because he came in.

'When can we take her home?' Simone said.

'I have no idea,' Edwin said. 'The Xuan Wu Serpent hasn't healed anybody for a long time, since before I came here; and nobody's ever been through what Emma has. We'll just have to play it by ear and listen to her personal monitoring device.'

'What monitoring device?' Leo said.

'Me,' the stone said.

'And what do you say?' Edwin said.

'I say, let her sleep. I'll let you know when she's up to more than just rest and putting herself back together.'

'Go home,' Edwin said. 'The stone and I can watch her. Go and eat and rest. It's been more than twenty-four hours, and you need to look after yourselves.'

'I'm fine here,' Simone said.

'Go,' I whispered. I struggled to make the words. 'That's an order.'

She pointed her finger at me. 'You do not order me around.'

'Go home.'

'Make me.'

I feebly raised one hand and dropped it on her arm. 'Go home. I'm not going anywhere. Leave Martin and Michael here to guard, then take shifts.'

'Do as she says,' Edwin said. 'She's safe here, we have guards set. She'll be fine.'

Simone tapped the stone on my finger. 'You keep an eye on her, okay?'

'Yes, ma'am,' the stone said.

* * *

531

Five days later, Simone wheeled me triumphantly into the apartment. Monica, Jade and Gold greeted me in the living room. After they'd said hello they didn't speak; they just watched as I was wheeled into my bedroom. Simone gently lifted me into the bed and pulled the covers over me. Monica came and stood inside the door, smiling like an idiot. Jade and Gold came up behind her with the same silly grins.

'How long before she can get around herself?' Gold said.

'Edwin says at this rate she'll be walking unassisted for short distances in three weeks. He estimates a full recovery at three to four months,' Simone said.

'She'll be out of action for that long?' Jade said, concerned.

'You didn't see her,' Leo said. 'If you'd seen her, you'd be saying "that soon?"'

Jade came to me and fell to one knee. 'My Lady. I apologise for not being here when you needed me.'

'Were you with Qing Long?' I said.

She nodded.

'The father of your children?'

She didn't reply, not even a nod.

I took her hand. 'Never apologise to me for spending time with your family.'

She grasped my hand. 'You are my family.'

I tried to lean forward to kiss her on the cheek but I couldn't do it. She kissed my hand, rose and went to the doorway.

'Is it twins?' I asked Gold.

'It is! We can't tell the sexes yet, but it's definitely two. They're still trying to work out what they're going to be — whether Amy should bear them as dragon or human,' he said with delight. 'The ultrasound is next week.'

'Is it possible they could be born stones?' Simone said.

'No,' he said. 'I fathered them in human form. They have normal human DNA from me. From Amy, however — they could be human or dragon.' He spread his hands. 'We just have to wait and see. It's even more exciting than wondering if they're boy or girl!'

Four weeks later, Chang came into my office and quietly closed the door behind him. 'There is a policeman here to see you,' he said.

'Lieutenant Cheung?'

'Yes.'

'Get Gold on the phone. If you can't get him on the phone, call one of the guys in the IT hub and tell them to contact him directly. I need him here right now, please.' I straightened the papers on my desk. 'Bring him in.'

Chang opened the door and spoke to Cheung. 'Come on in, please, sir.'

Lieutenant Cheung nodded to Chang as he came through the door, then stopped dead when he saw me. I wasn't surprised by his reaction: I was bald, my skin was bright pink and I was in a wheelchair.

'Sit,' I said, waving at the visitors' chair on the other side of the desk. 'How can I help you, Lieutenant?'

He pulled himself together and sat down, slapping the folder of documents onto the desk in front of him. 'We can't find anything to link you to the destruction of the boat. We're closing the case; the coroner has found it death by misadventure.'

'I knew he would,' I said.

Cheung leaned back and smiled. 'So that's all, Miss Donahoe. The case is over, you can go back to whatever you were doing. I just wanted to come and tell you that everything's fixed up now. You have a friend, a Mr Peter Tong, who has employed lawyers and the media to ensure your name was not linked with the case. He is a very powerful man.'

'I didn't want his help,' I said. 'I never asked for it.'

Gold came in, closed the door quietly behind him and moved to lean against the wall at my back.

'A terrible thing happened, Lieutenant Cheung,' I said, 'but continuing to come after me is pointless. I had nothing to do with it. I wasn't even there. Please, let it go.'

'Oh, I have, I have,' he said, still smiling. 'I have no choice. I've been assigned elsewhere; the case is closed.' He rose and his voice became menacing although his smile didn't shift. 'I'm sure that you have nothing to hide and that we will never meet again.'

'The families of the children on the boat have been compensated,' Gold said. 'Even Bevan's family are aware that it wasn't our fault. You really have no reason to come again.' He nodded to me. 'Ma'am.'

I nodded back. 'If you would.'

Gold wheeled me around the desk so that I was knee to knee with Cheung.

'Let me see you out,' I said.

'No need,' Cheung said. He picked up the documents, opened the office door and left.

'One day I am going to take him through this place and show him exactly what we do for people like him,' Gold said mildly. 'I'll throw a low-level demon at him and see how he reacts.'

'Did we ever have friends in the police force?' I said.

'In the past, but they've always been more trouble than they're worth,' Gold said. He wheeled me back behind my desk and I nodded my thanks. 'They came squealing to us every time something looked even mildly difficult, complaining that it was demons when it was actually human criminals and none of our business.'

'He didn't even ask about my injuries,' I said.

'He may not have noticed,' Gold said. 'And if he did, he probably didn't care.'

'It's okay to stay in the wheelchair,' Simone said. 'It's only been six weeks, and you're still bright pink.'

'No,' I said. 'I want to be standing for this. I want to show the Lion the respect he deserves. I can't be in Celestial Form like you, so this is the best I can do.'

We were in the square in front of the Hall of Purple Mist on Celestial Wudangshan, the Disciples standing in neat rows in their black uniforms, covering the whole area. The students around the edges of the square held black banners on long pikes: half were plain black — the livery of the Dark Lord; the other half were black with the silver motif of the Seven Stars of the big dipper, the most potent constellation in the Heavens and the symbol of his power. The banners snapped in a Celestial breeze provided for us by the dragons floating above.

The Celestial Masters stood behind us, most of them in Celestial Form. The human Masters stood in the front row of the assembled students in their black Wudang uniforms.

'If you need a hand let me know,' Simone said quietly, and I nodded.

Leo, in Celestial Form, walked up the centre of the students; Michael behind him on his left and Martin on his right as escorts, also in Celestial Form. As Leo passed each row of students they fell to one knee to acknowledge him.

He stopped in front of me and Simone. Martin and Michael moved to stand with the Celestial Masters behind us. Leo kneeled and saluted us, and we nodded back.

I held out one hand and the forge's head demon reverentially passed me Leo's new sword. I staggered slightly at the weight of it; the sword was way too big for an ordinary mortal to handle. Simone moved to help me but I shook my head. I held the sword horizontally with both hands and raised it. As I spoke, a stone amplified my voice for me. I wished my vocal cords were more healed; my voice sounded weak.

'Wudangshan welcomes its newest Immortal, Leo Alexander, the Black Lion. He has served the House of the North with integrity and honour and now takes his rightful place among the Masters of Wudangshan.' I held the sword out to him. 'This sword is a gift to you from the House of the North. You are no longer a Retainer, Lord Leo. You are a Celestial Master of Wudangshan.'

He stood and took the sword with both hands. 'I vow to use this sword in the service of the North and the Celestial.'

'Turn around and show them,' Simone said.

Leo shrugged slightly, turned and raised the sword for the students to see. He seemed surprised when they all jumped to their feet and erupted into applause, some of them whooping and whistling with delight.

'Well, how about that,' he said, his voice amplified by the stone, and the students cheered even louder.

Michael broke ranks first, coming to Leo and giving him a huge hug. The other Masters quickly followed and Leo was surrounded by a scrum of wellwishers.

I used the opportunity to take Simone's hand. 'I think I need some help.'

She caught me and I leaned on her as she helped me to my wheelchair.

'This is a turnaround,' I said. 'I'm in the chair and he isn't.'

'Oh, look,' Simone said. 'That's so cute.'

Martin had come to Leo and given him a hug as well, and kissed him on the cheek. For a long moment they gazed into each other's eyes, seeming to forget everybody else around them. Then they broke apart and grinned.

'About time,' Simone said.

I materialised in the living room. The furniture was gone, the carpet as well; the floor was bare concrete covered in dust. I went to the wall where my sword was usually clipped but it was empty. A faded rectangle showed where the photo of the family — Emma, Simone and me, Leo and the Tiger — used to hang. I went down the hall to my office; it was empty. The training room was devoid of weapons and the mats were gone; again there was just the bare concrete floor. I went to my room; everything was gone from there too.

I wandered through my home, alone and bereft. Where were they all? My Emma? My Simone? I dropped my head. Perhaps the Demon King had attacked them ... but surely I would have known? But I was so weak, so drained ...

Had I possessed my love again? I checked ... no. She wasn't with me; I was alone.

I raised my head and concentrated. My child, my Lady, where were they?

I couldn't see them. I couldn't find them. I fell to my knees with grief. Surely they weren't dead? I would have known. Where were they?

I changed and returned to the sea.

The Serpent takes its smallest form and drifts through an oil slick, choking on the filth in the water, suffocating on the debris.

The Turtle stands in the snow on the highest peak of the Western Heavens, gazing up at the perfectly black sky with its steadily brilliant stars, not sure what it is seeking.

They cry. There is no answer.

GLOSSARY

A NOTE ON LANGUAGE

The Chinese language is divided by a number of different dialects and this has been reflected throughout my story. The main dialect spoken in Hong Kong is Cantonese, and many of the terms I've used are in Cantonese. The main method for transcribing Cantonese into English is the Yale system, which I have hardly used at all in this book, preferring to use a simpler phonetic method for spelling the Cantonese. Apologies to purists, but I've chosen ease of readability over phonetic correctness.

The dialect mainly spoken on the Mainland of China is Putonghua (also called Mandarin Chinese), which was originally the dialect used in the north of China but has spread to become the standard tongue. Putonghua has a strict and useful set of transcription rules called pinyin, which I've used throughout for Putonghua terms. As a rough guide to pronunciation, the 'Q' in pinyin is pronounced 'ch', the 'X' is 'sh' and the 'Zh' is a softer 'ch' than the 'Q' sound. Xuan Wu is therefore pronounced 'Shwan Wu'.

I've spelt chi with the 'ch' throughout the book, even though in pinyin it is qi, purely to aid in readability. Qing Long and Zhu Que I have spelt in pinyin to assist anybody who'd like to look into these interesting deities further.

Aberdeen Typhoon Shelter: A harbour on the south side of Hong Kong Island that is home to a large number of small and large fishing boats. Some of the boats are permanently moored there and are residences.

Admiralty: The first station after the MTR train has come through the tunnel onto Hong Kong Island from Kowloon, and a major traffic interchange.

Amah: Domestic helper.

Ancestral tablet: A tablet inscribed with the name of the deceased, which is kept in a temple or at the residence of the person's descendants and occasionally provided with incense and offerings to appease the spirit.

Anime (Japanese): Animation; can vary from cute children's shows to violent horror stories for adults, and everything in between.

Bai Hu (Putonghua): The White Tiger of the West.

Bo: Weapon — staff.

Bodhisattva: A being who has attained Buddhist Nirvana and has returned to Earth to help others achieve Enlightenment.

Bo lei: A very dark and pungent Chinese tea, often drunk with yum cha to help digest the sometimes heavy and rich food served there.

Bu keqi (Putonghua) pronounced, roughly, 'bu kerchi': 'You're welcome.'

Buddhism: The system of beliefs that life is an endless journey through reincarnation until a state of perfect detachment or Nirvana is reached.

Cantonese: The dialect of Chinese spoken mainly in the south of China and used extensively in Hong Kong. Although in written form it is nearly identical to Putonghua, when spoken it is almost unintelligible to Putonghua speakers.

Causeway Bay: Large shopping and office district on Hong Kong Island. Most of the Island's residents seem to head there on Sunday for shopping.

Central: The main business district in Hong Kong, on the waterfront on Hong Kong Island.

Central Committee: Main governing body of Mainland China.

Cha siu bow: Dim sum served at yum cha; a steamed bread bun containing barbecued pork and gravy in the centre.

Chek Lap Kok: Hong Kong's new airport on a large swathe of reclaimed land north of Lantau Island.

Cheongsam (Cantonese): Traditional Chinese dress, with a mandarin collar, usually closed with toggles and loops, and with splits up the sides.

Cheung Chau: Small dumbbell-shaped island off the coast of Hong Kong Island, about an hour away by ferry.

Chi: Energy. The literal meaning is 'gas' or 'breath' but in martial arts terms it describes the energy (or breath) of life that exists in all living things.

Chi gong (Cantonese): Literally, 'energy work'. A series of movements expressly designed for manipulation of chi.

Chinese New Year: The Chinese calendar is lunar, and New Year falls at a different time each Western calendar. Chinese New Year usually falls in either January or February.

Ching: A type of life energy, ching is the energy of sex and reproduction, the Essence of Life. Every person is born with a limited amount of ching and as this energy is drained they grow old and die.

Chiu Chow: A southeastern province of China.

Choy sum (Cantonese): A leafy green Chinese vegetable vaguely resembling English spinach.

City Hall: Hall on the waterfront in Central on Hong Kong Island containing theatres and a large restaurant.

Confucianism: A set of rules for social behaviour designed to ensure that all of society runs smoothly.

Congee: A gruel made by boiling rice with savoury ingredients such as pork or thousand-year egg. Usually eaten for breakfast but can be eaten as a meal or snack any time of the day.

Connaught Road: Main thoroughfare through the middle of Central District in Hong Kong, running parallel to the waterfront and with five lanes each side.

Cross-Harbour Tunnel: Tunnel that carries both cars and MTR trains from Hong Kong Island to Kowloon under the harbour.

Cultural Revolution: A turbulent period of recent Chinese history (1966–75) during which gangs of young people called Red Guards overthrew 'old ways of thinking' and destroyed many ancient cultural icons.

Dai pai dong (Cantonese): Small open-air restaurant.

Daisho: A set of katana, wakizashi, and sometimes a tanto (small dagger), all matching bladed weapons used by samurai in ancient times.

Dan tian: Energy centre, a source of energy within the body. The central dan tian is roughly located in the solar plexus.

Daujie (Cantonese): 'Thank you', used exclusively when a gift is given.

Dim sum (Cantonese): Small dumplings in bamboo steamers served at yum cha. Usually each dumpling is less than three centimetres across and four are found in each steamer. There are a number of different types, and standard types of dim sum are served at every yum cha.

Discovery Bay: Residential enclave on Lantau Island, quite some distance from the rush of Hong Kong Island and only reachable by ferry.

Dojo (Japanese): Martial arts training school.

Eight Immortals: A group of iconic Immortals from Taoist mythology, each one representing a human condition. Stories of their exploits are part of popular Chinese culture.

Er Lang: The Second Heavenly General, second-in-charge of the running of Heavenly affairs. Usually depicted as a young man with three eyes and accompanied by his faithful dog.

Fortune sticks: A set of bamboo sticks in a bamboo holder. The questioner kneels in front of the altar and shakes the holder until one stick rises above the rest and falls out. This stick has a number that is translated into the fortune by temple staff.

Fung shui (or feng shui): The Chinese system of geomancy that links the environment to the fate of those living in it. A house with good internal and external fung shui assures its residents of good luck in their life.

Gay-lo (Cantonese slang): gay, homosexual.

Ge ge (Putonghua): Big brother.

Guangdong: The province of China directly across the border from Hong Kong.

Guangzhou: The capital city of Guangdong Province, about an hour away by road from Hong Kong. A large bustling commercial city rivalling Hong Kong in size and activity.

Guanxi: Guanxi is a social concept where people have built a network of others that they can call upon to help them when needed. The more guanxi you have, the more others will be willing to assist you when you are in need.

Gundam (Japanese): Large humanoid robot armour popular in Japanese cartoons.

Gung hei fat choy (Cantonese): Happy New Year.

Gweipoh: (lit: 'foreign grandmother') The feminine form of 'gweiloh', suggesting a female foreign devil.

Gwun Gong (or Guan Gong): A southern Chinese Taoist deity; a local General who attained Immortality and is venerated for his strengths of loyalty and justice and his ability to destroy demons.

H'suantian Shangdi (Cantonese): Xuan Tian Shang Di in the Wade-Giles method of writing Cantonese words.

Har gow: Dim sum served at yum cha; a steamed dumpling with a thin skin of rice flour dough containing prawns.

Hei sun (Cantonese): Arise.

Ho ak (Cantonese): Okay.

Ho fan (Cantonese): Flat white noodles made from rice; can be cither boiled in soup or stir-fried.

Hong Kong Jockey Club: a private Hong Kong institution that runs and handles all of the horseracing and legal gambling in Hong Kong. There can be billions of Hong Kong dollars in bets on a single race meeting.

Hungry Ghosts Festival: It is believed that once a year the gates of Hell are opened, and all the ghosts who do not have descendants to care for them are free to roam the Earth. Offerings of food and incense are left on roadsides, and in towns operas are performed to entertain the spirits.

Hutong (Putonghua): Traditional square Chinese house, built around a central courtyard.

ICAC: Independent Commission Against Corruption; an independent government agency focused on tracking down corruption in Hong Kong.

Jade Emperor: The supreme ruler of the Taoist Celestial Government.

Journey to the West: A classic of Chinese literature written during the Ming Dynasty by Wu Cheng'En. The story of the Monkey King's journey to India with a Buddhist priest to collect scriptures and return them to China.

Kata (Japanese): A martial arts 'set'; a series of moves to practise the use of a weapon or hand-to-hand skills.

Katana: Japanese sword.

KCR: A separate above-ground train network that connects with the MTR and travels to the border with Mainland China. Used to travel to towns in the New Territories.

Kitchen God: A domestic deity who watches over the activities of the family and reports annually to the Jade Emperor.

Koi (Japanese): Coloured ornamental carp.

Kowloon: Peninsula opposite the Harbour from Hong Kong Island, a densely packed area of high-rise buildings. Actually on the Chinese Mainland, but separated by a strict border dividing Hong Kong from China.

Kowloon City: District in Kowloon just before the entrance to the Cross-Harbour Tunnel.

Kwan Yin: Buddhist icon; a woman who attained Nirvana and became a Buddha but returned to Earth to help others achieve Nirvana as well. Often represented as a goddess of Mercy.

Lai see (Cantonese): A red paper envelope used to give cash as a gift for birthdays and at New Year. It's believed that for every dollar given ten will return during the year.

Lai see dao loy (Cantonese): 'Lai see, please!'

Lantau Island: One of Hong Kong's outlying islands, larger than Hong Kong Island but not as densely inhabited.

Li: Chinese unit of measure, approximately half a kilometre.

Lo Wu: The area of Hong Kong that contains the border crossing. Lo Wu is an area that covers both sides of the border; it is in both Hong Kong and China.

Lo Wu Shopping Centre: A large shopping centre directly across the Hong Kong/Chinese border on the Chinese side. A shopping destination for Hong Kong residents in search of a bargain.

Love hotel: Hotel with rooms that are rented by the hour by young people who live with their parents (and therefore have no privacy) or businessmen meeting their mistresses for sex.

M'goi sai (Cantonese): 'Thank you very much.'

M'sai (Cantonese): Literally, 'no need', but it generally means 'you're welcome'.

Macau: One-time Portuguese colony to the west of Hong Kong in the Pearl River Delta, about an hour away by jet hydrofoil; now another Special

Administrative Region of China. Macau's port is not as deep and sheltered as Hong Kong's so it has never been the busy trade port that Hong Kong is.

Mafoo (Cantonese): Groom.

Mah jong: Chinese game played with tiles. The Chinese play it differently from the polite game played by many Westerners; it is played for money and can often be a cut-throat competition between skilled players, rather like poker.

Manga: Japanese illustrated novel or comic book.

Mei mei (Putonghua): Little sister.

MTR: Fast, cheap, efficient and spotlessly clean subway train system in Hong Kong. Mostly standing room, and during rush hour so packed that it is often impossible to get onto a carriage.

Na Zha: Famous mythical Immortal who was so powerful as a child that he killed one of the dragon sons of the Dragon King. He gained Immortality by unselfishly travelling into Hell to release his parents who had been held in punishment for his crime. A spirit of Youthfulness.

New Territories: A large area of land between Kowloon and Mainland China that was granted to extend Hong Kong. Less crowded than Hong Kong and Kowloon, the New Territories are green and hilly with high-rise New Towns scattered through them.

Nunchucks: Short wooden sticks held together with chains; a martial arts weapon.

Opium Wars: (1839–60) A series of clashes between the then British Empire and the Imperial Chinese

Government over Britain's right to trade opium to China. It led to a number of humiliating defeats and surrenders by China as they were massively outclassed by modern Western military technology.

Pa Kua (Cantonese): The Eight Symbols, a central part of Taoist mysticism. Four of these Eight Symbols flank the circle in the centre of the Korean flag.

Pak Tai: One of Xuan Wu's many names; this one is used in Southern China.

Peak Tower: Tourist sightseeing spot at the top of the Peak Tram. Nestled between the two highest peaks on the Island and therefore not the highest point in Hong Kong, but providing a good view for tourist photographs.

Peak Tram: Tram that has been running for many years between Central and the Peak. Now mostly a tourist attraction because of the steepness of the ride and the view.

Peak, the: Prestigious residential area of Hong Kong, on top of the highest point of the centre of Hong Kong Island. The view over the harbour and high-rises is spectacular, and the property prices there are some of the highest in the world.

Pipa: A Chinese musical instrument, shaped like a mandolin, but played vertically with the body of the instrument held in the lap.

Pocky: A popular Japanese snack, which is a box of stick-shaped biscuits dipped in flavoured sweet coating.

Pokfulam: Area of Hong Kong west of the main business districts, facing the open ocean rather than the harbour. Contains large residential apartment blocks and a very large hillside cemetery.

Putonghua: Also called Mandarin, the dialect of Chinese spoken throughout China as a standard language. Individual provinces have their own dialects but Putonghua is spoken as a common tongue.

Qing Long (Putonghua) pronounced, roughly, Ching Long: The Azure Dragon of the East.

Ramen (Japanese): Instant two-minute noodles.

Repulse Bay: A small swimming beach surrounded by an expensive residential enclave of high- and low-rise apartment blocks on the south side of Hong Kong Island.

Salute, Chinese: The left hand is closed into a fist and the right hand is wrapped around it. Then the two hands are held in front of the chest and sometimes shaken.

Sashimi (Japanese): Raw fish.

Seiza: Japanese kneeling position.

Sensei (Japanese): Master.

Seppuku: Japanese ritual suicide by disembowelment: hari-kiri.

Sha Tin: A New Territories 'New Town', consisting of a large shopping centre surrounded by a massive number of high-rise developments on the banks of the Shing Mun River.

Shaolin: Famous temple, monastery and school of martial arts, as well as a style of martial arts.

Shen: Shen has two meanings, in the same sense that the English word spirit has two meanings ('ghost' and 'energy'). Shen can mean an Immortal being, something like a god in Chinese mythology. It is also the spirit that dwells within a person, the energy of their soul.

Shenzhen: The city at the border between Hong Kong and China, a 'special economic zone' where capitalism has been allowed to flourish. Most of the goods manufactured in China for export to the West are made in Shenzhen.

Sheung Wan: The western end of the Hong Kong Island MTR line; most people get off the train before reaching this station.

Shoji (Japanese): Screen of paper stretched over a wooden frame.

Shui (Cantonese): Water.

Shui gow: Chinese dumplings made of pork and prawn meat inside a dough wrapping, boiled in soup stock.

Shroff Office: A counter in a car park where you pay the parking fee before returning to your car.

Sifu (Cantonese): Master.

Siu mai: Dim sum served at yum cha; a steamed dumpling with a skin of wheat flour containing prawn and pork.

Sow mei (Cantonese): A type of Chinese tea, with a greenish colour and a light, fragrant flavour.

Stanley Market: A famous market on the south side of Hong Kong Island, specialising in tourist items.

Star Ferry: Small oval green and white ferries that run a cheap service between Hong Kong Island and Kowloon.

Sticky rice: Dim sum served at yum cha; glutinous rice filled with savouries such as pork and thousand-year egg, wrapped in a green leaf and steamed.

Sun Wu Kong (Cantonese): The Monkey King's real name.

Tae kwon do: Korean martial art.

Tai chi: A martial art that consists of a slow series of movements, used mainly as a form of exercise and chi manipulation to enhance health and extend life. Usable as a lethal martial art by advanced practitioners. There are several different styles of tai chi, including Chen, Yang and Wu, named after the people who invented them.

Tai chi chuan: Full correct name for tai chi.

Tai Koo Shing: Large enclosed shopping mall on the north side of Hong Kong.

Tai Tai (Cantonese): Lit: 'wife' but in this context it refers to a wealthy middle-aged Hong Kong woman who spends all her time shuffling between designer clothing stores, expensive lunches, and beauty salons.

Tao Teh Ching: A collection of writings by Lao Tzu on the elemental nature of Taoist philosophy.

Tao, the: 'The Way'. A perfect state of consciousness equivalent to the Buddhist Nirvana, in which a person becomes completely attuned with the universe and achieves Immortality. Also the shortened name of a collection of writings (the Tao Teh Ching) on Taoist philosophy written by Lao Tzu.

Taoism: Similar to Buddhism, but the state of perfection can be reached by a number of different methods, including alchemy and internal energy manipulation as well as meditation and spirituality.

Tatami (Japanese): Rice-fibre matting.

Temple Street: A night market along a street on the Kowloon side in Hong Kong. Notorious as a triad gang hangout as well as being one of Hong Kong's more colourful markets.

Ten Levels of Hell: It is believed that a human soul travels through ten levels of Hell, being judged and punished for a particular type of sin at each level. Upon reaching the lowest, or tenth, level, the soul is given an elixir of forgetfulness and returned to Earth to reincarnate and live another life.

Teppan (Japanese): Hotplate used for cooking food at teppanyaki.

Teppanyaki (Japanese): Meal where the food is cooked on the teppan in front of the diners and served when done.

Thousand-year egg: A duck egg that's been preserved in a mixture of lime, ash, tea and salt for one hundred days, making the flesh of the egg black and strong in flavour.

Tikuanyin (Cantonese; or Tikuanyum): Iron Buddha Tea. A dark, strong and flavourful black Chinese tea. Named because, according to legend, the first tea bush of this type was found behind a roadside altar containing an iron statue of Kwan Yin.

Tin Hau (Cantonese): Taoist deity, worshipped by seafarers.

Triad: Hong Kong organised-crime syndicate. Members of the syndicates are also called triads.

Tsim Sha Tsui: Main tourist and entertainment district on the Kowloon side, next to the harbour.

Tsing Ma Bridge: Large suspension bridge connecting Kowloon with Lantau Island, used to connect to the Airport Expressway.

Typhoon: A hurricane that occurs in Asia. Equivalent to a hurricane in the US or a cyclone in Australia.

Wakizashi: Japanese dagger, usually matched with a sword to make a set called a daisho.

Wan Chai: Commercial district on Hong Kong Island, between the offices and designer stores of Central and the shopping area of Causeway Bay. Contains office buildings and restaurants, and is famous for its nightclubs and girlie bars.

Wan sui (Putonghua): 'Ten thousand years'; traditional greeting for the Emperor, wishing him ten thousand times ten thousand years of life.

Wei? (Cantonese): 'Hello?' when answering the phone.

Wing chun: Southern style of Chinese kung fu. Made famous by Bruce Lee, this style is fast, close in ('short') and lethal. It's also a 'soft' style where the defender uses the attacker's weight and strength against him or her, rather than relying on brute force to hit hard.

Wire-fu: Movie kung-fu performed on wires so that the actors appear to be flying.

Won ton (Cantonese): Chinese dumplings made mostly of pork with a dough wrapping and boiled in soup stock. Often called 'short soup' in the West.

Won ton mien (Cantonese): 'won ton noodles'; won ton boiled in stock with noodles added to the soup.

Wu shu (Putonghua): A general term to mean all martial arts.

Wudang (Putonghua): A rough translation could be 'true martial arts'. The name of the mountain in Hubei Province; also the name of the martial arts academy and the style of martial arts taught there. Xuan Wu was a Celestial 'sponsor' of the Ming Dynasty and the entire mountain complex of temples and monasteries was built by the government of the time in his honour.

Wudangshan (Putonghua): 'Shan' means 'mountain'; Wudang Mountain.

Xie xie (Putonghua): 'Thank you.'

Xuan Wu (Putonghua) pronounced, roughly, 'Shwan Wu': means 'Dark Martial Arts'; the Black Turtle of the North, Mr Chen.

Yamen: Administration, as in Yamen Building.

Yang: One of the two prime forces of the universe in Taoist philosophy. Yang is the Light: masculine, bright, hot and hard.

Yang and yin: The two prime forces of the universe, when joined together form the One, the essence of everything. The symbol of yang and yin shows each essence containing a small part of the other.

Yellow Emperor: An ancient mythological figure, the Yellow Emperor is credited with founding civilisation and inventing clothing and agriculture.

Yin: One of the two prime forces of the universe in Taoist philosophy. Yin is Darkness: feminine, dark, cold and soft.

Yuexia Loaren (Putonghua): 'Old Man Under the Moon'; a Taoist deity responsible for matchmaking.

Yum cha (Cantonese): Literally 'drink tea'. Most restaurants hold yum cha between breakfast and mid-afternoon. Tea is served, and waitresses wheel around trolleys containing varieties of dim sum.

Yuzhengong (Putonghua): 'Find the True Spirit'; the name of the palace complex on Wudang Mountain.

Zhu Que (Putonghua) pronounced, roughly, Joo Chway: the Red Phoenix of the South.

CULTURAL NOTES

Animals on the edge of the roof:

Traditional Chinese buildings have upturned roofs and on official buildings there is always the same series of creatures. The point of the roof holds a man riding a chicken (or phoenix), and he is followed by a series of mythical creatures, with a dragon's head at the very back. The more creatures behind the man, the higher the building is in the Imperial hierarchy. Buildings in the Forbidden City have nine animals; in a small province there would be only one between the man and the dragon. The small vignette is a reminder and a warning to those working inside the building, that whatever they do, all of the mythical creatures on the roof are watching them, and will pounce on them and devour them if they stray from their official duty.

Ah Ting:

Part of the legend of the 'Creation of the Gods' involves the raising of all concerned to the Celestial. When it came time to choose the person for the job of Jade Emperor, the leader of the winning side graciously and politely didn't immediately take the position, he just said 'Ting, ting.' ('Wait, wait.') Legend has it that a rogue by the name of Ting jumped up and loudly accepted the post of Jade Emperor, and as it was what the leader had said, he was given the post.

FURTHER READING

I have expanded my library considerably while researching for the second trilogy, *Journey to Wudang*, and I have delved deeper into the mythology, as well as the texts and scriptures, of Taoism. Here is a list of some of the works that I have added to my collection, and may be of interest:

A Selected Collection of Mencius, Sinolingua, Beijing, 2006

A Selected Collection of the Analects, Confucius, Sinolingua, Beijing, 2006

Anecdotes about Spirits and Immortals (in two volumes) by Gan Bao, translated into English by Ding Wangdao, Foreign Languages Press, Beijing, 2004

Creation of the Gods (in four volumes), Xu Zhonglin, translated by Gu Zhizhong, New World Press, Beijing, 2000

Early Taoist Scriptures, Stephen R Bokenkamp, University of California Press, Berkeley, 1997

Journey to the North, Gary Seaman, University of California Press, Berkeley, 1987

Journey to the West, Wu Cheng'En, translated by W J F Jenner, Foreign Languages Press, Beijing, 1993

Secret of the Golden Flower, Lu Yen, NuVision E-book, 2004

Selected Chinese Tales of the Han, Wei, and Six Dynasties Periods, translated by Yang Xianyi and Gladys Yang, Foreign Languages Press, Beijing, 2001

The Origin of Chinese Deities, Cheng Manchao, Foreign Languages Press, Beijing, 1995

The Scripture on Great Peace: the Tai Ping Jing and the Beginnings of Taoism, by Barbara Hendrischke, University of California Press, Berkeley, 2006

To Live as Long as Heaven and Earth, a Translation and Study of Ge Hong's Traditions of Divine Transcendents, Robert Ford Campany, University of California Press, Berkeley, 2002

地球到地狱

JOURNEY TO WUDANG
BOOK ONE

KYLIE CHAN

BESTSELLING AUTHOR OF WHITE TIGER

EARTH TO HELL

EARTH TO HELL
KYLIE CHAN

A fabulous story of gods and demons, shapeshifters and martial arts ...

It is eight years since Xuan Wu, God of the Northern Heavens, living in Hong Kong as wealthy businessman John Chen, was exiled from the mortal realm. Emma and Simone, John's daughter, are facing a new series of threats, while their best fighter, Leo, sits in Hell. They must persuade him to come home ... but, in Hell, nothing is as it appears.

On Earth, Simon Wong, the Demon King's son, is no longer around to trouble them, but his associates have taken over Simon's underworld activities. The otherworldly stones are being targeted and are in danger of their kind being completely destroyed.

It seems that the Demon King is the only one Emma can turn to for help ...